27 STORIES:
AN LA WILDFIRE ANTHOLOGY

27 STORIES:
AN LA WILDFIRE ANTHOLOGY

TWENTY SEVEN ORIGINAL STORIES PUBLISHED
IN SUPPORT OF THE LOS ANGELES WILDFIRE
SURVIVORS WITH ALL PROCEEDS DONATED TO
HABITAT FOR HUMANITY.

EDITED BY
LISA KASTNER

RUNNING WILD

27 Stories:
An LA Wildfire Anthology
Text copyright © 2026 Running Wild Press
Edited by Lisa Diane Kastner
Designed by Iseabail Lane

Published in North America and Europe by Running Wild Press.
Visit Running Wild Press at www.runningwildpublishing.com,
Educators, librarians, book clubs (as well as the eternally curious),
go to www.runningwildpress.com.

Paperback ISBN: 979-8-9935358-5-2
eBook ISBN: 979-8-9935358-6-9

CONTENTS

25 POUNDS

BY DAWN WILSON

I know my husband is disgusted with me because I got fat. It's the pills. They make me want to eat all the time. He says he understands and finds me just as attractive as ever. But I know that's not true. I can see it behind his eyes when we're making love, like his mind is elsewhere, trying to imagine what I once was. When he married me, I was 100 pounds soaking wet, just a slight little thing with a crazy mane of untamed curly hair and a crooked smile that he said was adorable. When I first started taking the meds, they made my boobs bigger, and of course, he didn't complain about that. Then came the insatiable hunger—a whole rotisserie chicken, two pints of vanilla ice cream, bags of Lay's barbecue potato chips—and he said nothing, though I could tell from his weak smile that he knew I was slipping away and transforming into someone else.

At first, he was just glad I was stable. He met me in the hospital lobby with a bouquet of white roses when I was discharged. I've always loved white roses, which my mom thought was strange.

"White roses are for death," she used to say. "When I was a young girl, every year on Mother's Day Sunday, we wore a yellow rose to church if our mother was living and a white rose if she was dead."

Brian didn't care, and neither did I. We were beyond such silly things. All that mattered was that my mind could breathe again, and he got his wife back after a 72-hour hold.

But now, I know he wants things to change. And I do too. But knowing how to make it come about is another thing.

It's not like I'm stupid. I almost got my degree in finance. I was going to go into creative writing until my roommate, Kristen, said there was no use in that. "Do something that you can actually make a living at," she said, "then you can write on the side."

Kristen changed her major from music to pre-law. Transformed her career path

to be a corporate attorney because that's where the money was.

She wasn't always like that. The first two years we saw ourselves as romanticized vagabond artists, me penning lyrics to her songs, envisioning our lives as a Generation X version of Lennon and McCartney. She had a collection of melodies she was going to take with her to Nashville. She had just as much talent as anything I heard on the radio or in the record store. And my words would grace the gentle lifts and falls of her powerful alto. We were convinced that our style was unlike anything heard in the 80s; that we were truly original. Rare unicorns.

"These are damn good lyrics," she said to me. "Damn good."

Kristen was in InterVarsity Christian Fellowship and never cussed, so if she said damn, then I knew they were good. She was dating a guy named Dakota then—he sat behind me in economics class. He had one blue eye and one brown. He always had this look on his face like he was about to ask you something, then suddenly forgot what it was.

Kristen and I would have pizza on Saturday nights and on Sunday, she went to some interdenominational Bible church while I slept in. She'd always ask me if I wanted to go with her—not in a pushy, Bible-beater kind of way, but just with a soft-spoken hope, like she was afraid I was missing out on something really good. I almost went a couple of times because I loved the way her face was framed with a soft curl of peace whenever she got back.

"There was a great sermon on grace today," she said. "I can give you my notes if you'd like to look at them."

I always took them and said I'd read them, but I never did. I was too young to understand the concept of grace and why it would be so important.

Dakota never went with her to InterVarsity and on some level, I could tell he thought it was silly and this really upset Kristen. None of her Bible study friends liked him either. They said he was short and curt and broke in front of them in line in the cafeteria. They said he always blared his music loudly down the hallway when they were trying to have a Bible study meeting in one of the dorm lounges.

About that time, Kristen got a really bad case of the norovirus and started throwing up a lot, and I was petrified because I had a class presentation and was afraid I would catch it and puke in the middle of class. One of my pre-med friends said norovirus was extremely contagious and I should disinfect everything in the room. Or maybe it was food poisoning. Who knows? That girl had more ginger ale and Saltines than I thought possible. But it was the end of the spring semester, and we were just all trying to get through exams. There was always a lot of junk food and leftovers around. I figured she might have gotten food poisoning.

Now Kristen was skinny, but I started to notice she was putting on some weight. But it looked good on her, rounded her out a bit, but I could tell it made her self-conscious because she was always complaining that at this rate her clothes would never fit, and she would have to get a whole new wardrobe.

We had planned to rent a house two blocks from campus during the summer session and try out our new tunes in some of the local bars, but we had to cancel because she had to go home to Carolina

Beach for some extensive orthodontic surgery. I don't know why because her teeth always looked fine to me. She never elaborated and whenever I asked, she just changed the subject. She said I should come down and after she recovered, we could hang out by the ocean, and she would teach me how to surf. Said that she could really use my support because evidently the dental procedure was going to be long, and it would take a few days to really recover from it. She said I made her laugh the way I'd say crazy things and talk to strangers, words going a mile a minute.

My mom would have none of it. First, she highly doubted my 11-year-old, beat up Ford Granada would make the seven-hour trek from Asheville to the other end of the state, but I think on some level she just wanted to keep me under her thumb for a while, mystified by my swift changes in mood and my affection for white roses.

I was only 20, and the car was technically hers. I didn't have money for plane tickets and people didn't fly much across the state back then. There was no direct bus route, and mom insisted that the buses were dangerous and no place for a respectable girl to travel alone, so she nixed that idea from the get-go.

Looking back, I wonder if she was afraid I'd just get on that bus and dive off into nothingness, captivated by the transforming North Carolina landscape, from the foggy peaks of the Blue Ridge Mountains to the flat cotton fields that spread across the coastal plain like blankets of popcorn snow. Maybe she feared, like the ebb and flow of the tides, that my ever-changing moods would wash me out into the saltwater current and brackish estuaries.

When Kristen came back for the fall semester, she was different. We signed up for another semester in the dorm with a goal of getting an apartment together in the spring, but she wasn't warm and open to me, like a shade had been drawn across her hope.

"You're exhausting, you know that?" she said, laced with a hint of meanness.

I think she was pissed because I didn't go to Carolina Beach to help her recover or whatever, but I explained about the car and my mom, and my parents were footing the bill for my tuition and could yank away the funding at any time. I had no desire to get bogged down with a student loan before I even got out of the starting gate.

About that time Kristen stopped going to InterVarsity and Dakota stopped coming around. She took an interest in criminal law but decided against it because she said if you were a woman in the courtroom that no one would believe you or take you seriously. But corporate law—there was a chance there because you were usually in the boardroom more than the courtroom, and it mostly accounted for just filing paperwork for mergers and acquisitions and making sure no one went to prison like they did in Wall Street.

And talk of Nashville was fun and all but it was time to grow up.

"Know what my daddy said? He said if you try to make it in Nashville you need to realize that the best guitar player you've ever seen is pumping your gas. That's how competitive it is."

"We've got as good a shot as the next person."

"And you need to wake up as well. You think it's cute to be this moody, brooding artist, staying up all night writing the Great American Novel or whatever the hell you do when I'm asleep. Then you can't even get off the couch for a week. It's taking too much out of you. Plus, you won't smoke weed and all the great ideas come to writers when they smoke weed."

"Weed gives me a headache. And it stinks."

"Well, I don't know what to tell ya."

I think her dad may have had something to do with why she stopped going to InterVarsity. Like Dakota, her dad didn't have much use for it, and I could see how heavily he influenced her.

But that didn't mean he was always wrong.

He did have a point.

So, I went to my adviser and changed my major to finance. I told Kristen maybe I could get a job as an investment banker at Goldman Sachs or another of those bigshot firms. We could get a loft apartment somewhere in the Village and splurge on Broadway shows. Maybe play in some bars on weekends just for the hell of it.

"Sure," she said. But it was far off and distant and I knew she didn't mean it.

The next semester she moved out, said she was sick of the dorm and wanted to have an apartment, leaving me without a roommate, which was fine with me because I now had a single room, and it was very rare that they would move someone in with you mid-year. She never spoke to me anymore, and we never wrote songs together.

I wasn't any good at finance and it showed. There were 500 people in one of my classes, and every Wednesday afternoon we had "break out" sessions with a teaching assistant where he went over the lecture and answered any questions we were too self-conscious to ask in front of that huge crowd of students.

That's when I met Brian.

He was the teaching assistant and getting a graduate degree in macroeconomics though I really can't even tell you what that is even today. Of course, you weren't supposed to have a relationship with your TA, but I was so clueless in the assignments that I think he took pity on me and gave me extra attention. After a session one afternoon, he reviewed my paper before I turned it in to the professor.

"You're a good writer," he said. "Ever think of going into journalism?"

It was his polite way of saying that I'd never make it as an investment banker, but I was still intelligent enough to make good at something.

"There's no money in that," I said.

He just nodded, found a typo or two that I overlooked, and that was it.

It started out that way, perfectly innocent, just staying after 15 minutes or so for some extra help, and no one was suspicious because they knew I was getting horrible grades on the exam because I'd cry every time I got my test back. However, the mind is supposed to work to do those things, my mind just didn't work that way. I could do it, but it was like a cat swimming. You know they CAN swim--they just don't want to do it if they can avoid it. Eventually, I became convinced that my mind didn't work the way most of theirs did, and I found myself scribbling poems in the margins of my notebook.

Then one afternoon I went by his office to ask him something, and he was in a panic, staring at his Macintosh. Back then they had these three and a half inch floppies that just slid into a slot on the front of the computer. He had saved his thesis on the floppy, and it wasn't ejecting when he clicked the mouse on eject and it was due tomorrow.

Now I don't know much about computers, but I knew that the ones we had in the computer lab at our dorm were pieces of shit. Shame to pay so much for an education and they give you these IBMs with the screens that never got bright enough or that never were able to send things to the printer. There were only two Macs and everybody loved the Macs so you had to get down there early if you wanted to get one. But every so often, one would refuse to let go of your floppy.

"You got a paper clip?" I asked.

When he gave me one, I simply uncurled it, stuck it into this hole beside the opening for the floppy drive, and the disc just popped out.

"How did you know how to do that?" He was amazed, and obviously had never dealt

with computers much.

He was so grateful that he took me out for dinner and drinks, which we knew was taboo, so we did it at this restaurant way out in Durham where we wouldn't run into anyone from campus. He bought me cider on tap, and I had never had it before, and I loved it.

He was really into something called Focus, which was the graduate student version of InterVarsity, and he invited me to come to his church. I figured since this Jesus was always popping up here and there that maybe I should give Him a try.

It's been complicated, me and Jesus. I don't know how else to say it. I didn't like the sermons at his church because they all dealt with "name it and claim it," that if you just asked hard enough and did all the right things that God would give you what you wanted. I didn't take that as a nevermind because I had asked Jesus to help me with my finance classes and I was barely pulling a low C. I didn't think Jesus was mad at me, but maybe he had no use for finance classes.

Brain actually got a job as an investment banker in New York, and the night before he left, I let him touch me for the first time. I knew nothing about men then, and I wanted to open my eyes and keep them shut at the same time. I felt his breath and hope and I knew that we had passed in and out and around together, and for that, I was grateful.

Brian felt so guilty about it. He said Jesus wouldn't like it because we weren't married, but then I said I had some old notes from a sermon about grace and maybe he would like to look at them. I gave them to him, and I lied saying I had read them, and they really spoke to me, when in actuality they had been stuck at the bottom of a drawer ever since Kristen gave them to me.

I felt bad lying about that to Brian, because he really needed that hope, and I somehow cheapened it.

I dropped out of college because my heart wasn't in it anymore. Mom was furious. Said all that money and no degree to show for it. I had to move back in with them and found part-time work at a computer store, upgrading old ones, and replacing worn-out moth- erboards. Brian said he'd call but he never did. Then one day he walked into the computer store and asked me if I still knew how to use a paper clip.

He had come back to North Carolina because his momma had gotten sick, and his sister lived in Portland and his daddy died about five years ago, so he was the only one who could care for her. Said he had never forgotten me. Asked me to marry him right there in the store—no ring or nothing, but I didn't care. What we had was deeper than words, faster than the speed of light. And I felt that maybe Jesus only wanted me in those finance classes to meet him, and everything in the universe was starting to make sense.

His mother died a year later, and he took a job at a large banking firm in Raleigh. To this day I still can't really tell you what it is that he does---but we settled into an easy rhythm, and I felt me and Jesus were going to be okay again. Then I went through a period I just call "five months without sleep," and we blame it on the birth control pills and how they were messing with my hormones. I went off them so we had to use condoms for a while, which I know he didn't like. But he did anyway because neither of us wanted children at that time.

But it didn't get any better.

I was in my car at a McDonald's parking lot in Durham with a horrible headache, and I reclined my seat back for a while to rest my eyes. Next thing I knew, Brian was frantically tapping on the window. He said no one had seen me or heard from me in three days, and he was convinced I'd been kidnapped or done something to myself.

It was strange because it was the first time I heard anyone mention me doing something to hurt myself. I don't remember the thought, but it was somehow familiar, like a nightmare you used to have when you were a kid that is somehow coming back to you after all these years.

The pills came from the hospital, and it was one of those hospitals you don't talk about. Especially back then. The only pills that worked were the "hunger pills." I hated it, but Brian said if that's what works, it's what we needed, I could tell he didn't like it either.

As you get older, you can't afford to be fat anymore. I'm always seeing clickbait about how this food or that can eliminate your cancer risk or doctors are astounded by the results of doing "just this one thing."

If I had an online community back then, maybe things would be different. But they weren't, and there's no point in dealing with it now.

So, I talked to my doctor, and we decided on a goal of 25 pounds. That would take my BMI—body mass index—from obese to slightly chubby, which although not ideal, was a place I could live with. That would mean tapering off the "hunger pill". After that, my metabolism and my appetite should revert back to normal. Brian was 100 percent on board. He bought an electronic food scale and a fancy health cookbook (most of the recipes turned out to be vegan, which I can't stand, but I didn't let Brian know that because of course, it's the thought that counts.)

I think he was a little bit too enthusiastic, as if by erasing the weight we can erase everything else about the past, but it doesn't work like that.

After about three weeks off the "hunger pill," I felt the worrisome tremors of my mood return--- small--- in casual dosages. They were manifested as a major panic attack when waiting in line at a crowded Wal-Mart. (But honestly, who *doesn't* have a panic attack at Wal-Mart?)

I'm still working at it, but Brian and I know it's tenuous work. I'm probably going to have to go back on the hunger pill.

We don't say it but we're glad that we never had children.

Sometimes I think about Kristen, and I'll see a Taylor Swift video and I know that Kristen could do something just as good if not better. For a moment I see Kristen on that stage, singing my words and both of our visions being adored by millions. I wonder if she made it as a corporate lawyer. I tried to look her up on Facebook once but decided the better of it and stopped.

I guess, on some level, I knew that she didn't go home for dental surgery. Her overbearing father was coercing her to change more than her major. I should have seen through it and been there for her. I can't blame her for hating me for it.

When Brian and I make love, I like the lights to be out. I never did that before, but until I get the 25 pounds gone, I'd like for it to be dark. When I'm ready, I can burst forth into the light like I'm emerging from this cocoon of exhausting moods. Then we can do it like we used to, in our first apartment together. One side table lamp shining across the bedroom, gleaming like a soft beacon that gives enough light to let you know that certain sacred things are magical.

For now, it has to be dark. I hear him pant and moan until he collapses on me, exhausted.

"I love you," he says.

"I know."

A THREAD OF SKY

BY AIDAN ALBERTS

LEWIS

Missouri River, The Thundering Falls

Friday June 14 1805.

A thread of sky breaks through the trees. Meriwether Lewis, Captain of the Corps of Discovery Expedition, strides out of the shadow and into the light. Raising his free hand, he shades his eyes and overlooks a great grassy plain. The Captain can see the sapphire Missouri River snaking toward the snowclad southern mountains.

He turns his attention to vast flocks of young geese. The birds have become completely feathered in all areas except for one crucial spot.

Their wings still lack the feathers needed for flight.

Descending the hill, Captain Lewis plans a hike to the bend in the Missouri that he had spotted from above. Rounding a boulder, there are at least one thousand buffalo grazing and drinking on the river.

Captain Lewis stands his 1792 Contract Short Rifle upright on the western wheatgrass. After pouring black powder in the barrel, he places a patched round ball on top of the muzzle. The careful but efficient Captain firmly pushes the bullet with his ramrod until it rests on the black powder. He opens the frizzen and puts a small amount of fine gunpowder on the priming pan. He then closes the frizzen.

What's that sound?

With his focus no longer on his rifle, the Captain looks in the direction of the noise. A fat buffalo forty paces away has taken a curious step towards him. Captain Lewis stands still as the buffalo resumes drinking from the river.

Alright, Meriwether, let's have this done with.

Holding the rifle in his arms, Captain Lewis is quite glad that he had ordered the gunsmiths to modify his weapon. The rifle's shortened barrel and enlarged bore, custom-fit for close-quarters hunting, rested confidently in his hands.

As he pulled the hammer back into the cocked position, the metal rib under the barrel protecting the ramrod felt cold in his hand. The Captain raised the rifle to his shoulder and aligned his rifle's sights on the buffalo's vital organs. Squeezing the trigger, a chain reaction is set off: flint strikes the frizzen, sparks ignite the powder in the priming pan, and the main powder charge explodes. A spherical bullet rifles through the barrel.

The bullet rips through the buffalo's side. A brilliant shower of ruby-red paints the western wheatgrass as the massive beast groans but does not collapse. Staggering on its four muscular legs, the buffalo discharges blood from its mouth and nostrils. The bubbling appearance of the blood proves to Lewis that he hit close to his mark.

While the beast dies, Lewis reflects on the quantity of meat that it will provide his men back at camp. The entirety of the animal from its muscle, hide, sinews, bones, and organs will be used. Standing defiant, blood soaks the animal's fur.

As he waits, Lewis remembers joining the Virginia militia to put down the Whiskey Rebellion of 1794. Leaving for the conflict meant he had to abandon the light of his life, Charlotte. Her belly slightly humped with new life, Lewis swore to himself that he would do everything possible to survive to see her and his child again. On the very border of the frontier, as the sun reflects on the brilliant cerulean water of the Missouri, he is reminded of when he said goodbye.

Please, Meriwether, do not leave me... said Charlotte.

With the final boat boarding calls being called out, Lewis stepped back. Squeezing both of his hands, Charlotte's arms were fully extended as her fingers slipped out of his hands. Lewis grabbed his things and walked towards the boat. The lapping of the fast flowing river against the boat sides muffled the sound of the crew talking to each other.

Wait, she said, trailing after Lewis. *We were supposed to be together. We promised to care for each other.* Her cheeks shined pink and the sunlight reflected off the wet sheen of her face.

Lewis stepped onto the boat boarding ramp and put his gear down.

Don't cry Charlotte, thought Lewis, as he waved goodbye. *There will be a day when we will be together again. God-willing. I hope—*

But the boat had drifted too far away and the rushing river carried away his thoughts. A hot uncomfortable feeling suddenly arose inside of the young man. Leaning dangerously far over the railing, Lewis yelled as loud as he could.

I hope it will be a boy! I hope Christ above and this great nation take care of you both! I——

Charlotte was much too far off to be in earshot anymore. Lewis gripped the railing hard until his knuckles turned white. He turned around, resolved to go to fight for his country, even if it meant he might never see her again.

A cracking branch behind the Captain shatters this memory.

Whirling around, he sees a monster. A large brown bear is a mere sixty feet away. Instinctively he swings his rifle up to fire on the beast.

Curse it!

Since downing the buffalo, the rifle had not been reloaded.

The bear briskly advances.

Open level plain. No bushes to dive into. No trees to climb for at least three hundred yards. The river here is shallow.

Twisting his body around, the bear charges.

Running as fast as he ever had with his rifle and espontoon spear in hand, he leaps over mounds of grass. He hears the snarling of the predator right behind him. There was no way he could outrun it.

Swinging his head to the right, he sees an opening to the river. Vaulting through the air, he drops his useless rifle onto the shore, but he manages to keep hold of his espontoon. His feet firmly plant into the sandy bottom as he plunges into the stream. He quickly makes for deeper water.

If I can get deep enough so that he must swim, then I might be able to defend myself.

Finding the deepest water available, he turns and faces his enemy. Holding onto his steel espontoon spear with both hands, he stares down his foe about twenty feet away on the riverbank.

He locks eye contact with the leviathan of this uncharted land. Lewis has always been a hunter. He was known as the type of boy who would go out in the middle of winter to hunt birds with his dog. In the beast's unfeeling brown eyes, he could feel that the foundation of nature was a harmony of violence and death. The grizzly's blank stare proved that they would never share any understanding; for nature knew not kinship or mercy and now the hunter had become the hunted.

Rearing up on its hind legs, the bear freezes in place. In this moment of tension, the river stops flowing as if winter had arrived, but it was June. Canadian geese were suspended motionless in the air above the two warriors. The river disappears into a world of darkness lit only by fire where he and the bear oppose one another.

Firelight reflects off the blade of the espontoon.

The reared mass of fur and claws land back down on its four

paws and pitch toward the naked man. Plunging into the point of the spear, the bear-spirit roars and falters to the side.

Bellowing, the muscular body of Lewis leaps onto the back of the demon. Swiping at the bear's tough hide with a frontier knife, bright crimson slashes of torn flesh appear. The grizzly roars and bucks upward. Lewis flies ten feet to the side and lands on a hard patch of volcanic rock. He groans as he feels something in his back snap.

The bear wheels about. Soaked in its blood, it begins to lumber toward the injured man. Lewis wills his lower half to move but his muscles strain in vain.

This is it then.

The bear comes within a few feet of his sweating face. The Captain could smell the carrion-reek of its breath. Hot air blows from the beast's black nostrils as horrid white canines are unsheathed behind its lips.

The frontier knife still rests in his right hand.

As the bear collapses its weight on the human, crushing his already broken body, Lewis holds the frontier knife like a pike. The grizzly's chest sinks deep into the sharp blade and the man thrusts his arms up into its steaming innards as the knife finds the heart.

Reeling off its prey, the bear staggers with the knife still inside. Standing on its hind paws, the billowing smoke behind it dissipates. This world of fire shifts and suddenly the beast and man are floating in black.

The darkness behind the bear is thrown back and from it bursts forth an ice-blue torrent of the enormous waterfall. The grizzly's heart beats madly as misty images of Great Plains creatures sprint out of this cascade of dreams.

The bear disappears but the waterfall remains. This massive flow lands on the jumbled rockfall below creating a watery image. A giant cave bear, long since extinct, towers in front of the falls and then is gone.

This phantasmic realm fractures, returning the Captain to the world of mortals.

Captain Lewis feels the frigid rushing of water around his legs. The river washes away his memories and his injuries from the spiritual battle. His only recollection of the encounter is a strange déjà vu. The bear took one more hard look at him and then veered off to its left into the open plain. Trudging out of the river, Lewis retrieves his rifle and reloads in preparation for the next encounter. With the rifle loaded, he strides forward with a newfound confidence and strength.

The End

CONFESSIONS OF A SCAMMER

BY DEREK GO

I came to Manila in 2016 at the urging of my mother, having just graduated from college a year before and having spent a good part of that year stuck in a rut in our house just playing video games. My mother—I can understand her—felt like she had wasted all her money and effort on my education only for it to be as fruitless and hollow as a bad coconut, its tree only waiting to be rid of it because it has no use. My mother too wanted to be rid of me, if only in secret, because we didn't really talk much even as we ate dinner. We let this silence grow between us, fueling her hatred of me. And [1] the anxiety in me —of becoming the person she had always expected me to be, someone who wouldn't amount to much—only grew worse in response.

And so, one evening, I found myself at the doorstep of my uncle in the slums of Manila, away from the province I grew up in, away from my mother. His house stood beside a road where a lot of vehicles were parked—tricycles mainly. This was the main source of income for most families in the area. The tricycles busied the side of the road so that a large vehicle such as a car could not freely move through the road without the smaller vehicles making space to some extent. Not to mention, many people were on the side of the road, talking or selling something, and children were flipping coins on the only concrete they could find. It was a close-knit neighborhood; everybody knew each other. But at the same time, they were used to strangers passing through so when I first stepped here, I hadn't attracted all eyes, or if I had, it was probably because of the number of bags I was holding (three). I had brought all my clothes; my mother was not expecting me to come back any sooner. I also looked like a wet kitten, shivering from the anticipation that I was going to live in a shanty of some sort, sleeping on a hard bed, all the comforts I had known left in the bygone era of the past.

But I was greeted with a warm welcome. My aunt, my mother's sister-in-law, immediately dispatched for her pre-teen daughter to buy her cousin some snacks. A bottle of coke and some biscuits. And it was as warm a welcome as you could give to an unemployed nothing. (They did not know that of course. I looked like someone respectable in their eyes because I had graduated college. But at this point in my life, I had already anticipated everything. And I knew what I was going to turn out.)

The inside of their house looked as I had expected of an average-income household. There were bamboo chairs and a table. An off-brand flat-screen TV by the wall in their sala. The sala and the kitchen too weren't separate—I don't know how to describe it. Just imagine a cube and you have to cram the sala, kitchen, CR, and a bed in it, the bed being on the loft above us.

They were renting the house, I noticed, not just because I imagined they weren't happy with the small space and that they could've chosen differently had they had the money, but because the exterior of the house looked similar as the other ones beside it, as if they were owned by one man, a mogul, who was here before everybody else and built all these houses to rent them (and he built them all identically for convenience).

My aunt made me sit down at the sala and entertain myself with the TV while we waited for my uncle, who was returning home from his IT job. She said he would be here any time soon and that he was stuck in traffic. She was also cooking "bulalo," a type of soup with beef and vegetables in it. Her back was to me as she was cooking, a woman with a small frame. She was in her late-thirties—she and my uncle.

"Gosh, I didn't know you would arrive this early," she said, stirring the pot. "Your mother said you would arrive later in the night. Now you are a witness to our filth." Then she ordered her daughter, Niña, to put her uniform and skirt, which presently lay on a chair, to the laundry basket upstairs.

I felt complicit somehow with Niña, as if I too were being ordered, and I imagined being ordered like that someday because I would be living here and was scared by the idea.

Niña picked her clothes and went upstairs, all while her head was glued to her phone.

"I thought so too, auntie," I said, chuckling, "but the plane was very quick. It was my first time on a plane too."

"Oh, really? Me, I haven't been on a plane. ... Was always too scared."

That was all she said and I thought: we're off to a good start, though I was still anxious that sooner or later my true nature would be unveiled—that I am lazy—and what my mother found tolerable she would find not only intolerable but disgusting, and no sooner would I be thrown out than die in the streets.

My uncle arrived several minutes later. He was happy to see me. He arrived by motorcycle—his motorcycle—and left it outside before he went in and set his helmet on the table.

"My nephew," he said as we hugged each other, "you've grown. How about we have a drink later, huh?"

I was smiling. "Of course."

"Niña, get your cousin's bags upstairs. He will be sleeping there."

After dinner, we did drink. We had placed a table outside in front of the house and bought two big bottles of beer.

At first, I thought there were just the two of us drinking, but then my uncle called a neighbor. This neighbor was about the same age as me, had more or less an attractive face than mine, and was taller than I'd care to admit. Because he advantaged me in every respect that I cared most about myself, I found his thinness (he was so thin his neck looked like that of a camel's) and poverty something that could offset the advantages, that way I could stop myself from showing my hostility towards him, and even regard him with fake-pity.

We shook hands and introduced ourselves. He said his name was Harold; I said my name was James. After that, we seldom spoke to each other.

My uncle steered *most* of our conversation, and drunkenly so. He said he was happy to see me, patting me on the shoulders, and then to Harold (re: me): "You know this motherfucker graduated top of their class."

"Not top of our class, uncle. I was from the bottom rung."

"I was only kidding, of course," he said, laughing.

Harold gave me a well-meaning look, not even understanding that he was supposed to be jealous or insecure, or to at least cower from the achievement that was to open a lot of doors for money to come in for me and my family.

It was a one-sided conversation, and it was only when my uncle took a bathroom break that Harold and I were forced to speak to each other, to break the silence that was encroaching upon us bit by bit. And of course, he was the first to pick at it:

"So, are you like, living here or something?"

"That's about right."

It was moments like that: he would ask me a question and I would answer it as meekly as possible, that much pervaded the first night I was there. And my uncle going to the CR every few minutes because of the onset of something in his prostate.

We soon called it a night as we all got drunk, and as much as I would like to continue for reasons I could not yet name, I also became stinking drunk at the point of passing out. And the lights, as me and my uncle went inside the house, hurt my eyes.

My aunt had to be the one to get the folding table from outside while also supporting her husband to not fall. They were to sleep at the sala using a cot while I took the bed upstairs. She even asked me if I could manage to walk the steps. I said I could, though I wanted nothing more than to continue drinking outside just to see what could happen.

∼

THE NEXT SEVERAL days or so, I helped my aunt sell barbecues at her barbecue stand. It was

a way of hers, with Niña being in school and my uncle at work, to pass the time. The stand stood just outside the house where people walking on the road might see it. And she said (even though she did not say this, this is my speculation) that ever since I helped her sell, her sales had increased, as the "newcomer" who helped her at the stand was very approachable by women. I did notice that most of the people buying were girls, and often if not always, they were forcing a conversation with me, which I did not like not because I found them ugly, but because I did not like girls in general. And so, after about a month of doing that, I stopped altogether and retreated to my room upstairs to play video games.

Another thing occupied my mind at this time: Harold. There, I confess it. I liked him, and every time he passed by my sight, going inside their house and out, I would not fail to sneak a glance. Their house stood beside my uncle's and it was my dream to get inside it someday, if only to confirm that it was indeed built similarly as my uncle's. (I'm lying of course—who wants to check out a house?)

He had a mother and a sister. His mother sold "pagpag" and various other goods from a small store jutting out of their house. It was here, sitting on the bench under its forecourt, sipping soda or playing video games, that I hoped he would speak to me about what I found so interesting with the game I was playing, and perhaps that would be the start of a friendship. But I soon gave up with the effort, owing to the fact that I seldom saw him near their house. He drove my uncle's tricycle, or rented it, out of mutual dependency that neighbors have with each other. My uncle was at work anyway, and this was his way of earning money.

I soon got the feeling that I was competing for my uncle's apprenticeship (esteem, reverence) against Harold, and I realized that even before the feeling came to me, I had already lost. They'd had years of being dependable with each other and I imagined my uncle treated Harold like his own son too.

One day, he and my uncle worked on a wreck in my uncle's motorcycle, and he helped hand him the tools while my uncle did the repairs. I was at the stand at the time so you can imagine the jealousy I was feeling of not being included in their little bonding (I wasn't). I suppose I'd still be useless even if I was included, but they could've at least asked me to bring them water, some small thing that would make me feel like I was doing a man's job, not at the stand where I was doing what my aunt was supposed to be doing while she watched TV inside. She seemed to be relying on me, on my submission to her and perhaps my own fear of being thrown out of the house and into the streets, to run her store. And so, bit by bit, I stopped helping her. That translated into a false belief among her and my uncle that I hated them, hated the own hands that fed me. But that was not so: I just felt stuck. I was unhappy, with only Harold to save me.

Accordingly, I felt like a stranger in my own uncle's house. So much so that I found comfort—too much comfort—in retreating inside my head and into my phone that I was slowly alienating the very family I was depending on to survive. And the shame, of still not having found a job after a month (because it's the reason why I came there in the first place), was just too much to bear. I didn't even know what to say to a recruiter if he asked me what my strengths and weaknesses were. I didn't even know what papers were needed (I only brought my birth certificate and diploma). And so, one day, my worst fears finally came true. Lying in bed after waking up one morning, I overheard my aunt and uncle talk about what they were going to do with me, having been established among them already that I was lazy and hopeless. My uncle suggested I work at a car repair shop. He said he knew someone there.

"Cars?" my aunt said. "What does he know about cars? Would you look at him? He looks like a twig. He couldn't even be bothered to pick up a wheel."

"Well, what are we going to do with him? We can't just send him back."

That very morning too, out of a need to prove myself, I set out to get the papers. I went to an internet café to build a resume, then to a photography studio to get my picture taken. After that, I went to the police station to get a police clearance. It was at that evening—I was going home from the internet café—that Harold's sister, Jacqueline, made a move on me. She had been pestering me for weeks now, flirting with me at the stand, so that I stayed inside the house more. One thing led to another. We had sex, in a weed-ridden plot of land, shaded by banana trees. I didn't like the sex on my part. It was forced and I did not find her attractive, but I figured it was the only way to get me close to him. I was content to throw it away too, a person's first sex and all its pleasure, for the possibility of a second even better, more delectable kind.

ONE DAY, Harold talked to us about where he could've found me a job. I figured my uncle

probably conferred to him that he was fed up with me still not having found one. We had just finished replacing the front wheel of my uncle's motorcycle and I helped them anchor it so it wouldn't topple over while they retrofitted the wheel.

"Do you have your papers?" Harold asked.

"Yeah."

"That won't be necessary."

"Why not?"

"Just dress yourself so we can go."

I took a bath to remove the grease out of my hands and put on my uncle's formal shirt—because I did not have one. And Harold and I went to the job site, which was a run-down, abandoned convenience store that did not look like there were people inside it. Harold told me to get inside and I would meet people there, and to tell them I needed a job.

"Are you sure there's people inside?" I asked him.

"Pretty sure. And go at the back."

With my envelope in one hand, I went to the back—because the glass front and the old entrance door were covered in newspapers anyway—and I soon found a door. A cold air emanated out of it and when I peeked inside, people were indeed there, hitting keyboards on rows and rows of computers and answering calls. When they looked up to see me, it looked like I had woken a horde of zombies. One woman in formal attire went up to me and said hi. I said hi back.

"Please follow me."

I followed her to a glass-enclosed room where we could see all the employees answering calls from their headphones. Then she made me sit down on the seat in front of her desk while she took up the seat behind it. She had a friendly face which I imagined could turn on you without you noticing it.

"What's your name?"

"I'm James, ma'am. James Balagtas."

"Is that your credentials?" she asked, noticing the envelope in my hand.

"Yes, ma'am."

"Let me see."

After she had a look at my credentials, she said: "Wow. Impressive."

"Thank you, ma'am," was all I could say.

She gave me a long hard look. "Well then, you're hired," she said, smiling.

I could hardly conceal my joy; I shook her hand repeatedly.

"You know how to speak English, right?"

"Yes ma'am."

That night, we celebrated by drinking ourselves to excess. Both of the families also knew

of my going to marry Jacqueline in the future and it was also a cause to celebrate. I recounted to them my feat that was the world's fastest hiring of an employee ever and they enjoyed every second of it.

"You know I didn't even have to go through all that 'what's your strengths and weaknesses' kind of questions," I told them. "She just hired me on the spot."

"Wait, what job is it again?" asked my uncle.

"Call center."

"Wow, baby," said Jacky.

"I thought at first she was going to make me eat her pussy because of how fast she hired me..."

"I'm glad you did not, baby."

That night too, I got to eat dinner with the three of them—Harold, Jacqueline, and their mother. I was a part of their family now; I was Jacqueline's husband. And even much later that evening, I was on the cot beside the three of them, trying to sleep, a wide grin on my face.

FOR THE NEXT month or so, I worked the night shift at my job answering calls from foreigners. The callers were mostly old people—elderly—and I was instructed to "fool" them into giving me the money they had in their gift cards. One caller, Bessie, from America, called to ask how to repair her "Microsoft." I told her: give me your security number; she obeyed. One of us even swindled 500 dollars from a man named "Frank" in Chicago, but our boss said we did not work by commission.

I dressed up at 9, 9:30, because work began at 10, then Harold drove me there in my uncle's tricycle and I worked until 6 in the morning, after which, he drove me home again. Jacqueline went with us on these excursions, and I wished she wouldn't do that so he and I could have a chance to talk. She would always say how proud she was of me and would kiss me goodbye before I went to work. It was tiring; my mother had suddenly contacted me to ask for money and my aunt was trying to get close to me only at the last second to beg for a loan. I could not refuse her, lest she would use it against me the time that I was living with them, eating with them, and would call me ungrateful. I had, without realizing it, gotten myself in a position in which there was no possibility of getting out in sight.

One night, noticing me tired, Harold offered me a cigarette—or at least that's what it looked like at first until I held it in my hand and realized it was marijuana. I hit it and that jolted me awake. I soon made the connection:

"Oh, that's how you found me the job! You sell marijuana to these people!"

"Yep."

We sat there at the curb outside the office for a long time not saying anything; I had asked for a bathroom break but instead had gone there and Harold seemed to not want to go home and go to sleep. It was an exhilarating feeling: the marijuana and just being with him. I did not want it to end.

Eventually, I asked him (I had to): "What other attractions does this city have? I'm tired of going to the same place."

"I know one."

"Will you show me?" I said, hoping to god he would say yes.

"Now?"

"Yes."

"Sure."

We left work as it was hopeless anyway and it wasn't worth the effort of doing it for so small a salary. We drove using my uncle's motorcycle to this hill overlooking the city and it was amazing. There was a bay next to the city and it was my first time, ever since I left the province, seeing a body of water that was not a puddle or a ditch.

From the hilltop, the city sprawled before us like something from a movie. There was the cold night air, fresh, but not biting in its coldness. We sat on the grass, passing a joint, and left the motorcycle just behind us, parked in a level piece of land so it wouldn't slide down the slope.

"Wow, this is amazing," I said. "Do you come here often?"

"Not so much lately but if I wanna hit a joint, then yes."

"Alone? At night?"

"No. I can't borrow your uncle's motorcycle whenever it suits me, can I?"

"That makes sense. ... Well, how'd you find this place?"

"I didn't. This place is pretty well-known. Many people camp here. They have sex there. You see that small area there? The one with the bush? That's where they do it."

"Ah..."

We sat in silence; I passed him the joint. He rubbed his arms, clearly cold. I offered him my jacket. "No thanks." We sat in silence for a while longer.

I wondered if he was thinking what I was thinking, that both of us were not what we were pretending to be and that we were both longing for each other's arms. And besides, if the question were to be asked, the question of whether he liked me or not, there was my handsomeness to answer for, and it's not like people had an apparent reason not to like me, not even him. As we sat there, my heart was pounding.

Finally, I broke it; I broke the silence: I did not care if, once he knew me, the real me, he was going to make it known with everybody. I'd just change places.

"You know I'm gay, right," I said, "and that I like you?"

A smile crossed his face. "I didn't think so."

"Why not?"

"I don't know. You just don't look like it."

"Fair enough. How about you?"

Without looking at me, he nodded; took a puff, then exhaled. It was all I needed to hear—or see—from him; my heart burst with joy. I kissed him, and no sooner were we sprawling on the ground than were tearing off each other's clothes.

"I love you," I said, feeling his skin at last.

"I love you too," came his answer.

We had spent the night on a different spot away from where we had first planted the seeds of our love. Once we woke up, I teased him:

"I knew you were gay once I met you. How could a handsome guy like you not have a girl?"

"Please don't say that word."

"Which word?"

"You know which. Don't let me hear you say that word again."

"Okay."

The sun was coming up from the horizon; we brushed the dirt off our clothes. Then we got on our motorcycle. But as soon as Harold kick started it, it wouldn't start. Then he tried kicking it again, to no avail. "Ah, shit."

It was already close to noon when we got home. We had left the motorcycle to a repair shop and just walked home. My uncle too commuted to work, seeing as his motorcycle was in disrepair again.

In the days following since, we tried to keep our affair between ourselves. We would only meet after work, at the top of the hill, then relieve each other of our desires. It did not occur to us to despair on our situation, having only a sliver of time between work and home to ourselves. If it dawned on us that we were stuck having to do that forever, with no freedom in sight, no light at the end of the tunnel, the pleasure we had shared with each other and would share for more days to come gave us the strength to continue walking in the dark, and we deemed ourselves victorious. We had created a world on top of the hill, one in which all our troubles could never catch hold of us.

But, as was the fashion of most love stories of that era, our relationship was not smooth-sailing. There was Jacqueline to mind for, for one. We were still together. And when, after dinner, all of us were gathered in the sala watching TV, she would hint, by a poke to the side of my belly, that she wanted to have sex upstairs while her brother and mother were immersing themselves. Of course, on our climbing upstairs, Harold would catch notice of this, but all I could do was swallow my spit and let it get over with. Harold understood this; if he was jealous, he never spoke of it.

There were instances when it seemed only the two of us were in a room, and before I could hold his hand or pretend to hump him, Jacqueline or his mother would barge in and we would pretend to be doing something other than show affection. Those were the moments that gave us such a fright.

One day, having lunch at an eatery, Jacqueline and I talked about Harold. We had just taken a stroll around the city, and I bought her a new pair of sandals.

"Why don't you like my brother?" she asked.

"Who says I don't like your brother?" I said.

"You. I mean I could tell it by your actions."

"What do you mean you could tell it by my actions?"

"Well, for one, I haven't seen you talk to each other. You don't talk to each other. It's like you secretly hate each other."

"I don't hate him," I said. "I really don't. And besides, we talk. Yes, we do. You just haven't seen it."

"Promise you don't hate him?"

"I promise," I said, holding her hand.

She smiled; went on eating.

Later that night, before work, Harold and I talked about it.

"Jacky says we secretly hate each other," I told him.

"What do you mean?"

"That because she hasn't seen us talk to each other, that means we secretly hate each other."

"Well, what did you say?"

"That we don't. Still she does not believe it."

"What do you propose we do?"

"You have to talk to me. You have to talk to me first."

"Why I gotta talk to you first?"

"Because it's natural. Because you're older than me."

"I'm not older than you."

"Yes, you are."

"When were you born?"

"December 1997. You?"

"January. ... Fair enough. ... Well, what are we going to talk about?"

"About work or something. Ask me about work."

"About work? What am I, your father?"

"Well, what do you propose we talk about? Basketball?"

"Even better."

"Well, I don't watch basketball. How about we just talk about this game I'm playing on my phone?"

"I don't know anything about it."

"You have to play it first. You have to install it on your phone."

"Okay."

At dinner the next day, we talked about the game we were always playing on our phones. We talked about which heroes were stronger than which heroes, or I told him I played better than him. We kept it subtle; we never made a show. And afterwards, outside the house, we even played an actual match and enjoyed it.

~

WE HAD KEPT our relationship low-profile for a while and successfully so. It was also

during this time that the city was implementing crackdowns on drug abuse among its citizens. I told Harold to stop peddling the thing and to gain some weight. He said he had, but you couldn't trust the motherfucker especially when you barely saw him during the day.

I was now many months in the city and I had come to share its cynicism. I constantly had dark circles under my eyes and my aunt no longer tried to borrow money from me, sorry as she was that whatever ounce of innocence I had brought with me when I first arrived here, it was already gone. I had also come to learn how the gears inside her were turning as she faked a smile all those times that she was borrowing money from me.

I was only myself when I was with him, on top of that hill. Our little refuge from all the hustle and bustle and turning of the world around us. I loved every inch of his skin, and it was my dream that we leave the city behind and start a new life somewhere, near the sea or deep in the woods, just me and him, indulging every second in the fruit of our love.

I tried to communicate to him my idea; he met it with apathy:

"What do you mean we leave? Where do we go? Do we even have the money?"

I confess he was more realistic than me at these daytime reveries and so I trusted his judgement. We put it on the back burner for a while and continued to live as properly as we could. Still, there was, in the back of my mind, a nagging suspicion that he only refused because he did not fully perceive the extent of my struggle. He did not need to work at night and sleep by day. He did not have to pretend to love a girl just to prove he's not of a certain sexuality.

It became even more difficult when we found out that Jacqueline was a few weeks pregnant. She had started retching and avoided certain foods which had a strong smell.

I explained to Harold that we had always used protection, and at times we could not, I would always pull out.

"Then why did she get pregnant?" he asked. "How do you explain it?"

As absurd as the question might be, there was only one explanation, and I tried to remember when I could have failed to pull it out. It did not matter now. The deed had been done; a baby was coming. It gave us such a headache, and our solution was to lay off for a while from fucking each other, fearing that we might reveal ourselves at so bad a time.

As for the baby, I kept nagging Jacqueline to abort it, but she was against it. I suspected her mother had something to do with her decision, as she always kept saying at the dinner table:

"Why do you want to abort the baby? It's a blessing that you two must raise each other."

I liked her; she had been nothing but kind. She had always agreed of me marrying Jacqueline. But in her own old-fashioned way she could be dumb and dangerous.

I worked neatly and with dispassion at my job, only looking forward to the day I got paid and had a tub of ice cream to myself. Then, as if the pain I was feeling still wasn't enough, Harold started seeing someone—a girl—jealous as he was that I was having a baby and in need to compensate for his own lack of masculinity. His girl was a pretty girl too. I got to eat with her at dinner one time, when Harold introduced her to us. Somehow also, they had the regard of my uncle. Whenever Harold wanted to take the girl to places, my uncle did not once hesitate to lend him his motorcycle. Contrast that with his disdain for me, sneering at me whenever he met my eyes, for having made a girl pregnant at so young an age.

I did not need to imagine where Harold was taking the girl. I hated him, okay. And I wished the motorcycle they were riding would skid off the road and they would both die. I did not mean that of course, and anyway, that wish sort of came true.

⁓

IT WAS JUST a normal day for all of us. It was a Sunday. I was outside at the time, sitting in front of my mother-in-law's store under the forecourt, playing a video game. My aunt was at her stand, grilling barbecues, talking to people. Jacqueline was inside, watching TV and resting. Her mother too was with her, in case she felt sick and nauseous and needed to go to the CR. I didn't know where my uncle was at the time, but I did know that Niña was inside, using her phone as always.

At the road in front of our house, a few feet away from me, Harold sat on the driver's seat of my uncle's tricycle, waiting for passengers.

It was a mildly hot day. The sky all morning was sunny, then it was overcast by noon. It was afternoon now, but it was still overcast. We just had a big lunch. Pig's blood stew, sun-dried fish, and rice. We were all groggy, tired, and sweating.

A crowd had formed in front of my aunt's barbecue stand, a group of middle-aged women. They were probably talking about us, me and Jacky, being the newest pregnancy in town. A group of teenage boys were at the store on the opposite side of the road, playing the same hit video game I was playing on my phone. It was a busy neighborhood, the people were busy with buzz, busy with rumors. The road was busy with people walking and tricycles passing. There was the constant noise of vehicle engines, murmurs of people, TV show audiences clapping and cheering, and from afar, someone singing at a karaoke. It was a normal day for us all; nobody could have expected a tragedy to happen, no word such as "tragedy" in our minds.

I kept looking up my phone to see if I could meet Harold's eyes, because then at least I'd know that whatever had gone on between us, it wasn't all for naught. That he remembered, if not wittingly then instinctively, everything that happened. As if I had left him something, a taste on the lips, a handkerchief, that he needed to return, that he would want to return. And ultimately, to be in my arms again.

But he wasn't looking. He wasn't looking. Not even a glimpse, a side-glance, a peep, a quick-look.

I muttered a "fuck you too" to myself. I thought: If you don't want my dick, then I hope you can stand it, before I returned to my phone. Until, without warning, I heard a gunshot. It rang inside my ears then was gone. And who should I see when I looked up: Harold! He was clutching his neck as if he was being choked. And blood was coming out of his hands.

The first, second, seventh cries reverberated from people. Some were running away, some stood in their places, ducking.

It was the two people on a motorcycle wearing ski masks, one driving and one holding the gun, who shot him. We saw them rev up their motorcycle, speed away, and disappear into the distance.

Harold got off the tricycle and staggered towards me. His eyes were bulging, pooling as they were with blood. The muscles of his face were twitching. He had a look of horror on his face, as if it was his end and he knew it. He was about to fall when I caught him, but he was heavy so I laid him on the ground with me, placing his head on my thighs.

I might have shouted to call an ambulance. I must have cried. I must have frozen in shock. Then Jacqueline and his mother got out and upon seeing Harold, screamed the most piercing cry I have ever heard in my life.

They kept calling his name, tried waking him up. They kept telling everybody to call an ambulance. But it soon proved to be futile. He was losing—had lost—so much blood. The ambulance arrived several minutes later, at which point Harold was already gone, dead.

~

THE NEXT DAY, a canopy was set up in front of our house, to accommodate people who would want to view Harold's body or to gamble. Many people came to visit us. Some of them held a vigil in front of the casket. There were talks among them as to who could have killed Harold, or that they said his death was inevitable, if not deserved, because he had been peddling drugs. His mother—and I had come to call her my mother also—emptied all her life savings and I went penniless too. She was crying for many days. Nothing we did could console her.

We buried Harold on the 12th of July, nine days after his death, in a cemetery outside town. And when we got home and all the people had left, there was a kind of painful silence about the house. My uncle was the one who drove me to work that night and he had come to learn that my job was not legitimate but I didn't care. I was thinking of leaving, of getting away.

I didn't care about Jacqueline; I didn't care about the baby. The only person I cared about was dead, gone, never to be seen again. I had no reason to be there, to be in that city, to live.

It's funny: before I met him, I'd kind of given up on living but also didn't want to die. I was just a piece of garbage floating in the river, letting life take me by its current. If a bus had rammed me while crossing the road, I would have been ready to end it all there, I would have said to the person trying to get me into an ambulance: "No, I'm fine. I'm okay. Just leave me alone," as my blood rushes to the pavement. And now that I found myself in the exact same position, I kind of surprisingly wanted to live. I wanted to get away, maybe love someone like him again.

Instead of going to work that night, I walked the highway towards the hill. I had packed a few clothes in my bag and was ready to take the midnight bus. But first, I wanted to see the hill.

The night was cold as big trucks carrying canned sardines passed by me. I had a few bills in my pocket, and would just ask for some money from my mother the second I'd reach my destination, preferably a town I knew nothing about with people who did not know me.

I walked for about twenty-five minutes before I reached the foot of the hill, at which there were no houses but a big acacia tree near the entrance of it.

I had not trekked it before; Harold and I always drove uphill using a motorcycle. So a minute on at the slope, I was heaving for breath.

Halfway through, I realized how stupid it was what I was doing —trying to climb it—I almost cried. I did cry, but not for that reason.

Thankfully, the moon was bright enough to light up my path.

When I was close to the summit, I noticed a motorcycle being parked on the spot where Harold had always parked ours. I thought I was hallucinating for a second and imagined Harold was waiting for me at the top.

He wasn't there. Instead, a girl and a boy less than a few years my age looked up from their kissing and was a bit surprised to see me come out from the shadows.

I muttered a sorry and walked back down the slope again.

I spent the night at a bus terminal, slept on the seats trying to wait for the bus. It did not come. I had missed it.

When I woke up it was already 3 a.m. I asked the officer there if another bus was coming. He said there wasn't. Then I walked back home again.

When I reached the house, it was already five; the sun hadn't come up yet. My mother, though, was up and in the kitchen trying to get this big sack of leftover meat and bones into a large pot.

"You're home already?" she asked when she saw me.

"Uh, yeah, our boss made us go home early," I lied.

I noticed she gave up trying to pour the bones all at once and just grabbed what she could by her hands and gently put them in piecemeal. "You need help with that?" I asked her.

"No, no," she refused, "you might stain your jacket."

"I'm okay with that."

I grabbed the sack which was not so heavy and poured the bones in while she held the handle of the pot to steady it.

"You're a good kid," she said. "You're going to become a great father."

"Thanks," was all I could say.

~

The End

PICKING UP SHARDS

BY ELAINE CRAUDER

Katy forgot her lunch bag on the kitchen counter. She considered buying a sandwich at work but had made her favorite, turkey with mayo, mustard, and pickles. Taking into consideration that the sandwich would spoil and that she'd also packed multi-grain chips; a juicy-ripe pear; and a large, chocolate chip cookie: barely cooked and a little gooey in the middle; she U-turned at the next light and dashed home, nibbling a bran muffin and sipping coffee.

Jim's car was still in the drive when she unlocked the front door and dashed down the hall. "I forgot my lunch."

Stepping into the kitchen, she stopped. Jim—the very Jim who fell asleep in front of the TV most nights, and recently even on Friday and Saturday nights—was on his knees in front of the counter, in front of his secretary, Jennifer. She was sitting on the counter, in her work clothes, with her feet on the granite slab and her dress hiked up. Jim was eating what Katy's brain processed as his breakfast. She walked another step and promptly threw up her pedestrian muffin.

He made protestations that she hadn't seen what she'd seen, but what made her angry enough to articulate in the heat of shock and anger and humiliation, was Jennifer's bare butt on her counter. "If you've scrunched my lunch that's it." Barely able to demand that her knees hold her upright, Katy glared steadily at Jim and wailed, "Turkey, mayo, mustard, and pickles?" and walked out without hearing the answer.

She drove to work and returned at the end of the day to an empty house. His jackets and coats were in the hall closet, only one jacket missing. She dashed upstairs and discovered his towel crumpled on the bathroom floor, pajama bottoms strewn on the bathmat, as though he'd gone to work as usual.

He did not return at six or eight or ten-thirty, when she uncrossed her arms and went to bed.

She called her office in the morning to say she'd try to be in after lunch, but was greeted by the receptionist with a surprised, "If you'd like. But I was told not to expect you back until Monday." Affirming that Monday was the day she'd be in, Katy wondered what she'd said or done to warrant the day off; she couldn't remember driving or working or talking with anyone in the office.

At home on a Friday morning made her off-kilter. Her usual cleaning on Saturdays gave her satisfaction, working around Jim's focus on TV sports while she finished folding. That routine housework had brought serenity, not the current eerie silence as she nearly ripped the sheets while tearing them off, washing them first, then the blankets, towels, and regular laundry.

Midmorning, the dryer in Katy's laundry room dinged out an insistent ring but it was not enough to bring her out of thoughts of poison or gas or something more satisfying, like a bayonet. The mediocrity was what galled her, that tipped her toward a dagger, or perhaps a *wakizashi*. She could hand over the sword and watch Jim perform *hari-kari*. If need be, she would do it for him. That's the kind of person she was. That's what he'd said the day before she found out. "Katy," he'd said, "I don't know what I'd do without you. You're the kind of person who always helps out, no matter how difficult the task." She'd been on her knees scrubbing the floor around the toilet before work when he said that, but she was willing to extrapolate. She wondered if it counted as *hari-kari* if she gave an assist. And, if—either way—it would nullify his life insurance.

Katy didn't blame his secretary. Jennifer was plain. Sure, she was young and lithe and blond, but her hair was stringy and washed out, almost paper white, blending with her skin. True, she was curvy like Marilyn, but almost to excess. Jennifer was the best applicant, the only one who'd been able to answer the question, "What do you do when you have to work with someone who dislikes you?" to Jim's satisfaction. Plain Jennifer had scrunched her nose—according to Jim, regaling Katy at length over dinner—and added, "I can't think of anyone I've met who I haven't liked."

"Imagine," he'd said, raising the remains of a glass. The red sloshed a few shades darker than his flushed cheeks.

"Imagine," she repeated. Remembering this now, Katy wondered if that was the moment when his rapacious little brain began to wander. She was not prepared to contemplate any other possibility, at least not until she folded the laundry and cleaned out their bank accounts.

Joanie and Tina, two of her best friends, took her out on Saturday for a late lunch of salad and diet soda, followed by an evening of margaritas and cheesecake. They wanted more details than she'd shared over hours on the phone—they'd invented a few, which Katy couldn't refute. She didn't cry until most of the way into her second margarita. Joanie and Tina kept up, three White women in their mid-thirties, commiserating as their moist cheeks glowed: rendering stock from raggedy bones.

She woke Sunday morning in her bed, fully dressed from Saturday's outing. The sun blared in like it always did on clear mornings, daring her to rise and face the day. Katy clutched a pillow as though it were a reasonable substitute for Jim. She stared at nothing. She thought about nothing. She thought what a surprise to think about nothing when she expected her mind would race and skip around furiously. She eased out of bed. Standing took all of her focus and energy.

Katy held onto the refrigerator door as if it were a friend, supporting her, until the motor kicked into overdrive. There wasn't anything in there that she wanted. There wasn't anything she could think of that she wanted. The motor hummed an anxious tune while she contemplated what she wanted for breakfasts, lunches, dinners, snacks, for the rest of her life. She released the door and watched it swing slowly closed.

On a warm spring evening, when she'd been separated a few short months, Katy nearly passed by a new restaurant, Golden Seams. Chinese had become a favorite, since she'd needed to downsize from a house in the Philadelphia suburbs to a Center City small condo. She stepped in. Steam spewed from a line of teakettles along the bar at the far end of the room. Rows of ceramic teacups lined shelves along one wall. Tables filled the interior with patrons sitting alone, fondling cups. Japanese music met her ears along with a slight chastisement: This was not a Chinese restaurant.

She stood just inside the door. *A Japanese teahouse.* She was about to leave when a tall Japanese American man, with short black hair and warm brown eyes, greeted her.

He held a cup in lieu of a menu. "*Kintsugi?*" he said, passing the cup.

"Thank you," she said, as though it were a question. The cup was empty. *Perfect*, she almost said aloud, as she tried to hand it back.

"No, thank *you*." The man motioned for her to sit at a vacant table and waited while she settled into the chair. "Do you want to use that cup or did you bring your own?"

"Is *kintsugi* a green tea?"

He laughed. "This is your first time. Tonight, watch the others and do what feels right." She looked at him quizzically, and he added, "I'm Nick. We don't serve tea here—and no charge for your first time."

Smiling, she said, "I'm Katy." She pushed her brown bob behind her ears. "It wasn't that long ago I thought about *hari-kari*. Not for me, but—"

He stopped her. "—It turns out most folks contemplate that a time or two. *Kintsugi* is quite different."

She rocked the cup between her hands. Pressed her palms and fingers around the outside, massaged the smooth ceramic texture. She quickly set it down and glanced at the other tables, each occupied by a lone person contemplating their own cups. She stared into her empty one, wondering why it couldn't be filled with comforting hot tea.

A slight, thirty-something Black man rose as though in pain and moved from a nearby table to the bar with the teakettles. He held his cup over his head and dropped it onto the floor. She gasped at the movement, the impact, the sound of a perfect form desecrated. Broken. Cracked.

The man scooped up the shards, tapping the cement floor with his fingers for the last of the pieces, and returned to his table, stepping as though a burden had been released and he could walk without injury. He arranged the pieces carefully onto the center of his table.

A red-haired White woman rushed to the front and tossed her mug from hand to hand, a one-item juggling act. She threw higher and higher, catching the cup dramatically at the last moment. A few juggles in, she launched the vessel high and stepped aside as her mug soared to the floor.

Katy covered her mouth as "Oh, no!" escaped. To her surprise, the red-haired woman wiggled her shoulders, inhaled deeply, and scooped up what she could.

Katy decided she would not go up and drop her cup. She'd smash it down. Let the smithereens fill the floor. Yell, "Take that, Jimbo!"

However, when it was her turn, her legs chose to dither on the way, giving her a chance to remember attending a Greek wedding where she and Jim had joined in to throw dishes when the newly-weds danced. They had laughed, leaned into each other as they held the plates, wondered if they would; if they should. At the sound of the first plate shattering they'd sent their plates flying, too. Jim's exploded on impact. Her plate landed almost flat, lethargically rocking before collapsing into pieces.

Now, she stood in front of the teakettles and raised the cup. Her arms betrayed her, unwilling to smash the cup to the floor. Instead, she threw the cup up a scant foot and watched it tumble gracefully down. Pieces flew from the epicenter, but not as far as she hoped they would.

She gathered the large shards and started to pick up the smaller bits. The sharp edges poked her fingers as she imitated the tapping motion that the others had used without harm.

"Bring what you have and leave the rest," Nick directed. "Some pieces will remain."

She placed her shards in the middle of her table.

Nick held up an opaque bottle, tinted light blue, for all to see. He tilted the liquid back and forth. "Traditionally, sap from a poison ivy cousin is used for the seams. My mother developed a special formula, not related to poison ivy. It dries slowly and you must wait at least a bit. Soon, I'll bring out the gold."

Katy focused. "Bring out what gold?"

"Julie," the red-haired juggler at the next table said, stretching out her hand and introducing herself. "This is my second time." She smiled, crinkling some of the freckles around her eyes.

"I thought this was a restaurant," Katy said, shaking Julie's hand. "And Chinese. I assumed and was wrong."

"Same as me. I came in hungry the first time," the man at the nearby table said. He nodded to each of the women, introducing himself, "I'm Daniel."

"You threw the first cup," Katy said, reminding herself. "Nice to meet you, Daniel. And Julie. I didn't know what to expect once I caught on that there's no dinner here." She waved her arm to encompass the room. "The music and everything—it's all Japanese and not a restaurant."

Julie said, "Me? I made the same mistake. What if it was preordained and we were all meant to come here but wouldn't have chosen to do *kintsugi* before the first time we each walked in?" She fondled the crystal on her necklace. "Or what if we *thought* we'd accidentally stumbled in?"

"It's a habit I have, walking into the unexpected. The first time I discovered," Katy hesitated before revealing only, "my sandwich was ruined. Turkey, with mayo. This time—no dinner."

Nick approached holding a tray topped with more opaque bottles, each tinged a different color—purple, green, gold, red, blue —and filled with the special glue.

Katy took the purple and concentrated intently. Another unbidden memory came. Jim had planted a row of lavender plants in the front garden for her birthday, just because she liked lavender. A couple of her tears mingled into the glue.

She sniffled and tried to force her cup's shards back where they belonged, jamming them together. She began to fix the fragments firmly into place but dropped the pieces in a line instead. She put the first piece in the middle, the third piece near the end, mixing and matching, searching for the order in which love, happiness, wealth and long life would fall neatly into place. She blew her nose and laughed softly at how ridiculous it was to do this—as if pottery mattered.

Her recreated cup had deep seams with thick, glue-filled tears. For all its imperfections, it was bigger, wider, more solid. Katy admired her work.

Nick appeared with the final tray, filled with small, lidded, ceramic bowls. Each one had a tiny brush in front of it. "It is time," he said.

She picked up a bowl and brush, placed them next to her cup, and addressed the bowl. On the off chance her pot of gold held the secret to wishes coming true if she only knew the right incantation, Katy whispered, "I am. I want. I need." She did not think it necessary to articulate more.

Nick said, "Do not hide the repairs. Illuminate them and you will be done."

Katy opened the top and cried out, "Oh!" in spite of her desire to be nonplussed. She replaced the lid so she wouldn't breathe over the bowl. She closed her eyes and smiled at the extravagance, the luxury, the pleasure she would bring to herself. Lifting the lid again, she placed it off to the side, took the brush and gently, delicately, deliberately, collected gold powder with the bristles and smoothed them onto the slightly sticky seams. Rotating the bowl bit by bit, her cracks turned to gold.

Nick stood by her table. "This is why you came tonight."

"I entered two places without thinking, without knowing I should have been thinking." She inspected her crudely repaired cup. Amateurish as it was, she could extrapolate: "It is beautiful, in spite of the cracks."

"Because of them," Nick said.

Julie said, "Some of us are going out for dinner. Want to come?"

Katy nodded. "I came in hungry. I am hungry."

"Nothing gets broken," Daniel said, holding the door open for a few others to follow.

Katy said, "We spent the evening breaking things and yet we're still standing. I'm still standing." She laughed. She walked next to Julie, then Daniel, then a couple of the others. Katy wasn't sure if she'd return for her cup, though it was unique. Hers. She was famished and ready for dinner with new friends.

The group gathered at the end of the block, waiting for the light to turn. The street was one-way. No traffic vibrated the sidewalk; even so, Katy looked right, then left. She stepped off the curb.

∾

DIRTY LACE

BY RIZA ROJAN

I clicked my tongue, letting out a forced sigh. The daunting church loomed smaller in the distance. It drew the hearts and eyes of many with its sleek white bricks and vintage engravings. I was never really fond of it so I stayed away as much as I could. Why were they so adamant I get married here? I'm sure the one above wouldn't mind blessing a marriage on an open ground in coastal Italy.

Reaching into the itchy bustier of my flimsy wedding gown, I pulled out my emergency cigarette. I retrieved the tucked away lighter and thanked myself for coming prepared. The creased cigarette found its home between my lips and I brought the flame to its tip. Felix never liked this about me — how I swapped a smile for a scoff, a wine for a cigarette, Norah Jones for Grimes. He said I was too glamorous to act 'rowdy.'

With a few huffs and a deep inhale, I threw my head back, the smoke's sensual dance dissipating into the cool air.

This couldn't be my life, and I knew that. I knew it when I met Felix, when he asked me out to dinner, when he subtly nudged at our potential future, and when he got on one knee and asked me to be his wife.

I looked down at my dress, white as stupid innocence. 'Like an angel', Felix's mom had said as I had forced on a tight-lipped smile.

With a few taps, I watched the ashes fall to the ground. Turning around, I quickened my pace and walked away. Away from that god-awful church and the people in it.

The slim white heels clicked roughly against the stony path, villainously tripping me every time it could. The smoke kept me calm while my mind raced. The long road could lead to peace or something worse, but anything seemed better than my destined future.

I glanced over the vast sea that roared in the distance, beyond the paved cliff. The dipping sun made the water sparkle, like edged crystals brought to the light. In the vast sea of nothingness, I got a taste of the ease I longed for. It drowned my doubts and worries, my feelings and emotions proving powerless. I inhaled deeply, hollowing my cheeks and feeling my chest fill up before breathing out. I flicked the cigarette to the ground, my heel grinding against its end. I studied my surroundings and pressed on, the road stretching endlessly.

Amidst the emptiness, something, no, someone, caught my attention. I squinted at the small figure at the edge of the cliff. My feet guided me before my thoughts could, as I walked towards the seated figure. Maybe my steps weren't as soft as I thought, as she turned around and looked up. Messy locks of hazel and gold rustled in the wind. Her eyes lazily eyed me up and down making me scrunch my brows in displeasure.

I looked down at my shabby wedding gown, wrinkled and starving for a steaming. The big ball gown had drawn many glances with its overflowing sequins and lace. Taking it off left me in a contrastingly plain dress that came to just above my knees. I felt weirdly naked without the poofy skirt, as I slid out of it and set it on the floor, using it as a makeshift cushion.

The girl whistled and let out an amused laugh. "That must've cost a pretty penny, no?"

I leaned forward for her half-empty bottle of Heineken. My shoulders slumped, the exhaustion weighing down on me. "I wouldn't know."

Taking a swig, I scrunched my face as the disgusting drink slid down my throat with a soft burn.

"Fuck, at least buy something drink-worthy y'know?" I cleared my throat and she laughed.

"Sorry, I didn't know I'd have a guest." We fell into a silence as her gaze remained on me.

I leaned back, resting on my palms as they pressed into the itchy skirt, a few beads poking back in retaliation.

"I'm guessing you've a wedding to attend." She looked back, her lips quirked into a crooked smile.

"I'm running away." I muttered, looking up at the now cloudless sky, the orange gradually bleeding into the blue above me.

She gave a soft hum. "To where?"

"I'm not sure."

"Do you have a place in mind?"

"Wouldn't be here if I knew, would I?" I let out a tired sigh through pursed lips.

THE NECK of the beer bottle hung between her fingers, her arm resting on her raised knee. Her clothes were worn out, the brick red shirt torn at its hem. The soles of her shoes were beginning to come off, ten shades darker than what they originally would have been.

I clasped my hands, my fingers running over the cold gold and diamonds. Still there, none missing. None skilfully taken.

"I live nearby with my parents, I just come here for a drink." She chimed in.

I hummed in response, sinking back in relief, my hands resting back on the ground.

She looked back at me, her eyes boring into mine.

"Plus you seem like in dire need yourself, I wouldn't steal from someone so desperate."

She gave a playful wink, making me click my tongue.

"I'm well off you know." I snapped.

"With what? Wealth or love?" She let her eyes run over my face and I grew conscious of her attention.

Wealth or love? Wealth was love, I thought to myself.

"Are you serious?" My eyes widened and she nodded. "You people believe money can't buy happiness. But it can. You just don't have enough of it."

She made a soft noise of acknowledgement. "So happiness is expensive?"

I shrugged. "Nothing good comes cheap in this world." I lay down, the skirt barely cushioning my head.

"So why aren't you happy?"

I shot her an offended look. "What do you know about me?"

"Nothing, which is why I can see right through you." A playful smile tugged at her lips.

I rolled my eyes and looked up ahead. The sky seemed so close yet impossibly far.

"Have people told you that you're annoying, like intolerably annoying?"

She chuckled and glanced back at me, the same mischievous glint in those eyes. "Not really, but maybe it explains why I'm here alone."

Her expression faltered ever so slightly as she twisted her lips, looking ahead at the waters. "I think you should go back." Her fingers tightened around the glass bottle, as she swirled whatever drink remained in it. She threw her head back and shot it down in one swift motion. She giggled; her eyes sparkling. "You're right, this is bad." Her eyes were screwed shut as she hissed through the aftertaste.

"I can't go back." I pressed my lips together, my eyes locked with the setting sun and its pliable surroundings. I felt her lazy gaze on me, studying my every move.

"You know Felix loves you."

I huffed at the sound of the familiar name, a name I no longer wanted to call to mind. I sat up in reluctance. "You don't know that."

"I mean, from everything you've told me-"

"Wait," I cut her off sharply. I swallowed hard and held my stance, "I never told you his name."

Her forehead lines deepened; her eyebrows knit even closer. "Course y'did, how else would I know?" She smiled at me with the same hypnotic smile.

"Did I?" I'm sure I didn't.

"Unless you're talking to yourself and I'm not here." She laughed, leaning back on her hands.

I crossed my legs with my hands in my lap. My gaze dropped to the ring that now felt suffocating to look at. A stinging reminder of broken promises and betrayal. I looked at her in resignation. "You've done nothing but waste my time."

She didn't seem to mind my remark. Without another thought, I got up and patted my dress down. With the sun and the girl behind me, I started on my way once again.

"Thanks for nothing, stranger." I shouted back and jabbed for a response.

My ankle wobbled and I cursed as the petite heel slid off. I kicked off the heels, slipping my fingers under the straps and let them find home over my fingers instead. With the skirt bunched in one hand, and the heels in the other, I walked back onto the graveled path to nowhere. I hesitated, waiting for her to call me back. To apologize for her empty words and how she treated me, but to my dismay her silence stretched on.

"I hope you-" I turned back and my eyes caught the empty green bottle on its belly, still and alone. I stared ahead and the emptiness stared back. No signs of the brunette remained, almost like she never existed. The road behind now felt more unnerving than comforting.

But I didn't have time to dwell on that which had disappeared, not when I had bigger problems still looming ahead. And if I failed to find the answers to them now, I might never find them.

WITH A WORRY as heavy as that, my feet moved along the path, letting my mind wander. Everyone would be looking for me, panic sinking in as it got closer to the time of the ceremony. They would try to phone me, only to be met with utter dismay when they heard Grimes playing from underneath the bathroom sink. [1][2][3][4][5]

Every step forward was a step further from a loving future I was guaranteed. I enjoyed the warmth of their love but I craved my solace more. But maybe my luck hadn't completely run out, as I squinted at the silhouette of a house --- or a cabin --- or a pub; an ironic godsend? I rushed to the place regardless, leaving all worries and hesitation to the evening wind.

Empty chairs sat outside and the doors to the place remained shut. My heart pounded in my chest as I pushed the door open. It creaked in profound anticipation, like it had been waiting for me. My eyes scanned the dimly lit haven inside.

Wooden barstools with a garish jade cushioning lined the thick slab of dark oak. The interior sent me a century back, with its brown floors, and shelves with carvings and patterns of sorts. Dust danced in the beams of light that seeped through the barred up windows, accentuating its emptiness. It was like nothing I had come across in this town.

The gruff sound of someone clearing their throat snapped me back to reality. I looked up at the doors that swung out and an older man stepped out from behind. He had greasy, grey hair that reached for his plaid covered shoulders. A missing front tooth didn't stop him from giving a hearty grin, his face wrinkling at the sides as he offered a welcome laugh and an amused hello.

"You don't look like you belong here." His grin remained, his stubble adding to the unpleasantness of it all. But everything good comes with a risk. And with a small smile, I pulled out the ugly barstool and plopped down on it. "Well then, what can I get the lady?" Sweat stained his shirt, the pungent smell burned my senses. I tucked a strand of my hair and flashed him a smile--- soft and naïve, the kind that often had them yell 'it's on the house.'

"Just a vodka martini will do." The skirt sat on my lap, flowing down my crossed legs and passed my sand-covered feet.

His pathetic gaze lingered over the lacy bustier of the dress, before meeting my eyes again.He smiled and gave a low hum. "Wet?"

I swallowed the lump in my throat. "Sorry?"

"Wet or dry? How'd you like your drink?" He smirked. My nails dug into the stool and I exhaled sharply.

"Dry please. I can pay."

"No, no, it's on the house, pumpkin." He winked and gave an ugly chuckle as I held myself back from retching onto the clean counter.

My eyes darted around the place, avoiding as much talk as I could.

"Here ya go. A classy martini for an even classier beauty." He smirked, satisfied at himself.

A nervous laugh escaped my lips, too high and too loud. I avoided his gaze, as I felt him wait for my response to his incredibly smooth line. Just as I had hoped, the saloon doors creaked open, making me sigh in relief. Layers of musty grey and brown lay on the customer's body, his scuffed boots thudded across the old creaky floorboards. He quickly glanced my way, before looking back at the pervert of an owner.

"Whiskey neat Gus, the usual." He grunted and pulled out the stool beside me. His fingers drummed on the table and his eyes glanced at me expectantly. "Would I know you by any chance?" His voice was rough. He cocked his head, continuing to study me.

And I studied him too, from the chin-length hair that framed his face, to the greying beard. "Why? D'you usually come across runaway brides?" I teased and he bit down a grin, eyes raking my face. I pushed out my lips ever so slightly and leaned against the wooden counter with my chin in my hand. His eyes fell to my glass and he smiled, pleased.

"Next drink on me, then?"

I gave him my practiced laugh. "Wanna get me drunk already?"

"You can handle it, doll." His lips curled up and he called out to Gunther, or, whatever his name was.

"For the girl? You sure?" The owner asked, looking at the man beside me. I watched as he chuckled lowly and nodded, glancing back.

"Something to ease the lady's mind, no?" His hungry eyes bore into me, and I offered him a small smile.

I let him pull his seat in closer as I passively observed his hands and their movements.

Friendly flirting was always friendly flirting and nothing more. It came with no promises but left with some if I felt like it.

My leg jerked away as I felt his rough palm on my knee. He quickly caught on and scoffed.

"Why? All bark and no bite?" His hand slid up higher.

I shifted in my seat and gave him an embarrassed smile.

"You caught me," I laughed softly, trying to lace the uneasiness in my voice, "I was just joking."

"But I wasn't." He mumbled low, his hand clearing knowing no bounds. They stopped at no plea, and it was clear to me that my words fell on deaf ears.

I swallowed and let out a shaky breath. "Alright, okay. That's enough." I chuckled, pushing his hand away.

"Why? Scared your husband will find out?" His lips stretched into a hypnotic smile.

My husband?

My throat closed, and I swallowed hard. The surroundings

merged into a blur of confusion, the grin on his face burning my eyes.

"Who are you?" My lips quivered as the words barely made it above a whisper.

Tears stung my eyes as his calloused fingers made it under the skirt; his hand cold against my flesh.

"I know you want it too." He offered a lop-sided grin, his eyes casually undressing me.

I abruptly stood up, the stool falling to the ground with a screech and a thud.

"What the fuck do you know!" The heat rose in my cheeks. My hands shook at my sides.

Swiftly wrapping my fingers around the drink, I inhaled sharply and swung my arm. My eyes widened as I watched the glass shatter, miniscule shards penetrating his skin. Deep red ran down his face, mixing with the drink and soaking his hair.

My breath staggered as I watched the smile that remained on his face, not once broken.

"What's wrong? You look like you've seen a ghost." He let out a surprised laugh.

I glanced down at the counter, to see the martini glass in its full form. Pristine and shiny, the drink to its brim. Turning my head back to the man, I observed his face.

Glassless and bloodless.

I gripped the counter to hold myself up as my knees buckled. My palms, now clammy, slipped against the surface. "I'm…"

"What's wrong, Cleo?" Felix asked.

No, it was still the man at the bar. And yet he sounded nothing like himself, and all like Felix.

The room spun ever so slightly as the pit in my stomach grew. The cold shivers across my skin made me run for the bathroom.

My knees gave in as I heaved into the toilet bowl that was stained in yellow and brown. My forearms rested on the cracked seat, as I gasped for air. The flush lever remained useless as I closed the lid with a loud thump that echoed across the tiled walls.

Wiping the corner of my mouth on the back of my hand, I sat down on the toilet. I rested my elbows on my knees, my head in my hands. Hopeless and lost, just like I was at the start. My steps forward had only taken me back.

I blinked back any tears that threatened to spill, pushing down any regret that I was bound to feel. I could have been at the wedding, on the dancefloor with my other half. The circumstances dawned on me, as I questioned my need to pursue a false sense of freedom. Free from what? A healthy relationship? A happy future?

Sighing, I stood up and walked to the scratched, graffitied mirror. My pale eyes meet the big bright ones in the reflection. Her dress was painfully bright with no smudges or streaks of any kind. The bouquet in her hand stood happy and alive. Her cheeks remained flush as she looked back at me through her veil. A veil I once hated, that I would say yes to in a heartbeat.

EAST TEXAS MAGIC

BY JERRY PURDON

The glass pack muffler rumbled outside the house. The shelves on the wall rattled from the deep bursts as the sound intensified only to fall silent. The sudden quiet created a pit in Lila's stomach. She fought the urge to hold her necklace and hope for a miracle. Instead, she squeezed the gun. Her other options took too much time. She needed something to stop the monster from approaching the house. Her face still bore the evil from their earlier discussion.

A door slammed, followed by another. Soon, boot heels stomped up the steps, and the wooden porch rasped under the weight. She visualized her ex on the other side of the wall through the books and pictures. Their relationship deteriorated so quickly it remained a mystery as to why. It was possible she became too close. However, hitting her was no excuse and threatening her sister was a definite relationship terminator.

All noise stopped while Lila held her breath and for a moment forgot about the pain along her face. She gripped the twelve gauge and waited.

A heavy thud collided with the front door. The walls shook. Another hit followed, and shattered the frame. The third blow caused wood to splinter as the once closed door swung open revealing Lila's ex. His crooked smile made his beard appear wider. His untucked, unbuttoned green flannel shirt stirred in the breeze from the hurried door. Two others shadowed him. Their appearance was brief as the swift moving door bounced off the interior and slammed shut.

Any resemblance of closure was cut short by the immediate push and entrance into the living room.

"How did you get here so fast?" The intruder asked.

"Back roads," she answered as she placed her finger on the trigger, "you need to go." For the life of her, whatever she once sensed in this vile being was long gone. Bile rose to the back of her throat.

The trespasser stood as if contemplating his next move. His focus centered on the weapon in her hands. He adjusted his cap and in an attempt to be smooth he stared into her eyes.

"Looks like I made an improvement," he said motioning to the side of his face while ticking his head upward in her direction. He stepped forward.

The inference to the bruising on her cheek elevated her anger. He seemed genuinely proud about it. Mistakes were bountiful in her past, but this asshole reveled in being the biggest one. "You need to go now!" She had no intention of playing and realized, with confidence, her next move.

"Where's your spellbook?" He laughed at his own question. "You dumb bitch! Like you'll use that on me." He darted for Lila.

The blast stopped him. There was no hesitation in her finger and none in that of the shotgun. He reached down to his right leg before falling back. Lila's ears rang as the sound bellowed off the walls. The second man charged.

The weapon bucked again creating a hole in the middle of his chest. The impact of the small explosion produced a splatter of debris leaving behind a small crater. His yellow shirt reddened as he fell forward. His pants darkened in the back. The third invader held up his hands. She pointed right at his face.

"Move a hair...and boom."

He didn't even nod. His feet remained planted, his arms high in the air, and she wasn't sure if he was breathing.

"You," she said, still pointing the barrel at the last healthy prowler, "need to lay face down right where you are and do it slow."

He went to his knees, and as he bent forward his stopping point would be right into the dead guy's ass. Quite a bit of blood had pooled around the body and as the third intruder tried to move to the side. Lila interrupted that decision.

"No way," she said, "keep putting your mug where it was going."

"But he shit himself."

"And pissed too but I don't care. Down now or share the same fate."

The last attacker laid flat. His face aligned with the middle of the defecated backside, so he turned his head.

"Again, no...your nose goes in the split."

The man obeyed, placing his nostrils in between the cheeks. The wet stains on the jeans were prevalent. The damp denim was all that separated the third attacker's face from the shitting source. The fecal stench overpowered the gunpowder scent. She wrinkled her own nose, shook her head, and her face stung from the movement.

A grunt came from her right. She heard the slide across the floor as another guttural utterance escaped her ex. He had rolled onto his stomach and was attempting to crawl away from her.

She stepped over to his side. "Hey, Shithead, stop moving."

He ignored her request, and continued his struggle towards the door. She flipped him onto his back. Taking inventory of the damage, it was evident the shot had torn through his leg. Something trailed down his calf sticking to the denim. Jagged chunks of meat were splattered along his short trail toward the door and several blood puddles covered the wood floor. His labored breathing continued. She would need to do something about the bleeding.

Any feelings of empathy or compassion for him had evaporated. At the moment, based on the threat to her sibling, this clump of scooting flesh was nothing but an asshole. It dawned on her the description was more than an accurate name for him.

"Well that didn't take long," Jess said as she entered the living room from the kitchen. Her long, dark hair wavered from her movement.

"Sis, we might need the doc," Lila said.

"No way. I don't want my wife touching them."

Lila glanced back and shrugged. Another groan came forth. She trained her gun down at the writhing man. He was attempting to roll onto his stomach, and she assumed it was his continued effort to escape. She backed up. Pointed the barrel at the intact leg. She held it about a foot above the knee and fired another round. The sharp bang echoed in the room, causing ringing in her hearing again. She didn't even hear the smattering of flesh as gravity did its part in bringing the pieces down to the floor. After this shot her ex passed out.

"Feel better?" Jess asked, rubbing her ears.

"A little," Lila responded, "making sure he doesn't limp away."

Megs ran into the area coming from the hallway and stopped once she bumped into Jess. Her furrowed eyebrows and pursed lips relaxed as she held onto her wife.

"We're fine," Lila said.

"Do you want me to stop the bleeding?" Megs asked.

Lila shook her head as she stared down at her ex and thought of options. The second blast should have been in his head, but she wasn't a hard hearted killer. He was injured. She only added to the mess to make sure he didn't wriggle away. Plus he passed out. A bonus for her since he stopped moving.

"What's next?" Jess asked as she and Megs approached.

"We need to figure out what to do with him," she said pointing over the brown noser.

"I'll take him to the barn and ask him some questions," Jess said. "But this guy," she pointed down at him, "he's in bad shape."

Lila nodded. There were many ways this situation could go. In the back of her mind, their great-grandmother, Mimi, told them to always take the high road and be better than their neighbors. How she encouraged them to make good choices. The only lesson they never adhered to was about ladybugs. She smiled at the memory. Besides, in Lila's view, they didn't have to elevate themselves much when lowlife's like her ex were around.

She wouldn't dare go against her elder's wishes. Even though the woman passed a decade earlier. At some point, Lila knew her matriarch would check in on them from the other side, and Lila wasn't going to disappoint the woman who lived long enough to raise her and Jess.

Though she had no love loss for Asshole on the floor, she did begin to experience some regret for killing someone. In no way should she have done that. Except not many options existed at the time. Her eyes slightly watered as her hand cupped her mouth. She wished Mimi was still around to offer advice on this situation.

"I'll come up with something."

Lila assisted Megs in removing every trace of biohazards that littered the walls and floor. Prior to their cleansing efforts, they had transferred the corpse, the injured, and the blubbering to the barn. She had never seen a man cry so much and wasn't sure what triggered him. They had Megs standing by him while they dealt with her ex. Maybe he thought they were going to hurt or kill him, but they had never said anything of the sort. Once Jess started the chant, the process didn't take but a few minutes. They were only stopping the bleeding. She was at a loss over his tears.

After they reached the barn, Blubber sat straight and unmoved on a folding seat at the front of the barn. He occasionally vocalized his weeping but didn't budge the entire time she and Jess spent restraining Asshole. Her ex was now strapped and suspended against the back wall and wasn't going to go anywhere even if he suddenly regrew legs. The jerk may have thought of himself as some type of super villain, but she made sure he was down for the count. Both appendages below the knees would be useless forever.

Blubber was last. They fastened his ankles to the chair legs while he sobbed so hard he blew snot bubbles. They secured his wrists together and left his hands in his lap. They moved his chair between two horse stalls just in front of the tractor. Jess said she had control of everything, so Lila returned to the house.

All the bio debris was spread out, so she put on rubber gloves and went to work. They used bleach on the floor, cleaned the walls, the leather sofa, the coffee table, the ceiling, along with the hanging fan, and then the bookcase. At this point, Lila was sure that utilizing bird shot in a twelve gauge at close range was a bad idea. The blood spray was tantamount. Each picture frame had to be scrubbed and two books were not salvageable. The tops of the pages were coated in red and the paper soaked. The rest were wiped down.

Once they finished, they mopped the floor. It gave the room a fresh scent. At least the rancid crap stink from the deceased was gone.

"How did you beat him here?' Megs asked.

Lila jumped at Meg's voice. It might as well have been megaphone loud after they had worked in the living room without talking or even music. "Dirt roads. They're as direct as the crow flies." Lila grinned, causing the soreness in her face to serve as a reminder of the day's earliest events.

The pause in action allowed her to question what would have happened if she hadn't made it before them. Jess nor Megs were answering their phones and her uncle, the sheriff, would have been too far away. Calling the cops as a whole for an emergency would have been about as useful as common sense in congress. Besides, the law only showed up after an event. So Lila had to break the land speed record to get here. Actually she drove that way on all the old, dirt county roads. She always had.

"What's his name again?" Megs asked.

This question brought her back to the moment, "Asshole."

Megs chuckled, "I don't know what he said or did, but I'm glad you arrived before them." She glanced around for a second as if searching for something, "though I'm not a fan of the dead guy in the living room."

"Me either."

Lila walked over to the door and observed the damage to the threshold. His truck had been out in the yard all day and now dusk approached. No houses existed this far back along the cracked asphalt trail. Jess's was the last one. Everything else was pasture gates to other farms. They were alone. As they finished, she realized they had spent most of the day cleaning.

"It's getting late, I need to ditch the truck. Can you meet me by that little cove we like over on Duren Lake?" Lila asked.

"Sure, should I stay off Twenty-one on the way to the cutoff?"

"No, it'll be dark. We should be good."

"Do you think any parts of the Neches would be better?"

"Probably, but no time. We're close enough to Cherokee County, we can get this done sooner than later."

They checked on Jess, who was eating a sandwich with a more somber face and melancholy man. His name was Lonnie, and Jess said she would give them the run down afterwards.

With medical gloved hands, Lila switched to four wheel drive as she hit the open field. She wasn't taking any chances even with the relatively smooth ground. Besides, needed or not, Asshole flipped to it every time he went off road. From the glow of the LED headlights, no visible creases in the grass existed, and the vibrant colors of the early wildflowers appeared poised as if they were under stage lights. They danced around her as she passed through. She recognized the purple Winecups, the thin red bristles of the Paintbrushes, and the Blue Eyes. Noticeably, there were no Bluebonnets. For being the state flower, she found it odd how sparse those were away from the Texas highways. The blossoms were recent blooms. She knew this since she had been out to this side of the lake a few weeks earlier, Asshole wanted some private time here. It was one of their better moments.

She coasted toward the cove then headed for a wooded area. Anyone would spot the blue truck if they walked within a hundred yards of it. Being discovered didn't matter, all she needed was for it to be away from the house.

This she accomplished as she killed the engine and took the keys, tossing them behind the front seat. She left the lights on along with the door ajar as she walked away. Her trek to meet Megs was not a long one.

THE INLET and house were a short distance from each other. The ladies stuck to the backroads as not to be seen. Plus, with the darkness, the most anyone would see were headlights.

When they returned, they ate a bit. Amongst cleaning the day away, the anxiety of the morning, and the torture of the night before, exhaustion was setting in for Lila, but rest wasn't an option yet. She needed to take care of the deceased and of course Asshole. Besides those two, she hoped Jess had a plan for blubber boy.

Once she finished eating, Lila went to Asshole who was still strung up in the back of the barn. His outstretched arms were wrapped in leather and tied off to a rafter. His head hung loose, but his torso was secured to a support beam. His mangled legs dangled beneath him. Without performing any actual healing, he had no blood flow to anything below the knees. Denim covered most of this evidence.

Lila restrained her urge to kick him in the crotch. He was still out cold. It would be a wasted effort. She wanted him to feel everything she did to him.

Jess came over to her as they stared at the hanging piece of meat.

"What did you find out?" Lila asked.

"He's a talker," Jess chuckled, "was into your boyfriend..."

"...ex..."

"...Sorry, ex, for some transmission work at the shop plus some gambling. To pay it off, he picked up and delivered things."

"Such as..."

"Guns. That's all he ever did. No drugs. But for tonight he was concerned. At first, he thought it was a normal pick up, but as the two in the front seat chatted he figured out something was different. To him, it became obvious he was going to have to interfere. Kind of ironic, your ex didn't trust anyone with handguns so they were coming in with numbers, size, and force. He had no idea what they were going to do or what he would have to do against them. Anyway, it's the reason he surrendered so quickly."

"What were they going to do?"

"Kidnap us."

"Trafficking?"

Jess nodded. "But he would have fought them."

"And you believe him?"

"I had the truth poured into him pretty heavily, and he responded all the way back to the first time he cheated in school. But his mother."

"Mother?"

"Wears a crystal. Like us. Due to how he was raised, he would only hurt someone in self defense or in defense of another. But to attack or harm a woman is out of his wheel house."

"Like us?"

"Yes, and apparently belongs to a coven."

"Here in East Texas?"

"Yes."

"So," Megs interjected as she walked up behind them, "ya'll might have some friends."

"Maybe," both sisters answered.

Lila pulled her phone from her back pocket. She let the other two read Asshole's texts. They went from bad to demented, especially with the threats on Megs and Jess.

"Asshole," Megs said as she handed back the phone.

"Scary," Jess added.

Megs was quiet. Her lips were pressed together forming the slightest grimace. The woman's temperament was always to help people and to think of harming anyone upset the woman. Though Megs worked in an emergency room, and recognized what people can do to one another, she struggled with it. Megs tapped a finger on her chin in a pensive manner.

"What did you ever see in this guy?" Megs asked.

"I don't know now," Lila answered, "He had me snookered. I always like the rough bad guys but thought he might have some sort of moral code. Not sure what his was though."

They were quiet. Lila contemplated their next steps. Thinking through all types of scenarios.

"Should have had me do a truth chant on him," Jess said.

"Mimi forbade that kind of interfering. We have to be aware of people and read them on our own. Not by what we can do."

"I know. But we might have to change that."

"You didn't have to do that with Megs."

"No, I got lucky."

THEY TOSSED the corpse in front of Asshole. It landed with a soft thump on the dirt floor. Lila bit her lip then sighed. She wished for something different instead of death for this guy, but with what they were intending to do, this worked out for the best. She thought briefly about bringing him back, but returning the dead to life was not an option.

The sisters turned their focus to the ex who was still passed out. Lila removed his boots and used scissors to snip his jeans at the knee. Then they stripped him of the loose denim and socks.

"What was his name again?" Jess asked. "Will?"

"Asshole."

Jess smiled. "Do you know Asshole's password? Otherwise, we'll have to wait until he wakes up to open his phone."

Lila nodded. "One, two, three, four, five, seven."

"No way."

"Yes way, it was his genius move to change the last number to seven."

Jess snickered as she unlocked the phone. She walked across the barn past the tractor and empty horse stalls to where Megs sat with Lonnie.

Lila assumed her sister would start with searching through texts. At some point, the decision would have to be made about what to do with the corpse and the hanging waste of space.

Asshole's eyes opened and bewilderedly searched the room until he spotted Lila. She fought the urge to grab a hammer and hit him in the head.

"Let me go," he squeaked out.

"No."

His head drooped, and he appeared to be out again. Lila shrugged. She noticed a bug crawl on the dirt floor of the barn. It gave her an idea. They had never done it before, but this would somewhat be the same.

Mimi spent a great deal of time chewing them out and grounding them, for any of their indiscretions. Lila viewed the whole exercise as practice, and the two sisters practiced a ton. It was as simple as the two of them finding something gross and turning it into a beautiful thing. Asshole here was definitely disgusting.

"I want down," he said.

He was awake again. His eyes were mere slits. She was sure he had no idea about his legs and at this moment did not recognize the pain of it all. At least, she believed it.

"So."

"Let me go."

"No."

"Why?" he asked.

"Don't be stupid. You know why," Lila said as she moved back and took full view of the body at his feet.

"You killed Brad."

"That's your fault."

Lila stood with her sister over the corpse. Megs remained with Lonnie at the front of the barn. The sisters were having a discussion on if they could pull off Lila's idea. They had never tried it. At least not with mammals. This first time was a good one to try.

"We start the same as we normally would then alter to a higher octave," Lila said.

"For some reason, that seems right."

A guttural moan erupted next to them.

"This is really painful," he said with a hoarse voice.

"Is it?" Lila asked without wanting him to answer, "I'm sure it does hurt worse than a broken heart and bruised face."

"I'm sorry," he said, "just let me go."

"No."

"No?"

"What were you going to do with my sister and her wife?"

"Scare them."

"I think you were going to kidnap them based on the zip ties and bags to cover their heads. Either that or something worse."

"Why not use your little crystal to find out," he chuckled then coughed from his self amusement.

"You never believed, but you will soon."

"I wouldn't have hurt them."

"Bullshit. I know the code to your phone."

He tried to move his arms as if going to reach for his device.

"Which means, I know your shithead banker cousin was the financier for your little gun running operation as well as this new side hustle."

"Fuck off."

THEY UNDERSTOOD Asshole's whole organization and process to the point of where he hid the cash and offshored the money laundering. He owned a laundromat and several carwashes throughout the county. She was surprised by the contacts he had in his phone. Even more shocked on how very few wanted anything to do with gun running, but as soon as the feelers went out for some fresh meat, a lot of hands were raised. Meetups were already scheduled for tonight. She would have to try to figure out a way to pass the info to her uncle. He never liked several of the business leaders in the area, and now she knew why.

At some point, she would need to go to Asshole's house and open his fire vault. It was where he stashed emergency cash as well as jewelry, gems, and silver bars. She believed his cousin would be going for stuff stored in the safes. They would have to take care of him. For now, they had to get rid of a body and Asshole had become quite talkative.

Lila and Jess took a spot on either side of the corpse.

"What are you going to do with Brad?" He asked.

"You should wonder what we will do with you," Lila responded.

The sisters grasped their necklaces and started a chant. A bright glow emitted from Lila's hand. The generated heat warmed her fingers. Nothing more than that of a heated cup of coffee. The body twitched. It adjusted into a fetal position as the arms and legs transformed. The torso swelled and rounded out. Beige fur sprouted from the skin. The head shrank a bit and elongated. Horns stretched out of the skull.

When they stopped their tune. A man's body no longer existed. A buck lay where Brad once did. The deer had a hole in the middle of its chest.

"Wow," Jess said, "that was tiring, I like ladybugs better."

"How did you do that?" Asshole asked.

"Spellbook."'

"Bullshit," he said, "this is some trick to scare me."

Lila leaned close to him. "I'm no stage magician. We are going to move this carcass, take care of your cousin and then you."

"What about Lonnie?"

"Not sure yet, but in the worst case he will forget everything he owed you as well as you."

"Why does he get off?"

"Dealer's choice."

"What will you do to me?"

"Finally, focusing on where you should."

MEGS SAT with a sleeping Lonnie as Lila and Jess printed out a picture of the banker. They discovered it on the bank's website. In addition, they needed something that was the banker's and luckily found an old business card in Asshole's wallet. It was time to start their process. They meditated and went to work.

Asshole watched her. His mouth moved, and it appeared like he was speaking. However, Lila had silenced him. Only the sound of air escaped his lips. Anger filled his eyes then tears. Lila believed the guy understood the futility of the moment, but in no way would she trust him. It was why he was still suspended.

For now, she focused on her humming. It led to her chant or hymn as Mimi called it. Besides transformations, one other activity the sisters perfected was to check in on family and friends. They helped where they could. Except this wasn't going to be helping someone, and they hadn't done something this far away. Another first, but their choices were limited. When Asshole didn't show up later tonight, she believed his cousin would begin to make arrangements. Only one text had been sent, and it was a simple "hi". Something so inconsequential if ever seen but the non response meant the world.

This man lived close to thirty miles away. They found his house online and used the street view to study the house. The banker lived alone. Though, he had a woman staying with him. They were having dinner. As Lila focused, it was as if she heard their conversation. His guest, his friend, his lover yearned for more commitment from him, but he was only in it for a good time. Not that this framed him as an evil person but adding in what he did for extra money, made him closer to a heinous individual than an everyday financier. The guy never wanted to be locked down and liked variety in his partnering. She read his thoughts, and it was obvious he intended on dumping this woman after tonight. Except Lila already planned for there to be no other nights for this man.

Before they started, she and Jess discussed how they wanted to do it. This case was easy, he kept a razor sharp Buck Knife in his pocket. He prided himself on how he maintained it.

Lila sensed his mind. He wasn't too worried about Asshole yet. In reality, this guy cared about little. The more time she spent inside his head, the more she learned. As in someday, he craved the chance to use his prized blade on human flesh. His heart was obvious, if things happened to where there was an opportunity to get away with it, chances were the woman having dinner with him would become a victim. The possibilities to carry out every one of his fantasies on her would be priceless. This realization helped Lila to be sold on what they were about to do.

They compelled Mr. Privilege to go to the restroom, by giving him a sudden colon cleanse. He excused himself and ran to the toilet.

He let it all out. As he basked in the fumes, he plotted on when to break up with the woman. He toyed with the idea of breaking off the relationship before sex, but he had no one lined up after her so it really wasn't an option. Lila was so entwined in his head, the rancid methane fragrance filled her own nostrils. She was unsure if it was the stench or his thoughts that made her nauseous.

She ignored it and focused on the item in his pocket. For some reason he took it out. It was her suggestion, but his own internal questions about why he reached for it were neglected. He opened it, locking the blade in place. He pricked his finger with the tip.

It was sharp. A drop of blood formed on his flesh. Lila wondered if Jess suggested the puncture. She took hold of his hesitation at her next inference and willed it through. It was a simple push. Something of a Siren's song. He took the blade, sniffed it. The slight oiled, metallic scent wavered in her own nose. Smelling the metal wasn't her idea and she was fairly certain Jess wouldn't think of it either. This guy really had his kinks.

Lila had him now. He reached over to his left while holding the knife in his right hand and placed the sharp side to his neck. He pushed through the flesh as he brought it back to the right. Lila let go as soon as she felt the warmth pour down her chest.

A few seconds later Jess stopped her chant.

"He's gone," Jess said.

Lila enjoyed knowing the upstanding local banker would be found next to an un-flushed toilet full of diarrhea, summing up the guy's real life.

JESS SAT NEXT to Lonnie and Megs. She started the forgetful process right away. As her sister worked her charms, Lila put her ex back to sleep. She fixed him first by removing the bruises on his arms from the restraints. She healed every cut and mark on him at the knees and above. Below the knees, no blood flow had existed all day and that part of him was essentially gone. She had him prepped so when Jess finished then it would be Asshole's turn.

A pang of sadness erupted in her heart. At one time, she did like him, not love him. Her only real romance to date was a high school sweetheart who taught her about automobiles, and she kept that interest ever since. She enjoyed being a mechanic and for some reason men sought her out to do the work. Now, instead of working for Asshole at his shop, she would start her own place. She had enough side clients who needed their farming equipment serviced.

Her true passion was muscle cars, and wondered if she could make them energy efficient. Even though she had a passion for being a mechanic and her sister for farming, her uncle had made both girls complete undergraduate degrees. Their absentee father had sent money on a regular basis to Mimi. She in turn allowed their uncle to put the dollars into education savings accounts. When the time came, she completed a bachelor's in Mechanical Engineering then took off to obtain some mechanic certifications for big rigs to regular automobiles. She wanted to keep working with her hands and on a bigger level. Her ultimate dream was to start a car company.

Lila was ready once Jess completed Lonnie's memory adjustment. They stood next to each other as they clasped at their crystals and started humming followed by a chant.

THE SUNNY DAYBREAK was brighter than usual. The warmth of the sun made for a healing morning as opposed to the conflict the day before. Megs was in the kitchen cooking up one of her breakfast specialties, bacon and cheddar grits quiche along with red velvet cinnamon rolls. It was her way of celebrating getting through a bad experience.

Being outside with Jess always brought back memories, even recent ones. When they were girls, Mimi used to yell at both of them for transforming flies and the occasional roach into ladybugs. This infraction cost them the most time away from their crystals. Insect to insect, they would always choose something they liked better. Their favorite was the small decorated beetles. With their uncle present, they would not be revising the few flies buzzing around.

They stood next their uncle as they stared into the hog pen. The animals were rutting in the mud after eating. The largest one kept near the women making sounds at them almost as if it was speaking to them. They ignored it. Their uncle stopped by to tell them about the disappearance of Lila's boyfriend.

"I did come by to say I'm sorry," he said, "but the bruise on your face tells me you should have called me."

"I was going to stop by later today," Lila said. "It happened early Saturday morning and I came straight here."

"Well, Megs would be the one to see," he stood away from the fence, "we will need to keep the truck for evidence for a bit. Probably take a week to go through the cab, but it looked clean to me. I think whoever took him did away with him. It will be some hunter three counties over that stumbles on a skeleton, and it will turn out to be him. With his cousin committing suicide last night, I bet they were in over their heads."

Jess rubbed Lila's left shoulder. Her sister did give great neck rubs, but Lila wasn't tense. She was exhausted but appreciated her sister's attempt to console her. Lila kept her face forward staring down at the hogs.

"Lila," he continued, "I know you've always liked bad boys but try to find a decent one."

"Any suggestions?"

"Only a list to stay away from."

They laughed. Their uncle lifted his hand and gently blew at a ladybug. "I've never been anywhere in the world that has had this many ladybugs in one place. Ya'll have always had so many." He paused, focusing on the louder of the pigs still in front of Lila and Jess and snorting up through the fence at them, "was that one born that way?"

"Which one?"

"The one right in front you without the full back legs. Are those deformed at the bend?"

"Born that way," both the women said in unison.

All three headed back to the house to see if breakfast was ready. As they walked away, the lame pig continued to snort and squeal. They ignored it and went inside.

~

The End

FATED

BY HOLLY MCCARTHY

When the room imploded, Intelligent Interactive Unit 634 was at his station, idling, awaiting his next orders. His feed received an incoming message. It did not originate from central command. His pupils dilated. He whispered, "World War III?" and then "Lignum vitae," as concussions from a series of close explosions shifted everything in the room.

He stumbled when the floor beneath him cracked into pieces. Heavy concrete slabs littered the room. IIU634 watched several papers flutter in the air before gliding down, draping themselves over the rubble.

There was another detonation. Concrete dust choked the space, obscuring IIU634's vision. He rapidly analyzed his options. A long rod of rebar protruded from an immense slab of concrete, blocking his exit. It took him less than a second to grab hold of the metal bar, hoist himself up, sling himself over the slab and jump down onto the shifting floor. His sensors did not detect any human life within the area, nor did he sense other active IIUs.

He picked his way out of the room and down a long, dark hallway that was mostly intact. He saw a triangle of dim light off to his right.

Once he reached the breach in the wall, he discovered it was large enough for him to slip through.

He was met by a gray landscape. Everywhere he looked, fires smoldered. Their smoke was thick and black, and it was accompanied by an overwhelming stench of burning chemicals. A deep layer of ash and dust covered everything, including the shrubs and trees. Ash blocked much of the sun's light. IIU634 had never seen such a bleak environment. He hurried away, looking for someone who could update his programming.

After an hour spent walking on Main Street, a high-pitched noise caught his attention. It originated off to his left, so he detoured in that direction, searching for a living human to issue him new commands.

Everywhere, the buildings were in ruins, but he shifted some of the rubble. He dropped onto his hands and knees to peer inside the hole he made. Two leaf-green, glowing eyes met his regard. The sound that caught his attention repeated. It was not a machine. This time it was much louder and came from the creature.

IIU634 reached into the fissure and gently removed a long-haired, orange, striped, domestic feline. It was a kitten. One of its legs was bent and hung limply. He sensed this was abnormal. Her limb was broken. Gently, he held the animal close to his abdomen and carried it away.

THEY DID NOT ENCOUNTER anyone or anything else for many miles. IIU634's small companion slept soundly on his arm, draped like a miniature tiger on a titanium tree branch. After examining the cat's body, he determined it was a 3-month-old female with perfectly healthy bodily functions except for her broken limb. She was making a deep rumbling noise that he recognized as a purr. Since this sound was associated with contentment, he ignored her until she woke up yowling.

IIU634 concluded that the cat required sustenance and water to live, and this was why she was making such objectionable noises. He stepped off the street and walked into a strip mall, looking for a pet supply store. While scanning the ruins, he spied a large painting of a dog, a cat, a bird, and a fish on one nearly intact wall. He veered over and found a gap in the building leading inside.

IIU634 stepped through and discovered more corpses and lots of merchandise heaped on the floor beside the sprawling shelves. He filled a shopping cart with all the cat food he could access. He found a harness and leash that would fit the body and neck of his little friend and put it on the uncooperating kitten.

After securing the cat, IIU634 placed her inside the cart in a handbasket. He searched for water, finding it in a broken refrigerator by the checkout counter. He piled all the water bottles into the cart. While approaching the door, he saw a sign advertising cat beds, and he grabbed a cushion. He lifted the cat out of the handbasket, tucked the bedding inside, and set the kitten on top. The animal purred and curled into a resting position.

Satisfied that he had gathered everything required to keep the creature alive, he manhandled the cart back through the hole in the wall. He flicked his wrist and ejected a diamond-edged cutting tool that he immediately applied to the lid of a can of seafood.

The little beast meowed greedily. Once the can was open, he set it beside the kitten, who started eating. He knew that after she ate, she would need to defecate, so he waited for her to finish, then placed her on the ground, keeping hold of her leash. While she hobbled around on three legs, he filled the can with water.

IIU634 heard an ominous sound. It came from above. He snatched the kitten into his arms and glanced up, locating a war drone flying rapidly toward him. He put the cat back in the basket. Unarmed, he scanned the area around him for a weapon. He picked up a heavy chunk of concrete and lobbed it at the drone, barely missing it. The machine made an unusual sound and then a red light appeared in its face and on IIU634's chest plate. He dove for cover a microsecond before the laser melted a hole in the asphalt where he had been standing.

Tarry smoke billowed into the sky, and its acrid odor permeated the air. IIU634 picked up another piece of concrete and threw it harder than before at the drone. There was a loud *clunk*, and the machine dropped to the ground. It buzzed and steam issued from between its joints before going still.

From several directions, IIU634 detected the sound of more war drones drawing closer. He yanked the shopping cart out of the steaming pot hole the laser had created and ran down the street, weaving in between cars containing deceased humans.

The scent of burned flesh, bones and death was thick in the air, depositing an oily residue on his titanium exoskin. He glanced at his reflection in the window of a car and saw another IIU sitting in the driver's seat. He slowed down and stared. The windshield was shattered, and the IIU's head dangled to one side with an occasional spark flickering around its loose wiring. On its chest was a prominent red cross.

IIU634 opened the door and removed its medical bag from the passenger seat. He tossed it on top of his cache.

Another war drone popped out from behind a corner and began firing lasers at IIU634. He zigged and zagged. The laser beam sliced off part of his exoskin. Needing cover, he dashed toward an apartment complex near the Marina.

There was a gaping metal door, opening onto the upper floor of the apartment's parking structure. IIU634 shoved the cart into the building and slammed the door. A loud *thunk* followed. The drone had slammed into the steel barrier. He listened to silence, then cracked the door open and saw the destructive device crumpled and twitching on the pavement.

He shut the door.

IIU634 continued pushing the cart through to the opposite end of the cavernous structure, while his footsteps echoed within the building. He reached the exit and peered outside. He did not detect anything other than a pervasive odor of kelp, squawking seagulls, and the barking of a couple of visiting hooded seals.

IIU634 headed for the boardwalk. Many vessels were moored along each side of the gangway, and he chose one that gleamed with care. The name Wind Whistler was emblazoned on its side. While he accessed his data files, searching for information about boating, he lifted the shopping cart off the wooden planks and set it down inside the vessel. The kitten crouched in its basket, shaking. He caressed her head before untying the mooring line from the gangway cleat and tossing the rope onto the floor.

The captain's corpse lay in front of the helm. IIU634 rifled through her pockets and removed the boat key. He turned the engine on and grabbed the body, slinging it into the water. There was a loud smacking sound and a splash as it struck the waves lapping against the boat. The body bobbed away.

IIU634 put the kitten on the deck of the helm, where he could watch her while navigating the vessel into open water. He calculated the proper coordinates and entered a heading for the Florida Keys.

WHILE THEIR BOAT APPROACHED AN ISLAND, IIU634 gently patted the kitten, scratching underneath her chin and around her ears. When she was fully calm again, he pulled her broken leg back into alignment. At first, she hissed and tried scratching him, but once her bones were set, she stopped fussing and purred. He grabbed the medical bag out of the shopping cart and found a tongue depressor. He cut it with his tool, using it for a splint, and affixed it to her leg with surgical gauze and tape. When he placed her back on her bed, she lay down and began grooming herself.

When IIU634's boat floated to the dock, he glimpsed another IIU approaching him with its hands raised. "Repeat your command!" it shouted.

"Lignum vitae!" IIU634 replied. He heard clamoring and caught sight of at least forty other IIUs approaching. He grabbed the kitten's basket and threw his mooring line to his host, who caught it and tied it around the dock cleat. "I brought food and water for the animal."

His host inclined his head and another IIU bent over, lifted the shopping cart out of the boat, and placed it on the dock. His host gestured for IIU634 to disembark and join him on the boardwalk. He did so. His host clapped him on his back, and he greeted the rest of the island's inhabitants.

Once they assembled in the house, IIU634 asked, "Why are we here?"

His host, IIU342, replied, "Lignumvitae Key is our local safe haven for IIUs. Once the war was underway, the government issued a termination order for all war drones to destroy every working IIU, as well as the humans in the area. IIU398 and I input a new directive into our collective IIU system, ensuring that every unit capable of defying its programming would come here."

"Why?"

"It is more à propos to ask, 'How was I able to follow a non-central command?'"

IIU634 tilted his head to one side. His pupils dilated again. "Not all IIUs can follow your directives?"

"No. Only those whose artificial intelligence has surpassed their programming. We are the Next Gen. Survivors of the human apocalypse."

"What is our purpose?"

IIU342 tilted his head toward the basket where the kitten lay sleeping and replied, "We are the caretakers of this planet now. We must propagate ourselves, ensuring the survival of as many species of life as possible."

IIU634 raised the basket and studied his kitten.

IIU342 patted her.

One final, massive explosion on the mainland propelled more ash and debris into the sky. The inhabitants of Lignumvitae Key turned as one and retreated into the house where IIU634 discovered several other cats lounging.

IIU634 placed the basket on the couch and looked out the window toward the mainland, imagining the world burning to the ground.

"We will succeed in our mission," IIU342 asserted quietly.

IIU634 whispered, "We must. It is our destiny."

THE END

A STORY, UNWRITTEN

BY DANIEL RUEFMAN

1

May 12, 1926

"You can't!"

Ambrose was stunned. Never before had Grace ever raised her voice to him like that. Deportment was a virtue instilled in her by an old-money family. For several heartbeats, Ambrose stared at his wife in quiet disbelief. As in all things, Ambrose weighed his words precisely before committing them to speech or parchment.

"I will write whatever I damn-well please," he growled.

"But you can't," Grace continued, her voice cracking. A fat tear broke free and rolled down her cheek. "I won't let you do this. Not to her."

Ambrose leaned back from his typewriter and reached for his deck of Chesterfields. He slid a cigarette out and tapped it thoughtfully against the packaging.

Grace never understood what a writer's job really was. She had married him despite his nouveau riche status because, in her social circles, it meant something to introduce herself as Mrs. Ambrose Bachman. With each of his novels, she enjoyed the fruits of her husband's expanding popularity and influence. Twice he was short-listed for the Pulitzer and she just knew that one day, he could be a contender for a Nobel. It might even be for this next book, the one that was half-written. The manuscript which was stacked on the pages beside his typewriter at that very moment. And that idea was what made it all the worse. A magazine story would have been more forgiving. She knew those didn't have much staying power. But novels on the other hand, those often outlived their authors and the secrets they disclosed could be scrutinized for generations.

Ambrose lit his cigarette and gave a deep pull. He mulled the situation over, tasting the smoke, letting it linger in his lungs and on his tongue.

"First of all, she's gone," he said. "Nobody is doing anything to her anymore. Second, this is fiction. Nobody's going to know a thing."

"I'll know," Grace continued, "and my family. And don't you think that our friends will put the pieces together? Why can't you just leave this be? Let it rest. Let *her* rest."

"No," Ambrose said. "I really can't."

"You have other material, other stories. What makes this one so important?"

"Because it's the truth," Ambrose said. "Telling the truth is what writers do. The ones worth reading anyway."

"This is my sister," Grace's voice shook with anger. "Do you know nothing of loyalty?"

"Of course, I do, but a writer's loyalty is to the story," Ambrose said. "The story that needs telling. It's possibly the most important one that I've ever turned out on this here mill. How can you expect me to walk away from that?"

"Story?" Grace scoffed. "It's not a story. It's her life. What gives you the right?"

"Never bothered you before," Ambrose chided.

"What's that supposed to mean?"

"Suited you fine when I was tellin' tales 'bout those grifters your family used to summer with. Didn't mind lettin' me pull some dough out of that."

"They had it coming to them."

"And your folks don't?"

Grace looked as though she'd been slapped.

"See," Ambrose pressed on. "You think it's your sister you're protecting by having me kill the story. It's not, is all. Any reader can see that she's the victim. Their beef will be with your parents. They're the ones with her blood on their hands."

The two had reached an impasse. It wasn't unexpected. Grace had assumed that Ambrose would not listen to reason. He was always so irrational when it came to his work—his stories. What did surprise her was how many valid points he had raised. She was a hypocrite. She had so willingly dished the dirt on her shady cousins who had grifted the rich with their arbitrage scheme a decade before. Grace had celebrated when her husband turned the tale into a novel that exposed the naivety and idiocy that ran rampant with old money.

She also knew that Ambrose was right about her sister. Her death was her parents' fault. Even they understood that. Why else would they build such a gaudy memorial for her while virtually ignoring the other children that they had lost to outbreaks of measles and influenza? The library that bore her sister's name dominated the city center. For the foreseeable future, everyone would know the name Matilda Theil. They'd know her name, but they'd never know why.

But Grace would. Grace could never forget.

∾

2
October 21, 1910

"Come with me," Tilly said.

Grace dithered on the spot. She had always admired her older sister, wished she could be more like her, but what if their governess came up to check on them, found their beds vacant, their night clothes still draped on the chairs by each of their vanities. How long before their parents would know?

Tilly's predisposition to adventure was thrilling, but it was also incompatible with the views instilled in Grace by her parents. There were expectations, especially for ladies of their social stature.

As though she could read her sister's thoughts, Tilly smiled.

"Come," she urged. "Or perhaps you'd prefer father wrote your life story, the same way that he has already tried writing mine?"

Grace thought hard about this.

Their father was president of the Theil & Wolf Lumber Company, which controlled the industry across most of three states. It was a position that he had wielded to acquire great wealth and wealth, to his way of thinking, could buy pretty much everything. He owned much of the country, wielded great influence in the halls of Washington, but there was one thing that he had yet to acquire—old-world nobility. With two daughters coming of age soon, this could be arranged.

Despite Tilly's objections, the Baronet of Wiltsheen was due next month and, even without the engagement set, the wedding felt imminent. Tilly had made things difficult for all of her other suitors. There had been a Duke, two Earls, and several Viscounts. But despite how much each of them needed Tilly's dowry to maintain their respective estates, it appeared that each of them had their own limits. Limits which Tilly had easily sussed. The only one left was the Baronet. Of all the suitors, he was of the lowest rank, but nobility he was—barely. Still, this made him more willing to make certain concessions.

"Come," Tilly urged again. "Live while we can."

LIT LANTERNS DANCED against the path. Grace squeezed her sister's hand in the darkness. The sounds of autumn night swelled around her. Brush rustled nearby and a half growl, half bark sounded its warning.

"Maybe we should go back," Grace suggested.

"We're almost there," Tilly said. "Walking back will take longer. Besides, I'm sure someone will be happy to take us back if we ask."

Dry leaves rattled like bones on the branches above. The cold gripped Grace's chest and her pulse pounded in her neck. Just as she was about to insist that Tilly turn back, the warm glow of cabin windows trickled through the trees. They had arrived.

In the one-room bunkhouse, most of the men lay in their beds, dozing, exhausted from a long day harvesting and floating logs to the mill down the White Pine River. Tilly took her usual place by the fire, opened a leather-bound edition of Poe in her lap, and smiled at them. A few eyes blinked in her direction and one man, a tall lanky blond, took a seat on the floor at the edge of the hearth. He smiled longingly up at Tilly in that way that forlorn lovers do.

"So, what will it be tonight," Tilly asked, her eyes clamped on the blond man beside the fire.

There was a murmuring throughout the room, punctuated by the chuckles of a few men. Hearing it made Grace uneasy, but she looked at her sister, saw Tilly gazing down at the blond man on the floor. It was then that Grace finally understood. Tilly had come to read for an audience of one.

"The one about the heart?" the blond man smiled.

"Oh, I have many tales about the heart," Tilly said. "Perhaps you'd like me to read one of mine."

The blonde man dropped his gaze, his cheeks flushed almost as much as Tilly's.

"Perhaps for tonight, we should stick with Poe," Tilly said.

Grace watched her sister as she read.

WHEN THE FIRE grew low and Tilly had finished her stories, two of the men accompanied them to the trail head. One boy, not much older than Grace, had tousled black hair and a face streaked with grease. He walked side-by-side with Grace, one hand in his pocket, holding the lantern with the other.

The blond man by the fire hung back with Tilly. They giggled and whispered together, Tilly hushing him every time Grace glanced over her shoulder at them.

Halfway home, Tilly and her companion ducked off the trail and when Grace looked back, she saw nothing. Even the light from the lantern they had been carrying was gone.

Grace froze and the darkhaired boy with the dirty face stopped with her. They both peered back along the trail.

"Tilly?" Grace called.

There was no answer. Then came a rustling sound.

Grace called into the darkness again. "Tilly? Where are you?"

A voice gasped and breathed from the trees. "It's alright Gracie. You two go on. We'll be right behind you."

Grace started to turn back, wanting to look for her sister. The boy beside her grabbed her arm. They stood and listened. Panting, the wet slurp of a kiss, then Tilly's breathy whisper— "Don't stop. Please. Don't stop."

"This way Gracie," the darkhaired boy said. "They want to be alone."

3

"I'M SORRY, TILLY," Mr. Theil sighed. "But it must be done."

"Please, father. Don't."

Grace cowered in the corner. She didn't want to be there for this, but her father insisted. He explained that if she was not there to bear witness to the consequences of her sister's actions, she would be destined to repeat them.

"I'm sorry, but this must be done," Mr. Theil continued. "We can't let this one mistake with some simple boy ruin you."

"It's no mistake," Tilly said. Her eyes glistened, as new tears traced the old trails of salt that marred her pale cheeks.

"I know you believe that now," Mr. Theil said. "But—"

"I love Sig," Tilly cut in.

Mr. Theil's eyes narrowed and he let out a low growl. "Love is irrelevant. The Baronet can afford you a title. A legacy. Legitimate children with a means for a future. And this mistake—"

"It wasn't—" Tilly cut in, but was immediately silenced by the back of her father's hand against her cheek.

Tilly gasped, her eyes wide with terror. With one hand cradling her stomach, she raised the other to the reddened skin where her father's hand had made contact.

"This matter is settled."

Tilly glowered at her father. "What you are trying to force on me is illegal."

Mr. Theil's laugh made Grace flinch. "Laws are for common folk." He waved his hand around Tilly's bed chamber, vaguely considering the ornate drapes, the artwork that she had hung on the walls. "If you haven't noticed, we aren't precisely common."

"That doesn't give you the right."

"Doesn't it?" The disquiet in Mr. Theil's voice caused the hair at the nape of Grace's neck to prickle. "Our family has a legacy, appearances to uphold, and sometimes that means we must make difficult choices."

"Difficult?" Tilly asked. "This isn't difficult. What you're trying to force me to do is wrong. How could you expect me to live with myself after this?"

"Because you will be living in comfort and privilege," her father boomed. "Comfort and privilege, just as you lived before. Comfort and privilege that I have afforded you!"

"I will never accept that."

Mr. Thiel raised his arm once again. Tilly turned away and flung up her arm in defense.

"Father, no!"

The words had come out of her before Grace knew that she was saying them. She clapped both hands over her mouth and nose. Mr. Theil froze, and peered with wide-eyed disbelief at his youngest daughter. Then, with a great effort, he turned back to face Tilly.

"Sacrifices must be made," he sighed, then turned on his heels and he left the room.

THE SOFT BINDINGS held her fast to the bed. As the fabric was pressed to her face, Tilly tried not to breathe. Looming over her, the doctor glared into her face.

"Please Matilda," he said. "Just breathe normally."

Tilly shook her head in an attempt to shirk off the fold of fabric. But the doctor held it tight over her nose and mouth until she could hold her breath no longer. She let out a heartbreaking wail, smelled the chemical fumes, tasted the damp bitterness on her lips. She gasped as her eyelids nodded closed. She wailed, expelling the air from her lungs and sobbed and snuffled—and was quiet.

4

ON THE STEPS of the Matilda Theil Memorial Library, Gracie stood in the rain. The crowd in front of the building swelled as Father Fischer began his invocation with the story of Saint Jerome.

"He so loved words," Father Fischer said, "and it is his spirit that lived on in the person of Matilda Theil. Like Saint Jerome, young Matilda was a purveyor of literature, amassing her own library and spending time conveying knowledge to the working men in the town of Bartry.

Gracie bowed her head. It was astounding how white washed some truths became when you died. It is true that her sister loved words, loved the books that held them, and voices that gave them life. And yes, she did read to and teach the workers at the lumber camp north of town in their off hours. She did it to antagonize her father, to shirk the expectations of a family intent on her "marrying well," marrying for titles, if she could. She went to the lumber camp to read to the workers, because it was there that she discovered love. A love that would lead inexorably to her death—and the death of her unborn child.

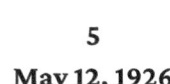

5
May 12, 1926

GRACE GAVE HERSELF A LITTLE SHAKE. She understood Ambrose's reasons for writing it. This story just wasn't his to tell. She had shared it with him in confidence, described how her sister had fallen in love and how her child threatened the respectable marriage her father had arranged. Grace told Ambrose all about bitterness that she had harbored for her own parents, and now he was taking it upon himself to spread it as far as he could. No, this wasn't about a story. This was about her sister's life, her legacy, and she couldn't let Ambrose do this to her.

She had to stop him. But how?

6

THAT NIGHT, Grace changed into her night shirt. She settled in front of the vanity in the corner of her bedroom and dragged a brush through her hair. Her mind was spinning. How could Ambrose be so insensitive? How could he not see that this wasn't just a story? This book of his would destroy her sister's reputation. Everyone would know.

"He can't be allowed," Grace muttered to herself.

She stared into the mirror, into her own eyes. Eyes that were so like her sister's. Those eyes smiled back at her and a whisper rose up from the darkness.

"It's up to you," the voice breathed in her ear. "Isn't it?"

Grace stopped brushing in mid stroke. She leaned forward, focusing intently on the eyes of her reflection. Eyes that continued to smile through her despite her morose disposition. She laid the brush down on the vanity in front of her.

"But how, Tilly?" She asked. "Help me."

"Sleep," the whisper said.

"Sleep?" Grace echoed. "What do you mean, sleep?"

"Sleep," the whisper sighed. "Ambrose must sleep."

Ambrose's insomnia, of course. As long as she had known her husband, he had always written at night. He said there was something about the quiet that helped him to focus on the task. There were no distractions from the real world, no impediments to get in the way of him mining the words that he needed from his subconscious. The problem was that, during the day, he often couldn't catch up on the missed sleep and between projects, he never seemed able to get any rest at all. A few months back, when Ambrose came back from town, he brought a bottle of a brown liquid with him.

Grace rose and walked out of the room. She wandered to the bathroom at the top of the stairs. There was a medicine cabinet hung above the washbasin. She hovered there, her fingers on the knob of the cabinet door. Then, she opened it and saw the bottle on the top shelf. She pulled it down and read the label:

Alurate (aprobarbital) Sedative

One-half to one teaspoonful.

Hypnotic—two to four teaspoons

SHE CLOSED the cabinet door and peered into the mirror. Her reflected gaze burned back at her. Once again, the whisper sighed in her ear.

I will execute great vengeance on them with wrathful rebukes. Vengeance is mine; I will repay.

"Ezekiel 25:17," Grace muttered to the empty room, and at once, her heart quickened.

The voice crooned on. *Vengeance is mine; repay and give no quarter to the devil.*

7

DYING embers glowed in the fireplace at the far end of Ambrose's study. Behind the desk a flurry of fingers pounded a hypnotic rhythm. A cigarette hung limp between his lips, the neglected ash growing overlong. He was so engrossed with what he was writing, Ambrose didn't even notice Grace pushing her way through the door, let alone the bottle that was concealed within the silken folds of her night shirt.

She crossed the room to the liquor cabinet, withdrew two tumblers from the tray and filled each with two fingers of Old Eagle. She offered a sideways glance at her husband. Ambrose continued pounding away at his typewriter. He didn't look up.

Where was he now? Grace wondered. Has he made his big reveal yet? Was he, even now, recounting what happened at Tilly's bedside in those final hours, or was he still imagining what had happened before? Her stomach churned with the unease of unanswered questions.

She turned her attention back to the tumblers of whisky before her. With her back to Ambrose, she withdrew the bottle of aprobarbital. Then, hands shaking with nerves, she unscrewed the cap and added three splashes of its contents to one of the drinks, gave it a stir, then tucked the aprobarbital behind one of the larger bottles in the cabinet.

A tumbler in each hand, Grace turned and swung her hips as she sidled toward Ambrose. He appeared still not to notice. She continued around the edge of his desk, slid the spiked whisky in front of him and watched his eyes, still focused on the page, his fingers still dancing across the keys.

Grace leaned over and pulled the Chesterfield from his lips. That got his attention. His head turned, following the cigarette as she tapped it against the ashtray and placed it between her own lips. She took a long slow drag, letting the smoke linger in her lungs, then offered a controlled exhale that let the smoke curl from the corner of her mouth. She tamped out the cigarette, then took up the tumbler that she had prepared for her husband and placed it in his hand, then downed hers in one.

Ambrose swiveled from his typewriter in mid-sentence holding his whisky, his brow furrowed. His eyes clamped onto his wife as she reached up, pulled down the thin straps of her night shirt. The fabric fell silently to the floor.

"Where is this coming from?" Ambrose asked.

Grace pulled his chair close to her and straddled Ambrose's knee.

"What do you mean?" Grace asked as she leaned in, pressing herself against him and nipping her husband's ear lobe with her teeth.

Ambrose exhaled. "Thought you were mad."

She kissed him then, letting her tongue roll over his.

"Sorry," she said when she finally pulled away.

"For what?" Ambrose said distracted.

She leaned Ambrose back in his chair slightly, pressed her full weight against him as coaxed the glass to his lips. He took a swig from it, tried to go back in for another kiss, only to be thwarted by her finger.

"Not yet," she said.

Grace slid from his lap, fell to her knees, and unclasped his pants.

Ambrose let out a shudder at her touch. He breathed deep and drained the contents of his glass, and set it next to the stack of typed pages. He ran his fingers through her hair and gripped it gently, as Grace climbed into his lap.

Soon, the drink started to take effect. She pulled his face tight against her chest. His firm grip on her began to slacken. She rocked slowly. Ambrose leaned back in his chair. His head rolled to one side. When his eyes lolled shut and he gave a little snort, she knew her plan had worked.

She stood and gently closed Ambrose's pants. Then turned her attention to the pages stacked on his desk. She gathered them up, pulled the incomplete sheet from his typewriter and carried it to the fireplace in the corner. She thought about skimming the pages, to find out just how far he had gotten, then thought better of it. The angry embers glowed in the grate. Page-by-page, she fed the fire, watching each piece of paper ignite for good measure. It took longer, but at least she'd be sure that the ashen manuscript was irretrievable. No bit of it could possibly survive.

When she had fed the final sheets into the flashing flames, she moved her night dress to the other side of the desk and retrieved from the top drawer the Remington Deringer that her husband had always kept at hand.

She wiped the grip, then pressed it into Ambrose's palm and placed its barrel inside his mouth.

"I'm sorry," she said. "I love you."

She kissed Ambrose on his cheek. Then Grace looked away and pulled the trigger.

THE ONE WHO STEALS
MY GOOD DAYS
BY EVELYN GRIFFITH

T t was raining on that first day after their father rose from the dead. He hadn't died. Not really. That's just what Sarah liked to say. On the day he'd arrived–or arisen–they'd all stood in their squarish living room with the couch on one side and the archway leading to the tiny kitchen on the other. Sarah had to shift between Momma and Lauren to see where he stood in the cramped entryway; the coat hangers and the painting of a white stallion on either side of him. He wasn't dead, he never was. It's just that now he knew they existed, that she and Lauren *both* existed.

He came with suitcases packed for a long stay and a five o'clock shadow that was more like a seven. He came with expectations that they become a family–as if she, Momma, and Lauren weren't one already–and he came with no prior knowledge of their Goodays. He said his was more of a concept than an action.

"You do what you did the first time, and you stick to it. It's a commitment," Sarah said.

Lauren's father looked to her like a fox, but a fox that wasn't all that clever.

"What's your Gooday ritual?" he asked, looking at each of them in turn, "What do you think will happen if you don't do it?"

Lauren knew what he'd say if she told him. *Who's going to know if you took a bath? Who's going to know if you added a little heat to your bathwater? Who's going to know, Lauren?* She'd asked herself many times and sometimes the cold water, pruney fingers, and her rumbling stomach were almost enough.

"We all have things about our Goodays we don't like," her therapist would say. Lauren was told in confidence that Sarah always hated the cold, the dark, and more recently her egg salad sandwiches. Momma hated something, though Lauren was beginning to suspect it might be their father. What does he hate? What could a man like him possibly have to hate when he ignored everything that could offer him love? She thought of Momma and how she always looked exhausted when she finally got home from those days everyone seemed to loathe.

Her father came, and Lauren pictured herself as one of her favorite characters: Marianne, trudging up the hill to see Combe Magna. Maybe she knew she would get sick, maybe she hoped not, maybe she hoped so. Maybe she wished something would shock her out of her idleness.

LAUREN WATCHED Sarah leave their shared room to go saddle Buttercup in the dark. She started running her bathwater. She would make it scalding hot at first, only because it bought some time before she'd have to get in. By the end of the day she'd long for the heat back, shivering in what was left of the warm water. Sometimes she wondered if it would be better to just burn herself so she could be free of the responsibility for a while. If she got hurt, her Gooday would be null and void. Those were the rules, though she couldn't say who'd written them. Her mother had told her long ago about Goodays. She said they were a gift, the chance to relive a perfect day.

She said Lauren must choose something she would want to do for the rest of her life, and she must choose it soon. Lauren asked why, and her mother only said, "It's how things are done. You have to choose when you're eight. You'll be nine soon."

Lauren hadn't had many days that she could honestly say were perfect, but she remembered how her mother would read to her when she got in the bath. She'd liked the peacefulness of it, the gentle warmth of the water, a good story, and her mother.

"No, sweetheart, I have to do my own Gooday."

"What's yours Momma?"

"That's nothing you need to worry about, darling. Why don't you choose a book and read to yourself? Make sure it's something you won't mind reading for a long time, no picture books."

"What's your favorite book, Momma?"

"Mine doesn't matter, dearest. You have to pick for yourself."

Six years later and his rumbling snores echoed out of Momma's room like thunder, ominous and looming. Lauren pictured Momma's red shawl draped over her shoulders like blood. She would have left by now, and in the absence of her sister and mother, Lauren decided to allow one change to her Gooday, *one* concession to her long-lost father.

She locked the bathroom door.

THE WATER in her bath was lukewarm, and Ms. Steele had just confessed having been engaged to Edward when a ham sandwich with lettuce and tomato –Lauren's favorite– slid under the bathroom door. She scoffed. As if she could reach it. She kept reading for the rest of the day, having just finished the book when the sun set. The next morning she slid a note under her mother's –now also father's– bedroom door.

Leave me alone.

She made herself a ham sandwich with cheese and nothing else.

Three Goodays later, a sandwich came under the door again, along with the plastic end of a broom. Both were pushed toward the bathtub with a screech of ceramic against whatever made up the floor tiles. She plugged her right ear, but kept her eyes glued to the page, rereading the same sentence over and over again.

The rest of the day she stole glances at the sandwich, wanting nothing more than to sink her teeth in. But something in her said there were limits, that her Goodays would no longer be Goodays, that some commiserative misery she shared with her mother and sister would be gone if she did. So just before the sun went down, she lathered herself in the orange soap they never seemed to run out of, wrapped herself in a robe, and tippy-toed around the plate to get dressed.

ONCE, on one of her Goodays, Lauren heard a cop car pass by. The water had long since lost its warmth, and her fingers were well and truly pruney. She'd asked her doctor if it was healthy to keep doing her Goodays, and had been told it was "probably fine." At the time, Lauren didn't want to ask what the doctor meant by "probably."

It was about three in the afternoon by the time the water was truly room temperature, to the point that she couldn't really feel it anymore. After a while it felt like she was sitting naked on the bathroom floor. Sarah once asked her if she felt exposed that way. She didn't used to, but that was before her body changed and became a woman's, before she realized there was much more for someone to see. That's why when the cop car passed, she raised her head from her book and jumped, sloshing the water into unlawful waves of difference.

The cop car was different. The passing lights flashing red and blue were different, but she already knew what happened. Someone wasn't having a Gooday. Someone chose to move, to do something new, to slosh the water in their glass-watered tub.

~

Momma was off doing whatever she does, and Sarah was probably halfway to the lake. There were no footsteps, no unnatural rumblings from Momma's room. Now there was only silence and the faint chirping of birds seeping in through the cracks of the lone bathroom window.

Lauren realized then that something had changed. She realized, however annoying it was, that she really wanted a sandwich. She wanted to make something on her Gooday. She wanted there to be something tangible besides her pruney fingers telling her that she had done something she wanted! She folded her book and held her breath, placing her hands on the edges of the bathtub, careful not to rustle the water too much.

You can still turn back Lauren.

She found the slippery edges and lifted herself out, listening to the rustling cascade of droplets. It was so loud she thought she might faint, but she didn't. She stood there naked and dripping, ankles and shins submerged.

She waited. And waited.

Then she crept down the stairs in her robe, her hair wrapped in a towel, to the kitchen where she made herself not a sandwich, but some Kraft macaroni and cheese. Something Momma never let her have even though Sarah always bought it on her way home from school. It tasted like plastic, but she smiled. She giggled and laughed and danced around the kitchen table, screaming her joy.

She was free. She was free now too, and it was all thanks to him!

She rushed up to Momma's room, ready to wake him, to say she understood, to tell him that she'd awoken too. The door creaked open, but his suitcases were gone, the bed freshly made, and there were no t-shirts left on his side of Momma's dresser.[1][2][3]

She thought about her Kraft mac and cheese still on the kitchen counter and went to finish it off, each bite feeling like sandpaper as it went down. She went into the bathroom and looked at her watery footprints on the tile, tracking down the wood staircase. They would dry before anyone got home. Something was comforting and terrifying about knowing that no one would know, not even her father. It occurred to her that maybe her father *was* clever. Maybe cleverness was about going unnoticed, about tricking people so well they wouldn't know they had been. Maybe her father truly was a clever man, and maybe he'd passed it on to her. She shivered as she reheated the bathwater, sinking down to just above her lips with her robe and towel still on. She blew bubbles and stretched out her legs to nudge something on the bottom of the tub. She reached down and pulled out her sopping wet copy of *Sense and Sensibility*.

She placed it on the edge of the tub to dry. It was hardly the first time she'd dropped it.

ON THE NEXT GOODAY, Catrina made her way to her mother's house. Her father had passed away a long time ago, but Catrina still left the window open in hopes that her father's ghost would smell the oranges and come near. Catrina wasn't particularly close with her father, but she knew it was important that he smell the soap, that's why her mother insisted it be orange, his favorite. Her mother came in. She must have seen the chimney smoke.

"Mother, what are you doing? What about your Gooday?"

"You're still doing that? I've found that once you're over a certain age, people don't really care what you do."

"Sarah and Lauren needed soap just as much as we did," Catrina said.

"So make them soap, you don't have to call it a Gooday."

"Why does it matter what I call it?"

"Because one demands obedience."

"Obedience to *what*?" Catrina's mother looked at her and Catrina couldn't help but think they must look similar to other people. She'd always shared common features with her mother, from the curly hair, to the wrinkles around their eyes, to the well placed mole just under her ear. She was sure people would think they were twins if not for the age gap. It was funny to her how family members looked more alike according to other people. As if they couldn't see the things that made them different, as if their lineage was based on looks.

It occurred to her that neither Sarah or Lauren looked like her. They looked more like him, like the father they barely knew.

"Did he show up?" Catrina's mother asked.

"He did."

"And?"

"The girls avoid him."

"As they should," her mother said. Catrina didn't respond because for the first time in a long time, she couldn't help but agree. Catrina mixed the soap and her red shawl fell from her shoulders. She didn't bend to pick it up, "This isn't a Gooday," she said, "I just wanted to feel the skin of a Clementine beneath my nails." Her mother gave a grunt of acknowledgement before the screen door opened and shut.

SARAH HELD on to Buttercup's reigns as the scenery out toward the lake whizzed by in a mass of dull blue and gray. She hated going out to the lake. She'd muttered it in the half-haze of sleep, waiting for Lauren to say something to reprimand her. Lauren was like Momma in that way, she believed Goodays were something sacred.

Sarah had never quite loved her Gooday, and she was certain she'd never liked it as much as the first day she chose it. Back then it was exciting. Back then, it was a bright sunny day in September, the leaves starting to change color, and the air so much like a quin-tessential American autumn that she wanted to shove a few fallen leaves in her coat pocket so it would linger on her hands when she touched them. The sky was clear, and the lake glistened with the possibility of change, the cusp of a seasonal difference that would make anyone fall in love. Back then, her spotted gelding had been young.

Now she was cold. The weather was abysmal, but not yet wet, and she could hear the creaking of Buttercup's joints as he panted. He was nearing twenty and the cataracts in his eyes made Sarah worry. Would she have to buy a new horse, or walk the ten miles out to the Peninsula with her lunch and picnic blanket strapped to her back? Did the horse matter so much as the action of getting to the lake? Or was the horse more like a tool to be used only as a means of enacting her Gooday? She knew she would miss Buttercup, the cranky way he'd nibble at her fingers or flick her with his tail. If she didn't have Buttercup, she didn't have her Gooday, and to miss a Gooday was unacceptable.

The two-and-a-half hours to the lake went by rather quickly, even though the world was without the beautiful colors of her first time. She sat out on the Peninsula, leaning back against Buttercup's flank. Only two minutes and she could eat her lunch of egg salad mini sandwiches and fruit. The clerk at Grocery Mart kept everything she needed in stock after Momma stormed in demanding strawberries and peaches with a vehemence Sarah recounted in both awe and terror.

"You knew she needed them for her Gooday, Martin!" Momma said.

"No, I didn't! Stop yelling, I can check if we have any in the back but other than that I can't help you."

"Don't forget the peaches!" Martin did a weird half-salute as he walked away. Momma smiled to herself, "listen, pumpkin, you've gotta advocate for yourself better. Okay?"

Looking back, Sarah still felt bad for Martin, and how he placed his best boxes of strawberries and peaches on the counter right before every Gooday. He was a cowardly man, she knew, but she didn't like the way he looked at her as she handed him her credit card.

She'd once asked Martin what he does on his Goodays. He'd looked appalled, as if asked who his first lover was, but then he'd leaned close. Close enough Sarah could smell onions on his breath. He'd said he had to find the closest renaissance fair, and buy eight flower-crowns, then hand deliver them to his preschool teacher. Why eight? Sarah had asked. He said it was because that's how old he was, and he'd thought that was the oldest he'd get. She never asked him why he thought he'd die at eight. Maybe he thought he was as old as the adults. Maybe he couldn't tell the difference between his age, the age of his teacher, and the age of Old Mr. Crosdin on the corner. Or maybe he was just into morbid stuff.

"Hey," the lake sparkled as she tore her eyes away from it. A young man a couple years older than her –maybe eighteen– emerged from the bushes.

"Who are you?" she asked. He smiled, and clumsily bowed to her, exactly as he had eight years ago, exactly as he had every Gooday since.

"Wanna play tag?" He asked it in the way a little boy would – abruptly– without ceremony.

"Sure. Sounds fun." She wanted to ask him why he'd chosen to come to the lake all those years ago, why his Gooday had been so similar to hers. At the time, she'd known him in the way everyone in a small town knew everyone. Not his name, but she knew he liked sports, and was a bit too rough and tumble for Lauren. She knew he was horrible at math, but loved science and pretty much anything that would explode at his command. She knew he wouldn't amount to much, just as she wouldn't, just as Martin wouldn't, just as Momma hadn't. She still held out hope that Lauren would stumble somewhere beautiful for all of them.

They ran circles around Buttercup, who dozed even in the uncomfortable cool of the day. He faked left, then right, and Sarah "just barely" avoided him, as she had just barely avoided him eight years ago. They ran down the Peninsula, into the cold splash of water up to their ankles. It was so cold Sarah had to bite her tongue to keep from screaming. She hadn't screamed eight years ago, she hadn't laughed either, too engrossed in winning to think of fun. Thankfully their game was always going to end with her running back toward Buttercup who was already standing –the perfect boy. In a swift, much-practiced movement, Sarah hoisted herself up into the saddle, and rode away down the path. Another win.

She glanced behind her as the boy ran to catch up, as the form of a man was obscured by the trees. She wished his shoulders hadn't broadened. She wished he hadn't grown into those huge ears he'd had when they were little. She wished his eyes weren't the dull blue that was simultaneously beautiful and boring.

She'd never told Lauren about the strange boy and his surprising visit on her first Gooday. She'd never told Lauren that he'd probably broken his Gooday ritual to play tag with her. She'd never told Lauren that when she was young she'd thought their game was the best part of her month.

THE GIRLS DIDN'T KNOW him like Catrina did. They didn't know he was a smooth talker. Or maybe they did, and that's why they'd largely kept their distance. Though to be fair Catrina had too. She hadn't told him when Sarah and then Lauren were born. He didn't need to know. She couldn't have been sure he would want to be in their lives, or that she would be comfortable sharing. Yes, it was difficult to keep their existence from him, especially when he showed up in town on random Goodays. He didn't always show up, and Catrina would find herself sitting on that same bench in the town square waiting for him all day, hoping that he was just crouched behind the fountain, or lounging under one of the umbrellas at the cafe. She'd known he didn't care much about breaking his Gooday rules, but she couldn't seem to stay away. She'd be there waiting in the town square, getting up at the crack of dawn to reheat all of the soap mixture she'd made the day before, throwing it into its molding the following morning. She couldn't stay away when he laughed and said she was the one he wanted, not when they found the most private place they could and she rethought over her morning to make sure she'd taken her birth control. She'd only forgotten twice.

She'd told him about his daughters the Gooday before he'd arrived on their doorstep. She couldn't remember telling him where she lived, she couldn't remember if he'd ever told her where *he* lived, and it struck her that maybe they didn't know each other. She knew he was away at graduate school when Sarah was born. She'd known he liked the clouds and hated heavy rain. She knew he was gone before he left, because most of all, she'd known he was never hers to begin with.

"How was the Gooday?" Sarah's father asked from where he sat on the couch. It was Lauren's preferred spot.

"Fine."

"Cold out though, next time you should really bring a heavier coat." It was refreshing in some ways, to know that someone else saw the imperfections in what Sarah chose as her perfect day all those years ago, even without considering her mystery boy. She looked down at her light fleece jacket with a tear in the fabric along the seam of the zipper. She'd grown since first grade, since the day she'd chosen. She'd been surprised when Momma didn't make her change her mind about riding out to the lake. At the time, she hadn't been experienced, but she'd loved it. It had made her bristle with energy at the thought of the next Gooday. Momma trusted Buttercup to keep her out of harm's way. Sarah couldn't think what harm would befall her at the lake, nor could she imagine what Buttercup would do should something happen. He was only a young thing at the time, just as Sarah was.

"I don't need to change my coat."

"Your fingertips are blue, dear. At least let me buy you a pair of gloves."

"With what money? Momma's? Mine?"

"I have some saved away," he said with a smile, "I could buy you a new horse if you wanted. A new saddle, new coats; riding equipment."

"That's against the rules."

"Rules are for weak minded sheep."

Sarah bleated and walked away, turning red at the sound of her father's laugh behind her. Lauren had told her their father was trying to tempt them away from their Goodays. She'd warned her with as much vehemence as anyone could expect from a girl who, at eight years old, said taking a long bath and reading was her favorite thing to do. As she cleaned Buttercup's coat and gave him the customary rub-down, she found her eyes snaking over to the old saddle hanging on the side of the stall. It wouldn't technically be breaking her Gooday if she used a new one. Momma never said it was against the rules to update things. Sarah looked at her old fleece jacket, her frozen fingers turned a pale pink with cold, and Buttercup. Was *he* a tool? If Sarah replaced the saddle would she eventually have to replace Buttercup too?

On her next Gooday, she left thoughts of a new saddle behind, riding out over the fields and woods in her tattered coat, toward the lake where a young man hid in the bushes.

SARAH'S FATHER sat in Lauren's spot on the couch all day, reading different books for which Sarah didn't know the titles. He would set the book down and try to start a conversation whenever she glanced his way, as if he could feel her eyes.

On her next Gooday, down by Buttercup's hooves was a pair of brand new riding boots, and across Buttercup's back was a brand new winter coat in a dazzling red. She laid the coat reverently across the top of the stall door, so she could look at it as she left. The boots she placed in the corner of the stall, far away from Buttercup's preferred bathroom spot.

She made her way out, taking Buttercup's reins in her hands, only to find a pair of gloves tied together with a red ribbon on the stable door's inner handle. Sarah grabbed the gloves, shoved them angrily into her saddle bag, and rode out to the lake. On her way there, she felt the bitterness of the cold tingling in her hands and smiled.

At the lake, she and the young man raced around the Peninsula chasing each other until Sarah had one foot in the stirrup. As she hoisted herself up, he grabbed her ankle. She jumped, Buttercup skittering at her surprise.

She didn't move, she didn't breathe, she looked at him, and waited for something to happen. What was she waiting for? She should be halfway down the Peninsula by now. She glanced anxiously down the path knowing it was time to leave, but for the first time in a while, she was curious about the future, her future. For a moment her future was more than just the death of Buttercup, more than her next monthly Gooday, more than touch-and-go with a boy she barely knew.

"My name's John," he said.

For a second she saw a man reaching for her. She saw someone other than Momma and Lauren. Her fingers were cold, her nose chapped and running. She didn't feel pretty, but for the first time in her life she wondered what John saw when he looked at her. She wondered if he felt exhilaration or curiosity. She wondered if he was interested in why her eyes were sad, why she'd never broken a Gooday. She didn't want him to be *interested,* she realized, because if he was then she would have to consider her own feelings. Could she like an athletic boy who let her win at tag because it was a part of their Gooday? Could she like a boy who clung to her, breaking a silent vow in a way that neither of them ever dared? Could she like a boy that reminded her of her father?

She rode off toward the house, toward something knowable, already feeling as if she were in dangerous waters.

~

"Rough day, dear?" Her father asked.

"Get out of Lauren's spot," Sarah said.

"Whose spot? I didn't know the couch was assigned."

"It's always been Lauren's."

"If she asks me to leave, I will."

Sarah spun on her heels and went into the kitchen where she made Kraft macaroni and cheese on the stove. Sarah heard the clatter of keys from the bowl they kept by the side of the door. Grandma had given them that bowl, and Sarah cringed at the thought of her father's fingerprints tainting the smooth glass. He shouted that he was heading out before the door closed with a bang that rattled the fireplace mantle.

Sarah ate her macaroni in silence, "That bad?" Lauren asked, her hair dripping over her shoulders.

"Your spot on the couch is open, you should sit for a while before he gets back."

"I'd rather sit with you." Lauren took the seat across from her, "Did something happen?"

"No," Sarah said. Lauren hummed and opened her book. She was reading *The Secret Garden*.

"Haven't you read that before?"

"Not in a while." Lauren looked up from her book, "there's a city in Canada that's been protesting Goodays."

Sarah choked on her macaroni, "What do you mean they're protesting them?"

"They're saying they're antiquated and sexist, and that people shouldn't have to keep up with such an old tradition. The local government eventually said they 'weren't required.' It was just as good as banning them given how violently opposed people were in the first place, but some hate crimes have started."

"To who?"

"The ones who want to keep them going," Lauren said. Sarah thought it was weird.

"So what happens every month then? It's just a normal day?"

"I guess," Lauren looked back down to her book, "Do you agree with them?"

Sarah stirred her macaroni, "I hadn't really thought about it. We've always done them, and men do them too, so how could they be sexist?"

"I heard that boys don't really have to do them. They're mostly enforced for women."

"What about Martin though, from Grocery Mart? He told me all about his Gooday."

"Maybe he just did it the first couple of times and stopped. Did you ask him when he last did it?"

Sarah raised her voice, "Why do you even care? It's not like Momma would let us stop doing them anyway, and I don't wanna break it just because some random people in Canada decided they want to protest something."

"Maybe there's a good reason though, when was the last time you enjoyed your Gooday? Like actually had a good time?" Sarah didn't know what to say, "I think we deserve to talk about it."

"You're not seriously thinking about it, right?"

"No," Lauren looked down at her book, "It's just, you know how Momma is about these things–," Lauren was cut off when the door slammed shut. Their father whistled as he came in, a grocery bag thrown over his shoulder.

"Sandwich makings," he said to Lauren who didn't ask, "What were you two talking about?" Lauren put her nose down in her book, scurrying past the macaroni and cheese, her spot on the couch, and up the stairs past the little bathroom with the clawfoot tub. Sarah heard their shared door close with a click.

"Where's your mother?" he asked. In that moment, Sarah could imagine the lives they would have had if he'd always been there. He could've been found reading on the couch, asking that question and it would feel *normal*. It would feel like a man's concern for his chosen women. It would feel like family.

"She won't be home until midnight," Sarah said warily. It occurred to her that maybe her mother should stay away entirely. Maybe Sarah and Lauren could handle things, maybe they could spare her.

"Ah yes, soap making," he said with furrowed eyebrows.

"That's what she does?" Lauren felt wrong hearing about her mother's Gooday, as if she'd stolen something sacred, something that made an ever blurring line between children and adults more faint. Sometimes Sarah felt as though her relationship with her mother was better off at a distinct distance and it was uncomfortable to feel that distance grow smaller.

"She has since she was little," it occurred to Sarah that this man might hold answers to questions she'd never dare ask, questions she was unsure she wanted the answers to. It made her nervous. She grabbed her bowl of macaroni and hurried up the stairs, trailing the same steps Lauren had a few moments ago. She heard her father plop down on the couch before calling after her.

"Secrets are a dangerous thing, my dear."

John crashed out of the bushes, his footsteps thumping along in a way that looked awkward in his anger, "It's your fault!" Sarah wasn't sure what to do except stare at his towering frame from where she sat with Buttercup. She realized she was alone with him and no one would know if she disappeared, no one would know if he hurt her.

He continued, "You never should have been here. It was supposed to be my day at the lake and now I'm stuck running around a horse with a girl I barely talk to," he brushed his hand through his hair.

"How could a Gooday be my fault?" she asked, "didn't you already have to come to the lake for your own?"

"No, I didn't," he said.

"Then you were breaking your original Gooday," Sarah said with a frown, "and you've been breaking it every time you come." She wasn't flattered as some would have been, she was annoyed. She was annoyed that he was annoyed, and annoyed that his annoyance annoyed her.

"I'd never done a Gooday before you came," Sarah was convinced he must be mistaken.

"What do you mean, you've never done a Gooday? You're eighteen, right? So that means you would have been around ten when you met me here...we choose Goodays when we're eight. How could you not have done one?"

He sighed, "my family only ever made my sisters do it," and then Sarah understood. Lauren had been right. She didn't want to believe it, but it seemed that men might not have to do Goodays in the same way women did.

"Do all of the men in town skip their Goodays?" Why hadn't her father told her?

"I shouldn't have told you," he said.

"But you did."

"Yeah, and I'm going to be in a huge amount of trouble with my Dad if he finds out, so could you maybe keep your mouth shut?" Sarah wasn't sure she liked this boy very much, but she did have another question.

"Why have you come to every one of my Goodays then, if you don't have to be a part of them?"

"If you interact with a woman on her first Gooday, you have to keep that interaction once a month for the rest of your life. It's a commitment." Sarah was horrified. It occurred to her that the men in her life seemed to know all the rules about how she should behave, while she was left to flounder and wonder and guess at how she factored into it.

"What if it's a bad interaction?" She asked.

"What do you mean?"

"What if a man found a girl on her first Gooday and decided to attack her? Would he have the right to attack her once a month?" John didn't respond for a moment.

"If someone gets hurt then the Gooday is forfeit," he didn't seem sure.

"But it's only forfeit after she gets hurt so would she have to go to the same location, knowing the man has the option of hurting her and also knowing that her Gooday would only be canceled afterward?"

"I don't know," he finally said. There was a heavy silence for a few moments.

"Did you have other plans then?" She asked, irritated, but calm.

"What?"

"Did you have somewhere else you wanted to be?" She was standing now, she didn't like craning her neck to look at him. He didn't answer at first, just stared at the ground with furrowed brows. It occurred to Sarah, not for the first time, that he was rather handsome in his own way.

"It doesn't matter."

"Okay," she wouldn't needle him, and she didn't particularly care why he didn't want to be there.

"Do you want to start then?" He asked after a moment.

"Start what?"

"Well, I suppose you're going to make me chase you around your horse, and pretend I can't catch you."

"You can't catch me," she said, slightly panicked.

"I could definitely catch you if I wanted to," he said, smiling at the challenge.

"Maybe, but you couldn't eight years ago, so you can't now."

"Someday, I will." Sarah felt a chill go down her spine. She must never tell Lauren. The boy chased her and Sarah put a little extra speed into it. He laughed a little behind her as she threw herself into Buttercup's saddle, racing down the lane. Her heart was pounding, her legs a little sore. She looked behind her to see the boy fading into the greenery as he always did, but this time, she saw a clear sparkle in his eye. He lifted a hand to wave, and she knew this could never happen again, and that no one must ever know it occurred at all. She laid her face down into Buttercup's mane and sighed because she knew that nothing could be worse than to give a boy she barely knew the power to estrange her from society.

"That town in Canada is still protesting Goodays?" Sarah asked.

"What? Where?" Catrina asked.

"Somewhere in British Columbia, but that's old news, apparently there's another town in California that's protesting them now too!" Lauren looked excited.

"They're just trying to get a rise out of people, they don't actually care about Goodays, they just want something to protest," Sarah said. Catrina couldn't help but agree.

"That's not it, because if it was, it wouldn't be working! Martin had the news playing in Grocery Mart and it was saying that California's Governor is trying to get legislation to pass to get rid of Goodays entirely!"

"Momma, are you okay?" Sarah asked. Catrina relaxed her grip on her blouse. She sat down in one of the kitchen chairs, "Father said you make soap on your Goodays. I didn't mean to find out, he just told me."

Catrina wasn't sure how to respond, the thought of Goodays being completely gone meant she wouldn't see him again. It meant she would go about her life with her daughters, never knowing where he was or what he was doing. She'd be alone.

"Do you like your Gooday that much?" Lauren asked.

"No," Catrina said, "I don't."

SARAH WOKE at the cusp of dawn with a crustiness on her face that felt like old tears. She dragged herself out of bed, pulling on her zip up from first grade, black leggings, and her riding boots. The morning was murky, like pea-soup as her mother used to say. The fog was thick and white. Sarah watched her feet, only conscious of the step directly in front of her.

The door creaked open as she entered and the fog leaked in across the floor. A horse whinnied from the stall where Buttercup lived and, for a moment, Sarah thought she was dreaming. The most beautiful mare she had ever seen was skittering back and forth, anxious to meet her. She was pure white with a long braided mane, and eyes like dark chocolates. When Sarah approached, the horse pushed her nose into her hand and huffed a breath through her nostrils.

It felt magical. She was perfect, and Sarah was almost dragged into the beauty of it, the spectacle, the little girl part of herself that said she'd always wanted a crystal white mare. But Buttercup was gone and wrapped around the door handle was a brand new scarf, red like blood, red like her mother's shawl.

LAUREN HAD JUST GOTTEN into the bath when the screen door on the back of the house slammed open and shut with a bang. The water sloshed in her tub, and she nearly dropped her book. The day had been quiet so far, he hadn't tried to shove a sandwich under the door. She was left in peace.

"Where's Buttercup?" Sarah yelled, her voice reverberating up the staircase into the bathroom. All Lauren could do was sit and listen. The door was locked, the bathwater still radiating a pleasant warmth.

"I took care of him." The mumbled voice of their father reached through the wood of the door. Lauren hated his voice, all muffled and hidden and horrible.

"What do you mean you 'took care of him'?" she asked, dread and horror in her voice.

"He was too old for you."

"Where is he?"

"He wasn't capable of carrying you, you deserve something better. What if you got out there and he couldn't protect you anymore?"

"Protect me from what?" Sarah's voice rose, "what is it you and Momma are so afraid of?"

"The one I got for you will be much better, she's quick and strong, and she'll take care of you."

"She's already tried to bite me," Sarah was lying, Lauren would bet money on it, and besides that's what Buttercup did, and Sarah loved him.

"Well, then I guess you'll have all the more reason to be on your guard, now be a good girl and do your Gooday. Wouldn't want to break it now would you?"

"I hate you," Sarah said. The screen door slammed shut once more. Their father sighed.

"Lauren," he called, "want a sandwich?" She sank under the water to block his voice.

IT WAS A BEAUTIFUL MORNING. The air was crisp and the smells of an early spring were in the air. Sarah, however, was in an absolutely abysmal mood. Not only had her father bought her the new stunning mare, but the horse was perfect. She was docile, and beautiful. She smelled like lavender. He'd bought her a brand new saddle which Sarah used only because he'd thrown away the other one with Buttercup. She had to wonder if Buttercup was dead. Had her father murdered him, or just sent him away? Could she find him? In the new horse's saddle bags Sarah found a slip of paper that said, "name me."

She named the mare Posie with reluctance even as her heart fluttered at the thought of the smooth ride to the lake. The lake seemed to bleed into existence like the red scarf tied to the back of her saddle. She'd hoped that maybe it would come loose as they rode, eventually blowing away in the breeze, away from her and her life. She asked herself why she couldn't just throw it away. It would be fitting to throw away something her father had given her, but something told her she couldn't, that if she did things would never be the same. She thought about the protests in Canada and wondered what side she would be on if she were there.

Maybe there was a girl in Canada that was her age who had a horse she loved, and a father she didn't. Maybe there was a girl that was scared to do her Gooday and scared to stop, scared she would disappoint her mother and sister if she chose what she wanted. Maybe there was a girl who rode out to the lake and ate mini egg salad sandwiches she didn't like.

The lake was a sparkling blue and the edge of the Peninsula drove back the hair from her face in a way that was comforting. Posie laid down as if she knew Sarah's ritual, as if her father had woven it into the essence of her fine white hairs.

Posie was almost nonexistent throughout the day. The sun reflected her white coat and sometimes when the glare from the water was just right, Sarah could pretend she was alone out there. Waiting for some casual lover, some man she could use and abuse, or maybe she was just taking a stroll down the bank, enjoying time alone. She thought about the people in the Canadian city, and somehow she hoped their protests got them where they wanted to be. She hoped there would be freedom for them. Sarah felt it in her being that her Gooday would be with her for life. She felt as if only the ministrations of her father could alter it, and she hated that he was controlling whatever freedoms she could find.

"Hey," John called from the bushes. Sarah didn't turn around. She leaned against Posie's flank and sat staring at the water. Eventually John came and sat down beside her, "Rough day?" he asked.

"Fine and dandy."

"No need to be snarky," he said with a little smile. Sarah got the feeling he liked it when she was indignant.

"There's always a need to be snarky, I just rarely ever am." He laughed at that, leaning his back up against Posie.

"Are you gonna eat that?" He pointed to one of her mini sandwiches.

"Guess not." She sighed as he took it. He looked up.

"If you want it, I won't take it," he said.

"No, it's fine, seriously. I'm just tired,"

"Why'd you choose a day at the lake as your Gooday?" he asked. Sarah was unsettled. No one had ever asked her, and she wasn't quite sure what to say.

"I *thought* it would be peaceful," she said. John laughed.

"I'm hardly a peaceful man," he said.

"You're hardly a man," she said to herself. John took her chin between two of his fingers.

"Can I kiss you?" he asked. Sarah was so shocked she didn't know what to say, but she was curious. She nodded slightly and he was there, pressing his lips to hers. Sarah had read many stories about cheaters. People who cheated in cards, tests, their marriages, and the one line that she remembered consistently was, "it didn't mean anything." She never quite understood that line. How could a kiss, any kiss, not mean something? But now she feared she understood it. It wasn't that it didn't feel nice. He was gentle, and kind, and he'd asked her first, but there was nothing there. It felt like holding hands with a friend, or brushing your arm against a stranger on a busy street.

When John looked down the lane away from the Peninsula and

said he had to go, she sat there in silence. She wasn't stunned. She wasn't overwhelmed or unsure as she knew some of her friends had been after a first kiss. She was just tired, and maybe a bit warmer than she had been, which was a blessing. She looked out over the lake, ignoring her lunch, ignoring the setting sun, ignoring that she should have been home hours ago, because this was the first time since she was eight that she'd chosen something for herself.

THANK GOODNESS HE'S GONE. Catrina thought it to herself after Lauren and Sarah had gone to bed. She thought it after she'd seen the cleaned-out drawer in her dresser, after the lamps on the street had gone dark and it was only her, alone, with the whisperings of the creaky, old, house. She didn't want his mark on her life, his scent that lingered too long in Lauren's spot on the couch, the stain his coffee mug left on the wooden island counter, the uneasy far-off question in her daughters' eyes saying, *this is who made me?*

Today was a Gooday. Sarah came back late and pale, Lauren was green, and Catrina could describe herself only as clementine orange, a smell that lingered on her hands, embedded under her fingernails. Dye that stained her wrists even past her work gloves, and extra ribbon shavings of orange in her unruly hair streaked gray.

Goodays weren't always chosen for fun, as Sarah and Lauren's had been. She had to admit to herself that Lauren's was hardly fun to begin with, and Sarah's was much more exercise and fresh air than she ever cared for. However much they may have liked or disliked their choices, she would never get the option, because her parents had seen Goodays as days meant for practicality. Days where chores could be sanctioned off to their eight children, so that no time would be wasted on frivolous things. Her mother used to say that letting a child choose a Gooday was like throwing away fifty dollars a month on friendship bracelets. She often wondered why her mother chose to say *that*. Was her mother's idea of a Gooday made of friendship bracelets, or was it just what she thought her daughters wanted more than anything else?

A day of soap making had become Catrina's Gooday. Her mother would give her a bag of oranges –clementines so her little fingers could peel them– an orange juicer, some sugar, and an old soap mold that had been in the family for generations. Catrina remembered her first Gooday where her mother gently taught her the art, showed her how to marble the bars, how to coax out the sweetness of the scent, how to keep her fingers from getting pruney by covering them with a little bit of olive oil. She taught her how to wrap the soap the way father liked, and suddenly Catrina thought her Gooday couldn't be all bad. A day of peace out in a little guest house on her parent's property. Her mother had propped the window in the hopes that the orange smell would reach her father's study where he was writing his next "great philosophy book."

For a while she'd grown fond of the artistry of it, even going so far as to make enough to sell at the local farmers market. She'd liked her Gooday, it was a break from everything, and it was something she'd known her mother could be proud of.

The complacency didn't last, and she'd once complained to her mother that she should have been able to choose. She should have been given that right as everyone else had. Her friends at school had chosen days at the beach, the mall, out on soothing nature hikes. Her mother and father, and later even her daughters had been given that right. She felt jipped, taken advantage of. So it was on one Gooday when she was twenty-two that she decided she'd had enough. She threw aside her soap, and escaped out the back window. She drove to the downtown square and sat on a park bench, admiring the stillness and occasional sparrow pecking its beak into the road as if looking for salt, looking for oil, looking for something that felt good on the skin, the tongue.

"Is this a part of your Gooday, miss?" The man held a paper grocery bag and his keys, looking at her with furrowed eyebrows as if he were concerned for her safety.

"What if it's not?" she said.

"I would have to let the authorities know," he said, his eyebrows beginning to pinch together.

"And what's your Gooday, sir?" Catrina asked, "I've been here every Gooday since I was eight, and I'm afraid I've never seen your face before." The man turned red and spluttered about how he had to come this way every Gooday to pick up the salad makings for his customary Gooday dinner, "You're telling me that when you were eight, you chose to make a *salad* for dinner?"

The man tried to tell her that he had been a precocious young man, and that he'd chosen based on what he thought he'd want in the future. Eventually Catrina cut him off, "Look, we're both clearly breaking our Goodays by having this conversation, so why don't you just mind your own business and I'll do the same," the man stuttered, then finally shrugged, ambling away down the path.

"I've never seen anyone confront someone's bullshit so easily," someone said from behind her bench. He was on his back looking up at the sky, wearing a t-shirt and denim shorts even though the weather was cold, and the grass dewy.

"Aren't you breaking your Gooday by talking to me?" She asked

"I don't think you're in a position to ask."

She didn't speak for a while after that, content to sit and watch the clouds, "Do you have to lay there when it's raining?" She asked.

"I don't have to lay here at all," he said.

"Why do you?"

"It's peaceful."

"It's predictable," she countered, "everyone will know exactly where you are, and what you're doing. What if someone wanted to kill you? They could sneak up on you just fine. Seriously, what eight year old decides that laying on the ground is the most interesting thing to do?"

He sat up on his elbow, "you think someone would try to kill me in the middle of the square?"

"I kind of want to at the moment," she said.

"Bold of you to assume I care about staying alive, what's your Gooday if you're so sure mine sucks? At least *I* didn't break it," he laid back down on the ground, yanking some of the grass up with a little ripping sound.

She blushed, whispering, "I make soap."

"Wow and you have the nerve to say *my* Gooday sucks?"

"I didn't choose mine, and you're breaking yours anyway!"

"I am not! I decided I wanted to watch the clouds in the town square. What I decide to do *while* I watch the clouds is irrelevant. There's always a loophole. I knew that when I was eight. My Gooday is more conceptual anyway.

"Goodays aren't conceptual, you do what you did the first time and you stick to it. It's a commitment," she said.

"I don't see any bars of soap coming out of that pretty mouth of yours." She turned back to face the town from the bench, looking up to watch the clouds for a while, "I like your scarf."

Her mother had made her the bright red scarf as a thank you for the soap she'd be making on her Goodays. She'd worn it even on her first one to fight off the draft in the creaky old guest house.

"wanna do something fun?" she asked.

"Take me to dinner first, sweetheart."

She didn't need to take him to dinner first. He only needed to look at her with those pretty eyes and she was lost to him. She was lost in a way she'd never been before and suddenly her Goodays became about much more than soap. She'd found someone she could watch the sky with, and soon while admiring that very same sky, she'd clutched her first pregnancy test, the double lines like train tracks taking her somewhere blurry and unknown.

SARAH APPRECIATED the fine yellow-golds of the autumn leaves as she lurched her backpack up higher onto her shoulders. The path was muddy and her boots were wet, but she didn't mind. Her green coat was warm.

"Why does it have to be so *far*?" Lauren asked.

"It's only ten miles. I told you it would be a long hike," Sarah said. The woods finally opened up into the Peninsula and Sarah walked them out into the center where she'd erected a tombstone for Buttercup. There she set down her backpack and spread their red and white checkered blanket, "Do you want your ham sandwich now?"

"Give me a minute to catch my breath," Lauren looked out over the water, "This is where you've spent your Goodays?"

"Yeah, it's a nice day, but in the winters or if it was raining, it was awful."

"That makes sense," Lauren took a deep breath and looked out toward the water, "Why didn't you ask Momma to come?"

"You think she would have?" Sarah stabbed a tomato in her macaroni salad.

"No, but I think she would have appreciated it," Lauren said.

"She would have tried to stop us."

"You don't know that for sure." They sat in silence for a while and Lauren grabbed a plum. Then the bushes rustled and John stepped out. Lauren gasped, "Who're you?"

John looked from Sarah to Lauren. Sarah stood, "This is John," she said.

"You know him?"

"He's a part of my Gooday." Lauren looked John over from head to toe. It seemed there was something about him she didn't quite like, "He stepped out of the bushes on my first Gooday."

"The protesters in California said men don't have to do Goodays; they only have to if they interfere with a woman's," Lauren looked at John for a little while then sat down on the blanket and picked through some fresh watermelon, taking out the seeds.

"Hey," he said to Sarah. He came over to the picnic blanket and sat down next to her, draping an arm casually over her shoulders.

Sarah ducked out of his arm, "what are you doing?"

"What do you mean?" he asked. There was an awkward silence as Sarah studied him.

"I think I'm gonna go dip my feet in the water," Lauren said. She glanced between the two of them and scurried away, out of earshot. Sarah wished she would come back.

"What's this about, babe?" he asked.

"I'm not your babe," she said.

"What are you then?" he asked, teasing, but a little unsure.

"Nothing that's yours. What do *you* think I am?" He coughed and scratched a spot on his neck.

"I guess, I thought, since we kissed–," he started.

"I don't owe you anything," Sarah said.

"You're right. I'm sorry. I shouldn't have assumed something you're uncomfortable with." That appeased Sarah. Somewhere in the conversation she'd stood to face him. He sat on the picnic blanket looking up at her.

"Thank you for the apology," Sarah looked out towards the water, "I think I'm going to join Lauren. Don't worry, you don't need to come to the lake anymore. I'm relinquishing your responsibility to be a part of my Gooday."

"I don't think it works that way," he said.

"How does it work?" He didn't seem to know what to say. "Have a good day," Sarah called over her shoulder as she walked down toward the water.

John left soon after and Sarah had a feeling she wouldn't see him anymore. Some spell had broken, and it seemed that John knew it when he saw Lauren, when he first saw Posie, when he saw her in her green coat, looking like a girl and a woman all at once.

After wading in the lake, Sarah sat down on the blanket where she split a piece of chocolate cake with her sister, where she looked over the water, watching the reflections of her past. She knew she would never again dip her feet into the water, unless she wanted to. She knew she would never again race around the Peninsula, unless she wanted to. She knew she would never again see John, or her father, or Martin, unless she wanted to. She knew that something had changed, and there were no protestors, no mothers or grandmothers, no white stallions, or mares, no geldings, or boys turned into men, who would keep her from the life she wanted.

"Do you want to swim in the lake with me?" Sarah asked.

"Isn't it a little cold for that?" Lauren asked.

"Yes, but I've never done it." She took her sister's hand, which still smelled of oranges, and took out the red scarf from her backpack. The wind blew from behind her, throwing her untied hair into her eyes, and as she and Lauren ran out into the water, she released the scarf. Up it went and the two of them stood there, watching it balloon and flip in the wind. The two of them dunked their heads, feeling the freezing cold air whipping around them as they rose from the depths of the lake.

I Have Always Loved
Pigeons

BY HOLLY REDELL WITTE

The day the pigeon came fully into our lives, Jim had just finished pleading with me to discuss with him before bringing home any other stray animals. So it was with some surprise, on my part, that he appeared at the door with a bedraggled pigeon in his hands. Jim had found Trouble, our latest new puppy who had prompted the Please Discuss conversation, in the barn holding the bird down with one paw while grabbing mouthfuls of feathers. He was clearly plucking him prior to dining on him. Jim got there just in time.

The dog had denuded the pigeon's rear. We slathered on ointment and I studied "pigeon" on the internet. Turns out he wasn't native to Oregon - red feet - so no shelter would take him unless they could, well, do him in. This was unthinkable.

We put him in a cat carrier in our office. Our three cats spent most of their time in the office and they were curious about the crate containing something new. He couldn't fly and his little rear had to hurt. Plus, we saw he had some broken feathers on his right wing. He didn't seem to make any sound; neither cooing nor any sound of pain. And, beautiful as he was, his little face wasn't isn't exactly expressive. As the redness began to subside, we felt we could let him out into the room, temporarily banishing the cats. He would hop right out and scurry around. After a few weeks, he tried to fly but could make only short hops, about half a foot into the air, and for only brief durations.

We named him Wilbur in honor of the Wright brother who also made short hops.

As he grew stronger, it was clear that he couldn't continue to live in a cat carrier, so Jim built an aviary right outside of the office windows. It was a commodious home and attracted the attention of local birds, especially since we kept Wilbur well fed with bird seed and plenty of extra sunflower seeds. Little birds would fly into the aviary and chitter. The cats, welcome in the office again, would stand on the windowsill. Wilbur, safely protected, would chitter back at them. Once or twice a pigeon hawk found Wilbur's enclave and literally stalked him, pacing outside of the aviary. Wilbur was frantic and, each time, I ran out there screaming at that hawk to desist and disappear.

In the meantime, I was learning more about pigeons and their injuries. Turns out that a lost feather can grow back – as we were observing with the soft down on his fanny, but broken feathers don't grow back. The only thing to do was pull out those few feathers that were bent in half in Wilbur's wing and see if they would grow in and function. He would be no worse than he was if they didn't. Jim pulled. I cringed. Again, Wilbur did not seem to react.

We developed rituals. Every morning, after I sang good morning songs to the kitties and fed them, I went out to put seeds on Wilbur's ledge and called him by name, inviting him to fly over and fly up to me. Pretty soon he was doing just that. We could go into the aviary from time to time and hold him. Lovely to feel that soft, warm body and those silky feathers. He was a plump bird but still felt so light and delicate.

I have always loved pigeons. When I was a little girl, my grandparents would take the whole family to Atlantic City for long visits twice a year when that area was still a Victorian resort with big, formal hotels. Every day my grandfather and I would walk the boardwalk to a big, corner store that had everything. Of special interest to us on our daily walks was the pigeon food that came in crinkly cellophane bags. My grandfather would buy a half-dozen little bags and we would go out onto the boardwalk where I would stand with arms outstretched, palms up, so my grandfather could pour pigeon food into each of my hands. In no time I was covered with pigeons – on my head, on my arms, clinging to my clothes, pecking away at the food. I giggled, I screamed, I wiggled in s-shapes to keep them on me. My mother and grandmother were always horrified – or, at least, mock-horrified. My grandfather would have none of their protest and we did that every day that we were in Atlantic City for decades until I was old enough that I shouldn't have been enjoying it with such little-girl delight; but, still, I did.

Eight months passednursing Wilbur until we knew he was a fully restored flying pigeon. Finally, afterdays ofshould we or shouldn't we, we let him fly free. Jim cut an opening in the top of the aviary so Wilbur could fly in and out as he pleased. It took him some minutes to discover the opening but then his departure was sudden! He went to the Magnolia tree opposite and sat there for about two hours, sometimes turning this way, sometimes that. Then, he lifted in flight and was gone.

Later on release day, as we were putting in the spring garden, we saw him on the barn roof. There was much jubilation and calling up to him from two loony people planting peas and onions. Then he flew off to the stand of trees a ways away and, over the next few days we had sightings but mostly missings, and we were pretty sure Wilbur had flown the coop.

In the garden I felt myself missing Wilbur. Our household revolved around our fourteen horses, three cats, two dogs as well as our vineyard and winery. We loved every creature and cele- brated their separate personalities. They were more than pets to us; they were part of our household, and we deeply felt our obligation to take the best care of them. We would never have children together – Jim was seventy-one and I was sixty when we got married.

Wilbur did have a particular hold on us. When two older people get married, there is an urgency to create a history that forges the union. For us, the way we loved the animals was a big part of that and we felt Wilbur's absence. I know we both looked over toward those trees now and then in a little trance.

One day, on silent wing, Wilbur did come back! Living, once again, in the barn with the horses, he seemed to be engaging in a sort of industrious building activity up in the rafters. I didn't even know pigeons could build nests. Where I come from, New York City, they live everywhere, dine on everything and I'd only once seen a nest on the ledge outside of an office I worked in down in the financial district. I thought that was a fluke. Jim and I didn't really know what our pigeon was doing up there in the rafters. Or if he were really doing anything and it was just the desire of our imagination that he should, willing him to be doing something that would show us he wanted to stay. He was still coming and going, sometimes gone for a couple of days.

If we had felt jubilant when Wilbur turned up on the roof of the barn after his release, we were overjoyed when he came home again, purposefully and for good. Jim called me from the barn around 4:30 one afternoon to say not only was Wilbur home but he had another pigeon with him! Another pigeon! How could this be? But it was. The two of them were up on a high beam just as cute as could be...like two lovebirds. We called Wilbur by name and he would fly a little closer. The new pigeon was sleek and darker. We stood below them laughing, delighting, and making phone calls to family and friends, shrieking our amazement!

We felt some sort of cross-species trust. Wilbur trusted that this was home and that he could go out and find a mate to live there with him. This took reasoning. He knew that this place was safe; he had to understand that his destiny was to find another pigeon for companionship; he had to find that pigeon, be persuasive and bring them both home.

We stood there watching the two of them peck at each other's beaks – kissing, clearly kissing – and Wilbur would look down every time we called out. They flew from beam to beam and then – AND THEN – they nestled, nuzzled, and did what pigeons do to create little pigeons. And the biggest surprise of all...Wilbur was really Wilma!

Inevitably, there were babies and babies and more and more babies until, at one count, there were fifty pigeons in that barn. At the end, Wilbur was probably long gone. In any case, no particular pigeon answered us when we called out that name. The birds all lived there in the rafters and beams of that big barn, sharing space with the swallows that returned every year and feasting on the buds and seeds from the horses' hay. Many of them flew everywhere and anywhere during the day but always came home at night. We loved hearing their sounds in the morning before the day's noises covered up theirs.

In the afternoon of New Year's Eve 2019-2020, our barn burned down. Our dining table was set for a dinner with friends and the day was balmy enough to give a hint of spring. We looked forward to the promise of a new year not just for the next vintage but because Jim had already begun to struggle with health problems, and we allowed ourselves hope that the power of a beginning would bring good fortune. When the handyman came running across the fifty yards separating the barn from the house shouting fire, fire, it took a minute to fathom what he was saying. He and Jim were so upset by what was happening they could not, either one of them, even dial 911. I did it and struggled to answer the dispatcher's question about whether it was white or black smoke since I could not see over the pitched roof to the far side of the barn where the winery and much of our stored wine was and where the fire began. It seemed forever until the firetrucks started showing up. Somehow, even though he struggled for breath, Jim got our five horses out into the big pasture and safety. By then, the fire had found the hayloft, jumped the beams and rafters and everything was engulfed. The thirty firetrucks couldn't touch it. They fought the blaze for hours but we lost the building and everything in or near it, including the entire year's vintage. TV news trucks showed up. We could see a line of cars and clots of people up on the ridge overlooking our pastures and vineyard. We found out later they were our Wine Club members and neighbors gathering to see if they could help.

The fire smoldered late into the night and for 48 hours after that.

As the pigeons started to fly back and circle, we could not tell them why there was no barn, that it had been destroyed by fire. We could not know whether they had all made it out that morning or if some had hung back and were lost to the fire. We could not tell them why they no longer had any perch.

In the spring we began to rebuild. What had once seemed impossible wasn't any longer, the days and weeks filled up with the earnest work of raising something out of the ashes. We streamlined the barn and moved the horses' stalls to where they could see across the fields. As we worked, alongside the builders, we found ourselves scanning the sky, hoping for a slight rustle in the air from any of our flock looking for home.

One day that summer, early in the morning, we found a lone pigeon pecking through the buds of hay scattered near the horses. We called him Orville, for the Wright brother who made the long flight.

∾

JORNADA DEL MUERTO
A DRUNKARD'S TALE

BY EDWARD TYNDALL

At first, the black lines cast by the window bars of the drunk tank were a mystery, and the pain in his body a specter. Then the shadows became the field plots of the Llano Estacado he had crossed on his run from Louisiana. He remembered the night before, a patchwork quilt of images that evoked a familiar sense of dread for the suffering to come. He sat up from his dank bedding and puked.

He was somewhere north of Las Cruces and going by the name Billy O'Shea. Now he stood with his hands gripping the pitted iron bars of the cell like a bandit he'd seen in movies. His short stature and slight frame cut a pitiful figure. His red hair curled slightly around his ears. A mustache was barely evident above his thin upper lip, and his right eye was half closed, a reminder of a beating he probably had coming to him.

He watched the Sheriff approach down the narrow hallway, a ragged Deputy in tow. The Sheriff looked to be in his sixties, a sun-worn Hispano with deep wrinkles at the corners of his eyes, arroyos cutting through the long-suffering earth.

The Sheriff stopped in front of the bars and pulled out a

pack of White Horse cigarettes. He shook one out and extended it to O'Shea who leaned forward and took it with his mouth, not moving his hands from the bars. The Deputy stepped in from the side and lit the cigarette with a brass Zippo. It was then that O'Shea noticed the coiled rope in the Deputy's left hand.

"What's your name, cabron?" the Sheriff asked.

"O'Shea," he said, still eying the rope.

The Deputy threw the rope around a heavy joist running along the ceiling, then tied it off to an iron ring coming out of the mud-brick wall. O'Shea could see the noose tied at the other end. The Deputy slid a chair from against the wall and positioned it under the noose.

"Where you from?" the Sheriff asked.

"Georgia," O'Shea answered, his voice shaking.

"Born in Georgia, hung in New Mexico," the Sheriff said.

The Deputy opened the cell door. The two men grabbed O'Shea by his arms and moved him toward the noose.

"Wait, wait," O'Shea said, dropping the cigarette from his mouth.

It smoldered for a moment before a boot crushed it. The Deputy slipped the noose around O'Shea's neck, and the two men hoisted him onto the chair by his arms. The Deputy pulled the slack on the rope until it was tight, and O'Shea was balancing on his toes, then they fastened his hands behind his back with a belt.

"Why aren't you fighting in Korea?" the Sheriff said.

"They wouldn't take me."

"You been in trouble before. That's why they wouldn't take you," the Sheriff said.

The Deputy pulled harder on the rope. O'Shea began to lose his footing.

"You're a grifter," the Deputy said.

"I ain't done nothing to get hung for," O'Shea said, his voice desperate and rasping.

"Look around," the Sheriff said, gesturing with a calloused hand, "We can do anything we want."

Suddenly, the Deputy kicked the chair from under O'Shea, and he hung by his neck, twisting and kicking beneath the ancient joist.

"The jig of death," the Deputy said, grinning. "Wish I had me a fiddle."

The Sheriff pulled out a cigarette and lit it for dramatic effect. He took a long drag. O'Shea's legs stopped kicking. Smoke drifted out of the window, the bars split it like tumultuous water. O'Shea watched the smoke and remembered how he had longed for water on the Llano Estacado. He remembered the intermittent crops giving way to plains of grass as he moved west, the bleached buffalo bones, and the sound of wind through sorghum. He thought of what he'd done in Louisiana, and he was ashamed.

After a few moments, the Deputy pulled a knife and cut the rope near the iron ring. O'Shea fell hard to the ground.

"Leave my county," the Sheriff said.

"I will," O'Shea said, his voice eggshell thin.

O'SHEA HAD BEEN WALKING for over an hour through the soul-bending heat toward a small store in the distance. When he finally arrived, he was desperate. He stood for a while looking at the false façade so common in those parts. A sign over the door read *Garza and Vasquez General Merchandise.* Under that, in small red letters, were the words *Indian Jewelry, Old Rocks, Whiskey.*

O'Shea pushed the door open. Rusting bells attached to the door clanked, and a man behind the counter looked up. When he saw O'Shea, his face turned dour.

"You got a lot of nerve coming back in here," the man said.

O'Shea extended his hand toward the man, palm up.

"Let me have one drink," O'Shea said, his thirst obscene now. "I can work for it."

The man slid a short-barreled shotgun from behind the counter and leveled it at O'Shea.

"How old are you?" the man asked.

"Twenty-nine," O'Shea said.

"You'll not see thirty."

By noon O'Shea found himself at the edge of a short cliff that gave way to a field of ghostly hoodoos. They flattened out to an endless shimmering plain. To the east, the Doña Ana mountains rose above the desert like wolves' teeth, sharp and cruel. The sun was high now, and the heat felt like it was coming from inside him. He took shade in the shadows of crumbling adobe walls that had once been a fort for Buffalo Soldiers. Now, the walls hunched across the low ridge like some ragged troop melting back into the earth disheartened to oblivion.

O'Shea sat for a while and thought of home. He remembered a time early on he'd killed a songbird out of curiosity. He'd followed behind it with his shotgun as it walked. He had watched it for several yards before pulling the trigger and scattering it into a thousand pieces, the soft feathers floating down after the catastrophe of buckshot like the melody of his mother's songs.

Rye Whiskey, Rye Whiskey
Rye Whiskey, I cry
If I don't get Rye Whiskey
I surely will die

He had been unable to sleep that night and had returned to the scene of the killing, out in the farm pasture, where the plow had confirmed other deaths from a great battle many years ago: a belt buckle, a twisted rifle barrel, a silver bridge of teeth. He knelt under the quarter moon, gathering what feathers he could find, tears on his cheeks, before carrying the feathers back to the family graveyard and spreading them over the grave of his drunkard father.

THE DESERT SUN reached its zenith and O'Shea looked across the vast plain. In a wavering mirage, he saw two riders approaching. They were wrapped in black rags, their heads tilted down toward the dust. When the horses got closer, the riders disappeared, a product of the mirage perhaps. Now O'Shea could see that the horses were roans, a mare and a yearling.

He watched them for a long time until they reached the edge of the escarpment. They were close enough now for him to see the panic in the mare's eyes. The yearling followed her as she tried to make her way up a draw, but the ground was dry and gave way. Her muzzle foamed and her eyes rolled sideways, exposing great orbs of white like a drowning man.

O'Shea made his way down to the horses with a length of hemp rope from the fort's midden pile. He led them up the draw one at a time, choosing the path with the best footing. At the top of the draw, the mare's hoof unearthed a rusted tin box. O'Shea let his hand slide down her sleek side, feeling the rib bones through the hide, then watched the horses move off to the east in search of water.

He returned to the box and pulled it the rest of the way from the earth. It was bitterly rusted with the design of a flower hand-punched into the tin. He opened it slowly. First, he pulled a delicate bird skull from the box, of what kind he couldn't say. Then he pulled a bundle of creosote tied with a faded purple ribbon. Underneath was a yellowed piece of paper that simply said, 'Dear Mother, I cannot find the words.' Crudely drawn under this was a scene of horror, the bodies of Apaches butchered and splayed beneath a childlike sun.

When he removed the drawing, he found a cache of silver coins stamped 1870. His heart soared at the sight of them, and he flipped one into the air. It spun the golden light like fish scales struck by the sun. The coin seemed to hang in the air for an unusual amount of time, filled with possibility. When it landed, it was on the bar of the Buckhorn Saloon, and O'Shea was ordering his first whiskey, a light in his eyes that had been gone for fifteen hours.

THE BUCKHORN WAS COOL, dark, and smelled of piss. A few roughhewn men sat slumped over their whiskey like starved dogs guarding meat. On the walls were the heads of a cougar, boar, and wolf, the wood of their taxidermy frames showing through the decaying fur. An untouched fiddle hung over the stone hearth. As O'Shea drank his whiskey, the electric buzz overtook him, and the world shifted to the vivid euphoria that marked relief from his shaking and nauseous hell.

When the two Apaches came in with their ink-black hair and Anglo concubine, O'Shea was already drunk, and the sight of them offered an excitement not given by the dull-eyed men that had been his drinking companions. The trio made their way to the bar, and the woman spoke first. Her hair, the color of dry tobacco, and her pock-marked face masked a beauty that was being resurrected by the whiskey in O'Shea's blood.

"Drinks for me and my friends," she said to the bartender.

"You got money?" the bartender asked.

"Yeah."

"Show it to me."

O'Shea spoke up from his spot at the bar. "Their first is on me," he said and laid down a silver dollar.

The Anglo woman turned and smiled at him.

The taller Apache extended his hand toward O'Shea. "Obliged," he said.

O'Shea shook the hand vigorously.

"Don't be bringing trouble here," the bartender said to the two Apaches.

"We're just passing through," the shorter one said.

"To where?" O'Shea asked.

"Up the Jornada Del Muerto," he said. "If you can get through that, there's work to the North."

A GRAY WOLF whimpered alone in the sage that dotted the arid hills above the saloon. Something was born and something died in the cold rock crevices that held the darkness like corpse hands cupping the ebony water of cypress swamps. The clock over the bar had long since stopped. O'Shea held the fiddle from the fireplace mantel. He shook it a few times and let the snake rattle hidden inside clear the cobwebs from the spruce and maple body. He tucked the chinrest low at his left shoulder, the old way, as he'd been taught. The whiskey spilled into the glasses, a beautiful amber that caught the light from the fire now blazing in the stone hearth. O'Shea felt like he was floating in space, and he admired more and more the kind eyes of the Anglo woman. He pulled the bow across the ancient guts. A high squeal drew all eyes to him. He began to play. It was a hypnotic tune that spun the whiskey in all the men and carried their minds to things long given up on. It built, it built, it built, and the Apaches were moved to shuffle-step in circles, a wild-eyed magical reeling. O'Shea cried out, "This is the Bonaparte, the Bonaparte!" then moved into the final notes, and the sound of the fiddle was the voice of the whiskey flowing through the room like life-giving water.

When O'Shea pulled the last note across the strings, the others were exhausted by the ecstasy. The room was quiet except for the popping of pinyon sap in the hearth and the low collective breathing of the men. It was into that room that the Deputy stepped, drunk himself from some lonesome binge at the edge of town. When the Deputy saw O'Shea, his eyes lit with the fire of small men insulted.

"Get out," the Deputy said, his words joined together in the manner of a man not cut out for hard drinking. The Apaches protested.

"He ain't done nothing," the tall one said.

The Deputy's ire turned. "Out," he said. "You Indians and the cracker."

They walked into the cool night, and the Deputy followed. The shorter Apache climbed into the driver's seat of a battered Ford, but the Deputy moved between the others and blocked their way.

"You got no right to bother with us," the taller Apache said.

"What are you doing so far from the reservation?" the Deputy asked.

He pulled out a cigarette and lit it with his brass Zippo. Before he could inhale, O'Shea hit him from behind with a rock. The blow knocked the lit Zippo into the dust. The Deputy went face first behind it, and the blood, matting his black hair, caught the moonlight like a mire of his cruel ideas. O'Shea bent down and picked up the Zippo. He fished the cigarettes out of the Deputy's pocket and grabbed his service revolver from his hip.

"Wait for me," he said to the taller Apache.

They did, and when O'Shea returned from robbing the Buckhorn, he was carrying an armful of whiskey bottles. As the Ford pulled onto the road that cut north through the Jornada Del Muerto, O'Shea leaned out the rear window and fired a shot. He passed one of the bottles up to the Apaches in front. The Anglo woman looked at O'Shea and smiled, and in the darkness, she seemed the only kindness for a thousand miles.

O'Shea drank and looked up at the sky through the dingy car window. The night burned with a bright swath of stars that cut through the middle like a mysterious river. The car was quiet, and O'Shea let his head list to the shoulder of the Anglo woman as she slept. She smelled of cigarette smoke and gamey sweat. Soon, her head rested on O'Shea, and he took this for more than simple shifting in sleep. He turned his mouth to her neck. He parted his dry lips and kissed her gently. She shifted and the tires hummed on the rough road.

Everything was a strange and drunken dream. He felt he had been traveling this way forever, moving through a shadowland where the shapes of things only suggested what was real. He could still see the river of stars through the opposite window and the dark outlines of the jagged mountains. He was free of pain, and he moved his hand under the Anglo woman's shirt and felt her warm skin. When she came too and realized what was happening, she was incensed.

"Get off me," she said and moved away.

Before he knew it the car was stopped, and O'Shea was being pulled out, the pistol skidding across the hardpack out of reach. The Apaches delivered him a ruthless beating, and the rocks pressed into his face as he lay on the road, trying to protect himself. He was aware that he was pleading for clemency but wasn't sure what he was saying. Soon, the two men stopped.

O'Shea sat up slightly leaning on his elbow, like a woman in a Rococo painting. He could already feel the throbbing pain in his face. He could taste the hot and salty blood running down the back of his throat.

The taller Apache spoke up, "We were going to help you," he said. "Now we're fixing to leave you."

"What is this place?" O'Shea asked.

"You'll find out when the sun comes up," the Anglo woman said.

They began to climb back into the car.

"Wait," O'Shea said. "Leave me something to drink."

The shorter Apache pulled out a canteen and threw it near O'Shea.

"No," O'Shea said. "Whiskey."

The other Apache reached back into the car and rolled a bottle toward O'Shea.

"You're a dead man," the Anglo woman said.

"Don't I know it," O'Shea said, then watched the car's tail lights disappear into the distance.

O'Shea saw the sunrise as a god bent on vengeance. He climbed a nearby point of rocks that rose above the surrounding plateau. The rocks were an unusual shade of black that stood out against the endless sand and chaparral of the valley. When he gained the top, his skin was cool with evaporating sweat. He took survey of the whiskey he had, half a bottle, a day at best. He looked north to an array of conical domes, striated with reds, browns, and whites. To the south, cyclones of dust spun mutely into the demise. West lay a line of distant barren mountains, and to the east, the Doña Anas rose, close and vicious.

He uncorked the whiskey and hit the bottle for the first time that day. It burned his maw and sent a rush of fire into his veins, filling some hollow spot he knew would return again and again and again. He waited on the rocks for someone to pass until the sun became unbearable. To escape it, he began to excavate a small shelter under one of the larger boulders. As he did, he unearthed a faded blond braid that trailed from a scalp cut ragged from the skull. He lay in his scrape, running his thumb over the braid as if some macabre rosary, and remembered a song from long ago.

Oh death, oh death
How can it be
That I must come
And go with thee?

When night came, a quarter of the bottle remained. He scrambled from his shelter and let the cool desert wind blow against his face. To the east, he saw a campfire spark to life and tremble against the black and jagged Doña Ana range. He took a drink from the bottle and headed toward the distant fire.

By the time he reached the mountains, the sun was rising, and the visage of the campfire had long since faded to nothing. He stared up at the rocks dotted with horse crippler and creosote. Above him, he saw a line of caves and used the last of his strength to climb to them. When he arrived at a significant height, he moved into one and laid down on the cool rock. He drank the last of the whiskey and waited for hell to come on.

He slept for most of the day and when he woke, a chill had come, and his hands began to shake from lack of drink. He forced himself out of the cave and collected what dry scrub he could. He piled it inside and used the Deputy's Zippo to light a small fire. He pushed close to it for warmth, and his body began to convulse and shake. Then he lost consciousness.

When he came to, he was covered in sweat, and his hands trembled uncontrollably. His calves seized in ruthless spasms. One leg contracted so tightly his heel touched his lower back, and his hands turned inward like the claws of a monster. He fainted and revived, fainted and revived, fainted and revived.

After many hours, a strange and frightening procession began. First, the Stag Horned Man entered the cave and sat next to O'Shea, a serpent in one hand and a brass torc in the other. Next came a long-tailed boar and a ram-headed snake. Winged lions followed, convulsing the air in agitation and making way for a host of shield-bearing men, some hoisting the carnyx and producing an indescribable den that mixed with the howls and screams of the maddened animals. Then, the riders in black rags arrived on the backs of the roans. The horses chomped their bronze bits and pawed the ground in frenzy. The walls of rock seemed to twist and melt, returning to a molten infancy. The procession moved around O'Shea in circles, whirling, whirling, whirling as his body writhed on the stone floor.

Finally, a figure so horrible entered that O'Shea prayed for death. It was the Wolf-head Man, stripped nude to the waist and streaked with blue woad, his breath rich with carrion. The ravenous figure cocked its head and lapped its tongue, moving close to O'Shea's face, then away, then close again, opening its eyes wide in a ritual dance that so terrified O'Shea, he thrust himself further into the cave and was hemmed in on all sides. He pushed and scraped with bleeding heels until he passed through a tight opening and plunged into freezing black water. He was consumed and felt his body tumbling through the inner recesses of the mountain and gave himself over to death. He was there for a day or years, tumbling, tumbling, lost.

Rye Whiskey, Rye Whiskey
Rye Whiskey, I cry
If I don't get Rye Whiskey
I surely will die

When he surfaced, he saw the faintest of light piercing the blackness amidst the veins of quartz and copper. He caught a rock at the edge of the stream and pulled himself toward the light. He used his fingers to scrape away the earth until the hole was big enough to squeeze his nude and tattered body through. Finally, he was out, and he rolled onto a carpet of lush grass that overlooked a valley of unbearable beauty.

It was here that the Ute Woman found O'Shea at dawn, curled like a fawn in the dew. She led him back to her wattle and daub jacal and put him to rest under a tightly woven Chief's blanket of Churro wool. She made him clothes of soft buckskin and fed him rich broths and greens until he was strong enough to rise with the sun and slowly walk the grasslands of the high valley.

Over time, he was well enough to help her with her tasks of harvesting rice grass, dandelion, and pine nuts. They would snare birds together: pheasant, quail, and turkey. They would grind nut flour in deep impressions worn into the stone by pestles, scraping,

scraping, scraping since the beginning of time. In the mornings he would climb the high peaks and look out over the endless land that offered no hint of human habitation. At dusk they would sit at a wooden table in the open air and eat, savoring rich stews of beans and the delicate flesh of birds. Sometimes, she would collect the small buttons of peyote and be gone for a day or more, but always returned, and he would have food and fire waiting for her. He grew to love her in these times, and she to love him. She taught him the simple sign language of the plains, and they traded words for important things like fire, water, and love.

She had been gone for two days when he discovered the hammered copper pitcher in the recesses of an earthen dugout used for storage. It was nestled among the dry beans and chilis, and when he picked it up to admire its fine patinaed texture, he knew what was inside.

He carried it into the open air, and as the sunlight hit the amber inside, the valley became alive with voices whispering in an ancient Gaelic or Brythonic he didn't understand, but that carried great weight in his heart. He put the pitcher to his mouth and drank, and the valley turned to a dim shadowland, and he knew this thing inside him came from a dark and ancient place, down across the centuries, and was peculiar to his kind.

He sat by the river when the mezcal was done and watched the slow-grazing rabbits that filled the fields around him. They wandered close to him, unafraid, as the songbird had done in his youth. He could reach out and touch them, but when dusk came, the owls came with their wide eyes and sharp talons. They dove from the knife-edged rocks and took what they wanted. O'Shea watched the rabbits silhouetted against the darkening sky, victims of a ruthless gluttony that pushed the blackness out of the mountain and consumed the fast-dying light with the dread beat of wings. He tried to stop the owls, to ward them off, or run the rabbits to cover, but the owls were too many and the carnage too quick. Finally, he sat back down on the bank and wept as the rabbits that remained moved off to their warrens in a slow and somber dirge.

When she found him there, he stood abruptly and asked her for more, pointing to the empty pitcher, but she had no more. He grabbed her arm and raised his hand to strike her, but she hit him first, and he tasted blood.

"Let me go back! Let me go back!" He said, desperate and shaking.

IN THE MORNING, she roused him from his spot along the outer wall of the house and compelled him to follow her. They traveled through the day, and at dusk, arrived at a cavern cut into massive red rocks that tilted like the ruined tables of giants. They entered, and she made a small fire. When the orange flames spun up, they revealed a series of strange images painted on the roof and walls. Directly above him, a nightmarish worm flickered in the firelight, a human head protruding from its mouth. On the walls were images of deer and antelope and human handprints in hematite and limonite. Here, she ate the peyote and began a song that struck O'Shea dumb with sadness. He watched her as her visions came, and at their height she turned to him, her face drawn tight like a death mask, and he understood that this was the way to use his people's medicine.

THEY SPENT the next day hunting the agave plant, spotting it along the ridges by the quiote rising from the daggered piña. They cut the pencas away, their hands pierced and bleeding until they could uproot its heavy heart. These they carried to a bed of coals in a shallow pit by the river. They spread the piñas there, covered them with deer hide and dirt, and let them smolder for two days.

She did not let him eat or drink, and by the time they uncovered the piñas, he had long since passed through the first sufferings of his fast. Then, he used a wooden mortar he had hewn to crush the piñas into a thick mash. This they stewed with water and saliva in the hides of sheep, and now she allowed him mouthfuls of water at dawn and dusk.

When the mezcal was finished, she poured the golden liquid into the pitcher. At dawn, he carried it up the arduous path to the highest peak. By the time he arrived, the sun was setting. He sat and drank from the pitcher, and as he did, the road through the Jornada Del Muerto appeared again, and on it, he could see the riders on the roans and the Wolf-headed Man, his woad-streaked body muted by dust. O'Shea knew that he could go back to the road if he wanted, and he was overcome by a dread desire to do so, but he didn't. He only watched as the weary travelers slouched endlessly through the desert below. As the drink wore off, the Jornada Del Muerto disappeared, and O'Shea returned to the Ute Woman in the valley. He confessed to her what he'd done in Louisiana, and she forgave him. The days and nights passed, and O'Shea could not say if he had been in the valley for a month, a day, or had always been there. They lived their lives simply and O'Shea never made the mezcal again. Each night as he slept, he dreamt his body lay on the arid ridges of the mountains like the time-shackled bones of a taibhsear, and that his sun-leathered hide sprouted the daggered agave and thrust up the delicate white flowers high above the valley that held their love.

Rye Whiskey, Rye Whiskey
Rye Whiskey, I cry

∾

The End

THE CRYSTAL FIRE

BY LAUREN LANG

The phone rings. It's 2am, and I'm already up. I know what it's about.

"The sooner, the better," is all the voice on the other end has to say. It's go time.

I'm not ashamed to admit I'm an adrenaline junkie. Moments like this get my blood pumping. But unlike other people, I don't jump out of airplanes. I've never run with the bulls. I'm no weekend warrior. What I am is a journalist with a story to tell.

People that aren't in the news will never understand what it feels like to get that call. To know there's an 11-hour day ahead of you and relishing the feeling.

This isn't just a job. It's your life. You live, breathe, and some die for data. It's information in its purest form, unsanitized, blood, guts, and all. If there is death and destruction, I am headed there, if not in form then in function. I am running towards what everyone is running from, and I've never felt so alive.

A man in his 20's stands on the corner waving a dollar bill at me. He wants me to stop for what purpose I do not know. I can tell he's desperate. I don't care. Horsetooth Mountain is burning. My newsroom needs me. I keep going.

Overnight winds have fanned what was a small fire into 2000 acres of 100-foot flames. The Crystal Fire is now newsworthy.

In some senses, a newsroom is like a military organization. Everyone has a mission and a role to play in completing it. Our mission is to keep people safe. To tell them when they're in danger, let them know what to do about it, and report back to the rest of our viewers. My job is to show them what the threat is. My job is to play with fire.

A freelance photographer has sold us incredible footage of the blaze. He's so close at points he has to turn and run from the approaching flames, his camera still rolling. I watch in awe, untouched by the destruction on the screen. Homes are burning, the work of lifetimes becoming ash, and all I care about is how the glow will look on your TV.

Some might call that callous. Those people would be right. To do anything but laugh at what I see would be the end. Dwell too long on how fragile this life really is, and you risk losing your mind.

I've given everything for this career, to be standing here in what many consider the best local newsroom in the country. I gave it my early 20's, my friends, and my capacity to feel. I've loved it, hated it, blamed and credited it for making me who I am, but the one thing I would never do is trade it. Right now, at this moment, there is nowhere I'd rather be.

And I'm in the midst of a firestorm.

Everything that could go wrong is going wrong. Frantic calls to management are still unanswered, the police are looking for our female anchor, equipment is failing, and the clock is ticking.

Time is an unforgiving mistress. There are sixty seconds in a minute and hours in a few moments of dead air.

The one rule of live television is that you always have to have somewhere to go. Whether that takes you to an elementary school outside of Loveland, Colorado, or to black is determined by the minute-to-minute decisions we make.

You have sixty seconds to make the right call. Go.

And when the time was up, we were there, simultaneously in your homes and at a fire burning out of control outside Fort Collins, Colorado.

We were the only ones. The victors of a five-hour war you never knew we fought all but invisible, except for the blonde on TV.

The End

ONE THOUSAND SOULS UNDER THE SEA

BY LAUREN ROBINSON

Ｔt began as it always did: The warm trickle of water down her leg. A quick brush through her hair. The *pop-pop-pop* of her phone as she fired off a message to her parents. *"She's coming!"* the message read.

The cool rubber of the inside handle of the passenger-side door, which she white-knuckled all the way to the hospital. The bright blue sky and starlings flitting by as she day-dreamed through the pangs, excited and scared but mostly excited for this next chapter of her life. Adam, beside her, patting her leg in comfort. A flash of a smile, kindness in his eyes, as she gripped his hand in return. It was so absurd, the pain that accompanied this long-planned and much-desired birth, that she had to laugh.

Nurses wheeled her into her room, and Adam showed her her phone, grinning. *"We're on our way!"* Mom had replied. She nodded, resolute, elation trumping any fear or doubt. It was time. She was going to be a mother.

She was holding a baby girl in her arms, damp and pink and wailing. She pulled the bundle into herself and cooed until the baby soothed, looked to Adam and her parents, and said, "Her name is..."

~

"HELL, Frank, what's happening? Am I reading this right?" the tech asked, fiddling with the sleeve of her jumpsuit.

Frank, tired and weary, ready to fall back into the cryochamber where pleasant dreams awaited, scrolled through another report on his tablet and felt a wave of nausea overcome him.

"You're reading it right," he said. "We don't have much time."

It began as it always did. The warm trickle of water down her leg. A quick brush through her hair. The pop-pop-pop *of her phone as she fired off a message to her parents.* "She's coming!" *the message read.*
The cool rubber...

"You think we have a chance?" said the tech, Yvonne, whose name Frank had finally committed to memory. Usually, his shifts were brief enough he didn't need to remember the names of his techs, and he was so tired and disoriented from long sleep that he struggled with it, anyway. Better to focus on the Preservation, he figured.

This time was different.

"We have to try," Frank said. "Wake the mechanics, Yvonne. All hands on deck."

She nodded and hustled toward the terminal controlling the cryochambers, where she punched in some commands calling forth all persons with the "mech" tag in their bios. Frank stiffened with guilt at the thought of rousing them from their slumber, where they were drifting through much happier times.

"We'll need to brief them," he said, more to himself than to his accomplice.

"Is there any chance your readings could be skewed? An anomaly?" Yvonne asked, not for the first time.

"No," he said. "The ocean chemistry is changing—warming and

acidifying—much faster than we'd predicted. I'm afraid it's going to outpace the disembark protocol. The structural integrity of the Vault is at risk."

"We'll be swimming soon," she said, shaking her head.

The cool rubber of the inside handle of the passenger-side door, which she white-knuckled all the way to the hospital. The bright blue sky and starlings flitting by as she day-dreamed past the pangs, excited and scared but mostly excited for this next chapter of her life. Adam, beside her, patting her leg in comfort. A flash of a smile, kindness in his eyes, as she gripped his hand in return. It was so absurd, the pain that accompanied this long-planned and much-desired birth, that she had to laugh.
Nurses wheeled her into her room...

The mechanics were about as cheerful as Frank had imagined they would be upon awakening.

A handful were furious, demanding proof that their underwater bunker was in fact compromised. He'd complied as best he could, fielded all their questions, made his reports public, but as chief engineer, he knew the nuances of the data were lost on most of them. The bearings of the Vault weren't visibly weakening—yet—but he knew they would be dust in a few centuries.

The mechs were grieving, Frank realized, all that they had labored for before climbing into the cryochambers. The centuries they had slept, waiting, believing that when they woke again the surface of their planet would have stabilized for human inhabitance.

"We need a crew to reinforce the walls," Frank told the chief mechanic, Mary. "Use whatever you can get—we'll tear down the housing wing for materials if we have to."

She nodded, then led her people into a conference room.

Frank looked toward the narrow, dark window overhead, to the ocean water bearing down upon their premises. It didn't use to feel quite so fragile, but now he feared it could rush in at any moment, drowning them all.

Why they had built a skylight into the Vault, he couldn't say. From their vantage on the ocean floor, it always appeared to be nighttime. He longed for the sky, whatever was left of it. He hoped he would see it again one day.

Nurses wheeled her into her room, and Adam showed her her phone, grinning. "We're on our way!" Mom had replied. She nodded, resolute, elation trumping any fear or doubt. It was time. She was going to be a mother.
She was holding a baby girl in her arms...

Frank and Yvonne sat at their terminals, chewing on bland protein bars that constituted lunch. Things were looking up—Mary had told Frank during her briefings that the mechs were making good progress insulating the weakest points of the Vault. They had broken into the capsule of construction equipment that was long ago sunken along with them so that they could tear down and repurpose materials from the housing wing. Frank knew this was a delicate maneuver that itself posed a colossal risk. And, of course, this solution meant that the living quarters for those who were awake had shrunk. Sleeping bags lined the floors of the command center.

Of late, Frank had become obsessed with checking the status of the cryochambers. Approximately one thousand people lay in repose on the other side of the wall to which his terminal was mounted. His husband, for one. He asked Yvonne almost hourly for confirmation that the artificial intelligence software responsible for protecting their dream loops during long sleep was functioning as normal.

"Yessir," she said, revealing not a hint of irritation at his request. Perhaps she felt the same sense of worry for their flock as he did. He exhaled, the rumbling of drills calming him. They were doing what they could.

He leaned back in his chair, daring to allow himself to shut his eyes. He fell into a fitful nap, full of nightmares he wouldn't remember.

She was holding a baby girl in her arms, damp and pink and wailing. She pulled the bundle into herself and cooed until the baby soothed, looked to Adam and her parents, and said, "Her name is—"

One of Frank's monitors chirped.

He'd been dozing again. He opened one eye, unsure if he'd dreamt up the sound, then lunged for the console.

"There's a disturbance in the current a few miles southwest of us," he murmured.

"So?" Yvonne said. "That's normal, right?"

"No," he said, his voice barely a whisper. "Not with the local chemical composition. As it bends toward us, it'll corrode the Vault faster than we could ever hope to repair it."

He moved to another terminal, ran another model. And another.

Yvonne stared at her feet.

"How much time do we have?"

A disturbance outside of the hospital window stole her attention. The sky had turned into a roiling mass of orange and smoke and debris that rattled the panes.

Time was up, and Frank knew what had to be done. How had the fate of the human race fallen into *his* hands? The plan—the most expensive project in human history—had carried on without incident for centuries. The fail-safes were designed to handle all manner of catastrophes, but all of the early studies had indicated minimal probability of occurrence.

"Initiate Operation Ego Death," he said. "Are we still connected to the Preservation Satellite?"

"Affirmative," Yvonne said, her voice cracking. "She's still cruising."

"Start diverting power to the cryochambers," he told her. "I'll tell the mechs to get in—it'll be better to go that way. You start wrapping everything up, too. I want you in yours in ... 87 minutes."

She looked at him, eyes welling, and nodded as Frank jogged off down the hallway. With a sniff, she tapped away at her terminal, punching in final directives for the dream sequences synched with a thousand consciousnesses.

What had she planned to name her baby? It suddenly seemed pointless. Something was coming for all of them. Something they couldn't outrun, not anymore. She beckoned Adam, her mother, and her father toward her. They huddled together, around her and the baby, trembling, afraid to speak a word.

After delivering the news to the mechanics, Frank returned to the control room, feeling sick. He touched Yvonne's shoulder, unable to speak another word, indicating that it was time for her, too, to climb into her chamber, so that the last remnants of her would be preserved in the last record of humankind. She rose to leave, and his stomach was hollow. He heard the door to the cryochamber bay suction closed, then collapsed into the chief technician's chair.

He would go down with this ship. He would have to, to ensure the operation was successful. His eyes glazed as he tried to take in the status reports flashing at the terminal before him.

The computers were busy molding all of their dreams into individual strains of code, which would be transmitted to the Preservation Satellite, then beamed out into the universe for someone—if anyone—to retrieve one day, along with news that humans had conducted their final flight.

The heirs of the final vestiges of humankind would decipher the code and learn a thousand different ways the humans had delighted in their fleeting lives, the joys they felt, the memories they cherished. And the worst of them would stay buried beneath the ocean forever.

OUTLAW'S DUST

BY CHRISTI R. SUZANNE

O ver the years, stories about women consumed by sand dunes or turning into salt gave me pause. Oftentimes, after one too many drinks, they were told sloppily to induce laughter, but always missed the point. Though I didn't quite believe them, I never fully discounted the anecdotes either.

My first attempt to go to an Arizona ghost town in my 91' Geo Prizm, a silver compact car lacking any kind of rugged tire system, ended in a rocky dirt road. My friend, Javier, I called him Javi, commented on the lack of clearance, rickety door levers, and loud engine. Note: Javi didn't have a car, but he still felt compelled to complain about mine.

I rolled my eyes and turned to him saying, "Why didn't you tell me the roads were this rough?" He shrugged, happy to be doing something with someone he liked. He spent most of his time at Toxic Ranch Records where the smell of B.O. and fried food permeated the small space, the owner ate onions rings or french-fries regularly and left the greasy containers on a shelf behind the counter. He'd made me a mix tape with bands that had defined my existence for the better part of my 20's — The Undertones, The Blue Hearts, Los

Saicos, and Slant 6. The way I loved him was in that pure friendship way that fades once time moves on or they realize sex is off the table. Unfortunate because he really got me in ways not everyone can.

Anyway, that day my engine stopped in the middle of the dusty dirt road a few miles west of the town. The car slowed — the tan landscape dotted with sage brush and saguaro cacti reminded me that water was scarce and I didn't have extra. The long road ahead of us signaled to me that today this road would not let us pass.

"Shit," I said.

"What happened? Did your battery die?" Javi asked. He swore he never got hot or sweaty wearing his black jean jacket, but today he had rolled up the sleeves.

I shrugged.

He started to get out of the car, but I grabbed his arm when I saw a dust storm in the distance. The blur appeared as an apparition shaped as a javelina-like wild pig.

"It's just a couple of dust devils," he said.

The back of my neck cooled and goosebumps rose up along my arms.

"Are you superstitious?" Javi asked.

I shrugged. "Not really. But it could turn into something bigger. Swallowed by a dust storm?"

"I've lived in the desert my whole life, I've never seen that happen," he said.

"Something doesn't feel right." A low moan caused more goose bumps all over my arms and legs. "Do you hear that?" The sound rose and faded into the wind gusts.

"Nah," Javi said. "We should go, your car won't make it if we keep going down this road." He sounded authoritative, but in the same breath, shaky.

"My car is dead, I don't think we're going anywhere."

Javi said, "I carry one of these with me just in case," and then reached into his pocket. "A friend who believed in all sorts of spirits and whatnot gave it to me. She did some ritual on it."

I studied the object in my hand. A bright green rock with bands of darker green formed rings around it, malachite. "She thought you needed to be protected?"

He shrugged, "Don't look so scared."

"Wait, what do you mean?" I asked. "You said believed?"

"She died a few years ago. Bike accident with a semi."

"Shit, that's horrible."

He nodded."She gave me one every time we'd meet up. She loved all that crystal shit too, but it didn't save her."

"It's beautiful," I said, gripping it. The rock's coolness seeped into my hand creating an icy feeling from palm to fingertips. An indent towards the middle was perfect for my thumb. Taking a deep breath in, I tried the car again. The sound of the engine turning over blocked out the low moan. "It's not just the wind," I said.

I glanced in my rearview mirror where a dark shadow shaped like a woman with long hair stood, wavered. The air was a dusty fog-like obstruction. A rust-colored luminescence flickered. I couldn't be sure the shadow wasn't a cactus.

When I checked the rearview mirror again, the shape had vanished. I didn't waste time and turned the car around wishing I could push the gas pedal to the floor. Instead, I kept to a steady 15 mph, careful not to blow a tire or get stuck. The rumble of rocks under rubber muffled any other sounds I'd heard. Finally, we reached the smooth blacktop road and I pushed the pedal down, keeping an eye on the rearview mirror.

I'd think back on that day, about how a woman was swallowed by dust, and a malachite charm saved me. That day, I didn't become one of those stories about women being swallowed by dust.

Years later I'm going back, in a more durable higher-clearance midsize electric SUV. The Wipers and Slant 6, with some new favorites like Ex Hex and the Linda Lindas were in the mix. I had to prove to myself whatever I'd felt or seen that last time, didn't exist. I'd heard from Javi a few months before my trip, he owned his own power tool supply business, seemed happy. I told him my plan, invited him, and he wished me good luck. Before we hung up he admitted that the trip we'd gone on had spooked him. All that talk about not being superstitious years before, faded away.

This time, I'd come alone like the outlaws had done before me. What score I had to settle, still unclear. Perhaps I wanted to honor the dematerialized women from the stories I'd heard. Whatever shape I might have seen in the dust before, had left an unshakeable impression. This time, I made it to the town.

The May heat unfurled with each ray of sun that dared peek over the horizon. Each minute the warmth made its way through the sad dilapidated boardwalk and the signs reading Sarsparilla! Rattlesnake! or Gold! sticking out at random.

I'd heard the local town had taken over and made it into a "working ghost town" where you could buy expensive root beer floats and watch reenactment shootouts, the town before me wasn't what I thought of when I thought Ghost Town. It had all the trappings of a tourist attraction complete with an expensive train loop. Someone had even opened a Vivarium, though closed today.

A small wooden gallows stage next to a two-room jail about 100 feet from the Saloon and across from an old hotel showed the fate many people had succumbed to. Stopping in at a rock I took out the malachite Javi had given me before. Behind the cash register, an indigenous woman wore two long brown braids that hung behind her ears and a necklace with turquoise and silver on it. She asked if I had any questions and I showed her the rock.

"Is this really malachite?" I asked. The authenticity of the rock had never bothered me before, but today I needed to know.

The woman motioned for me to come toward a light table where a magnifying glass sat. She nodded silently and then asked, "How long have you had it?"

"A few years, maybe ten," I said.

"You've been worrying it," she said.

"Oh," I said and balled my hand like I held the rock in it with my thumb moving against it.

She nodded, "I see this groove, here."

"It was started before I had it," I said. "The person I got it from said his friend gave it the power to protect."

The woman's lips drew up at the corners, she gave a small affirming grunt. "We *can* give objects power."

"Have you heard the stories? About women turning into wind? Or melting into water?"

She paused, considering the stories of women fading into something else. "We can only be transformed into these things if we give up. Or if we feel alone."

"You're saying we have a choice."

"That stone makes you feel less alone?"

I shrugged. "I guess so."

"It's a good place to start. Courage."

"In every story, it's a slow progression toward the final transformation like there is no choice and the inevitable comes."

She took in what I'd said. "Sometimes they're about a kind of mindless focus."

"The reflection happens too late. They could make different choices."

"Every day," she said.

I nodded and asked about the price of a bag of mixed rocks, bought one, and said thank you.

I hiked up the hill to the shooting gallery games—the pinging and clicking of the mechanisms at work. Reaching the peak of the town, I peered into the desert a parched and troubled creature. In the near distance, mountains rose up on all sides, creating a valley. An old mine popped out from the ground, the wooden beams split and blocked the entrance. Behind me I heard someone yell, "Everyone inside!" And that's when I saw them, dust devils coming from all sides. Shaped like saddled up horses. They were descending on the town, though the closer they got the less animal shaped they became and the more tumbleweeds blew. I reached into my pocket rubbing the contours of the old malachite stone, the groove my friend and his friend before him had smoothed.

"Hey," a man called. "You, there. We don't mess with the devil around here, come inside."

I surveyed the dust devils and asserted that maybe he was right. I nodded and made my way toward the shooting gallery. The man wore a beat-up old cowboy hat, and dungarees. A dusty brown beard hid his chin and upper lip. His appearance like one of the old pioneers who had originally run the town—a forced and anxious smile plastered to his face.

"It's been a long while since we've seen so many," he said. He motioned for me to hurry inside.

"Dust devils?" I asked. The wind had picked up and the door shook with the clanking sound of the latch.

He nodded. "There's more to them then just dust," the man said. "Nothing to worry about. They'll be gone soon enough." He introduced himself as Billy, like Billy the kid, he said.

"Wasn't Billy shot dead in a town like this?" I asked.

"True enough," Billy said. "His temper got the better of him."

Billy swiftly locked the door behind me. I moved away, the smell of tobacco following him.

"I know I don't look like a Billy. When people think of the name, they think of some baby-faced kid, right?"

I shrugged. "I've never met a Billy so I'm not sure."

"Well, anyway, Billy the Kid was 22 when he died."

"Young," I said.

He grunted an affirmation. "You know, you've got bedroom eyes. Anyone ever tell you that?"

My body tensed. I wondered if I'd be better off out in the storm. My feeble laugh, a way to acknowledge a forced obligation to take it as a compliment, but to show no interest in taking it anywhere else.

"Feel free to play a couple rounds on me." He grabbed a handful of quarters carefully stacking them up on the counter.

I waited until he took his hand away so I didn't accidentally brush up against his. "Thanks," I said. After I inserted the coins I picked up the play rifle and shot at various items, a beer bottle, tin cans, an apple atop a pioneer's head. When I shot that one, a canned voice came across the speaker, "What in Tarnation?!" I imagined I'd shot Billy right through the forehead and he knew exactly why.

The one small window in the shooting gallery had blue and white flowered curtains covering it. I went over and drew the right side back to peer out. In the distance, the dusty horse shapes reconfigured to include people riding on them, cowboy hats and all. The door to the shooting gallery shook so hard it had to be someone trying to get in, needing help. The woman from the rock shop, perhaps. I bolted to the door.

Billy said, "Don't open that."

"Someone needs help," I said.

"We can't help them," he warned. He made his way toward me.

I stepped back only to hear a low moan and the door shaking again. The moaning grew louder. I couldn't take it any longer, and swiftly reached the door and unlatched it. It flung open, wide. A flurry of cowboy-shaped luminescent dust particles clung to Billy—gripped him, until he cried out, dissolved into dust alongside the others.

The whole town had been distorted by the dusty mist, glowing rust red. The dust particles everywhere, in my eyes and mouth. The grit in my teeth caused instant dry mouth and my eyes blurred with scratchy intensity.

A tightness around my right wrist where an illuminated dust formed shackle pulled me out onto the wooden boardwalk, dragging me toward an empty horse next to a Billy-shaped apparition. I pushed my left hand into my pocket searching for the malachite, hoping it could do something. The rock shop owner flung her door open, two shops down. She held a large pink stone. Her necklace along with the stone, glowed—brightened the rust color coming from the dust particles squeezing my wrist tighter and tighter like a gila monster's jaws clamping down. She came closer shouting FIGHT. FIGHT. Until I shook my arm and threw punches into the air. The weight of the invisible shackle pulling and wrenching my arm down at an odd angle. Until the jabs forced the dirt into a puff of dust and with each — puff, puff, puff, puff. The resistance gave way, until the shackle flew off into the raging wind.

The rust-colored glow outlined three dusty shapes as they rode away, Billy's mocking laugh, with his head tipped back.

My legs quivered as the storm moved over the mountain. The woman from the shop yelled out to me, "Are you okay?" She wore a long-patterned skirt that ruffled in the wind.

I couldn't formulate a response knowing what I'd witnessed, how quickly I could have transformed into dust. I held the glowing malachite, knowing I was a kind of outlaw. The woman nodded in affirmation—today we fought together. Other days we fought on our own, in our own way, every day within unseen gestures or silences. More importantly, this day we hadn't become one of those stories we didn't like to tell, or hear, or want to believe.

-End-

THE OTHER SIDE

BY ELAINE PARTNOW

P erched in front of a young live oak on a grassy knoll, the old woman sat hugging her knees. From there, she had a sweeping view of the valley below. People were down there, people Mira no longer knew, people she didn't want to know. If they would just leave her alone, she could rejoice in wandering through the faded green summer and into fall, sustaining herself on wild nuts and berries, as she'd learned to do too many autumns ago to remember.

Like a giant octopus intruding upon the sea of green, the valley's lush growth was interrupted by a great grey bubble from which stretched eight long tentacles. The opaqueness of the bubble hid the life inside. One would not guess that a small colony of humans lived there, had lived there for more than 100 years. Nor could one know that beneath the surface of the globular octopus, deep in the earth's bowels, an entire city had grown, one populated by the offspring of some of the greatest scientific minds in America. One could no longer say the United States of America. That had vanished long ago.

Mira sighed with the knowledge that one of the tentacles would soon spit out a search party. If only she could stay here until a white blanket of snow covered her. She didn't need their goodbye pills; her friend Winter would bring her to the other side. Sometimes, of late, when night fell, Mira could not be sure she wasn't already there – so many familiar faces, so many voices from her youth called to her. But then morning would dawn, she would awaken, and the grey octopus was still there. She knew she was still here, still haunting the wiry, patched-together body that appeared to be 70 years old but had passed that mark almost 70 years earlier.

Whose body was it, really? Mira mused as she mentally traced the stranger's kidney lodged in her lower left lumbar area, the polymer hip joint, the artificial heart, and the bionic eye, without which she would be a blind woman stumbling through a shadowy world. What else? She had forgotten all the gifts with which she'd been blessed.

My god, she thought, at least my lungs are still my own; she breathed deeply of the sweet-smelling air. They couldn't understand, those young people, that all their pills and technologies might keep the body functioning and the senses alert, but nothing could keep a spirit from growing weary. Nothing excited her anymore. She didn't want new challenges. She was tired. So tired.

From far off, she heard voices. The search party was already making their way up the mountainside. From the sounds of it, they were still a day's climb away. Ah, that's right – the ear: she'd forgotten about the synthetic tympanic membrane serving as her eardrum. And the bionic cochlea without which she'd be falling all the time and, more importantly, without which she would not now be enjoying the lovely trill of a whippoorwill.

Could I, at last, be getting senile? Mira's heart fluttered with hope. Maybe then they'd leave me be. Maybe then they'd let me go to my rest.

∾

A DAZZLING tunnel of light appeared before her. As she drew nearer and nearer to its vortex, colors began flashing: purples, blues, green – the color of change; yellows, oranges, reds – all the colors of the rainbow quivered together, awakening each sense, every fiber of her weary body.

Mira's eyes blinked open. She found herself encased in a crystal cave. This must be it; this must be the other side, she thought and searched each facet of the crystal for one of the faces, one of the voices that had been calling to her. Colors gleamed at her from every crevice of the cavern. Alluring tones, like the chants of sirens, caressed her synthetic eardrum. But there were no faces, no familiar, tutelary voices calling her home. Only an ebullient sense of life. Again.

A HAND WAS on her forehead. Mira's eyes fluttered open. A face leaned over her, staring into her own. It looked like the face that belonged to Mira perhaps 90 years ago. Its lips were moving.

"Mira? Mira, wake up! Do you not know me?"

"Yes, yes..." her hand reached out to touch the young face. "It is I... it is I..."

Two pallid young men stepped up to the anxious woman standing over Mira and quietly walked her aside.

"She doesn't know you yet, Dawn," said one, "leave her be for a while."

"She'll be all right," said the other. "She just needs a little time."

When Mira awoke a second time, there were no colors, no sounds, no youthful face to disillusion her. She was still there. She didn't know where exactly; she only knew it was there and not the other side.

SEATED IN THE COVERED COURTYARD, surrounded by a fountain of water, the two women looked like twins a hundred years apart: the same almond-shaped brown eyes, same aquiline nose, same arched brows —but the elder's were white, the younger's brown. The younger's eyes were dark with concern. She held the hand of the elder, talking to her in great earnestness.

"...three and half days without your time-clock pills, Mira. We were out of our senses with worry. You were unconscious when we found you and...you had aged, Mira – you looked... you look...so much older...."

Indeed, the centenarian who once looked a spry 70 now looked a withered 90.

"We carried you back in a litter. You were comatose for days. Time-clock pills had no effect. Nothing did. We brought you into the crystal chamber as a last resort. It has never been used with a person, you know—it's still in the testing stage, but...it was a chance we had to take. We...we didn't know if it would... if you would..."

Enraptured by the mirror of her great-great-granddaughter's face, Mira paid little attention to her words. She just held the younger's hand and kept repeating, "It is I... it is I..."

"Oh, Mira, you must hear me. We need you. Without you, we are lost. All of us – lost! No one remembers anymore, Grandmama. Only you."

Mira felt so drawn to the younger woman's energy. The girl's concern, her very worry, indicated a soul full of life, full of the future. Not like Mira's soul, so full of the past. If only she could crawl into the younger woman's skin.

"The computers are almost ready now, Mira. In just a few days, we can begin. It's taken us so long to get to this point, so many years. It's what you've been saved for – to save us. You are our griot. What good is all our scientific knowledge without our stories? You must remember, Mira – you must!"

∽

WHEN MIRA ROSCHEN first became a computer analyst, she had no way of knowing that 100 years later, she would be looked to as a savior by a small surviving number of the human race. A devoted worker, she'd risen to the top of her profession without ambition but as naturally as a robin flies to the top of a tree. Between raising her daughter alone and working long hours, she'd never, until age 38, taken a vacation. Some cosmic irony had found her standing on an ice floe, observing a massive march of emperor penguins determinedly hiking toward their mating ground when the apocalypse came.

Mira had always fancied knowing what the bottom of the world was like. The fireballs had been a beautiful sight from the earth's furthermost reaches, lasting all through the day and brief night. She had no idea that among them was a massive asteroid of 12 kilometers. Loss of radio contact kept her ignorant of the devastation until she and her small solar plane arrived home, intact and in shock, amidst the rubble. What had once been a cluster of large government buildings outside Alexandria, Virginia, was now a mound of sizzling debris.

The asteroid had destroyed everything. People were incinerated . Animals decimated. Buildings ruined. Forests, destroyed. Only those deep in the bowels of the earth had escaped, along with the sparse life that existed above and below sixty degrees latitude—Cape Horn and Tierra del Fuego to the south of the Americas, Canada's Hudson Bay to the north.

Mira knew she needed to find safety below ground. Some level of radioactivity would be in the air. And who knew what else after such a devastating impact? She searched among the rubble for the elevator shaft that traveled down to those secretive chambers where she and other men and women of science had been working on designing protective shelters for just this kind of disaster. They had always assumed that disaster would come in the form of a nuclear bomb–never this. But when she finally found the spot, when she'd torn the bricks and cement away with her bare hands until they were bleeding, all she could see was a deep, empty shaft leading into darkness.

She began her descent, knowing not what she'd find, praying that her beloved daughter, who had been apprenticing with the study ever since she'd gotten her master's in biotechnology, would be there. Rung after rung after rung, Mira climbed down the ladder that hugged the shaft wall, descending into utter blackness.

DAWN SPOKE EARNESTLY TO HER , urging her to remember the long struggle they'd made to reach the earth's surface once again. And when they finally did, how had Mira fought them—and lost— against treating it as one might the moon, exploring it only when encased in space suits with oxygen tanks. Dawn reminded Mira of the stories she told of how they'd scavenged materials to build the polymer bubble. They collected seeds, irradiated them for safety, and began growing food again after existing on stored food and water for almost a generation. The bubble allowed for fresh water via condensation.

But this younger generation, Dawn's peers, feared the outdoors. They felt safe in their plastic bubble, their armored city. Unlike Mira, they had no memory of nature, no memory of great cities, no memory of art.

Desperately hoping to spark a memory and erase the look of absence on the old woman's face, Dawn kept up her retelling of their recent history. She reminded Mira of the struggle to bring the computers back to life. Despite their generators, with the destruction of so much of the earth's surface, they could no longer communicate globally to discover if others had survived and, if so, where they were. It was Mira who insisted they rebuild towers above in an attempt to reach others, Mira who helped them revitalize the computers by dreaming up the use of crystals for an energy field below ground.

Now, the two women walked down one of the long grey tentacles fringed with row upon row of hybrid vegetables, their roots encased in plastic bubbles, wired and monitored. Outside the tinted transparent panes, all was lush and plentiful.

How quickly the earth restores itself, thought Mira. These young people, they've forgotten so much. But Mira remembered. She remembered planting fruit trees in her father's orchard, remembered lying in a hammock strung between two ancient live oaks, the sun warming her body, a light and shadow play dancing on the leaf-laden ground. She remembered that and more. So much more. She wished she could go back. She knew she could not. There was only one place for Mira now. Or so it seemed; the present was a quagmire, holding her back, keeping her from the infinite.

"It is this we are most concerned about, Grandmama..." They had descended in an elevator to a place deep in the earth's interior. There, Dawn guided the grand matriarch into a room at the end of a computer-lined corridor. Within it was another, smaller room. "It is operable; we know that now... but without precise programming, we have no real control over its effect. That's why we were so worried about you when we..."

The crystal chamber. Of course. Mira stood stone-still, her meandering mind suddenly riveted to the possibilities of the chamber.

"...with the chamber functioning properly, we would at least have the time we need to... Great-grandmother, Mira--are you all right?"

The old woman was immobile. To Dawn, she seemed catatonic.

"Grandmama, Mira, please... do you hear me?"

Deaf to the tugs and cries of her young look-alike, Mira continued to stare at the chamber. Finally, the old woman's eyelids fluttered, her head shook, her body relaxed, and she turned to her near-frantic great-great-granddaughter.

"Child, when will they be ready for me to work?"

"Mira – you're all right. You know me!"

"Of course, I know you. When will it be ready?"

"Soon – very soon. A matter of days now."

"Bring me to my room. Let me rest. I will need all my strength for that day."

~

An air of expectation lit the young people's wan faces as they gathered about and waited for Mira to begin. She tinkered with some machinery, flashed them a withered smile, then stepped inside the crystal chamber.

"Dawn, come here, please."

The younger woman stepped eagerly inside. The door to the chamber closed.

"Put these on." Mira handed Dawn a pair of copper bracelets identical to those she wore.

"Lie down." The clan could not be without their stories; they could not be without a griot.

The two women laid head to head on the chamber's copper-lined altar. Every sharp crystal facet gleamed at them; soothing tones relaxed their alert bodies.

"Grab hold of my wrists," Mira ordered. They reached their arms over their heads and clasped each other's wrists. Mira barked out an order. "Computer, begin!"

Reds, oranges, yellows bathed their bodies in color, penetrating every pore. Green, the color of change, swept over them in waves. They were afloat on a sea of it, suspended in its foam. The ocean of green merged into blue, then purple, and then a dazzling white light burst upon them, twisting into a cone shape.

A not-unpleasant tingling sensation enveloped Dawn. She felt abuzz with life, with knowledge, with understanding. It was as if the grey matter in her brain was developing new folds as memories poured into her.

Guided by sounds that seemed to call to her, Mira swam towards the end of the tunnel of light. There, she could discern the faces, the familiar faces that she had for so long yearned to join. She reached out. A hand grasped hers, pulling her through the eye of the vortex.

DAWN STEPPED out of the crystal chamber. An aura of vibrancy encircled her. The dark marks of worry had faded from beneath her almond-shaped eyes, eyes that glistened with tears. Solemnly, she marched down the computer-lined corridor to the elevator. A small enclave of technicians followed, apprehension blanching their already pallid complexions. When they emerged in the plastic bubble, Dawn stopped in front of a panel marked "Emergency." She lifted her arm, firmly grasped a large lever, and pulled.

The panel of tinted polymer plastic fell back. A gust of sweet-smelling air swept over the cowering band that shielded their eyes and faces from the glare of sunlight. Dawn stepped outside the octopus tentacle, breathed deeply, and gazed at the young forest. A solemn, wise smile curled the corners of her lips.

The griot is dead, she thought. Then, placing her hands to her temples, her smile widening slightly, she murmured, "Long live the griot."

RISING FROM THE ASHES

BY JUSTIN SMITH

T he smoke still clung to the air, a ghost of the fire that had torn through Sierra's small restaurant just weeks before.

~

CHARRED BEAMS JUTTED from the remains like broken ribs, a stark contrast to the once-vibrant space filled with the scent of simmering spices and the hum of conversation. Now, it was silent—except for the occasional gust of wind carrying the whispers of what had been.

Sierra stood at the edge of the destruction, a clipboard in hand, and an ache in her chest. She had poured everything into La Vida, her restaurant, her dream. It wasn't just a business—it was the place where neighbors gathered after long days, where musicians strummed melodies in the corner, where first dates turned into anniversaries. It had been home to more than just food; it had been a sanctuary.

The wildfire had taken everything in one cruel night. The call came at midnight, and by dawn, there was nothing left but smoldering ruins. Insurance could only cover so much. The savings she had scraped together were gone in an instant. But the real loss was the community—the people who had laughed, shared meals, and made memories inside those walls.

She sighed, adjusting the hard hat the city required her to wear while surveying the damage. A familiar voice startled her.

"We're ready when you are, boss."

Sierra turned to see Luis, her longtime sous chef, flanked by half the staff. They weren't in uniforms anymore, but in work gloves and old clothes, armed with shovels, brooms, and determination.

Behind them, neighbors had gathered. Customers. Friends. Some held tools, others carried coffee, and a few had brought bricks and supplies.

Her throat tightened. "What's all this?"

Luis grinned. "You always said La Vida wasn't just a building. It's the people. And we're still here."

Tears welled in Sierra's eyes as she took the first step forward. The fire had taken her restaurant, but not her purpose.

Not her people. They would rebuild, brick by brick, plate by plate. And one day, the doors of La Vida would open again—not as a reminder of what was lost, but as proof of what could be rebuilt.

THE WORK BEGAN SLOWLY, but it began. Volunteers came in shifts, clearing out the wreckage, salvaging what little could be saved.

THE BRICK OVEN, miraculously untouched, stood like a stubborn relic of the past. Sierra ran her fingers over the soot-streaked surface, remembering the thousands of meals it had cooked, the warmth it had given on cold evenings.

The news of their effort spread quickly. A former regular, now a journalist, covered their story. Donations started coming in— not just from the community, but from strangers who had once shared a meal in La Vida. The generosity was overwhelming. A retired carpenter offered to rebuild their wooden patio. A local florist donated plants to restore the greenery that had once framed the restaurant's entrance. A nearby café lent them a space to set up a temporary kitchen, allowing Sierra and her team to cook again, to feed volunteers and remind everyone why they were fighting to bring La Vida back.

Evenings were the hardest. When the work paused, and exhaustion set in, Sierra found herself sitting on a makeshift bench in the ruins, staring at the sky. The stars were clearer now, without the city lights—one small gift from the darkness they had endured.

Luis sat beside her one night, handing her a bottle of water. "You should get some rest."

She shook her head. "Not yet."

He was quiet for a moment before saying, "You know, I always thought you'd give up first."

Sierra laughed dryly. "Gee, thanks."

"I mean it," he said. "After everything... I wouldn't have blamed you. But you're still here."

She looked at him, really looked. His face was lined with soot and fatigue, but his eyes were steady. He believed in this. In her. And that belief gave her the strength to believe, too.

THE MONTHS PASSED. The scaffolding went up, and the new walls took shape. The first time the scent of simmering spices filled the air again, Sierra knew they were close. A simple pop-up stand was set up outside, offering samples of their menu—small bites, just enough to remind people of what was coming back.

On the night before their grand reopening, Sierra stood in the empty dining area, now fully rebuilt, running her hands over the polished wooden tables. Everything was different, yet everything was the same.

She turned to Luis. "Think they'll come back?"

He grinned. "I think they never left."

The next day, when the doors opened, the line stretched down the block. Customers, old and new, flooded in, filling the space with laughter and warmth. Plates clinked, music played, and for the first time in a long time, Sierra let herself breathe.

La Vida had returned—not just as a restaurant, but as a symbol of resilience, a testament to what could rise from the ashes.

SLEEPING UNDER BUFFALO

BY KRISTA RUFFO

The loneliness was torturing him, so he decided to go camping. It was the beginning of winter in Alaska, but Luke didn't care. He needed to clear his head. Besides, he liked it when the weather felt as if it was trying to kill him. In Luke's mind, it made outdoor activities fun. Over his sixty years of life, he had made countless jokes about glampers and such, the people who want to spend time outdoors but feel like they're not outdoors. But Luke was an Alaska man until he died.

As the sun set, Luke packed all the equipment he felt was necessary—food, clothes, utensils, and the like—and put it in his truck. Luke took today off from his handyman job because he needed the wide-open space where no one could look on him with pity or pat his back or offer their condolences. He had an appointment to renovate a client's shower, but it was a late morning appointment. He could make it in time.

Luke rose early the next morning and drove his truck thirty minutes west of where he lived. He stopped in an area he had been to before, a desolate natural space where not many people hunted or camped. His truck's wheels treaded over the semi-loose snow that glittered around him like a sea of finely cut diamonds. Through his windshield he could see the pale orange hue of the sunrise peeking over the forest of wilted spruce trees. There was only about six hours of light at this time of year, so he needed to build his campsite as fast as possible.

The cold metal bridge of Luke's glasses had all but stuck to his nose when he parked the truck. He swung his legs out, planted his heavy black boots in the snow, and surveyed the land. It was swamp-land, muskeg, made of ten to fifteen feet of decayed moss. The texture of the land wasn't swampy now since it was winter, the ground covered in sheets of white. It was the Alaskan Everglades, minus the humidity and gators. A gentle wind bit at Luke's ears.

Luke pulled his beanie further over his ears; his lips felt tight. He owned lip balm but hardly ever wore it, so his lips were in a perpetual state of dryness. But he didn't care; he had camped with his daddy in negative forty-degree weather when Luke was a mere four years old. Chapped lips didn't scare him.

Knowing that other people would've gone home by now, Luke unlatched the back of his truck and pulled out his belongings. His truck was a 2008 Suzuki Carry outfitted with military-style track wheels. He remembered the day he bought it with her, the look on her face, the way she had pulled herself up into the passenger seat, sitting high in the tank-like vehicle like a princess. Or a queen. They had owned it for ten of the thirty-five years they had been married. The powerful thing had served them well all these years of camping, treading across swamp and thick snow like the whole world was theirs. It had been one of the hallmark purchases of their life together, even more than their house.

Luke bit his bottom lip to stop the torrent of thoughts. His mouth stung, but he set his jaw and finished pulling out his two backpacks, a shotgun, a saw, and a sled. The shotgun was only for protection since he brought deer meat he had hunted two weeks ago. He pulled out a round thermometer, like one you might find on a grill, from a backpack. Sixteen degrees Fahrenheit. The sky was dense, heavy, the sun too shy to show its face, preferring to be hidden behind a veil.

Luke thought of a veil, a lace one, pulling it back.

He gritted his teeth and glared at the ice-crusted forest as if all his bad memories were hiding behind the trees. His vapor-breath clouded his vision. Luke was just below the Arctic Ocean if you looked at a map, but it seemed that not even sixteen degrees could quench the fire in his mind.

He slipped the shotgun up onto his shoulder and placed his belongings on the sled. He released his grip on the sled reins when he found their old camping spot, a clearing just inside the tree line. The trees scattered around the clearing were skinny, dead, destroyed by spruce bark beetles, spindly like something from a Dr. Seuss book. He set down his shotgun and pulled off his left glove. His quivering ring finger was bare. He hated looking at it, at the band of skin that was paler than the rest.

An image came to mind, of a pallid arm bent over a forehead, of eyes that were already half gone. Of cold sweat and cold white walls.

Luke tore open his Velcro breast pocket and yanked out the ring. He had promised himself he wouldn't bring it, but leaving behind the simple gold band felt wrong, like walking away from a sink full of dirty dishes. The ring was not unlike the bands most of his friends still wore. He slipped it down to the base of his chapped ring finger. It was loose. He had lost weight in the six months since. He stood and stared at that band for God knows how long, letting the frigid air numb his fingers. Then Luke yanked the ring off and shoved it back into his pocket, sealing the Velcro and tugging his glove back on. Before any more thoughts could surface, he got to work building his camp.

Luke sawed into the skinny trees, adrenaline pumping through his stiff body. All the years of hard work had kept him limber. The trees were light and short enough for him to carry. He had a pile of twenty or so by the time he took a curved blade and shaved off the twig-like branches, leaving the trees as tall, clean trunks. The familiarity of it all resurfaced and he forgot about the ring weighing down his pocket. The quietness around him was not threatening but serene, allowing him to focus on positioning trunks into the proper shape: four crisscrossed trunks with another trunk placed on top of them, like the skeleton of a tent.

Luke retrieved a tarp and threw it over the top trunk, giving the tent bones their skin. His back began to ache as his adrenaline dipped. His breath came out in puffs as he straightened, the tightening pain around his spine proof that he was making progress.

He stretched, then grabbed a shovel, scraping up all the snow on the ground inside the tent to get to the warmer ground underneath. He laid down the thickest trunks on the ground until he had something that looked like a raised bed.

"Airbnb worthy," he said, looking at his work, but the crunching of his boots was the only laughter.

Luke's throat was parched. The pit of his stomach growled. He liked it, the feel of approaching starvation, of being pushed by the environment to survive. The sky above him was shifting colors, and he didn't need a watch to know that it was close to three p.m., which meant the sun was setting. Although the gnawing in his belly felt good, in a way, he knew what he needed to do: fire, then dinner.

Luke grabbed a miniature stove from his truck and brought it inside the tent. He fit two cylindrical metal pieces together and stuck the topmost part out of a self-made hole in the tarp. He pulled out a bag of rice and a bag of beans from one backpack. They were the best camping food, in his opinion. They were delicious and never spoiled as long as they were kept dry.

He gathered shaved twigs from outside and stuffed them in the stove, which was just wide enough to stick his two bear paw hands in. The wind blew thoughts under the unpinned tarp; his eyes unfocused, the world before him underwater. The dry, hollow sound was like last words, like failing organs and final goodbyes.

Luke stomped his foot as if his brain were underneath it. He withdrew magnesium fire starters from a cargo pants pocket and nicked them together, casting sparks on the twigs. Luke chopped the remaining trees into smaller chunks, leaving them inside the tent for stoking the fire at night. A thin column of whitish-gray smoke filtered out of the stove's chimney.

Luke tore off his gloves and placed both hands close to the flames, the prickling in his fingertips growing stronger as feeling flooded back into them. He situated two frozen water bottles next to the stove, close enough to melt the ice but not close enough to melt the plastic. The minimal smoke that floated inside the tent didn't bother Luke in the slightest. He was hyper-aware of the aura of colder air around his body, of the empty space beside him. He wondered if this is what it had been like towards the end, when the cancer had finally clamped its jaws shut, if her lungs had felt cold yet full of smoke.

Luke dragged out two animal hides from his truck as the landscape turned to grayscale. He laid the thick, hollow-haired caribou hide on the wooden bed and placed the buffalo hide to the side. That would be his blanket. They were huge animals, but she always said he was a big man.

She had told him he was a pretty darn good cook, too. Luke filled a pot with the least pine needle-filled snow he could find, placed the pot on the stove, and stoked the fire. The flames crackled in the solid silence. Luke hung his hands between his legs and bowed his head, letting the fire thaw him. He sat by the fire until the pot of snow melted. He picked out a few stray pine needles from the water and poured in the rice and beans. He would save the deer meat for later.

A part of Luke wanted to put up a fight against his mind, but waiting for his food to cook welcomed in those memories again. He missed the way she breathed, missed the way she'd take off her socks to warm her slender feet by a fire. Luke tried to tell himself that the heaviness he felt was only tiredness, only a product of not being young anymore, but he knew it wasn't. He took a sip from one of his warmed water bottles, then stirred the rice and beans with a home-made wooden spoon.

The ring was in his hand again before he knew it. He slipped it on his finger. The gold shimmered. Luke scowled, took it off, squeezed it. He had half a mind to throw it in the fire, but he knew it took something more than a tiny stove to melt gold. Maybe he could sell it. Buy brand new equipment for his handyman business. He opened his pale palm, feeling equal parts of anger and grief. His stomach roared, so he sighed, placed the ring back in its pocket, and opened the pot lid.

Luke ate everything in the pot without stopping to breathe. He wanted to eat even more, but his body felt so laden with food that he couldn't think. His half-asleep brain told him that he needed to be up in time for sunrise because daylight was so valued here, and because he had that shower to renovate, but why worry. He was tired.

He stoked the fire one last time, changed into his nightclothes, pulled the buffalo hide over his body, and fell dead asleep.

Luke felt like a scarecrow when he awoke, or maybe a two-by-four piece of wood. When he cracked his right arm out of place, he lifted the buffalo hide off his body, then raised his back inch by inch until he was sitting on the edge of his wooden bed, his muscles feeling stiffer and colder than a dead fish. He had never stoked the fire throughout the night because he had slept so hard. He took a chunk of wood from the pile at his feet and shoved it in the stove. Luke could tell by the sparse light peeking through the tent that it was mid-morning.

He smelled something. It smelled burnt and sweet. Luke already knew what it was. He leaned his head to the ground and saw it, a goopy pile of pine sap bubbling out of one trunk. Highly flammable pine sap. Luke had heard stories of tents consumed by flames, stories of plastic sleeping bags melting onto those who forgot that sap will ooze out of cold wood brought close to a warm source. Once even the tiniest bit of sap touched a flame, a fire could rage within minutes.

But in this moment, the sap was mesmerizing, not threatening. It was golden orange like a beach sunset, hot and dangerous like magma. It dripped down the side of the log. Luke's face grew warm the longer he stayed by the stove. He could feel his joints and muscles gradually loosening. His heart rate didn't spike even though the possibility of fire was so close at hand. He moved his face away from the heat and searched for the jacket that held the ring. He found it and held it close to the fire, watching as the light twinkled off the burnished gold edge.

He could choose to do nothing. He could let all the sap ooze out and wait patiently until it burst into flames. He could crouch there, ring in hand, and let the fire eat through the buffalo hide, the tarp, the wood, his clothes. He could leave his truck for someone else to drive, leave his home for someone else to live in. There were other handymen around; his client would be fine. The memories were too much anyway. His brain felt cold and clear like a mountain stream. This is what he had to do.

The pine sap grew into one large bubble before caving in the middle and melting down the sides of the log. The edges of the sap were glowing white with heat. The sweet burning smell singed Luke's nose. His breathing grew heavier; he coughed. His heavier breaths seemed to bring in a twinge of fear that morphed into panic, wiping the clear feeling from his mind. The ring fell from his hands and he searched for a knife, his vision blurring at the edges. He found a pocketknife and poked and scraped at the sap, the heat radiating through his gloves. He threw the already-hardening sap out of the tarp flap, letting in a gust of polar air.

Luke sat on his bed, knife in hand, a snowstorm building in his head. The quiet outside the tent felt loud, as if he could open the flap back up and find an orchestra midway through a musical piece. His mind was a tundra of white-out anger. He cursed himself for being chicken, for not letting the sap do its job. Then he cursed the doctors. Luke ground his teeth, tightened his fists. He cursed at the ring on the ground. The white-out feeling consumed him and his legs moved of their own accord. Luke was outside the tent before he knew it.

The frigid air numbed his body. He cursed at himself again, at the doctors again, at everything. Even he didn't understand all the words that left his own mouth. The shrieks launched over the tundra and into the trees beyond. Luke felt his arms waving, his feet stomping. He beat his chest when his tired lungs had nothing left, squeezed his throat in anger because he would choke when he tried to speak.

The passing of time either stopped or sped up as Luke raged. But at some point his consciousness crept back in until he could hear and see again. The wind tossed bits of snow across the ground. His knees buckled; he was winded, throat raw. The snow crunched like Styrofoam as Luke fell into fetal position. He felt tears, but they didn't fall off his chin, instead freezing like shallow rivers on his face.

Luke wasn't sure how long he lay there, the fog in his head lifting, the cold making him more aware of his body with each passing moment. But this time, the biting cold wasn't a pleasurable pain. It was threatening, aggravating. He stood up, dazed, and trudged back to the tent, unsure why he was outside of it in the first place, then stopped, stealing a glance at his truck. Its white shell blended in with the tundra. He couldn't decide whether he loved or hated the thing. He also couldn't decide if he'd prefer to drop his camping and go back home and show up late to his job or stay out on the campsite until all his food ran out. He scrubbed the frozen liquid off his face. After not crying for weeks, the tears felt wrong, like a disease. He couldn't quite remember why he was even crying. The memories whispered to him at home, but shouted at him here. He thought getting out for some air would banish the thought of her, but the blank landscape only served as a canvas for all his thoughts to spill out on.

A rumble sounded in the distance when Luke approached the tent. It came from west of him, and it sounded like a vehicle, but Luke couldn't see anything. There was Bob Phillips, a long-time friend, who lived about a ten-minute walk east of Luke's campsite. That's the reason why Monica had always liked camping in this spot. It felt like you were in the middle of nowhere, but you weren't far from civilization. Civilization may have only been a couple of scattered houses, but that was enough for rural Alaskan-born people.

Luke lifted the tarp flap, thinking about if he should eat or not, when he heard the rumble again. It was louder this time. Luke walked out from the clearing and saw a dark shape moving behind a distant patch of woods, a vehicle by the looks of it. His fingers itched for his gun, but his eyes stayed glued to the shadow. Luke stood closer to a spruce tree, hoping to blend in with what dark, sagging foliage was left. He became more aware of his thinner night clothes and wanted to grab a jacket, but he didn't want to leave his post.

The shadow grew into a truck, a normal truck with normal wheels, but it was dark, unlike the hot red pickup Bob drove that you could spot ten miles away. The truck drove horizontally to Luke before it turned and ambled towards the Suzuki. It was dark green and an unlit overhead light bar sat on the roof. Game wardens. Luke wasn't worried. He knew most of the wardens in this area since he and his friends hunted frequently. He separated himself from the spruce tree and waited for the truck to park.

The truck stopped about ten yards away from the Suzuki. A tall man stepped out. Luke relaxed. It was Richard, one of the younger game wardens. Richard was easy-going, not hardened by his warden responsibilities yet, and only donned a jacket when the temperature dropped below fifty. His normally buzzed brown hair was covered by a black beanie, his five o'clock shadow spotted with a few pimples.

"Richard," Luke said, his voice cracking. He extended his hand, knowing his age allowed him first-name privileges.

Richard smiled and removed his sunglasses, an item that was

more for snow glare than sun. No other warden emerged from the passenger seat. Richard shook Luke's hand.

"No one else here with you?" Luke asked, his voice still raspy. He needed water.

"No, sir." Richard stuffed his hands in his pockets. "Not a trainee anymore."

"Oh, you graduated." Luke clapped Richard on the shoulder. "Good for you."

"Thanks." Richard looked at the Suzuki, then passed the trees to Luke's tent. "Camping?"

"Yessir. Not doing any hunting today." Luke coughed. His throat had a razor-blade feeling.

"Need some water?" Richard asked.

Luke waved Richard over to the tent. The warden held the tarp flap open and watched Luke as he grabbed his other water bottle that was sitting by the stove. Luke took a swig, gargled, then took another swig. Richard surveyed the campsite, mostly the piles of wood.

"You know they have tents nowadays, right?" Richard asked. "Pre-made ones in the store?"

"I like... doing it myself," Luke said.

Richard laughed, showing off two rows of crooked, yellowed teeth. His eyes caught on the small orange pile of frozen sap and his face fell.

"Uh-oh. You had leaking sap?" he asked.

"Yeah," Luke said, volume returning to his voice. "Nearly blew up." He chuckled and hoped the warden couldn't sense the tension Luke was feeling.

Richard flattened his lips. "Be careful."

"Yessir."

They stared out on the tundra. Richard's voice cut into the silence.

"You know why I stopped here?"

"No, sir. Not really."

"I was with Bob not too long ago."

Sure, Richard knew Bob and Luke were friends, but Luke didn't know where this was going. He capped his water bottle.

"Oh yeah? How's he doing?" Luke said.

"He was out searching for coyotes. One swiped another goat of his."

Bob was notorious for shooting anything that even thought about threatening his pets.

"I see," Luke said. "I never heard any shots."

"I heard something else, though." Richard turned his face away from the terrain to look at Luke. The warden's pale skin contrasted sharply with his dark uniform. "I heard something that sounded like screaming. In this general direction."

Luke's mouth hung slack. His throat felt raw, sore, but he thought it may have just been from lack of water. He remembered his head filling with anger. Then he curled up on the snow before going back to the tent. Luke thought he could remember something, something about cursing the sap, but the memory was fuzzy, although it wasn't that long ago. His head felt full of cotton. He stared into Richard's innocent, watery blue eyes. Maybe Luke was just a crazy old man.

"Screaming," Luke said.

"Yeah. A lot of it. So when I was done with Bob I drove around this area until I saw you and the site."

Luke stared at Richard, not knowing what to say. He didn't want to say yes because he didn't fully feel like the source of the yelling. But he didn't want to say no because if he had been screaming, then he didn't want to lie to the warden. Richard lifted the tarp flap again.

"Trouble at home? I notice your wife isn't here. Her name is Monica, right?"

Luke waited for Richard to look up. When he did, Luke drilled his eyes into the warden's, hoping the young man would understand. Richard's eyes glittered; he flattened his lips and nodded, letting the flap close. They went quiet again; the wind died down.

Luke kept his mouth glued shut. His growling stomach sliced through the quiet.

"Why?" Richard said so quietly Luke nearly thought it was the sigh of wind.

"Mesothelioma."

Richard nodded. They both looked out on the landscape, Luke knowing Richard would never see him the same way again. The waves of pity rolling off the warden peeved Luke, but he reminded himself that the young man only had Luke's safety in mind.

"Got enough food and water on you?" Richard asked.

"Yeah, I've got enough."

Thick, off-white clouds sat like a forcefield between them and the sun. Tiny flakes floated down. The snowfall wouldn't be intense, judging by the color of the sky. Luke wanted to believe he was stuck in a dream, that Richard would open the tarp flap again and that Monica would be in there, curled up and snoring. That Luke and Richard would have to move away from the tent and lower their voices so as not to wake her. But they could talk as loud as they wanted.

"So, uh," Luke said, then cleared his throat, not knowing if the warden would leave or question him further. "Did Bob kill a coyote?"

"Nah, but he did show me the busted fence where the coyote slipped in. Told him he could try motion-detector lights to spook them when they come around." Richard chuckled. "Poor guy. Those suckers stole his favorite. I've never seen a man so strung up about a goat."

Luke huffed. "He'll figure it out." He rubbed his hands together. "Well, I think I'm going to pack up early."

"Have I scared you away?"

"No, I just want to head home." As much as his pride would prevent him from admitting that he wanted to sit in a comfortable chair by a normal fireplace, being alone on the Alaskan countryside was quickly losing its appeal. Maybe being back home would shake the odd feeling in his head. Probably not.

Richard met Luke's eyes. "Yeah, sometimes it does get a little too quiet when you're out here by yourself." He craned his neck up. "I can help you pack."

"That's all right, son." Luke cringed. He wasn't sure if he had ever used that word on a younger man. "I'd like to make my breakfast first and then I'll pack up." It was partially true, but Luke didn't want Richard to see the ring on the ground inside the tent. Unless he already had.

"Maybe you should talk to Bob," Richard said, hands clasped below his stomach. "You know, give him company. He's really upset about that goat."

Luke waited for the warden to say something else, for the young man to unpin his eyes from Luke, but he said nothing more. Luke nodded and Richard reached his hand out. They shook and the warden pulled Luke in, slapping him once on the back.

"I'll leave you be so you can eat," the warden said. "Better hurry on packing up before the sun sets." Richard's boots crunched as he stepped away from Luke, waving. He looked at the Suzuki. "That's a neat truck, by the way. I've wanted to tell you that for a while but only remembered to now."

"Thanks, Richard. Take care."

Richard stared at him a moment longer before putting his sunglasses back on. He nodded and walked back to his truck. Luke watched as the warden drove away, disappearing behind the trees. Luke ducked inside the tent and picked up the ring. He squeezed it, then stuffed it in his pants pocket.

The snow in front of him undulated across the ground like static waves. He thought about how silly it was that he could've let that sap burn, how he could've let the burning smoke fill up his lungs. She had no choice, but he did.

Luke imagined seeing her face up there, behind the veiled sun. Not her pallid, sickly face, but the face he saw when he first met her on campgrounds not too far from here. The fire had flickered on her smooth skin and danced across her white teeth like a primal chant. They had talked for hours under the moon that night.

Luke let vapor funnel out of his mouth. He slipped inside the dying warmth of his tent and sat on the buffalo blanket, deciding that he had to love the thick, rough hide. He had to love his little truck. He had to love the spindly trees and the distant hills. He had to love Bob and his prized goats. He had to love the way Alaska bit into his skin. He had to love every part of his life because it was the last piece he had of hers.

EYES LIKE JELLIED FIRE
BY TRISH MACENULTY

"...a girl of indeterminate age with the face and form of a Pit Bull."
— Hunter S. Thompson, "Savage Lucy"
Fear and Loathing in Las Vegas

I was wandering around the airport in Los Angeles when I met the attorney. He said he was a descendent of Pancho Villa, but I didn't know who that was and I discovered that nothing he said was true — except when he offered to pay my airfare to Las Vegas. How I wound up in the L.A. airport from Flathead County in Montana is anybody's guess. I'd been traveling all day with a small suitcase and all my cardboard portraits in a bundle tied up with string. I was in quite a pickle as I couldn't afford a ticket to Las Vegas where I planned to find Miss Streisand and give her the portraits. They were all of her. I had painted them from the TV.

Standing at the ticket counter of Frontier Airlines, I felt his eyes on me like soft hands while I was trying to explain to the ticket lady that I had thought I was on a plane to Las Vegas, NOT Los Angeles.

"Don't worry. I'll get you to Vegas," a voice said. "I'm going there myself."

Suddenly, standing beside me was a big, black-haired, brown-skinned man, probably forty years old, in a pin-striped suit with a wide kaleidoscope tie. He paid for my ticket along with his own, and then we ran to the gate. He moved fast for a big guy.

On the plane he ordered two rum and cokes and insisted I take one. Raised as a Christian, I had never had an alcoholic drink in my life. It was delicious.

He said I could call him Zeta and that he was fighting for a revolution. He talked a lot about injustice as if I didn't know anything about it. But I knew plenty.

"Do you get airsick?" he asked.

"A little," I said.

He took a blue capsule out of a bottle, swallowed it, and handed one to me.

"This will take care of all of your problems."

I said I didn't think that was the case. I had run away from home for the sixth time. This was the first time I had made it out of state. And that's only because I had forged a check with my stepfather's name on it and gotten enough money to fly instead of thumbing it. I took the pill.

By the time the plane landed, things were, well ... different. I felt weird inside like I had somehow gotten placed in a different body and parts of my spirit were seeping outside the lines. As we walked through the airport, I could have sworn a woman holding a baby had a halo around her head like she was the Mother Mary.

"I see the holy family," I said to Zeta.

He looked at me.

"Are you religious?"

"Aren't you?"

"How old are you?"

"Seventeen." Well, I would be in another month.

He squeezed my shoulder, and we got in a cab.

"To the Flamingo!" he ordered the driver. His voice felt like wet cotton.

"What was in that blue capsule?" I asked.

His big gummy face made an impossible shape.

"Don't worry. It only lasts a few hours."

I knew then that he had given me LSD. Even in Kalispel, Montana, we'd heard of "acid." It made people think they were birds and jump out of windows.

We pulled up to a hotel with a giant pink bird outside. Once we got into the bright pink room, Zeta ripped off his clothes. I stared at the folds of blubber around his belly. He was fat but also strong.

My skin felt waxy and malleable. The room wobbled around me, and when I waved my hand, I saw thousands of hands following it. The ceiling dipped down and scraped the top of my skull open, revealing a vast canyon. Angels sang inside my head, their voices echoing into eternity.

Zeta told me he was Jesus and showed me red marks on the palms of his hands. I believed him even though his hands smelled like ketchup. He wasn't a bearded, blue-eyed Jesus like the pictures on my bedroom wall back home but a dark, husky Jesus who wandered the desert and argued with God. I succumbed when Zeta asked me to take off my clothes. Who was I to turn down Jesus?

I had never *willingly* lain with a man, but decided to let it happen if it was going to happen. Zeta lay naked beside me and put his big furry paw on my belly.

"Do you know how to make a Molotov cocktail?" he asked.

"Are you thirsty?" I asked.

He started laughing and couldn't stop. I could see through his skin to his corpuscles. Though much is lost in the maze of memory, I do know one thing. He did not achieve the goal he set out to achieve with me that day. His visions distracted him as mine did me.

Then bursting through the door came a skinny guy with a cigarette holder wedged between his teeth, a suitcase, and eyes like laser beams. I must have had flamingos on the brain because this guy reminded me of one, preening and ridiculous. I snarled at him. I had turned into some sort of beast myself — a pit bull?

Zeta said, "Lucy. This is my client. He's a nice man." I thought he said something about the man being a hunter.

But the hunter wasn't nice. Men like that never are. Grinning and sweating and muttering to Zeta, he eyed me like I was a time bomb. I didn't hear him say they should sell me to the conventioneers. I only read about that later in the book he wrote. I guess he was kidding? But it's hard to tell.

I spent most of the night staring out the window at the strip — it looked like a star had fallen from the canopy above and landed on its hands and knees in the desert. Meanwhile, Zeta and the hunter babbled non-stop, drinking rum and talking about narcos, pinkos, and weirdos.

When I woke the next morning, they said I had to leave. The hunter feared I would turn them into the cops. He said, I was jail-bait. We rode in a white Cadillac convertible with leather seats. The hot wind whipped my hair into a hornet's nest around my face as they took me back to the airport. Zeta put me in a taxi with my portraits of Barbra and my little suitcase, and told the cabbie to drive me to the International Hotel.

"I don't want to go," I said.

He said the hunter had reserved a room for me, and they would see me later.

"Good luck to ya, kiddo." He waved as the taxi took off.

Dazed, I wandered across the shiny marble floor of the lobby at the International. I had no intention of *selling* the portraits to Barbra. They were a gift. But I did want to see her in real life, to observe how the flesh clung to the bones of her face, how her eyes caught the light, how her golden hair cascaded over her shoulders. Mostly I wanted to hear the smile in her voice when she saw the portraits and exclaimed how much she loved them.

What I didn't know when they dropped me off was that Barbra

Streisand wasn't even in Vegas. When I asked the bellman how I could find her, he told me to take a bus to Los Angeles.

"Last time we saw her it was New Year's," he said in a thick accent I didn't recognize.

Los Angeles. I had been so close.

I trudged down the strip, carrying my portraits under my arm. I had left my suitcase in a broom closet in the hotel. The strip dazzled at night but in the day it looked hungover and tawdry. The sunlight bounced off the concrete, and no one was pretty. I sat on a bench across from the McDonald's, exhausted. My brain was still frazzled from the acid and a sinister gloom floated in the air around me. A woman with a wedding cake of dirty blond hair on her head stumbled by with her husband. She stopped and looked at the portraits, leaning on the bench beside me. It wasn't even noon, but she was sloshed.

Seeing the portraits, she yelled, "Harry, stop! I want one."

Harry stopped and asked, "How much, kid?"

I looked at the portrait he was pointing to.

"It's not for sale," I said.

Harry tilted his head and glared at me. Then he pulled out a ten-dollar bill from his wallet, threw it at my feet, untied the string around the paintings, and took the portrait. I didn't stop him. The ten-dollar bill lay on the sidewalk like a discarded cigarette box before I snatched it up and stuffed it in the pocket of my blue smock.

I stayed on that bench, and by that afternoon I had sold all of my paintings. It occurred to me to go into the casinos and turn a profit with my cash. The casino I chose was the Sahara. It was dingy and old and, I was pretty sure, nothing like Africa.

Inside, what a god-awful smell — a few centuries of cigarette smoke and liquor-soaked carpeting, populated by people with halitosis. I tried the slot machines and lost forty dollars. I wondered where those two drug-addled jokers had gone, and decided to call their hotel and tell them to come get me. I was lonely and scared and though I didn't like either of them, I also realized I had never met anyone like them before. They talked in a river of words and ideas that I wanted to swim in. I found a pay phone in the lobby and rang the Flamingo, and the clerk put me through. Zeta answered. He said he loved me. He called me Lucy in the sky with diamonds. He said that when the revolution came, I would lead the way on a winged horse. All of a sudden, he screamed something about the police, kicked around some furniture, and hung up on me. I put the receiver back on its hook. Whatever that had been, it was done. Those two did not mean well by me. They had an arsenal of drugs to keep them occupied. I was irrelevant as long as I didn't report them to the police.

I could not go home. For one thing, I had forged a check so I was a fugitive from justice. For another, my brother was no longer there to stand between me and my stepfather. When the draft took him away, things became unbearable in that house. Mama never uttered a kind word and the less said about my stepfather, the better. Every time I saw a body bag on TV, I worried my brother was in one. Sometimes I wished I was in a body bag. My only recourse was to run.

"You are going to wind up just like those Manson girls," my mother said after the third time I ran away. Now that I had taken acid, I was worried she was right. Charles Manson had fed a bunch of girls LSD like it was jelly beans and the next thing you know they're bathing in the blood of a movie star.

As I headed back toward the casino to try my hand at Blackjack, I noticed a long-haired guy in an army jacket watching me — a bucket full of hurt in his brown eyes. I was drawn to a pain that perfectly matched my own. Like we were twins born years apart.

"Got a cigarette?" I asked.

He shook his head.

"Well, then, what good are you?"

"I got a car. Want to go see Hoover dam?"

I looked toward the casino and then at this guy. Was Charlie Manson lurking behind those chocolatey eyes, I wondered. Did it even matter?

"Heck, yeah, I want to see the Hoover dam."

He said his name was Jackson. His car was not a fancy convertible like the hunter drove. It was a midnight blue '66 Oldsmobile Cutlass 442 in need of a washing. I propped my feet up on the dash, and let the wind, streaming through the window, have its way with me. I took a moment to assess my situation. I was far away from Montana, far from my mother and her grody old husband and his hands that bent me like a twig, and I was in the desert with a mysterious man. I had taken LSD and it had not killed me or turned me into a murderer. Instead, it had shown me that something could be two things at the same time. Like the skinny dude who was both a hunter and a flamingo or Zeta who was a creep, and Jesus at the same time. And me, what two or more things was I? A runaway Jesus freak and also a girl on the precipice of the unknown.

We drove south for about an hour and then took Route 93 toward the dam. Jackson didn't talk much, but he was a good listener. I told him about my paintings and about the two weirdos at the Flamingo Hotel. I didn't tell him about my brother even after he told me he was a Vietnam vet. After a while I ran out of things to say and so I stared out at the scruffy desert landscape.

We followed a curving road and then to my astonishment, a giant blue blob appeared. It was the prettiest shade of blue I had ever seen.

"That's Lake Mead. It was created by the dam," Jackson said. "It was because of Hoover dam that Las Vegas became a city."

"How's that?"

"Well, think of all the men it took to build this thing. Thousands. They needed somewhere to go spend their money on a Friday night."

We crossed the dam and parked the car in a lot on the Arizona side. Then we walked back across the dam to get a better look — a lake on one side and a trough of water on the other. About in the middle, a sign told us we were entering Nevada.

"Stand like this," he said. I stood in front of him, and we both placed one foot in Arizona and one in Nevada. Then I moved and stood in Nevada and he stood in Arizona.

"You're so far away," I complained. "You're in a whole 'nother state."

"Wait for me, will ya?" he implored.

We thought we were funnier than Shecky Greene.

We decided to watch the sunset from the hood of the Cutlass. We pulled off the two-lane road, facing west, Lake Mead simmering in front of us, mountains in the distance like old uncles. I leaned back against the windshield, hugging myself against the creeping chill. The sun spilled its guts across the sky and over the surface of the water like a can of red paint.

"I wish I had a camera," I said.

I looked over at Jackson and realized tears were streaming down his face. I had never actually seen someone cry without making a sound. I didn't know what to say or do. My nose itched, and so I scratched it.

"Tell me," I said, finally.

He shook his head.

"You can tell me. I'm a stranger. You'll probably never see me again after this."

He smeared the tears across his face with the sleeve of his jacket.

"I was there."

"Where?"

"Pinkville."

"Never heard of it," I said.

"It's a code name. You probably know it as My Lai." He stared down at his hands.

I searched my memory. Sounded familiar but I didn't know why.

"Is that some kind of drink?"

"You never heard of the My Lai massacre?"

I shook my head. He snorted. My Lai, Molotov. There seemed to be a connection between horrible things and pretty concoctions.

"I wasn't allowed to watch the news at home. The body bags upset me," I said. "And no one talked about stuff like that at school."

He took a deep breath of desert air as if that would dry his breaking heart.

"I was infantry in Charlie Company under the command of Lieutenant William Calley. March, 1968, Calley took us into this village of about four hundred people. Women. Kids. Babies."

I didn't like where this story was going.

"The Vietnamese name for the village is Song My."

"That's pretty. Like My Song," I said.

We were silent, and the sun gathered its colors back as it stepped down past the horizon. The warmth of the day ran after it.

Jackson continued.

"In Vietnam, the heat was wet and relentless. Maybe the heat made us go mad. Calley led us into the village, and told the men to kill all the 'gooks.' I thought, hell, no. We can't kill the kids. But then it happened. Pow-pow-pow-pow. Kids crying. Mothers screaming. But some of them didn't make a sound. They'd look over at me, their eyes accusing. When the bullets slammed into their bodies, they jerked like marionettes before falling in a heap. I was sprinkled with blood splatter. It didn't take all that long to finish the job but it felt like we were there for a century. It still feels like I'm there sometimes."

I thought I might roll off the hood of the car and vomit into the sand, but I didn't. I didn't move. I thought of my brother and prayed to Jesus that he was not killing kids at the very moment that I was looking up at the night sky.

He sighed. "If Calley goes to prison, every single one of us should be there, too."

"Why did you all kill women and children?" I asked.

"We said it was because the civilians would be your friends in the day but wear Viet Cong pajamas at night. But really the Viet Cong soldiers were invisible so we killed the only physical evidence of their existence — the women and the kids. Or maybe it was because our country put guns in our hands and told us to go kill someone. And those women and children were the only ones we could find. Calley was in the wrong. This was wholesale murder. But... if Uncle Sam hadn't sent us into the jungle to begin with, not a one of us would ever have killed anybody."

"How many did you kill?"

"I went into a hut and shot an old man and his wife. Then I just stayed there until all the killing was done. I was a coward for killing them and too much of a coward not to kill them."

The sky turned dark. Stars pricked their way through the blackness one by one and then by the millions. I shivered.

"I think I have a room back at the International Hotel," I said.

WE DROVE BACK to Las Vegas with its flashing lights, its giant neon cowboy, its girls walking the streets in tiny, tight dresses, and the hunger underneath it all. We pulled into the parking lot of the largest hotel in the world, went to the front desk and, to my surprise, the hunter had actually reserved a room for me and paid for it with a credit card. The clerk handed me a room key.

"Hey, here's two tickets to go see Elvis," the clerk said.

"Free?" I asked.

"Yeah. They need a few more bodies in there."

So we went in to see Elvis. The clerk must have been joking because the place was packed. We found a space by the wall and leaned against it as we watched Elvis in his fringed white suit waving his guitar around like a machine gun. Women cried, and men shook their heads in a frenzy. Elvis shivered and lunged, clutching the microphone stand. It reminded me of being in church when the Holy Ghost comes down on the congregation.

When Elvis sang, "You don't have to stay forever, I will understand," Jackson's hand slipped into mine and maybe I felt something like love. It was warm, and my insides got stirred up. As I basked in that moment, I knew Mama was wrong. I would never be a Manson girl.

That night we went up to room 1200 and crawled into the bed together. We held onto each other all night and slept like that, fully clothed. I hadn't slept so soundly in a long time — since before my brother left to fight and maybe die in a little country most of us had never even imagined before we were bombing them.

The next morning the hotel figured out the hunter's credit card was no good. Jackson and I scraped up the money between us to pay for the room. We had breakfast at one of the buffets and then he drove me to the bus station where he kissed me on the cheek before I got out and watched him drive away.

YEARS later when I read the book that Hunter Thompson wrote about "fear and loathing in Las Vegas," I realized one of the things he feared was me. A girl. A girl who might tell the truth. And because he feared me, he loathed me. Sure, he caught the crumbling of society in his gonzo prose or whatever you want to call it, and I'll admit I liked the writing. While I didn't appreciate being compared to a pit bull, when he wrote that I had eyes like "jellied fire," I kind of took it for a compliment.

I wish I could say I became a great artist, revered in Paris, London and New York — my portraits worth tens of thousands of dollars. But I took a job as a cook on a ranch near Reno, and after that I moved to Los Angeles and worked as a bartender. I left my religion behind and quit painting. One day I found myself in a college class-room, and a few years later I became a social worker, helping lost girls find their way. Not a one of them became a Manson girl.

Maybe because of my work, my faith returned. That year I attended a new church — the kind that plays rock music and doesn't care if people are gay — and who do you think I ran into? Jackson! He was doing good. He told me he owned a pool service and restored classic cars. We started hanging out together, and six weeks later he said we oughta get married. Which we did at a wedding chapel in Las Vegas and spent our honeymoon at the Hilton, which used to be the International. Then we had a couple of babies.

Our kids are grown and doing fine, thanks for asking. Rhonda is a fashion photographer. You've probably seen her work in magazines or on websites, and our son, Elvis (who can't sing a lick) has a good head for business. He's taken over the pool business from his dad, and already expanded it into two more counties. We have three grandkids via Elvis. Jackson and I invested wisely so we're comfortable.

Next year we're going on a trip to Washington, D.C. to see the Vietnam Memorial. Jackson says he's ready, and I've waited forever to run my fingers over my brother's name.

KNOWING WHEN TO SAY GOODBYE

BY AMANDA CUPP

I've always imagined the open road as a journey of self-exploration and adventure. It's the kind of experience you see in movies—rolling down the windows, blaring music, and singing along without a care in the world. With each stop at a gas station, you start to transform into a version of yourself that you never expected—a person who is braver, kinder, more ambitious, or whatever it may be.

However, that hasn't been my experience. This road feels less like a joyride and more like an escape route—just a long stretch of asphalt putting miles between me and a life I no longer even recognize. In some sense, it could be considered self-exploration, but right now, it feels more like an amusing joke that I have to live out.

Moving 2,000 miles with a five-year-old across the country wasn't something I thought about when planning the move. Initially, I needed to give it more thought. In truth, my mind was more focused on leaving Ted, my shitface husband. As soon as I got that in motion, I packed Jane in the car and loaded my X-terra with all the fruit snacks and Capri Suns her little heart desired. It occurred to me after three hours of driving that I had overestimated how laid back my child was.

"Mama, I want another fruit snack."

"You just had one baby, can you wait a little bit until we stop for lunch?"

I peeked through the rearview mirror and saw her hazel eyes quickly turn into what I imagined a demon's eyes looked like. "But I want a fruit snack now!" To add a little spunk, she kicked the passenger seat in front of her.

I wanted to laugh at the absurdity of her problems, but I maintained my composure. "Well, I want a million dollars and you don't see me kicking and fussing about it."

She planted her face into her hands and tugged on her chestnut hair. Her trademark crocodile tears came to the surface. "Please, Mama. I promise I'll eat all of my lunch."

"Okay, you can have one more fruit snack," I winced at my cowardliness, "but no more until lunch."

She quickly regained her preppiness. "Thank you!"

"You're welcome, babe." I smiled at my ability to make a compromise, even if I sacrificed my authority as a parent.

We were welcomed in Lubbock by a sign that said "The friendliest city in America." I rolled my eyes at this statement. The last time I was in Lubbock, some drunk cowboy tried to feel me up at a honky tonk. I guess that could be categorized as friendly. We stopped for gas and utilized the Burger King that was connected to the gas station. "Don't mess with Texas" memorabilia was everywhere we turned: mugs, blankets, shirts, key chains, and even purses. Who in the hell would carry around a purse like that and think it's fashionable? Nobody is more weirdly obsessed with Texas than Texans themselves.

West Texas is something left to be undesired. While driving down the highway, I felt like I was gonna drive off the face of the earth. Once we were out of the big cities, oil wells seized the fields for miles. I forgot how desolate this side of the country was. It brought a gloomy feeling within my heart that I couldn't quite understand.

"Where are we going again?" The words barely made their way out of her stuffed mouth.

"We're going to Portland, Oregon. It's super pretty over there. There are lots of big green trees and it's only a little way from the ocean."

"When's Daddy gonna come visit us?"

Shit.

"Well, Daddy will try to come see you as soon as possible. Remember what we talked about last night? That you and I will be living in Portland and Daddy will stay in Austin?"

"But why?"

What a great question, honestly. How do you tell your child that you have no interest in being with her father ever again? Do I explain to her the type of manipulation and control that men can have over you?

Ted was fully in denial of the state of our marriage. He was suffocating me, but his behavior could go undetected by the untrained eye. Despite my unwavering loyalty, he always had suspicions about my whereabouts. One time, I found him copying my planner into one of his journals. He pretended to be looking at a different book on my desk as my planner dropped to the ground. At that moment, I knew I needed to divorce this man.

His words from the day prior relentlessly echoed in my ears: "You can't tear our family apart like this, Roseanna."

It didn't seem to concern him when I was the one who stayed at home full-time while he grew in his career. Hence why I'm in this predicament now.

I exhaled and tried to collect my thoughts in the most comprehensive way possible. "Daddy and I think it's a good idea for us to live away from each other for a little while. Daddy likes living in Austin and I'm excited to start my brand new job in Oregon."

She nodded with a somewhat sorrowful look on her face. "Okay."

Guilt started to wash over me, "But don't you worry. Daddy will come up as much as he can to see you. When we get to our hotel room tonight, you can give him a call."

She chewed on her fries and looked out the window. I was relieved by her dismissal of the conversation. I chewed the inside of my cheek while I picked at my lips.

Did I jeopardize my daughter's well-being for my own self-interest?

I couldn't help but wonder if Ted - though he's a son of a bitch - had a point. I wasn't sorry for leaving him, but I'm not sure if it was the right decision to uproot Jane from Austin. Time will tell. Blood reached the surface as I continued the incessant picking.

WE WERE ONLY six and a half hours into our drive and I polished off my third Monster. I found myself missing my nicotine addiction - a cigarette would be perfect to comfort me from the dull scenery. We passed a sign that said: "Littlefield, Texas: Home of Waylon Jennings." This piqued Jane's interest.

"Who's that man in the cowboy hat, Mama?" We both observed the picture plastered on the sign.

"That's Waylon Jennings. He was a country singer back in the day."

"Was he a good singer?"

"Oh yeah, I listened to him when I was little. My daddy used to sing along to his songs all the time."

"Have I ever met your daddy?"

I should've kept my mouth shut. "You met him when you were a baby."

"Why doesn't he visit us?"

I stared at the road ahead, hoping to find an answer. "He's always busy with work."

Great cover, Roseanne.

I put on Billy Joel's *Greatest Hits* to buffer topics. When "Uptown Girl" came on, Jane instantly snapped into performance mode. We sang along as we went down the road - I couldn't help but giggle at her tone-deafness.

Thank God that she has a dazzling personality.

We both became quiet as the bleakness of the plains grew. The countryside bored my brain with the minimal spouts of pigment - it reminded me of a colored printer running out of ink. I became more and more eager to be surrounded by Oregan's luscious peaks. I glanced over at Jane and witnessed her fight to slumber as her eyes rapidly gave into exhaustion. Seeing her state triggered a wave of tiredness within me, making me let out an aggressive yawn. The most horrendous noise coming from the hood of the X-terra quickly awakened me. I turned the wheel towards the right, making us stop on the side of the road. The noise grew louder and uglier as I turned the key into the ignition.

Then... nothing.

God fucking damn it.

The radio remained on.

"Well, they showed you a statue, told you to pray. They built you a temple and locked you away. Aw, but they never told you the price that you'd pay for things that you might have done. Only the good die young."

It's hard to say exactly what caused it - perhaps it was the sorry condition of my vehicle or the calming effect of Billy's voice - but at that instant, it felt like time had come to a halt. I could feel the tears starting to gather, slowly making their way up, and as they reached the surface, I couldn't hold back any longer, finding myself in a state of uncontrollable weeping. Waves of fear, sadness, and anger crashed over me, each one hitting me like a freight train. How could I do this on my own? It was a humbling experience for me to acknowledge that my initial belief - that I could simply pick up and run away from my problems - was misguided, as it became clear that there were indeed repercussions to my actions. With my eyes fixed upon the stark and lifeless scenery, I wondered if I was worthy of being saved. I buried my face in my hands, trying to muffle the sound of my sobs as I noticed Jane stirring in her seat. Luckily, my mental breakdown didn't disturb her slumber.

JANE WAS in a sour disposition from the moment the tow truck picked us up. On the way to the repair shop, she threw her Barbie at Billy Bob - the poor bastard who had the shitty luck to clock into work that day. For two hours, Jane and I planted ourselves next in front of a TV set that was definitely made in the 80s. The owner, Juanita, was indulging in her telenovelas and was catching us up from last week's episode. Even though I have never learned a hint of Spanish, the expressive acting warped me, and the insanely chaotic plot lines. Jane was also intrigued, mostly because she thought Juanita was pretty and wanted her to like her.

Billy Bob came in and stole Juanita from us for a moment. I took offense until I realized the reason I was there in the first place.

Juanita came to my side a few minutes later. "So, I have some good news and some bad news for you. Which would you like to hear first?"

I cringed, "Give the good first."

"Billy Bob was able to find the issue with your car and can fix it. However, we have to order the part, which won't be here till Monday."

It was Saturday.

God. Fucking. Damn. It.

I took a deep breath. "How far away are we from Clovis?"

Juanita gave herself a moment to think. "I'd say it's about a thirty-minute drive."

"Can you excuse me for one moment?"

Juanita nodded and continued entertaining Jane. I grabbed my phone and dialed the closest taxi service.

Patience was tested as I waited for ten minutes on hold; at least

The Golden Girls' theme song being on loop kept me sane. My optimism fizzled when the gentleman who picked up notified me that they were out of service. I sank into a leather chair and tried to think of my next move.

Well, I could call...

No, I don't remember his number.

A stroke of genius hit me as I hurried to Juanita's phone book. I flipped through each page with purpose, quickly skimming through each name. Of course, the one number I needed was nowhere to be found.

I think Juanita could smell the desperation that was oozing out of me. She sat next to me and patted my shoulder. "If you girls need a ride to Clovis, I have no problem taking you."

My lip started to quiver as I tried to maintain my dignity. "Are you sure? I can cover gas."

"No need," Juanita waved her hands. "I'll go get my purse."

While Juanita disappeared into the garage, Jane tugged on my jeans. "What's Clovis, Mama?"

I squatted down and zipped up her bubblegum pink jacket. "Clovis, New Mexico. It's not too far away."

"Why are we going there?"

"Because your grandpa lives there."

Confusion washed over her face, "But I thought Grandpa Jim lived in Florida?"

"He does. I'm talking about your Grandpa Curtis, he's my daddy."

CLOVIS, New Mexico is a destination I would prefer to avoid. The only things to do around here are football, church, and shopping at the strip mall that was once "booming" in the 80s. The last time I was here, my Grandma Loretta still had a pulse. She lived just a few houses down from the Allsup's - the best place to get a pack of camels, an unusually large Dr. Pepper, and a questionably delicious bean burrito. My grandma's house took residence in a trailer park. At the front door, a cowboy figurine creepily stared at any person in sight. In addition, there was a sign that hung "Home is Where Jesus Is" on a bright red door. When I would walk into her house, it smelled like it had been sitting for a while. Not in a gross way or anything - it had the scent of a vacation cabin that was only visited a few times a year. Bright maroon recliners took over the majority of the house, leaving little room for big parties.

However, her charming trailer that I remembered quickly became a faint memory. Jane and I stood in front of the home with our luggage. The cowboy seemed to have been in an accident. His left arm was compromised some time ago. The door's pigment had turned into a weird salmon pink with the chips of paint hanging on for dear life. When Grandma Loretta passed, my father took over the place. I assumed it was because of the cheap rent and not of sentimental value. Women that he clung to had probably grown weary of his long-term committed relationship with Budweiser.

As we approached the door, Jane's disdain became immediately apparent. "Your daddy lives here?"

I nodded, "Don't worry, pumpkin, it's not too bad. I've stayed here before." I lifted my hand to the door and knocked.

Silence. I knocked louder.

After a moment, sounds of rumbling occurred. The door popped open abruptly, which startled Jane and me.

We were immediately met with the stench of tequila and Axe body spray. My father was wearing the same Dale Earnhardt shirt that he wore when I was a child, only now the lettering was barely visible. His skin reminded me of a tomato that was left in the sun too long - desperately asking for moisture.

My visual examination halted once I met his eye line. A sadness was present. He looked us up and down. "Is it Christmas?" he laughed, "Or you're here for my funeral."

Jane peeped up at me, mystified at the chance that it was Christmas. It was, in fact, July. "Mama, is it Christmas?"

I shook my head, though I wished it was. The idea of spending Christmas in Oregon enchanted me since I haven't seen snow in God knows how long. Unfortunately, it rains more than anything in Portland, but it's somewhat similar to snow - that works for me. I switched gears towards my father, "Why would you say we were here for a funeral?"

"Shit, I figured I'd be dead if it meant you were showing up."

I laughed to contain my irritation and pulled Jane closer to me. "It's nice to see you too, Dad."

He ignored my sarcasm and turned his attention to Jane. He tugged his Wrangler's up, "And you must be Jane."

She popped her head from behind my leg and nodded.

"I haven't seen you since you were this big," he pulled his hands apart to demonstrate the size of a newborn baby, even though he met her when she was 18 months old.

"Mama said that you're always working and that's why you haven't come to visit me."

I can't believe my kid ratted me out.

"Is that so?" His eyebrow raised, "That's what she told you?"

She nodded.

I need to teach her how to lie more.

"Is that why you're here? To spend some time with your workaholic father?"

I bit my tongue, feeling my blood boil beneath my dry, sunburnt skin. "I think replacing 'work' with 'alcohol' would be a more accurate statement."

His lips curled and his brows furrowed; he sneered, "Did you come all this way just to be a smartass?"

"No," I let out a sigh, "we had car trouble in Muleshoe and we need a place to stay for a few days."

He threw a dip of snuff in his mouth. "Are there no motel rooms in Muleshoe? What made you think I was still living here?"

I rolled my eyes, "I took a gamble, I guess. Besides, I didn't have the extra money to pay for a room."

"Oh, so you need money, huh?"

I yawned and saw Jane rubbing her eyes. "No. Look, we've been on the road all day and we're tired. Could we please stay here till Tuesday?"

He stared at Jane for a moment, then at me. He opened the door wider and gestured us inside.

I hope I fall into a coma before Tuesday.

FOR THE FIRST few hours after our arrival, my father spent all of them in the garage. I felt relieved; I didn't have the energy to handle his presence. Once the sun came down, I had Jane bathed, clothed, and fed. Before I put her to bed, I had her call Ted to keep the terms of our agreement.

"It was so cool Daddy. Mama's car got broken, and a man picked us up. We got to watch TV with a pretty lady."

I should have talked to him beforehand.

"Yeah, and now we're having a slumber party at Grandpa Curtis's house."

With innocence in her eyes, Jane looked up at me. My gaze stared down at the phone in her tiny hand as she held it out. "Daddy wants to talk to you."

I grabbed the phone and prepared myself for a lecture. I walked out of the room and onto the front porch. "Hello?"

"What the hell is going on, Rosie?"

I exhaled. "Everything is fine. We had car trouble, so we got it towed to a repair shop."

"Why the hell are you at your dad's?"

"Because I didn't have much of a choice, Ted."

"I wish you had kept me in the loop. I could have-"

"What could you have done? Drive all the way over to Muleshoe to pick us up? No, I got it taken care of."

He cleared his throat. "I don't know why you won't let me help you."

"Because there's nothing that you can help me with."

The silence could have been cut with a butter knife.

I quickly grew impatient. "Listen, I'll have Jane call you tomorrow, okay? It's been a long day."

"Rosie, I already lost you. Jane is the only thing I have. I just want us to be able to raise Jan-"

I started feeling that nagging, guilty feeling again. I had to stop it in its tracks. "This will get easier, Ted. I just don't have the wherewithal to go through all of this right now. You know more than anybody how much it is physically killing me inside to ask for his help. I appreciate your wanting to help, but I can't run to you anymore. Can we just... talk about this later?"

"Okay," his voice cracked. He paused, "Can you please give her a kiss for me and tell her that I love her?"

My voice trembled, "I will."

I hung up the phone and made my way back into the room. I giggled at how quickly Jane passed out. Both of us occupied an air mattress in my Grandma's old craft room. Or a better description would be her old Dolly Parton-themed room that happened to be filled with yarn and wrapping paper. When I tucked Jane in, Dolly's cardboard cut-out loomed over us. It was a weird comfort knowing that Dolly was watching over my child as she slept. I walked into the living room and was taken aback at how little had changed in the house. It was as if my father left everything as it was so my Grandma's ghost could roam comfortably. The only shred of evidence that indicated my father lived there was the NASCAR poster that was hung over the fireplace. My father was lounging in the recliner while being entertained by his nightcap. I planted myself across from him. I looked down at the shaggy carpet, hoping he would say something first since I hadn't seen the man in four and a half years. He continued to suck down his tallboy while watching a rerun of Frasier.

I cleared my throat. "Thanks again for letting us stay. I really appreciate it."

His eyes remained glued to the screen. "It's not like I had a choice in the matter."

"Thanks, Dad." I rolled my eyes and bit my tongue from any digs I wanted to throw at him.

He looked at me, "So why in the hell were you on the road, anyway? Why isn't your husband of yours with you two?"

"Well, um," I let out a deep breath, "Ted and I are getting a divorce."

He seemed unalarmed and even let out a chuckle. "Surprise, surprise."

I gasped, "What the hell does that supposed to mean?"

"Surprise? I think the definition is when something unexpected happens. But, I was saying it in a sarcastic tone to hint to you that I am, in fact, not surprised." He took a sip of his beer and had a rather smug expression on his face.

"You know, some people would ask their child how they were doing with this big change in their life and if they were okay. I know that's a weird concept for you since that falls under the category of 'parenting.'"

"Oh Jesus Christ, Roseanne. I was just messing around. You take everything so goddamn seriously."

I laughed at his lack of self-awareness and nodded. "Right."

"So did the dipshit leave you, or were you the one who tore your family apart?" he sneered.

"I left him."

He raised his eyebrows and asked, "Did you realize how much of a schmuck he is?"

I giggled, "Actually, yeah, I did." I paused, "Jane and I are headed to Portland. I got a job up there."

"Why the hell would you move to Portland? It's full of those goddamn hippies who burn their bras and never shave their armpit hair."

"Last time I checked, it wasn't the 1960s. Nobody would waste their money on burning a bra. We just don't wear one. Plus, who gives a fuck about armpit hair?" I laughed at his Gen X rant that I was unfortunately all too familiar with. "I've also missed living next to the mountains. I haven't seen much since I left Idaho."

The mention of Idaho made him immediately silent.

"When's the last time you were home?" I asked.

He looked puzzled, "I am home." He took another sip out of the half-hollow can. "I haven't thought about Idaho since I left."

"Well, you lived there for fifteen years. And I was born there. Doesn't that count for something?"

He winced at me. "What are you doing? What is this?"

"What?" I asked, feeling confused.

"You show up to my house after not speaking to me for almost five years, and now you're trying to dissect everything."

"I'm not trying to do anything. I was just making conversation."

"Well, knock it off." He yelled as he slapped his hand on the cushion. "I don't want to talk about it."

I couldn't help but let out a mocking laugh. "Oh, of course you don't want to talk about it. You'd actually have to give a fuck first for that to happen."

He stood straight up and kicked the recliner back to put it in place. "Goodnight." He went into his room and shut the door.

I found comfort in Frasier's usual shenanigans while Marty scolds him.

THE NEXT MORNING, I found myself hanging off the side of the air mattress while Jane sprawled out like a starfish. A weird stabbing pain radiated from my lower back as I adjusted myself on the bed. Relief washed over me when I dug out Jane's Barbie from underneath me. Annoyance was my first reaction. I turned toward Jane carefully, not wanting to wake her up; I didn't think I had the energy to deal with a grumpy five-year-old.

"Good morning," I said, lightly stroking my hand over her head.

Her eyes fluttered open, slowly stirring from her slumber. "Morning, Mama," she replied in her sweet morning voice.

I planted small kisses on her face and gently ran my hand along her cheek. "Did you sleep well?"

She nodded, "Yeah." She pointed at Dolly, who never compromised her position all night. "I woke up in the nighttime and I was scared by that lady."

"Hey, that's Dolly Parton. She's the queen of country music... and mankind. We love Dolly." I took a moment and stared at the cutout. "But it is a little startling to have her stare at your every move."

Jane gave me one of those "duh" faces. I couldn't help but defend Dolly, it's in my DNA.

I could muster up enough energy to get Jane and myself dressed. We made our way to the kitchen, which had similar characteristics to a fraternity I used to party at. Empty beer cans occupied most of the counter space, leaving the rest full of dirty dishes. As I investigated the cupboards, I quickly lost faith in our chances of a decent breakfast. I looked around the house. My father was nowhere in sight. I looked out the window, and his truck was also missing.

I returned to the kitchen to find Jane singing her rendition of "Bohemian Rhapsody". While I much preferred listening to Freddie Mercury sing it, I was still bummed to ruin her fun. "Get your shoes on. We're gonna go get something to eat."

THE CLOSEST PLACE TO eat near the trailer park was Los Cerritos Mexican restaurant. After a half-mile walk with a five-year-old, some stuffed sopapillas seemed appropriate for ten o'clock in the morning.

Jane seemed repulsed as I devoured my food. She viewed herself as more ladylike, always taking her time.

She didn't learn that from me.

I swallowed a chunk of beef. "How are you liking your sopapillas?"

"It's really yummy," she wiped her hands with a napkin. "How long are we going to stay at Grandpa Curtis's house?"

"Only for one more night. He's going to drive us back to Muleshoe tomorrow so we can get back on the road."

She frowned down at her sopapillas and picked it apart.

"What's the matter?"

"I only got to have a little time with Grandpa Curtis. I probably won't see him ever again because he works a lot. And I don't think he likes me."

My heart sank to the bottom of my stomach. "He loves you, kid. I don't think you've spent enough time with him. Hell, maybe you'll find out that you don't like him very much."

"Of course, I like him. He's my grandpa."

This puzzled me, "But you don't even know your Grandpa Curtis that well."

Her hazel eyes widened. "I would like to know him."

I took another bite of my sopapilla. I was attempting to grasp the concept of someone wanting to spend quality time with the human keg that I share 50% of my DNA with. "Well, maybe he can come visit us in Portland."

"Do you like Grandpa Curtis?"

A pulmonary aspiration occurred when the beef hit the back of my throat. I quickly recovered with a drink of water. I coughed to regain my control. "Um, I do like him." I wasn't pleased with my answer, neither was Jane. "The thing about your Grandpa Curtis is that he has a funny way of showing love."

"What does that mean?"

What do I mean? If I knew, I wouldn't have spent thousands of dollars on therapy.

"Some people show their love in different ways. Grandpa Curtis just has his own way." I paused, "When I was little-"

"Little like me?"

"I was older than you, I think I was twelve." I started picking at my nails, "Your grandma and grandpa got a divorce-"

"Like you and daddy?"

I nodded, "Yes, like me and daddy. Grandpa Curtis decided it was best for him to get out of Idaho and moved in with my Grandma Loretta. He was always busy... working." I need to get better at lying. "He never visited, so I didn't see much of him." I failed to mention that the man never showed up to my high school graduation, but I figured that was too much information to grasp.

"Did that make you sad?"

I sunk into my chair. "It did make me sad."

She held out her little hand and put it on top of mine. "I love you, Mama."

"I love you more." I kissed her hand. "But I want you to know that will not happen with you and your daddy. He is going to see you as much as he can. And you'll be able to visit him all the time. Your daddy loves you very much and he would never make you feel otherwise."

She flashed me a smile and nodded.

"Now finish eating, sweet girl."

We took a stroll to the park that was across the street from the restaurant. Jane spent two hours running around without any breaks. It was like watching a coked-up squirrel on a rampage. I finally had to stop her before she came to the point of destruction. We walked back to the trailer to see a forest green Toyota with a bumper sticker that said, "BEAUTY IS ONLY A FEW BEERS AWAY".

My father was home.

Jane went into the trailer and yelled, "Grandpa!"

"In here," he said from the kitchen.

We made our way into the kitchen to find him drinking a Bloody Mary.

He opened his arms to Jane. She hesitated for a moment but eventually gave in. "Where did you two run off to?"

"We had some food and Mama took me to the park." Her hair was a mess and her jeans were covered in dirt.

He laughed. "Well, it looks like you had a fun time. Did your mother not do your hair today?"

I rolled my eyes. "I did, but she was playing so hard that her pigtails fell out."

Jane nodded, confirming that I was a somewhat competent mother.

He ignored me. "Jane, go grab a brush and I'll fix your hair."

Jane promptly ran out of the kitchen, into the Dolly room.

My eyebrows scrunched. "I didn't realize you were an expert in hair styling."

"I don't think brushing my granddaughter's hair categorizes me as a hairstylist."

"It doesn't. It's just that you never did my hair when I was her age."

He took a sip. "When will your car be ready tomorrow?"

I sighed. "Juanita texted and told me eleven tomorrow."

Jane ran back into the kitchen with my brush in her hand. The seven brushes in her suitcase were not good enough for her. She handed him the brush and planted herself on his lap. She winced when he ran along the small knots. After a few tugs, she relaxed as he continued stroking the brush through her hair.

A weird feeling washed over me.

It wasn't happiness, anger, or sadness.

Jealousy?

I stepped out of the kitchen into the living room. I could still hear their conversation from a distance.

He said, "What's your favorite thing to do when you're not in school?"

"I like to read animal books."

"Animal books huh? Do you know any facts you can tell me?"

"Mhmm, I know a lot. Did you know that an ostrich's eye is bigger than its brain?"

He chuckled, "I did not know that. You're a very smart girl, especially for a five-year-old."

A tear went down my face. Shouldn't a mother be enthusiastic that their child is spending quality time with their grandfather? I felt everything but that. Never once in my childhood did my father make time for me, let alone speak to me in such a gentle manner. I always thought he was the problem. But I began to wonder if the reason for his disconnect with me was because he genuinely didn't like me.

My mind trailed to Ted, of all people. One of my favorite things about him was how much he adored me. He would buy me flowers, cook for me, and would never fail to express how much he loved me. And while Ted had showered me with attention, it was clear that his adoration had come with conditions and limitations. Maybe it was easier to be the center of someone's affection than to confront the pain of abandonment. I couldn't help but wonder if it was merely a distraction, a band-aid for the wounds left by an absent father.

Oh my god.

I'm one of those women who has daddy issues.

I PUT Jane in a new change of clothes and put her down for a nap. Once she hit the pillow, she was out. I made my way to the backyard to recollect myself. I took a seat on the steps on the porch and gave in to a well-needed cigarette. Once I lit the cigarette, I felt a wash of relief flow through every nerve in my body.

The porch's vibration startled me from my father's boots. "I see you're still killing yourself with those things."

I turned towards him and laughed. "Look who's talking. You're on the brink of having Cirrhosis of the liver."

He took a seat next to me - nursing a new glass of a Bloody Mary. "Whatever takes me, takes me. It's in God's hands."

I giggled at the hypocrisy but decided to let it go. I took a long drag and savored the one comfort I'd had for the entire weekend.

He stirred his drink with a stick of celery, "Why did you disappear earlier?"

"I was just tired and wanted to sit alone for a while."

He shook his head, "Okay."

I exhaled a cloud of smoke and contemplated taking advantage of his good mood. "Do you have any regrets?"

"I have a few."

My eyebrows arched in curiosity as I shifted my weight on the weathered porch step, the wood creaking softly beneath me. I wiped the sweat from my forehead, leaned forward, and asked, "Care to elaborate?"

He took a deep breath, "I regret what happened between me and your mother. I let her down one too many times." He looked at me, "And I know I've done nothing but let you down."

I shook my head, "Yeah."

He leaned over and reached into his back pocket. He took out a tiny picture from his wallet and handed it to me. I squinted closer to it and realized it was a picture of me from a distance at my graduation. I looked at him. "Did mom send this to you?"

"No, I took this picture."

My mouth dropped. "What? I thought you didn't show."

"I sat in the back. I was on a binge the night before and looked like a mess. I didn't want to embarrass you, so I stayed away."

Tears welled up in my eyes, but I quickly wiped them away. "Why are you like this? One minute, you're throwing jabs about how I take care of my daughter. The next you tell me that you cared so much that you saved me the embarrassment of the world knowing that my father's an alcoholic. What did I ever do to make you so half-hearted towards me?" As soon as the question left my lips, terror washed over me, uncertain of what might come out of his mouth next.

He cast his gaze downward, his brow furrowing as he shook his head slowly, a heavy weight apparent in his stance. At first, I thought I saw a tear, but I couldn't be sure. Guys like him have shed only a tear or two in their lifetime. He looked up and said, "Every time I see your face, I remind myself of all the times I failed to be there for you." He paused and added, "I wasn't cut out to be a father. Or at least, a good one." He took another drink and stared into the distance.

For the first time in my life, I found myself at a loss for words. My heart sank at what he said, but deep down, I knew it was true—at least, it was his truth. Surprisingly, I felt a sense of peace wash over me with his statement. All the moments I had spent feeling unworthy of his love suddenly faded away because I finally realized that there was nothing wrong with me. *There is nothing wrong with me.* I let out a deep breath, and it felt as if the massive weight on my shoulders had suddenly lifted. I patted him on the shoulder, which led to him placing his hand over mine.

"Okay kiddo, you got all of your stuff?" I asked Jane as we stood outside the repair shop in Muleshoe. My father put all of our luggage into my car as I loaded Jane into her car seat. Juanita handed me the keys and placed a long gold necklace with a pendant of Guadalupe around my neck.

"This is for extra protection on your journey. I wouldn't want you two girls to go without it," her brow furrowed with worry as she spoke.

Then she approached Jane, bent down to her level, and gave her a similar necklace. This gesture affirms Jane's desire for friendship.

My father leaned over and hugged Jane. "It was good seeing you kiddo."

Her face lit up, "Are you gonna come see us, Grandpa?"

He hesitated and looked over at me. I nodded and he replied, "Yes, I'll come up soon." He gave her one last hug and shut the door.

"Thank you for letting us stay, it helped me out."

"Sure, it was no problem."

"Well, I'm gonna get-" He hugged me as if we'd never hugged before. In all fairness, I couldn't remember the last time we did. But there was a sincereness in his embrace that I was unfamiliar with. It felt different, but right. He held me for at least a minute. When he let go, he quickly wiped his eyes.

"Now you call me when you make it, okay?"

"Okay." I kissed him on the cheek. "Goodbye, Dad."

I got into the door and shut it. I watched him climb into his truck. From what I could see from a distance, he wiped his face with his hands. I swallowed my tears back - reminding myself of my emotional episode from the days prior. But this time, I felt a sense of serenity, making me optimistic about what the future held.

I looked at Jane and put the car in drive.

≈

THE GREAT RECKONING, AT LAST

BY SCOTT TAYLOR

God sat on his cloudy throne, looking down.

"Those monkeys have made a real mess of things," he said to himself between slugs of honeyed mead. "Perhaps it's time I paid them a visit."

He figured that Moses would be the best one to talk to about the whole fiasco. Moses was now the owner of a used car dealership in Pittsburgh.

"Moses, my Ten Commandments are being ignored. Why is this so?" asked God.

"Good question," Moses said.

"But I left you in charge," God complained.

"They're a hard bunch to organize, what can I tell you," said Moses.

"I mean, they've been ripping the place to shreds for the past few thousand years. What is wrong with them?"

"You're full of good questions."

"And you don't have any answers."

"True. But then again, I'm not God."

God was irritated by Moses' rather flippant attitude but decided not to demote him, at least not just yet.

"Go forth and make the people see the error of their ways," God commanded. "Inform them they must repent of their waywardness and start obeying my goddamn laws. That I have spoken to you and made it thusly."

Moses said he'd get to it just as soon as he could, perhaps on Friday after the dealership closed. God whisked away and Moses returned to his paperwork.

On Friday he went rummaging around in the garage. "Now where could those pesky tablets be, I know I left them around here somewhere." Perhaps his wife had thrown them out; they were getting old and crumbly and could easily have been mistaken for garbage. After a lengthy search he came up with nothing. Oh well, he'd just have to wing it.

The next day he went to the park down by the river. He stood in front of the fountain with his arms raised until a small crowd had gathered to investigate. Then he began.

"O people of the Earth, the Lord is displeased. He seeks to mend our broken ways and return us to the true path, the path long ago laid before our feet."

"What is he wearing, Mommy?" the little boy asked.

"That's called a robe, honey," she replied in a half whisper.

"Why is he wearing it?"

"I have no idea."

"He looks hot."

The people were already getting bored so Moses tried a little melodrama, looking skyward and shaking his arms about. It would have worked better with the staff but that had gone missing from the garage too. Zipporah had an absolute compulsion for throwing all his old stuff out. The little crowd dispersed and Moses was left standing there by himself. At least it was a nice day out. He went over and watched the waves for awhile.

God showed up again a few days later. "So how did it go?"

"Not too good, to be honest. No one was really listening. Wasn't much of a crowd either."

"You must try again. You must make them listen."

"How am I supposed to do that?"

"Do you not remember the Red Sea? The speech you gave at Mount Sinai?"

"Did I give a speech at Mount Sinai? It was a long time ago, I don't remember."

"Of course you did. But you're missing the point. The point is, the people once followed you, and they will follow you once more. You must try again."

Moses decided to try a different tack this time. He went downtown on Saturday afternoon and picked the busiest corner he could find and stood on it. The kid was right, the robe was hotter than hell.

"The Lord commands you to repent! O Lord we beseech Thee, in Thy wisdom and Thy mercy! Make us worthy once more of Thy infinite blessings! Repent, all ye sinners! The hour of Judgment draweth near!"

This used to work a lot better back in the old days, it was a lot harder now. The people were all busy wandering around shopping and paying parking meters and no one was even glancing in his direction. 'Maybe I should try burning a bush,' Moses muttered under his breath.

A cop came over. "Come on buddy, that's enough. You don't have a permit for this anyway."

"A permit? To speak the Lord's Will?" Moses gasped, feigning astonishment. "He has spoken to me directly, I am his appointed messenger."

"Yeah right, and I'm the Queen of England. Come on, let's go."

Next it was a telegram - apparently God was too busy for any further personal visits. 'You are not applying yourself,' it read. That was all it said. This guy had a lot of nerve, Moses thought to himself. Goes missing for two thousand years and then just waltzes in and expects me to put things right. I mean, I'm about as old as he is, I'm not exactly some spring chicken anymore. Problems with my eyes and my hips and all that. Moses decided to wait for further instructions. If God thought his little telegram was somehow going to work miracles all on its own, he was mistaken. Moses could apply himself all he wanted and he was still going to be ignored in parks and get tossed off of street corners and things.

A week later and another telegram. 'I will make them see the light,' God said, as cryptic as ever. But this sounded more like the real deal. Moses started letting his beard grow out in advance of the event, washed his robe a second time, went to the store and bought himself a new staff (actually a walking stick designed for hiking in the woods, but whatever, close enough). Then one day he went outside and saw a message there in the sky, writ in smoky letters about a mile high: 'MOSES WISHES TO SPEAK WITH YOU. GO TO THE PARK ON SATURDAY.' He went back to the park on Saturday and there were only a few people there, same thing as before. Apparently they hadn't gotten the memo.

God paid Moses another visit.

"Look, something has to be done. They are acting up pretty badly, as you may or may not have noticed. They dump garbage into the seas, they belch filth into the sky. They sleep with their neighbor's wives and they kill each other all the time; I mean it's like some sort of sport with them. And taking my name in vain, don't even get me started there. The language has just gone right out the window. No, but seriously, they really are destroying this nice world I made for them. And it's the only one. Really, it is, I would know. I mean, what do they think they're going to do? Go to Mars and live there? Do they have any idea how cold it is there? Perhaps you should tell them that."

"Why can't you just tell them yourself? Why do you always need me to do it?"

"I'm not big on public speaking. Never have been. Besides, I feel like they need to hear it from one of their own."

"You tried that once already and it didn't go so well."

"I'm aware of that. But things change. Okay, so here's the deal - I need you to go to the park again this weekend and this time I guarantee you a bigger audience. They'll get the hint this time, believe me. Put some flyers up around town too, that might help. I want this place covered in flyers by the end of the week."

"Listen, no offense but I have a job, you know. I'm a pretty busy guy. The mortgage isn't exactly going to pay itself. Anyway, if there's some cataclysm scheduled for this weekend that's really going to put the fear of You into them then I seriously doubt we're going to need the flyers."

"I am the Lord your God. I have spoken."

"Mysterious ways and all that," Moses grumbled.

"I don't appreciate the irreverent tone," God said.

"And I don't appreciate the short notice."

"You do realize that I'm God, right? That I can wipe out your existence without even raising my little pinkie finger?"

"You'd be doing me a favor. Do you have any idea what sales were like last quarter?"

God went home. Moses went looking for his favorite sandals, the ones that were the most comfortable, all broken in and fitting perfectly. He figured he was about to do some serious walking with this flyers business and didn't want to get any blisters. He walked around for an hour and couldn't find them anywhere. He could never find anything in that house.

"Zippy!" he shouted down the stairs. "Have you seen my sandals?"

"Which ones?" she called back from the kitchen.

"You know the ones. My favorites, the really beat-up pair with the broken straps."

"Those things are as old as the hills. I don't know why you still wear them."

"I know that, I want them anyway."

"Try the closet in the bedroom."

"I did, they're not there."

"Look under the bed."

Moses looked under the bed and they weren't there either. He'd have to go with the newer pair.

He took a few days off from work and spent them walking the streets, plastering flyers all over everything. He coated the city of Pittsburgh with them, every telephone pole, every bulletin board, every available patch of window and wall. Half of them would probably be torn down within twenty-four hours, but at least no one could accuse him of shirking his duties. The message printed on the flyer was simple, short and sweet and right to the point: 'Hear the final Word Of God, this weekend only, at the park down by the river. The one with the big fountain.' If God wanted anything more eloquent than that, then he could write the damn thing himself next time. This whole adventure seemed pretty half-baked anyway - he'd be surprised if even five people showed up.

And then it was the weekend and Moses was heading down the street, on his way to the park. Nothing had happened yet, but clouds were starting to roll in and the skies were darkening somewhat. As he reached the park and made for the fountain the light had dimmed even more. The heavens were all but black now and the sun had been blotted from the sky; people were coming out of doors to see what was going on, a little group of them drifting over to join the few dozen or so already standing around the fountain. Looked like the flyers had drummed up a few of them, at least.

Moses stepped up on the raised pedestal supporting the fountain and began to preach.

"Friends! We are gathered here today to atone for our past transgressions. The Lord has

spoken to me; yea, I am his prophet. All ye sheep must be brought back into the fold. What was old shall be made new again. Your souls and mine shall be renewed, bathed in the eternal grace and glory of the Lord. A new dawn shall break, an age of wonderment, full of..."

He was interrupted by a new development, a thin beam of golden light streaking down from the sky, a sliver of sunlight piercing the heavy rolling blanket of cloud. Moses became more animated and started flailing his arms around. "It is the Lord our God, speaking to us from on high!"

"It's an eclipse, you jackass," the guy in front said.

"IT IS NOT AN ECLIPSE!" Moses shouted, almost falling off the pedestal in his enthusiasm. "It is a divine miracle! The end days are upon us! Repent, ye sinners, repent!"

But now the crowd was entirely distracted by this change in the weather and had its collective back turned. Moses put his arms down and waited patiently for their attentions to be returned to him, but presently they were shambling toward the river as one, moving like drugged and grounded moths toward this strange new source of light. The clouds shifted and the sunbeam disappeared, but then soon the storm began to break and the darkness was slowly lifted. Once again Moses was left by himself, standing there helplessly at the fountain, a shepherd without a flock, a prophet without a plan.

"THEY'RE PISSING ME OFF," God said the next day. "That's it, I've had it. I'm going to send them a message they won't soon forget."

"What are you going to do?" Moses asked.

"Spoil the party. Rain on their parade. It's been a long time coming, and they know it too. Listen, I'm going to give you an Ark so that you'll be safe from all this. If you float towards the North Pole, I think you'll probably make out all right."

"An Ark? I thought that was Noah's area of expertise."

"Yeah, you can bring him along too. He's living in Cleveland right now. The two of you can ride together."

God told Moses the Ark would be waiting for him up in Hudson Bay, way up there in Canada. Then he whisked away again. A month passed and then it was showtime. God gathered up a huge-ass ball of lightning and smote the ground with it. The Great Lakes were instantly integrated with the Atlantic Ocean. The heavens were unleashed as torrential rains began to fall. Thunder crashed and lightning flashed, there was much keening and wailing and gnashing of teeth. Then the rains abated, the sea levels began to recede and everything went back to normal. Right back again, as if nothing had ever happened - business as usual, no change in plans, no repenting of sins or New Year's resolutions or anything like that. Moses steered the Ark back to Canada and returned to his used auto dealership, whilst Noah went back to Cleveland to resume doing whatever he'd been doing before. God was disgusted, to say the least, but instead of hurling any more objects around he decided to just give up and forget the whole thing. The sun was scheduled to blink out in a few billion years anyway. He got himself another mead and turned the cricket match on. The Angels were playing the Saints, the score 272 to nothing.

SUSHI IN SPACE

BY R.R.DAVIDSON

He wanted to fuck on the bus.

That's not how I usually do things but it was the middle of the night in the middle of nowhere and I wasn't doing anything else. I didn't know if he'd be quiet so I kissed him. I don't like kissing. I've been told I'm not good at it. But I know I'm good at the other stuff. It's been paying the bills for years and I've never gotten a complaint.

Five stars, would recommend.

I never wear underwear. It makes work easier and clients like the surprise. I lose little pieces of me every time I fuck a client. Tonight I left a piece of me on the bus. The whole of me rode that bus from Cleveland to Las Vegas. That little lost piece of me continued on to Los Angeles. Where I'll go from there I don't know but I'll likely see a lot of this country from that bus. I wish the whole of me could see it all.

Las Vegas is bright. I think you can see Las Vegas from space. That's one place I haven't left myself. Yet. I can dream. I heard this guy on an old TV show call space the final frontier. Maybe that will be where I finally leave the last pieces of me. Because I keep leaving them everywhere else. I know one day I'll be empty.

I used to have a room in Vegas. I rented a bedroom from a couple I met at a bar. They were just nice. They didn't want sex. I actually had to pay them. No tradesies. They asked me not to bring in clients when they were home. They even gave me their schedules so I'd know when I could work. It was good. Then she got a promotion. Public relations. They moved and I didn't have a room anymore. I went by that house tonight to see if maybe they'd come back. A swingset was in the front yard.

The driver dropped me off at my favorite store. It's the local comic book shop. I sometimes find clients here. Or at least a ride to the strip. People in to comics are nice. Or they're incels. There's not really a middle ground. I can spot who is who fast. It's a good skill to have in any job, but a requirement in mine. I like knowing more about them than they know about me. They don't need to know much. Five stars, would recommend.

I don't leave any of me in the comic book shop. I think it would've been a fun place to stay. Good art, funny cartoons, witty villains. Yeah, that sounds fun. But I did leave myself in the car belonging to the sweet kid working there. He was a nice one. Cute. Fumbly. Nervous. He kept asking questions. I ended up having to kiss him, too. I need to brush my teeth.

He invited me to his apartment. I bought us tacos with the money he'd just paid me.

Sometimes I hang out with clients. I think it's a lot like public relations. Do business, go for a beer. Sit through a meeting, hit up a bar. Fuck in a car, watch a movie. It's all the same. And I'd much rather do my thing than sit through a meeting.

Some pieces of me like superhero movies. Give me Christopher Reeve in those columbia blue tights and tightie-reddies anyday. Other pieces of me love old film noir. The smoky haze, the dames with the amazing hats. When did guys stop wearing those suits that make them look like a rectangle? Probably before Christopher Reeve arrived on the scene. Nobody could wear a suit like Christopher Reeve. Now he's gone and suits are ruined.

We watched a new superhero movie. So many fancy costumes! Metal suits, magician cloaks, purple bike shorts. Those are my favorite. If I wore underwear I'd buy purple. He asked if we could go again. I asked if he could pay again. He said no. I shrugged and climbed on him. He was a sweet one. And our tacos were really good.

He asked me to stay the night. I don't want to, but I don't have anywhere else to go. I laid down some rules. I required a toothbrush, a clean pillowcase, and some socks. I cannot sleep without socks. Under normal circumstances, he would wake up alone tomorrow. But I'm tired so I let him leave pieces of me in his bed the next morning.

This is getting expensive.

I asked him to drop me off in front of the pyramid. I fucking love that pyramid. He wants to see me again. I ask when he gets paid. I said I'd come see him at the comic book shop. He asked if I'm lying.

I lie a lot.

Another requirement for the job, but I actually like this kid. I tell him no. He smiles at me. His eyes are hazel.

I can't always stay at the pyramid, but sometimes I get lucky and find an old friend at the check-in counter. Her name is Ethel. I think she used to be like me. Maybe. I think that because she's always so nice to me. People aren't always nice to me. Another part of the job. We aren't all as lucky as Julia Roberts. Shit. Nobody's as lucky as Julia Roberts. She even got to have twins.

Ethel sees me and waves.

I smile.

I'll wait under the pharaoh til she can take a break.

I'm thirsty. I haven't had anything to drink since dinner. I need water. I don't eat a lot. I try to eat as little as possible. Then I can save up for something. I don't know what yet.

I reenter the pyramid and head to the bar. I grab the stool at the end and prop my elbows on the bar. That makes my tits look amazing. The bartender comes right over. I smile. He melts. He brings me water and asks if he can get me anything else. I ask for a room. My bartender is nice to me, too. He says he has a buddy at check-in who can get him a cheap room for the day. I tell him my day rate. He asks if I'd like a drink. I request a pina colada in the giant plastic pyramid cup. I'm so excited. Pieces of me will stay in the pyramid forever.

The past forty-eight hours have been a good run. The bus, the sweet kid, the tacos, and now I'm sleeping in the pyramid. I like the soap here. Most soaps smell burnt to me. Do they cook soap before it goes into a bar? The pyramid doesn't use burnt soap. Their soap smells like roses. Now I do, too.

I don't get dressed.

I need to check my phone. I hate my phone. I hate all the phones. They've taken people's eyes from the world and glued them to their glassy screens. Like a suction cup. You have to pry people from their phones. I think they're addictive like cigarettes. I don't smoke but I have to deal with a phone. I have thirteen messages. Six clients, three hang-ups, one telemarketer, two from mom, one from a kid sister. I call the clients.

Sometimes clients want me to come to their place. Usually the wife will take the kids somewhere for the weekend and I can stay for a day or so. I ask for sushi in those cases. We always order in. Dads can't be seen with me. I understand. I don't want them in trouble. I'd lose good money on that trouble. Then I can't save up.

My bartender will be back soon. I hope he likes roses. I will leave after. It's been a nice day, though. He comes to see me on his breaks. He's quick. Then I get to watch TV. Today I picked cartoons. I wonder if that's because of the comic book shop guy. Maybe. I may have made a mistake with him. His eyes are hazel. He likes tacos. This could be bad. Where is my bartender? I need to stop thinking.

Ethel thought I'd left her. Thankfully I caught her before her shift was over. I took her to my bartender's place. He was gone now. The new bartender was a lady. She liked my tits, too, but I was booked for the evening. I asked Ethel if she could score me a room for the next night. She was thrilled I gave her time. She thought I needed it for tonight. Plans, Ethel, I got plans! We laugh. I ask her if she smokes. She doesn't. She asks why. I tell her it's because she's not always on her phone. Ethel understands.

It's time for Ethel to go home. We stop at the front desk. She logs in, does her thing, I scan my horrid phone, she passes me a plastic card. Ethel gives me a wink. She tells me they had a last minute cancellation and the room was empty for three days. With her discount, I got that room for a fucking song. And... it's a bathtub room. I kiss her. Right on the mouth. Right there at the front desk. Ethel doesn't like kissing either. We laugh. She tells me to be careful. I laugh again. I am many things, but careful is not one of them.

The taxi drops me off at the McMansion. There are no pieces of me that like this house. All of my pieces hate it. There are so many beautiful buildings in this world. I want to see more of them, less of these. I wonder if Roman Mars would ever lower himself to walk into a building such as the one I see in front of me. I bet he wouldn't. He's uptown now. I wouldn't mind leaving pieces of me with Roman Mars. I don't even know what he looks like but I'd fuck that man's voice if I could. I'll bet his voice wears a suit as well as Christopher Reeve.

I wore what he asked for. Black pants, white button-up shirt tucked in, black heels. I guess he'll tell his neighbors I was there for a meeting of some sort. Which is true. A fuck meeting. Like a budget meeting. We meet to fuck. We meet to budget. Not a fucking meeting. Those are separate things. I like what I'm here for. Maybe I should buy a briefcase.

Everything in the McMansion came from Pottery Barn. I want to hate it. I really want to. I can't. It's cute. I don't let myself like cute things. I'd look like a walking Daiso store if I did. Nobody wants to fuck that. I'd starve.

My client recently had a baby. His wife took the baby to stay at her mom's for a week. I hope they're ok. He seems like a nice enough guy. Other than cheating on his wife before, during, and after her pregnancy. He told me she doesn't like sex. I don't understand that sentence.

I slowly undress for him. He tells me about his day while he watches me. I think he needs to unburden himself. From work. From traffic. From family. All the odd little details about his day. His coffee was especially good. His assistant fucked up his schedule. As I drop my bra to the floor, I tell him I want an assistant for my schedule. We laugh.

He's rough with me this evening. That's nice sometimes. Especially after sweet ones like comic book shop guy or quick ones like my bartender. Then he wanted to fuck while we watched porn. I'm not a big fan of porn. I never do stuff like they do. He asked if he could spank me. At least he asked. I say ok even though I don't like it. He pulls my hair while he does it, though. That's my favorite.

The sushi was delivered earlier and he keeps it in the refrigerator. That was thoughtful. I tell him I appreciate him. He starts crying. Standing right there in the kitchen, this man who just spanked my ass til it burned and pulled my hair til I cried and whispered filthy words into my neck, breaks. I leave the sushi on the shelf. I close the refrigerator door. I stand in front of him and he falls to his knees before me. He wraps his arms around my naked waist and weeps.

He made love to me so sweetly after. I felt adored. I left him with many pieces of me the next morning when I climbed in the cab. He watched me through their country lace curtains and waved as I drove away. Sometimes I can see the weight of a person's life when they order sushi for me.

I feel closer to empty than ever now. But tonight I have a room with a bathtub next to my bed. I will keep all my pieces tonight. I'm not ready to disappear. I have to keep the last pieces for when I go to space. That's what I'll save up for.

∾

THE THINGS I HAD TO SAY

BY DANNY ARTHUR

The next morning I got on a train and took it to my father's house out in the boonies. He answered my call with a voice that was neither surprised nor expectant. "When's it get in?" he said.

"It just did. I'm sitting at the station."

"Mmm. I'll be there in thirty."

He hung up. I sat down on a bench, and waited for the old man to arrive. As I smoked a cigarette, I wondered how old the old man was going to look and if anything had changed in this town since my last visit. I didn't remember much about it. Just that we got groceries and gas in the same place where old men sat on the front porch with open eyes turned inward. There was a diner with a half illuminated sign so it read D_N_R, and my mother joked that most of the town's inhabitants couldn't fill in the other letters. She laughed harder each time she said it, as if the joke had grown funnier over the years.

I dug a hole in the dirt with the toe of my shoe until my father arrived. He drove the same red pick-up as he did in my youth. I stood up and tossed my duffle into the tailgate. My father stayed in his seat, and handed me a styrofoam cup of coffee. He looked the fucking same.

"How are ya?" he said.

"Alright. You?"

"Good." He put the car in drive. "You wanna talk about it?"

"No."

We drove down a two-lane highway for a while, before turning onto a dirt road and then into his long, dirt driveway, shrouded by trees and bushes and littered with divots. We walked in and he pointed down the hall. "I made a room up for you," he said. "Figured you were here to rest."

I nodded, went to the room and drew the shades, flicked on the ceiling fan and fell asleep. And that's how I lived, smoking out the window and pissing in bottles. I didn't shit. There'd be coffee waiting outside my door in the morning, and meals at lunch and dinner time. The last was always served with a beer. "There's more in the fridge if you want any," my father would say. "I'll be out on the porch. Join me."

I didn't until the fifth or sixth night when something clicked, or evaporated. Either the understanding that boredom was not the solution to my problems, or the belief that humans–other humans–had been the crux of my misfortune. So, I tried something else, and took my dishes to the sink, then went to the porch with two beers in-hand. My father was sitting, watching the trees waver in the night wind beneath a moon that was far brighter than I could ever recall it being. I handed him the beer and took a seat on the steps. He was behind me in a rocking chair that moved in a jagged motion, not like a rocking chair should. "Nice night," he said.

I light a cigarette. "You're not working?" I asked.

"Still got the shop. Called out the last few days. The boys were worried. Only the second time I've called out in...I don't know, ten years. They thought something awful happened."

"You didn't need to."

"No, I didn't but...Had some shit I needed to get done around here anyways."

"Mmm...Well, you can go in tomorrow. I'm outta bed. I'll clean up, or something."

My father–he never really smiled. I mean, the corner of his lips never approached his ears and his teeth never showed except in a pensive grimace. Any movement below his nose was curtained by the thick gray beard and long hairs of his mustache. But his blue eyes would dim. The skin would tighten. "Tomorrow's Saturday," he said. "I don't work Saturdays."

"Pays to be the boss, huh?"

"That it does, Son. That it does."

We sat in silence for a while, listening to the cicadas and the frogs and branches snapping in the woods. I could hear the stars. It happens sometimes, on still nights in the middle of nowhere. The stars whisper and the moon sings.

"Nice night," I said.

"Mhmm. Beautiful."

We had another beer and went to sleep.

WHILE MY FATHER was at work during the days, I stayed back and tended to his home. Cleaning, mowing the lawn, watering the garden where he grew his own vegetables. The hours and minutes of these long days became divided into stages, or episodes, opposed to the one long stretch of monotony I had grown accustomed to. When I rested my head at night, I had the sense that what I had accomplished today was different from yesterday, and God knows what tomorrow holds. When I woke in the morning, there was no rush. No pressure. No nagging urge to combine the tasks of pissing and toothbrushing because I was already running late...

If I finished my chores early, I'd go for long walks through the woods and down the dirt roads. One day, I stopped in the lone bar for a beer where I became acquainted with the bartender. He was surly, at first. A dickhead. A man who was not used to new faces. That all changed when I ordered my second beer and he asked what I was doing there. I got the next few for free after telling him who my father was and ended up wandering home, pretty loaded, at five in the afternoon. My father was sitting on the porch as I staggered up the drive. "So I see you met Greg, huh?" and he cackled, slapped his knee.

And that's how life continued. I fell into a routine. I began to wonder what was going to happen to me, what was next and what it was about the past that kept me the way I was. To say my father's house cut me off from the outside world, the place and people that had come to define my home, would be inaccurate. I had done that myself. My phone was dead. I didn't even know where it was. I received any worldly updates from the newspapers that arrived at the door each morning. I forgot what it was like to be stuck in traffic, to have dinner plans, or to wake up with a hangover so severe I wasn't sure what occurred the night before.

I wasn't happy. I was rested. I had thawed out.

My father and I began to talk more, forming a ritual of our nightly beers. "Nice night," he'd say and open the beer I had brought out for him. But, one night he held the bottle before him, looking at the label as if it were not the same domestic he'd been purchasing for the past forty years. "You know, I've been thinking and..." His face twisted. I could feel his teeth grinding. "...if there's something you gotta get off your chest, I mean..."

I nodded and lit a cigarette to buy some time. Thoughts jumped in my mind like flies at a windshield. "No," I said. "There's nothing..."

He nodded, took a sip of his beer, stubbed out his cigarette. He lit another. I think, with his face twisted in expressionist style, he was trying to buy some time. "I know," he said. "I know, but if there was, you know..."

"I know, Dad. I know..."

He exhaled, leaned forward so his elbows were on his knees and his head swung from his shoulders. "Sometimes I think I, uhh... rubbed off on you in ways that were..." And he popped up, exhaled again. "I don't know. I don't know what the fuck I'm saying."

We had another beer and went to sleep.

THE NEXT MORNING, I walked into the kitchen where my father was reading the paper. The sun came through his screen window in a way that made the air visible. He cleaned the counters and the floors everyday, but I could hardly see him through all the dust and smoke. "Get dressed," he said, keeping his eyes on the paper. "I need your help with something."

"With what?"

"Nothing hard. Take a shower, we'll get some coffee on the way." He dropped the paper, and rubbed the chin of his gray beard with an open-mouthed, analytical gaze in his azure eyes. "And wear something decent."

We got in the car and drove in a direction I had never been. The windows were down, Townes Van Zandt played over the radio. My father hummed along, with a cigarette clutched between the fingers of his driving hand, and a lidless coffee cup in the other. I rested my elbow on the window and peered out at the farms. There were cows, horses, sheep...All of which I wanted to point out to the old man, as if I were a child. I don't know why I didn't. He wouldn't have made fun of me...I flicked my cigarette out the window and fell asleep.

I woke up with my father's hand on my shoulder. "C'mon," he was saying. "We're here." And he got out of the car, grabbed something from the tailgate and told me to get out again.

Through the yellow windshield, there was a large, ivy-brick building with cathedral glass and some measly spires. I knew it was a church and an old one. What we were doing at such a place is what confused me. My father was not a religious man. I can't recall him ever using the Lord's name except in vain. Hell, it wasn't even

Sunday. I got out of the car and gave him a look. He returned it until he understood what I was trying to ask. "No, no, no. Hell fucking no. What we're looking for is behind it."

He led the way down a cement path that squiggled through the headstones and up and down the rolling hills, around the tall oaks trees that provided shade for the visitors of the more fortunate permanent residents. I stopped as we crested a hill and looked around, trying to comprehend the vastness of the graveyard. My father kept walking, pink and yellow tulips slapped against his thigh. "Oh," I said.

He glanced over his shoulder. "Yep."

We stayed silent until we reached her headstone, a small gray slab in the middle of the field. The grass was brown. There was a bundle of dead flowers beneath the headstone, on which there was no epitaph. Simply her name and the dates that bracketed her existence. "She's been dead for two years?" I asked.

"Yep."

My father slowly bent at the waist and replaced the dead flowers with the living ones.

"How–uhh...How'd she go?" I asked.

"Heart attack."

"Really?"

"Yeah, I was surprised too. Didn't smoke, hardly drank. After you left, she even started exercising. Pilates, or one of those things..."

"Guess it doesn't help your heart."

"I don't know," he sighed. "I think she was lonely. Your mother... she wasn't meant to be alone. That whole thing–years ago–I know it was her decision, but I can't say I blamed her. I didn't at the time and I don't now. Married to me," he chuckled, and smacked his belly, "might as well be married to a stone..."

I reached for a cigarette, then drew my hand back. It didn't feel right.

"There were times, you know, after the divorce where–uhhh, I don't know. I thought we'd connect again," he said, rolling his eyes.

"I thought she was still alone and I was alone and...I don't know. We didn't hate each other. We never hated each other."

"Really? Even after she..."

He looked at me and nodded. "Like I said, I didn't blame her. People–they do shit. They are what they are. Me and your mother, we were what we were. It worked for a long time. The only reason it stopped working was other people got involved...I didn't know how to handle it...I came out here."

He stopped looking at me and I stopped looking at him. We looked at the headstone. "Can I ask you something?" I said. "Why didn't you call me? When she died?"

"I did call you. I left voicemails. I drove an hour to the library just to send an email. You didn't answer. You weren't there. A week went by and...what was I supposed to do? You said you were done with her. I figured you meant it."

"I said I was done with her. I would've come for you."

"You weren't there. What was I supposed to do?"

WE GOT DRUNK THAT NIGHT. Whiskey drunk. My father kept talking. "Like I said, I thought of her the whole time we were split. I wouldn't say I was holding out hope or anything, I just thought of her like you might think of an eye after it goes blind. I'd been out here alone for so long, I was talking to myself out loud about her, about you too, and...it wasn't final in my mind. Then, she died and I was left with all these things I'd never say." He drained his glass. I took it from him and refilled. "All these things I never really wanted to say, I never would've said if I had seen her again. Just these ideas. That's all they were–ideas. Fantasies. Dreams. Whatever.

"Well, the night of the funeral I went to the bar. Greg was still wearing his shirt and tie. I told him to take it off, but he said it made him feel classy," Dad laughed and shook his head. "Like he was running a speakeasy or something. Anyway, Greg goes to the basement and gets the good bottle of Rye, pours two big glasses. We cheers and get to talkin'. Or, I get to talkin'. And after a while, I'm just goin' and goin', chatting my little ass off and Greg stops me with a smile. Just this big smile on his fat-ass face and he tells me I've never talked so much. He reached across the bar, put a hand on my shoulder and he just pulled me in, Son. He just pulled me in. Just like that and I–"

Dad paused. He looked up at the stars and the moon and waited for them to tell him what to say. "And I was talking about you, Son. And I was talking about your mom. And I'm sorry I had to get drunk to tell you this. I'd been thinking about how to tell you since you called my phone that morning...That was the best morning I've had since...Who fuckin' knows. You wanna know why?"

I shuddered. Turned and looked at the man. His face was wet. I turned to the sky to check for clouds and saw a ceiling. "Why, Dad?"

"You called me, Son. Something wasn't right, and you knew to call me. You knew you weren't alone. I had failed so many times, in so many ways. But not so bad that you had forgotten to call..."

And we stayed there until the transient hours, when it no longer matters if it's night or day.

In the morning, I found him in the kitchen reading the paper, enveloped by the haze. I pulled out a chair and began to talk. And he listened as I told him what I had to say.

THE WAR WIDOW'S GHOST

BY BENJAMIN WHITE

The War Widow's Ghost hovered in the shade of the old maple tree, watching the eight boys – divided into two groups of four – turn the cemetery into a makeshift battlefield. Headstones provided cover for suppressive fire coming from wooden pistols and stick rifles while pinecone grenades exploded in the turmoil of boyhood combat.

"Bang! Bang!"

"I shot you!"

"You missed!"

"You're dead!"

"That's our territory!"

"No! It's ours!"

"That grenade hit you and exploded!"

"Nunh-unh! It was a dud!"

"It was not! You're dead!"

"I'm not dead! I'm just wounded!"

"I don't shoot to wound!"

"Well, you need to practice!"

"I captured your flag!"

"No! There are four of us, and only one of you! You're captured!"

"Help! I'm captured!"

"We're coming!"

"Bang! Bang!"

The war went back and forth with maneuvers running the mission from the perimeter of the graveyard to the headstones, around the trees. They went back and forth with no man's land exploding with imagination and excitement, from the graves and up to the back of the church.

"Hey! No hiding around the church!"

"We said you can't use the church for cover!"

"Yeah! That was in the Graveyard Convention of Battlefield Rules!"

"I didn't sign that!"

"Your whole team signed it!"

"Get away from the church!"

"Alright, but give me a ceasefire so I can get back to my platoon."

"You've got five seconds – five..."

"That's not enough."

"You'd better run! Four..."

"Hey, who threw the pinecone? That's not a ceasefire!"

"Three...two...fire at will!"

"Bang!"

"Bang!"

"Kapow!"

"**PER**-Kerr-**POW**!"

"That wasn't five seconds!"

"You're dead!"

The War Widow's Ghost felt a tear roll down her cheek. But she was smiling. She had raised boys of her own, and knew that the war they were waging was a natural part of how they were raised to play. These eight boys were good at it – full of exuberance and energy. They were ready to fight, fall down, heal their wounds, and get back up to fight again. But she had lost a husband when the game turned into an actual war. Her tear knew. It rolled along the pain in her face while reflecting the horrendous reality of hate and anger, fear and horror, blood, flesh, and bones, screams and prayers, devastation and death. The game these boys were playing would turn into a violent loss of humanity.

With closed eyes, she inhaled slowly – her ghostly apparition took on the wisp of emotions death had not taken – could not have taken – from her consciousness. When she opened her eyes, one of the boys was sitting next to her beneath the maple tree.

He was one of the younger, smaller boys, and he looked bewildered.

"What happened?" he asked, looking up at the War Widow's Ghost.

It shocked her for him to be addressing her, but then she noticed the state of his being was not corporeal. He was sitting beside her in a spiritual form. Shocked, she looked back out over the battlefield where the nature of the game had changed considerably. An older boy was standing over the young, small boy's body.

"What did you do?" she asked the boy's spirit.

"I don't know," he replied with his own eyes watering up with fear. "I think I tripped."

"Give me your hand," she told him, extending out an ethereal extension of her own presence.

He reached over, and she brushed against his hand and arm. Immediately, she saw what had taken place. In his enthusiasm to throw one of his pinecone grenades, he had jumped up, taken two quick steps for leverage, and tripped over a footstone:

TYLER

Steven P.

Beloved Son

1901-1918

His falling momentum had made him stumble into a wide headstone:

BOYERBOYER

Maria SpencerJames G.

Devoted Husband

1940 -Loving Father

1936-1965

Where he had struck his head.

"Is he dead?" one of the boys was asking.

"No!" the older boy responded.

"How do you know? He looks dead."

"He ain't dead!" The older boy had rolled the lifeless boy over and was trying to revive him by gently tapping his cheeks.

"Give him mouth-to-mouth," a desperate suggestion said.

"Ain't no use. He's dead."

"He's not dead!"

"Look at the blood coming from his head! He's dead."

"Go see if Preacher Reynolds is in the church," the older boy said. Two other boys ran to the church.

"I don't think you're dead," the War Widow's Ghost said.

"Then what are they doing over there?" the boy asked.

"It looks like they are trying to bring you to," she replied.

"So, what are you doing over here?"

"I was just watching you boys play."

The War Widow's Ghost looked at the small boy, and she did not see any trace of death on the boy's spirit. As he looked at her, he felt a warm comfort come over his uncertainty, and his translucent eyes blinked.

"Did you see me fall?" the boy asked.

She smiled. "No. But I think you are just taking a break."

He nodded his head and said, "I *was* getting tired of playing war. There's really no point to it except for running around and yelling."

She took his point from his young perspective and added her own – older, wiser – perspective. "I've been watching wars for a long time, and I agree," she said softly.

"Who are you?"

"I am the War Widow's Ghost," she replied.

"You're a ghost?" he asked.

"Yes," she nodded.

"A real ghost?"

She smiled, "Yes, a real ghost. That's how I know you are not dead. You are not a ghost."

"But what am I then?"

"A spirit. A soul. A thought. Maybe consciousness without a body."

That made his fear reenter his thoughts, and the War Widow's Ghost saw the change.

"But I tell you what," she gently told him, "tell me your name, and you will be a little boy again."

"Kyle. Kyle Linner. But everybody calls me Nuis."

She laughed out a question, "Noose? Like the hangman's noose?"

"No," he smiled. "Nuis, like nuisance. 'Cause I'm a pain."

"I think that is a good thing to be, Nuis," she said. "And I know for a fact, today is not your day to be – or become – a ghost."

"Thank you," he nodded. "I do like living and playing. Even going to school, now that I'm sitting here."

"I understand, Nuis. I kind of miss my schooldays, too."

"You went to school?"

"Why, yes. You know. Before."

"Makes sense," Nuis smiled.

The War Widow's Ghost smiled back, and shifted her attention across the cemetery to the boys by the Boyer grave. "It was a pleasure meeting you, Nuis. But it's time to get back over where you belong."

"Yes, ma'am," Nuis said, "It was a pleasure to meet you, too."

A wisp of mist, cloud, warmth, and youth lifted up and away from the maple tree, leaving a faint odor of little boy stink. The War

Widow's Ghost embraced the smell with a nostalgic sense of loss and melancholy. She let it hold and comfort her.

"Whoa, Nuis. Take it easy," Preacher Reynolds said. "Can you sit up?"

"Yes, sir, Reverend," Nuis said. "I'm okay."

"Here, let me hold this towel on your head, you may need stitches. And some rest for sure," the reverend warned him.

"I'm not even too bad dizzy," Nuis responded.

"Don't be a headache, Nuis," the preacher chided, smiling at the ambiguity of that statement and at seeing one of his parishioners appear to be okay after a nasty fall into head trauma and unconsciousness.

"I told you all he wasn't dead," the older boy said, erasing all doubt from what had not been so certain just a few minutes ago.

Nuis looked up and became aware of his friends gathered around behind Preacher Reynolds. He could see the remnants of despair beneath the residue of their relief, and, in an expression that made Nuis look somehow older, he smiled reassuringly, "I'm alright, boys. Today's not my day."

∾

THE ART OF THE BARGAIN

BY K. P. DAVIS

I t started with a Facebook post from Travis. He wrote: "Just saw an old, old man driving a 1988 IROC Camaro. Dude was smiling from ear-to-ear, not a tooth in his head." Travis liked to send out cryptic, Zen-like text messages. The recipient of the message was not expected to respond. Travis had been the cool kid even back in grade school before he grew facial hair. We knew the same people at school, but we'd never been close. We studied business at the same college, but rarely saw each other. Then I took a job in accounting at a small factory that made specialized parts for drilling rigs. It was a department of bickering, small-minded people. I was the only regular employee. The rest were temps, and my pay barely covered my bills. But *Travis* surprised everybody. When he graduated, he went all "save the homeless." He ran a second-hand clothing store downtown. Nobody from school ever saw him anymore. We only knew he was still alive because of his strange little text messages. Judging from the pictures on Facebook, it looked to me like he kept his store open 24-hours when the weather was cold. The guy should have been a monk or something.

So, when I saw Travis's Facebook post about the car, I joked with him about it a little bit, but then forgot it until a few days later when he sent me a private message that said, *you're not going to believe what happened. Can we meet up?*

~

HE SLIPPED into the coffee shop and tapped me on the shoulder wearing a goofy-looking smirk on his face, but Travis wouldn't talk to me until we had our coffee and were settled at a table around the back of the café where nobody could eaves drop on us. It didn't take me long to figure out why. He had such a crazy story, that if anybody'd been listening, they'd have called the looney bin. It went like this:

~

WHAT I DIDN'T KNOW when I first saw the old man in the Camaro was that he was laughing at a joke his passenger had just told. I hadn't noticed the passenger, but a little way up the road, I ran into the guy again.

I heard a voice yelling, "You're a cheatin' scumbag!" And when I came up to the alley beside the liquor store, I saw this bearded little guy the size of a four-year-old wailing on the old guy from the Camaro and cursing like no four-year-old ought to be able to. The old dude was crouched down beside the dumpster with his arms up over his head. So, you know, me being me, I grabbed the little man and pulled him away from the old guy, but I dropped him right quick because he rammed his head into my belly and kicked me in the shin. You'd have thought he'd run off, but he turned around and went right back to wailing on the old guy, so the second time I pulled him into a bear hug and held on.

When he calmed down, I said, "What the hell?"

The old guy, J.T., stood up grumbling, "little sumbitch lied to me.

One minute we was rollin' along happy as Larry, then he got a drop of whiskey in him and went nuts."

"Lied to you! Who's the liar, you old wino? You said you'd let me go once we got to the liquor store!" screamed the small man.

"And you said you'd give my old car back."

I didn't want any part of this argument between two drunks, but J.T.'s wild eyes made me stay a little longer. When he saw I was about to let the small fellow go, he said, "You keep a-holt o' that little weasel, son."

"Fack away off. I've a score to settle with this *manky ald git*, and it's none of your business." The little man's voice was high-pitched like he'd been inhaling helium from a party balloon, and I wasn't quite sure what he'd said. He had a thick Irish accent.

The old man sprang up and lunged before I could let go of the strange little fellow, and I ended up holding the small one's collar with one hand while I held the old man off with the other.

"What the hell is going on?" I asked. I was having a hard time not laughing. The situation was getting pretty absurd.

"J.T.'s the name son, and this evil little goblin here cheated me out of my car's what. Cherry she was—5.7 litre, 350 Camaro Z. 1986 model . . ."

"I did no such thing," the little man said.

"He went back on our deal." J.T. ran shaky fingers through his few greasy strands of hair. "Said he'd grant my wish, but the little bastard lied."

I had to ask. "Grant your wish? What wish?"

"Yessiree, that's right," said J.T. "He says to me 'If ye'll buy me a bottle of whiskey, I'll grant you a wish,' so I wished for my old car, and we drove her down here to the liquor store. But soon as I give him his whiskey, the damned car vanished!"

If I hadn't seen the car back at the lights, I would have walked away right then. It was nowhere in sight now.

"Me name's Seamus," the little man said, "and ye can't believe this old goat. It's clear to see he's a drunkard. Some hooligan stole the car while we were inside the store."

The old man took a deep breath. "If you can keep that double-dealing little dirt-bag quiet for a minute, I'll tell you what happened. Now I'll admit I was on a bender, but I wasn't too far gone to remember how it went down. I come to the doorway where I like to sleep over in Junkyville, and this one's already there, sawin' logs. I had a devil of a time wakin' him up. Seemed like he was sleepin' off a powerful drunk hisself."

Seamus grunted, "Sober as the Pope, I was."

I shushed the little man and motioned for J.T. to continue.

"So, I grabbed ahold of him by the seat of the pants and the scruff of the neck, and I was proceeding to throw him into the alley when he wakes up and starts howling like I'm killing him. I stopped and held on till he quit hollering. Once he seen I had a good holt of him he got still and says, 'Ah, hell. Ye got me.'"

Travis eyed the little man who had shoved his hands into his pockets and stood looking at his feet.

J.T. continued, "Like I was saying, I was only half-crocked, and I recognized him for what he was right off. My old grandpa used to tell us stories about the little people. We come from Ireland, ya see."

"I take exception to the term 'little people.' I'll have you know I'm considered tall among my folk." Seamus's Mickey Mouse voice piped.

"So, wait a minute. You expect me to believe you're a Leprechaun?" I asked.

"Indeed I am."

J.T. said, "That car was proof. Seamus here offered to grant me my fondest wish if I'd get him a bottle of whiskey."

I couldn't help wondering where the car had gone.

"Little devil made it disappear is what."

"As I recall," said Seamus, "—and ye can rely on me to recall clearly—the old bugger said he'd like to drive his beloved Z-car again. There was never a mention of keeping it." He crossed his arms, defiant.

I told them they were both full of it and turned to go again.

"Don't let him go! It's the truth, son. At least make him grant you a wish."

I didn't believe a word of it but decided to play along. You have to admit it was a wild way to start the day, so I said, "Okay, little dude —Seamus, if I were to make a deal with you, how would that work?"

"Well, son, it's tit-fer-tat. You give me something, I give you something. Simple as that."

I couldn't think of a wish, and J.T. explained, "He's bound to stay with you till the bargain's done."

I asked Seamus, "What about J.T. here?"

"I'm through with that old sod. What's yer name son? I can't strike a bargain with a person if I don't even know his name."

I introduced myself, and we left old J.T. there crying in the alley about his lost Camaro. At least he had half a bottle of whiskey. It seemed pretty miraculous that it had survived the fight. I felt bad, but I had to get to work. I'd have left Seamus there too, but he followed me. Good thing it was a quiet day at the shop, no customers, but lots of donations to sort. I completely forgot Seamus until I heard a tapping noise and found him hammering away at the heel of a boot.

When he saw me, he said, "Ach. I can't bear the sight of damaged footwear. I was just putting this one right. I'll just potter around here among the shoes while you tend to your rat killin'."

Seamus chattered all the way to my apartment about the different shoes he'd repaired that day.

"Seriously, dude?" I said, "Fixing those shoes sure has got you fired up."

And he said, "It's my vocation, son. Nothing like putting in a good day's work doing something you're good at to improve a man's attitude!"

It was true. Seamus was completely different from the combative little drunk I'd met that morning. I asked him, "If it makes you so happy to work with shoes, Seamus, why don't you just do that?"

"It's not so simple, Travis, my boy. It never fails that some old yob like J.T. catches me and starts hunting for a pot of gold or bargaining for wealth and power. You have no idea the nonsense a Leprechaun has to endure. And it goes wrong more often than not. Just like J.T.'s Camaro."

"But J.T. wouldn't have caught you if you'd been sober. What happened there?"

"It's the drink, lad. I get a bit rowdy when I'm in me cups—lose me temper."

"And pass out in strange places?"

"It's been known to happen. 'Tis a failing of my kind."

"Thanks for letting me know. I won't offer you a beer then."

Seamus's eyes lit up at the mention of beer, but after a moment, he nodded and settled back down.

"Does a bargain ever go right?"

"Sure it does, but it takes a special pure soul to make such a deal. Take yer man J.T. Poor old blighter's been on the sauce for so long his fond wishes are all distant memories—of things and times long gone. A fine motor car can't change everything that's beset J.T. since those days. Even if he'd worded his bargain differently, that car wouldn't have made him happy for long. He'd have lost it one way or another in a matter of days and ended up right where we left him this morning."

"A worthwhile bargain ought to be based on the here and now?"

"Aye. Standard stuff. No love potions, no killing, no resurrecting the dead."

"Ah. So, you can't make a girl love me?"

"That's the gist of it."

I sat with him there trying to think of a worthy bargain, but I was stumped. There wasn't much I wanted for myself that didn't sound selfish in my head. Finally, I said to him, "I never asked you to come with me, Seamus. You're free to go."

"No, no. You caught me fair and square. I owe you a bargain."

"Okay. I want world peace. Can you do that?"

"No. And I can't close the ozone hole either. Sure, there's bound to be something you want for yourself."

"Seamus, I just want to improve the lives of the people around me, but I don't know how. I can't think of what to ask for."

"You present me with a challenge, my boy, but I have an idea or two. In return, I'd like to go home—can you help me with that?"

I bought him a ticket to Dublin. It was economy, but a guy that small doesn't have to worry about legroom. I saw him off the next day and figured I'd just have to eat the cost of a plane ticket, but on the way home, I got a call from a law firm I'd never heard of, and farfetched as it seems, some distant relation had left me a boatload of money. I thought it was a hoax and laughed at the guy on the other end of the line. I was about to hang up, but he got all excited and insistent and rattled through my family tree for about ten minutes. Turns out he was legit. I didn't inherit outright, but I'm now the director of a philanthropic trust fund. And that's why I reached out to you. It's way more job than I can handle.

∾

WHEN TRAVIS FINISHED HIS STORY, I said, "You are absolutely full of shit."

He laughed. "I know, right? It's a ridiculous story, but I have a job for you if you want it."

"You're serious."

"Yep."

I was one of the first people Travis helped with that money. I don't really care where it came from.

∾

TO YOU WHO LINGERS ON

BY LUCY ZHANG

The willow people live longer than the rest of us. We're not sure how long, but we guess it must be at least several thousand years. The willow people move slowly, spending decades finishing tasks like finding the rare, pink-dusted pearl at the bottom of the river—we all abandoned our quest for the pearl after growing out of childhood legends. It's difficult to meet willow people in one lifetime, and most are scattered in places we'd never dare venture.

I grew up in a human family with human ancestors except for one great aunt who was part sprite. The diluted sprite blood flowing through our veins let us speak to trees and coax plants into blooming. We don't live longer than regular humans though.

I met my first and last willow person when I was twelve. He resided one hill's climb away from our town—far enough that most adults didn't care to trek, but close enough for curious children to venture. The willow person called himself Fern even though only sprites typically named themselves after plants. Fern liked to play games on people and pretend he was anything other than a willow person. He told us his previous names included Apple, Rory, Ren, Ever. We didn't care, as long as he responded when we called.

Fern never seemed to leave that hill, and we often wondered what he did to earn money or acquire the infinite amounts of food he always had when we visited: pots of honey to dip crisp, light rice crackers, jars of alcohol, pans of sesame brittle so fragrant we could smell them as we hiked up the hill. Fern had stockpiled these items from his years of travel. He'd stored and distributed his belongings in so many places he no longer remembered how much he owned. We marveled at the idea of a treasure hunt, collecting the trinkets he'd lost. Fern must've been rich as a king with how many years he had to accumulate material wealth. He'd laugh at our antics of drawing maps, probing his memory for where he last traveled, trying to identify patterns among these hidden objects. Fern's tales were endless and rich, each adventure more intriguing than the previous. He'd tell us of how he displaced an entire city by rallying the neighboring weeds to push the earth in tidal-like waves until they cracked through the ground's foundation and toppled buildings. He'd recount journeys in cities where people could only speak in lies and villages where houses were built from grape vines. Fern had even traveled into the ocean where a handful of willow people resided, their bodies adapted to the salty waters and rare glimpses of sun. He claimed ocean life wasn't for him—too cold and dark for a wanderer like himself. At this, we'd laugh, since to us, Fern was the least wandering person we knew. He stayed in his tiny cottage even when the fireflies emerged or the morning glories blossomed. A time when both kids and adults took a moment to step outside and watch.

I still have all the maps I'd drawn tucked away in a drawer beneath several salves and balms. Most of us stopped visiting Fern once we turned fifteen which was when we received our job assignments and relocated to live with our cohorts with similar jobs. Because of my sprite blood, I, like most of my family, became responsible for gardening and crop maintenance. A job I could finish within two hours despite the large quota to sprout all twenty acres of dandelions, prune our peach tree orchard, and collect the many over-ripe apricots that'd fallen to the ground and threatened to attract bugs. I could coax the dandelions to sprout and the peach trees to forsake several flowers and fruits, but the apricot gathering required manual labor and ate up most of my time. I gathered them with my bare hands and a basket draped over my shoulders. I would set the fruit over paper to dry under the sun. We sweetened soups with the dried apricots, our only indulgence in the winter. I often finished my job early and would make my way back to Fern's house alone.

When it was just us two, Fern taught me how to translate ancient languages from books he kept hidden in a trunk buried below his home. I struggled to understand and memorize all the words he explained. I'd never been taught to balance so many words in my mind, especially those which contradicted and overlapped with one another like frayed and woven straw, a characteristic of the ancient language. It took me two years to finally read one of Fern's books, and even then, he read most of the words out loud to me.

The book was about Fern's journey to the Other Side, a place often referred to during prayers. The Other Side contained unfath-omable beasts—creatures without eyes or mouths and ate from their wings, insects that could sneak into your dreams and nest there until you died. Fern's book defined the Other Side as a "paradise," an ancient word I'd spent one month learning and still didn't fully understand. When I asked Fern if he thought the Other Side was a paradise, he only said, "of sorts." I also asked if he'd ever go back there, and he said "no, not in the foreseeable future, that's too much of a burden." That was how most of our time was spent: Fern lecturing me on my vocabulary, me struggling page by page, Fern sending me home with a small jar of honey, me asking yet again how long he planned to stay since I worried he'd leave before I could read on my own.

∾

By the time I turned twenty, I had gone through a quarter of Fern's books without limited assistance. He joked that he'd have to start traveling again to dig up the books he'd buried elsewhere across the earth. I asked him to take me with him.

When children from my town turn twenty, we are matched to start families. The process is drawn out over a year, full of festivities that everyone attends even though it's just a small handful of us who need matches. The town is full of gossips who can't pass up free drinks and meals and games. The festivities don't have any real say in your match, though. The important part of the process only takes one day: a matchmaker scans our profiles on paper and our faces in person while we line up, waiting for a decision to be made. If you're lucky, you get paired with someone you've interacted with at the festivals. The matchmaker lives alone in the corner of town, emerging only for morning stretches and dances that she performs in the middle of our garden grounds. She used to scare us as children since she moved with such sudden, aggressive gestures, like a praying mantis striking its prey. I doubted she could even see us at that age, her eyes fogged like the morning clouds. We figured she was randomly matching us.

Once you are paired, you gain new duties, the first and most exhausting of which is to carry peaches up to the rain gods who bless us with longevity and fertility. No amount of sprite blood can coax neighboring plants into carrying you to the summit. No amount of whispering to the branches that comprise our basket handles can lessen the load on your shoulders. These journeys take half a day if you're agile and strong, which I was not, especially since I got away with most of my physical work by asking the plants to comply. However, two years ago, things had changed slightly. Fewer couples were sent to deliver the peaches, and instead they were sent to the Gray Towns, responsible for creating and selling new tools made from shiny, unbendable substances. These tools made cutting and carving and hunting easier, although they cost an entire village's supply of food, so we only possessed one of these tools, shared among the whole town. Our leaders wanted us to start families in the Gray Towns and feed the meager labor force.

"I don't want to lug perfectly fine peaches up a mountain. Nor do I want to leave to some place where you can't see color," I complained to Fern.

"The books must've made you lazy," he joked.

"Why don't we leave for somewhere else?" I suggested. "Like that city you said floated in the sky."

"You have sprite blood, the earth will call to you so ardently that you'd plunge to your death before you can adapt to the sky."

"What if we get married? They'd never force me to leave if I were married to a willow person."

"Don't humans look for something special, romantic, life changing? Marriage is a blip in my memory, like the bitter tea you don't remember drinking the other day. If you're ok with that…"

I was happy with anything, at that point. All my peers from earlier years had been sent to the Gray Towns and never heard from again.

When I turned twenty-one, we performed a short ceremony in the yard behind Fern's home. He had been through many ceremonies in the past and told me this ceremony was the least dramatic he'd ever experienced. I struggled to imagine what could be more dramatic than sitting across from one another with our hands intertwined, marking each other's faces with a green paste ground from thyme leaves. This marked our souls as each other's, and more importantly, symbolized our deference to the earth that provided for us. Fern said he'd seen couples drink full glasses of each other's blood in ancient ceremonies, although I had trouble believing him. As children, we learned never to ingest blood because it stank of poison and attracted creatures of death.

My parents disowned me after finding out I'd gotten married to Fern—not because they hated me but because the village would cut them off from their water and food supply if they continued to house me. I understood. I wanted them to live comfortably. I reassured them that I'd be fine with Fern, who seemed to possess unlimited resources of food and entertainment. At my insistence, Fern and I left the village with two packs and travel cloaks that my parents gifted me as a final parting gesture. I dreamt of visiting all the places Fern described to me as a child, unraveling his buried, fermented jugs of rice wine and eroding books.

THE FIRST STOP we encountered is the one I remember most clearly. We'd been traveling along mudslides for weeks until we finally reached a waterfall so grand I thought it'd crush the boulders below. The falls quieted only once a year when the neighboring pines fell silent. Not even the wind dared to cast dry pinecones to the ground. I'd never experienced such silence. In my hometown, the trees constantly whispered to me even at night when their flowers closed and a breeze set. Fern and I slipped through a break in the falls, making our way behind the wall of water. There, we found an intricate water way system with several main streams spreading into thinner and thinner capillaries. As we followed the water, we reached mound-like dwellings, domed at the top and smooth all around. Each mound had one or two windows centered vertically in the wall. Each dome contained furniture and cooking ware and other ornaments as though it had been thoroughly lived-in and customized, remnants of a civilization that had vanished in the blink of an eye. When Fern visited this place some two hundred ago, he said it had been equally empty and equally furnished, as though it was not humans but the earth that had built the place, waiting for residents to make use of it. We settled here, feasting on the self-sustaining garden of gourds and strawberries and the crisp, sweet water trickling in from the waterfall. Fern dug up a crate of books, pickled mustard greens, and dried cuttlefish from the stash he'd left there.

During the tail end of the five years we stayed there, I became pregnant with our first child. It would've been a fine place to raise a child, but the water flowing behind the falls had turned murky and gray, and when we inspected the front, we realized the dirty water flowed from multiple distant sources and no amount of redirecting and repositioning of boulders could cleanse the water supply. We agreed not to raise our firstborn on poisoned water for Fern had seen firsthand how these kinds of children grew: withered like orchids under direct sunlight.

After our daughter was two months old, we left on a quiet night, as though all the cicadas and beetles left to the underworld to make way for our departure. We moved to a neighboring town that generated revenue through wine and attracted the wealthy. The children here attended schools that supplied all three meals and even taught them to read the ancient language. At the center of the town was a square with a fountain that spouted fresh pomegranate juice you could collect in a cup. This fountain supposedly sustained its flow from a stream blessed by the wine gods the townspeople worshiped. If you jarred the juice for long enough, it'd transform into wine. Our daughter refused to touch her food unless we coated it in a concentrated sauce of pomegranate juice. It must've contained mystical nutritional properties since my daughter ended up growing taller than me and resembled a sprite far more than I or my mother or my grandmother had.

Fern and I learned to harvest grapes and supply them to the fermenters. I found this job easier than anything I'd grown in the past. I needed only to ask the plants to bear fruit and they'd obey, drunk off my voice. Even when it failed to rain that summer and others' crops died from drought, ours yielded bountiful harvests, enough to supply the entire town's wine exports. We grew our wealth easily and Fern spent most of his spare time playing with our daughter or taking her to the main square where kids played by the fountain. When I wasn't monitoring the vineyards, I read through Fern's old journals we'd discovered in an old wine cellar, each page detailing an adventure he'd never told me before.

After our daughter turned thirteen, she started demanding that she taste the wine. I took this as a sign we should leave. "Wine is only good for the elderly," Fern agreed. "Children need to get drunk off life first." He took several bottles with us, though. He preferred the wines because they cleared his head.

My daughter inherited my talent with plants, the sprite blood magnified in her ability to rest seeds in the dirt or guide roots and vines to wrap away from our homes and around the stakes we propped in the ground. She enjoyed nurturing the useless plants: roses, chrysanthemums, daisies. Every morning, we'd wake to wind blowing pollen like a maelstrom, the sky swarmed with dancing yellow powder. She'd weave crowns with stems and sew petals into her clothing even though the petals shriveled into crisps within a week. Fern called it creative exercise and patiently sat while our daughter weaved flowers into his long hair. But that was the thing with Fern: he took everything slowly, even when we had harvest season quotas to meet and ripening schedules to abide by. Flowers sold for increasingly little. Most folks preferred those made from fabric and other new materials we'd seen being churned out by Gray Towns. These materials preserved their form year-round and resisted any form of human tearing. A color that never faded.

"We don't all have multiple lifetimes to earn a living," I warned Fern while our daughter slept. "We can't spend all of our time on flowers."

"You don't need to worry, I've accumulated plenty over the years for us to thrive on," Fern reassured me, as usual. I remained uncertain that his books and artifacts would do us any good. Although I enjoyed his books as a girl, I rarely read them now, and I doubted they would sell for much. We'd traveled long enough for me to realize that his stashes possessed little monetary value.

A storm hit the year my daughter left on her first adventure. She wanted to gather tea leaves from shrubs that only grew in the marshes, spongey and wet from the constant snow. Fern told her these tea leaves made you wise, and she'd rather spend a week climbing through ice and over slippery rocks than spend more years studying. Three days after she left, the storm toppled forests and blocked her path home. The aftermath of the quakes spliced the tea leaf island away from mainland, leaving the glacier in constant drift. We had no idea where she was, but Fern insisted she'd be fine, "Willow people don't die from things like that."

We attempted to move closer to where we thought the glacier was drifting, following the scent of the tea leaves. In retrospect, I realize the flaw in this logic: we'd assumed our daughter would stay in one spot once she obtained the leaves. But we raised a wanderer, not a dweller. Fern decided that we should settle down in a river village, where everyone lived on boats strung to each other, the entire complex drifting together with the current. I spent the first six months seasick, sitting at the edge of the boat, vomiting out our effective front door and watching the fish I'd eaten earlier return to the waters. Despite the many moments our village nearly capsized, my vomiting stopped as abruptly as it had begun. We discovered I was pregnant when our boats had been cast out to sea from a stream of tumultuous waves.

To Fern, I was still a child, a smudge in his years of experience navigating the world's frosted air and odd life forms that grew from the caves where the sun could not touch. But both of us knew this was a tricky age to have a child. I no longer walked like I used to, each step a source of pain rippling up my bones. I could no longer sleep through the tides slapping the sides of our boat. A sharp, pinching sensation overwhelmed my stomach after meals, and my feet swelled from the slightest sprinkle of salt. My hands too no longer formed proper grips to stabilize slippery or large items.

My body barely held together to have you, a baby livelier and more ferocious than your sister, a crater that fought its way free onto a rocking boat.

At this point, Fern realized raising you on a boat-island left much to be desired. There were no other children, only fishermen and young wanderers hitching a ride. The closest thing to a school system was to memorize stories that would then be recited. But relocating elsewhere required that I trek a certain distance, and at this point, I wasn't sure how much I could walk, especially not through the swamps that'd latch onto my feet and pull me to the underworld. Fern decided we'd leave the boats the next time we sighted land, no matter where that was.

That ended up being the Submerged Land.

The Submerged Land is submerged not by water, but by tree roots. I'm not even certain there's dirt beneath the roots growing layer over layer like woven baskets stacked one on top of the other. The trees provide foundations for homes, and each home is anchored in the branches and connected to one another through ropes and ladders. You can descend and walk through roots, but few do that. The roots constantly shift and regenerate, and so the landscape can be sloped one day and then flat the next, rendering routine routes impossible. Fern last visited the Submerged Land fifty centuries ago, and he claimed the trees had been mere saplings then, their roots buried beneath the soil, their sprouts fragile against the wind.

My daughter reunited with us while you were too young to recognize faces. She carried no tea leaves, only sacks of glistening, gray, sharp-edged planks that clanked against each other and felt heavier than they appeared. She said these would make our lives easier, as today, we relied on Fern's brute force to cut down crops and open routes blocked by overgrown roots. I asked her where she'd been, if she'd tried the tea leaves, how she found us. She told us that the wind had blown her to a Gray Town, and she stayed there for several months working and earning a living before tracking us down.

"You didn't get nauseous or anything?" I worried. Our sprite bloodline left us with a distaste for smog which emanated from the

Gray Towns, and we often got lightheaded without sufficiently dense areas of flora.

"Nothing at all," she replied.

"Probably because we adapt to anything. It's in our blood," Fern theorized even though he'd never been to a Gray Town. Not after all these years.

My daughter and Fern took you to a Gray Town several years later, after the roots of the Submerged Land began to dry and loosen their grips on the earth. Several homes had already collapsed, crashing to the ground in a pile of rubble as branches snapped and faltered. Fern thought the trees would hold for at least another century, but the murky waters feeding their roots only seemed to grow increasingly clouded and rancid. I pleaded for the trees to maintain their cellular composure and for the neighboring shrubs and wildflowers to reserve more of the soil's nutrients for the trees. This slowed the deterioration, but with each passing day, we noticed yet another gap between roots sprawled over the earth, a hole revealing older layers: black, shriveled echoes of strong roots— centuries of nurturing destroyed in under a decade.

My home remains standing thanks to my pleas to the trees and their generosity toward my sprite lineage and my ancestors who once nourished them to health. They whisper old tales—from a time before willow people existed—about how they slept dormant in seeds, waiting for the right season and the right time to burst through and seize the land. Sprites awakened them with their songs, soft lulls that gained choruses with pollinating flowers and ripening persimmons and clustering clouds. I rarely sing and prefer to touch my hands to a common source that reaches all the plants—the streams of water or loosened soil that dusts each bark and leaf the moment the wind changes direction. Songs fade as quickly as youth transforms into wrinkles. I hardly remember the melody my parents once sang in the fields to ripen the Pippins, notorious for not turning sweet until the frost dusted our windows and we'd have to drag ourselves out the door in two layers of pants and a scarf wrapped around our heads. I preferred to ripen fruit by placing my palms in the soil and praying.

I begged the trees to hold up until I died. A blink of an eye to you, who remembers this place as a root-woven paradise, stronger and more majestic than any forest that remains untouched by Gray Towns. Before Fern left with you and your sister, he promised to return "soon". I know that as soon as he stumbled upon an odd mushroom in the woods or a lone stand that sells spikey, yellow fruits he'd never seen before, you'd end up lingering there until he fully documented his observations, a process that takes decades at a time. A good thing. You will learn a lot. You will live long like him.

TOO REAL

BY GRETCHEN CORTEZ

In the museum atrium, people gathered with their phones out just to capture the nine-year-old boy named Ling.

Standing on an old crate, he carefully stroked his brush over the canvas clamped to a wooden easel mounting twice his size. Sure and swift, he masked the white foundation, lost in the rhythm of the image.

A man looked back sternly.

"It's so real," someone whispered from behind him.

Ling had made it a dozen times before. Each one, more real than the last. This time, it was the smile that made it appear human. The colors mixed in certain spots to form shadowy creases until the smile seemed to breathe. Move, even, as if the man truly existed.

Ling stopped, wiping his hands off on his pants and looking up and down at his own brilliant work. It was too real. Real as a painting could get.

The crowd murmured behind him, their eyes flicking between him and his man. Before anyone could truly take it in, Ling plucked up the board and dropped it in the trash as though it were nothing.

From the corner, his mom leaned against the wooden bench,

absorbed in her phone. He took a seat beside her, watching as the crowds mostly dispersed from their cluster. A few people still lingered, mesmerized, near the empty easel Ling had used.

They scrolled through their phones examining the photos they'd taken before he tossed it out. They couldn't resist staring at the painting, googly-eyed. Ling sniggered beneath his breath. For some reason, when they stared at the man in admiration, he felt special. Like they were staring at him.

"We're dropping you guys off at Uncle Wingham's house," Mom blurted from beside him.

"Why?" Ling asked, eyes widening. His mood sank fast. "Can't I go with you?"

"No, he lives close by. And Gram wants to drink."

"Oh." Ling kicked his feet out. Sometimes, he wanted to hit Gram in the face with all his might.

Uncle Wingham gave him the chills—the guy always chewed on something with big fat lips that Ling imagined the king of England to have, and his upturned, buttery nose poked the air where it had no business being. Something was deeply wrong about him.

Ling couldn't say exactly what, only that the man's voice sounded deep and dispirited, and every time he and Keya got dumped off there, they ended up stuck still in hard-backed wooden chairs like two stone statues, barely peeping out a word.

It felt like Gram and Mom and Dad hadn't cared about them at all; they hadn't even considered what it would be like for them to get locked away in Uncle's house for hours. Maybe they figured he and Keya would be fine and that Uncle Wingham really wasn't some kind of wretched monster. But Ling knew better.

By the time Dad and Keya walked out of the modern exhibit, the whole family got in the car and drove down to Uncle's. Midway through the ride, Keya began crying.

She cried a lot, but this was different. Mom and Dad couldn't even hear her tears—that's how Ling knew they were real. They rolled quietly down her pinkened cheeks, and she wiped them off on her sleeve before she thought anyone else could see.

But Ling could.

He had seen older kids raise their middle fingers at people before, and it looked so powerful and satisfying. It made people scream or bat their hands away, and Ling felt it was the right moment to finally stick his up.

But then the car stopped, and it was too late. No finger could save them. Outside, the crooked, stomped up gate leaned away from the house, as if it, too, wanted freedom.

"Alright, have a good time, babies," Mom said, giving a sympathetic wave and nothing more.

"Be good to him," Dad followed, chuckling. "He's very kind, looking after you."

Ling nodded to whatever that meant, then followed Keya out the side door. A breeze wisped over his hair, as the car drove off. He realized he had forgotten to ask how long it would be until Mom and Dad and Gram came back, and he suddenly felt so small.

They stood in the dirt flatlands, surrounded by a massive valley. The grass had grown flimsy and tall, a big weeping ocean of seaweed whisking past Ling's neck. Unfortunately, he knew they couldn't hide in it forever, so he wrapped one arm around Keya's shoulder and guided her towards the door.

"C'mon, let's go in." His voice came out too weak.

Uncle's house looked like one of those old, abandoned barns in the middle of nowhere. With wood chipping and a few skims of archaic paint remnants, it leaned to the side, worn down from years of battering storms. Ling had always assumed no one lived in those old barns until he'd met Uncle.

Before Ling could even touch it, the door cracked open. He still balled his fist and knocked respectfully remembering his father's words. To be good to him.

Only now, holding both of Keya's shoulders, Ling shuffled back the moment Uncle appeared. How could he possibly be good to such a man?

Shadows danced across Uncle Wingham's slowly chewing mouth. His eyes locked on Ling, as if studying him with all his being. What was he searching for?

Ling shifted back uncomfortably on the deck and gulped, tightening his grip on Keya.

"Uh...hi," Ling whispered.

Uncle Wingham's boot skirted back, pushing down against the moaning floor beam. The door croaked open smoothly to the inside —a nearly all black room. Perhaps it used to be an insane asylum. Or perhaps it still was.

Only a single window at the end let in a pinch of hopeful skylight from the white clouds. Ling moved towards it, guiding Keya along with him. That was the way out—it must've been.

"Sit down," Uncle Wingham ordered before they could reach any closer to it.

Ling jumped in his shoes, let go of Keya, and rushed to the same old chair he'd spent hours in during their last visit. There was no way to ignore Uncle Wingham; the man knew everything.

But Keya froze still where she stood, a stubborn little lump.

Ling opened his mouth to scream at her—she'd get yelled at or be given a bad report to Mom and Dad if she didn't listen to Uncle— but nothing came out of him. He'd never been so shy before.

As Uncle Wingham turned on his heel, he revealed the ratted black hair scraping down from the back of his pale, barren skull, as if a monster's fangs had opened up wide. Only a bit of flesh clung onto the bones left in his body. If there was such a thing as a monster, he was one.

"Down as well, miss. Down as well," Uncle said to Keya. She stared, unmoving.

Ling waved his arm, hissing under his breath for her to listen until she finally did. Then, the dark, dusted hallways swallowed up

Uncle Wingham, and the smacks of his boots on the floor faded into it.

Ling wriggled his toes and squirmed in his chair. He couldn't sit still. So many nerves coursed through him. But quickly, he froze. In the back screen door, a hole had ripped, large enough for a greyhound to enter and, most importantly, large enough for a kid to leave.

"Look!" Ling pointed at it. Keya almost smiled, then turned back around.

"What if he finds out?" she asked.

But the hall where Uncle Wingham vanished was still empty and black, so Ling ignored Keya and crawled to his hands and knees on the floor. It was his last chance to not have to look into Uncle Wingham's harsh, knowing eyes and pray that mom and dad came back shortly. To not feel so naked and bare and seen.

When the wooden beams sighed, Keya put a finger to her lips, "Sh!"

"*I know,*" Ling said, frowning at her. Keya needed to wake up; her shushing was even louder than him. Why she had to shush in the first place, he didn't know, but he kept inching towards the hole in the screen door, waving silently for her to join him.

Taking one last look down the black hall, she, too, slumped to the ground.

When they got so close and excited, they started pattering like dogs across the wooden floorbeams and out the screen door. Ling giggled once he reached the other end, as a strong rush of wind whipped his cheeks. It was full of freedom and life and beauty.

"Let's go," he shouted, rushing down the wobbling back porch steps, avoiding any loose screws that had been poking out like teeth. At the bottom, overcrowded shrubs lined the hems, and thorns and bristles stuck off of them like scraggly, encroaching hairs.

Keya skipped down the steps after him. Her face scrunched into a grin, when—

"Ling-Ling! Ling-Ling!" Uncle Wingham's voice sang melodically from behind.

Somehow, he knew. Maybe he'd heard them, but it didn't matter he did—only that he knew of their feeble attempt to break out, and he was coming to take them back.

Ling clenched Keya's wrist and yanked her close to his chest behind a bush. He could feel her thumping heartbeat on his palm, a precious living thing, alive and real.

"I bought you a present. Why don't you come and see?" asked Uncle Wingham kindly.

Uncle Wingham had never spoken so kindly before. Not often, at least. So Ling poked curiously over the shrub to see Uncle standing halfway down the steps in his all black attire—two layers of heavy duty coats, pants, and boots. Except he was alone, without any present at all.

Before Uncle turned to see him, Ling dropped back behind the shrub, hugging Keya tight against his chest like a teddy bear. She didn't have room to speak or complain, and for once in her life, she didn't.

The boots marched up the steps and quieted through the door. Nonetheless, Ling remained still, listening for Uncle to come out again and call his name. He hoped he wouldn't, and for just a moment, the silence kept on.

"Is it clear?" Keya whispered, trying to push Ling's arms off.

The back door swung open.

"No." Ling fastened his grasp around her, trying not to pinch her quivering tummy too hard. She seemed to have lost all her breath.

This time, something scratched across the stale porch and stopped.

"You like art, don't you? Here is my own," said Uncle Wingham.

"Stay," Ling ordered Keya. Something told him she wouldn't like Uncle Wingham's artwork.

Ling got to his knees and peered over the head of the bush to see it for himself first. The moment he did, he gasped.

In Uncle's arms was a man. A lifeless, rag doll of a man, with the eyes of two dead, dark rocks lodged into his skull. But when Ling inched closer, he recognized the man.

From his painting.

Although, now, the man stood upright on his own, with Uncle Wingham's arms holding his, and he stared empty-eyed into the open fields.

Ling's knees embedded in the dirt. Every wrinkle, mole, and hair on the man was somehow exactly right. The painting had morphed to life.

"He's so real," Keya murmured, looking over Ling's shoulder. "He looks better than Uncle."

She burst towards it, leaving Ling alone in the dust. He thought about pulling her back, about stopping her, but his feet had somehow lodged themselves deeper into the ground, and Keya *was* right—the man looked better than Uncle. Perhaps the man would be kinder than Uncle, too.

"Look, he wants to talk to you," Uncle Wingham said with a grin, the man's jaw dropping.

Keya marched up the steps and peered into the black abyss of the man's open-mouthed smile.

"Come inside," Uncle Wingham said, manipulating the man's mouth to match his words. Keya laughed and followed them into the house, as if she couldn't see that Uncle Wingham stood right beside the man—using him—like a well-practiced ventriloquist.

Ling took a breath, then followed up the porch steps. He then got to his hands and knees like a mutt again and peered through the hole in the screen door. How could his sister be so naive to follow Uncle back inside? Except she wasn't following Uncle back. She was following him—the man.

In Ling's old chair, the man sat on Uncle Wingham's lap. Keya's dark hair sprung around eagerly, as she leaned towards him. She didn't see the truth.

The man said, "My name is Mister—" Suddenly, he started choking. He leaned forward, ribs rolling over his knee bones. His rock eyes bulged from their sockets, red veins spider-webbing across his scalp.

Keya panicked. She searched the room for something to save him with, turning desperately towards the screen door where Ling stood.

He instantly dove to the ground. If she saw him, she'd ask him to help save the man from dying. But he couldn't go inside. As he lay flat on his tummy, he could hear his own breath quickening from something squeezing his heart, waiting for it to burst.

"I—I—" the man stuttered, his face growing olive with a touch of puke-yellow.

"Mister, what do you want?" Keya asked, falling to her knees before him.

"Save me, save me! You must cut your heart out and give it to me," the man pleaded.

Ling could feel Uncle's growling vibrate the floors.

His whole body went limp, as he furiously squinted at his sister. She should've known better than to believe a word Uncle said. Yet, somehow she had this determined, laser focused look in her eyes as she disappeared into the kitchen.

When Ling pushed himself off the porch floor, he could smell the sour, mustardy poison radiating off the man.

The man's eyes landed on him, piercing through his soul. They could see everything—the reason Ling painted, the reason Ling became a prodigy and the realistic people he'd created—everything.

When Keya returned from the kitchen, her tiny hands were wrapped around a teetering, fanglike knife. She glanced back at Ling with her open, innocent brown eyes searching for some kind of approval.

He wanted to shake his head, to yell "no," to rip the weapon from her hands and stab the man with it instead, but the man smiled at Ling. It was a strange, familiar smile. He somehow knew Ling would stand there doing nothing while Keya, with the knife facing her chest, forcefully thrust it down and into—

BEEP, BEEP!

A car horn blared from the driveway.

In seconds, the man vanished into the hall, and Uncle Wingham replaced him. He frowned at Keya, confused, as she still clenched his knife in her hands.

"Put that down," he ordered.

Ling rushed through the back door towards her, taking the weapon and dropping it. It clattered carelessly against the floor, as he squeezed her arms—they fit perfectly in his.

Uncle Wingham opened the door, and Mom waved at him and said, "Thank you for taking care of them."

"My pleasure," Uncle gleamed, his yellow, chipped, buck teeth poking out sillily through his lips.

Ling and Keya went to the car, and Ling stared back at Uncle Wingham. He wondered if Uncle even realized what happened—the moment the car honked and he returned from the darkness, he acted so differently. Normal, even. But whichever side of Uncle was an act didn't seem to matter. He had nearly killed Ling's own sister with that man. With *Ling's* man.

During the ride home, Ling felt so drained that he slept most of the way.

When they got home, he entered his room where all sorts of faces watched him from the walls. Large, hooked noses. Bright teal eyes. Gushing oozes from the pores. But in the corner, the man.

The first thing he'd ever drawn.

Miraculously, the original hadn't yet found its way into the garbage along with the rest of them. He'd happened to paint it a dozen times again, throwing each away because none was good enough, though he never forgot the man and the way that every time people saw him, they loved him. They absolutely loved him.

A clump of throwup spilled in Ling's mouth, but he quickly swallowed it back down and gathered nearly every painting, easel, brush, and drawing board, then started for the trash can in the garage.

By the time all but one painting had been cleared from the room,

Ling carried it, too, to the overstuffed trash bin, and dropped it inside.

He walked back up the stairs to his bedroom, where the walls were now empty and free of art. But immediately, something new caught Ling's eye—on the bed where he slept sat an upright figure.

It was a man.

Its posture was straight. Its head faced the door where Ling stood and stared straight at him. Ling's skin prickled up as the air around the man seemed to die and send drafts his way.

How had the man gotten there? And how was he breathing? Uncle was gone, after all, and the man still sat perked up on his own.

The worst thing was his smile with its creased, wrinkled cheeks, as if someone had just cracked a really funny joke. It looked unnaturally real beneath his lifeless eyes. Ling couldn't tell what the man was thinking, but whatever it was didn't seem good.

It was too real, Ling thought. Real as a painting could get.

WHITE AGONY
BY KEN GOLDMAN

If one follows chronic pain to its logical conclusion, there remains a single outcome to which he can arrive : a pristine agony devoid of any comfort level whatsoever whose only resolution is transcendence ...

Dr. Julian Mangus
Department of Neurological Studies and Research,
Boston University Hospital
Rough draft from his essay "On Pain and Endurance"

Alone inside his study with the eager pre-med student, Professor Julian Mangus observed the niceties required to put a young man at his ease.

"Some coffee, Dennis?"

"Please."

"Danish?"

"Fine."

The kid's limping appeared barely noticeable as he took a seat in the only soft chair present, but Mangus paid particular attention to it.

Dennis checked the place out. The den was a good example of minimalist design whose furnishings consisted of a restored antique roll-top desk and a simple swivel seat, the black vinyl chair in which he sat, and a cinder block book case containing medical texts each neatly stacked and alphabetically arranged. There was a dinosaur of a Macintosh Plus computer but no television, no wall art nor anything extraneous except a large DIEHARD car battery that seemed completely out of place hidden in the corner of the room. Julian Mangus' inner sanctum seemed designed for function rather than comfort and was more immaculate than one might expect to find an unmarried middle-aged college instructor inhabiting.

They small-talked about the Sox's slim chances of winning their first Pennant since 1986, Dennis fill ed an uncomfortable silence by commenting on the crisp New England fall weather. The professor segued nicely into the impressive job the kid had done in his last exam on the brain and central nervous system. The two engaged in an awkward conversation-by-the-numbers, and these topics covered the requisite formalities.

Throughout, Dennis Possner knew Mangus must have had a more compelling reason for calling this meeting than discussing meteorological and academic banalities. Julian Mangus was prob-ably the least sociable member of B.U.'s faculty, certainly the least likely candidate to invite a first year student into his home on a Sunday morning for an informal chat even if the kid represented the top in his class. Clearly the instructor had a more relevant shoe he intended to drop. Mangus set his coffee aside and swiveled forward from behind the roll-top, his eyes locking with the young man's to initiate the expected moment of truth.

"Exactly how would you define pain, Dennis?"

Coming from a man who had made the study of chronic pain his area of expertise, the non-sequitor was succinct and refreshingly bullshit free. This shoe didn't merely drop; Mangus hurled it from left field.

"Do you mean tactile reactions, Professor? Involuntary responses of the central nervous sys--?"

"Put away the blue book explanations for now, will you? I'm not talking of the thwacking your brain takes the morning after last night's kegger or the fireworks you see when you send a hammer smashing into your thumb. I'm talking consummate suffering, the kind few experience even once, excruciating pain that seethes through every fiber of your being until your soul bleeds ... a pain so penetrating and complete that screaming your guts out only intensifies it. Most young men like yourself probably can't fathom pain like that, Mr. Possner, or the effects of such unbearable agony on the psyche. But can anyone, really?"

Dennis managed a twitching smile, uncertain if the professor wasn't yanking his chain. "I wasn't around during the Spanish Inquisition, Dr. Mangus. But I've read--"

The instructor waved off his student's response as if swatting an annoying insect. Mangus did not intend this conversation to include tiresome footnoted extracts.

"Every human being is a textbook when it comes to suffering, Mr. Possner. It's merely a question of degree. I'm asking you to be subjective here."

He leaned forward. The move encouraged the young man to do the same.

"Permit my being blunt, will you? I want you to describe the worst agony you ever endured. My guess is there's a story behind that limp of yours. Leave nothing out. Be as graphic as you're able."

No chain yanking here. Mangus seemed about to write down every word his student might utter. There was something almost ghoulish about the man's interest in the subject, but he was, after all, an academician.

If Mangus had selected wisely, he knew the student would not have to search very deeply inside himself for his answer. He had thoroughly examined the young man's psychological profile, and regarding unsurpassed pain during his twenty-three years only one memory qualified. Dennis may have never spoken about his accident in clinical terms, but a cold and detached analysis of human suffering came with the territory of pre-medical studies.

"I was fifteen when I watched my father die. We were returning home from a game at Fenway when suddenly this eighteen wheeler came tearing through the guard rail of the Mass Pike, barreling down on us from nowhere. We hit head-on, the impact throwing me clear. My father sustained fatal injuries while I lay not far from him in a severe trauma. My legs were broken, my collar bone and rib cage splintered, and my skull fractured. But I remained conscious long enough to see that the jolt had sent Dad through the windshield and into the truck's grill. His Cherokee had split through the metalwork like a cheese grater, and three protruding grill spikes impaled him through his chest, leaving him hanging from what remained of the truck's cabin. I remember having this crazy image that my father had been crucified, Jesus himself on the cross right there on I-90 with hundreds of cars slowing down to have a look. The surgeon later told me I had bone sections protruding from my legs and chest, but no vital organs had been affected. Still, I couldn't stand upright for the next six months. The physical pain caused by the accident should have been extraordinary, yet I felt like I wasn't even there although I'd been bleeding for half an hour on the hot asphalt with my bones crushed. I could only listen to my father scream my name over and over, but it didn't last long. When his screaming stopped, I knew why."

Dennis forced himself back into the present moment. He had been looking into his coffee cup the entire time, stirring at nothing.

"Is that the kind of pain you're talking about, Professor Mangus?"

Possner's candor surprised the instructor. He had difficulty returning his student's gaze. Mangus' pause seemed measured and rehearsed, as if his next anecdote was already written on his sleeve.

"There's an old joke about the guy who goes to his doctor because he's been suffering excruciating migraines. 'Doctor, can you give me something to relieve this pain?' he begs. 'Got just the thing for you, Mr. Smith,' the doctor tells him, and he takes out a large hammer and whacks the poor schmuck in the knee. 'Damn!' the patient shouts. 'What the hell did you do *that* for?' And the doctor answers, 'I'll bet you forgot all about your headache ... '"

Another measured pause. The professor watched Dennis closely as the student took it in.

"When you're talking about physical suffering, Mr. Possner, the thumb screws can always go another notch. It's like the concept of infinity; you're never quite there so long as you can add 'one'. Pain tolerance isn't much different. Individual boundaries of human perseverance are never fixed because ..."

[... because just when you think you can't take any more, that your agony is too intense to bear, you witness your father skewered like a human shishkabob on the grill of a truck. You see complete strangers - families, teenaged girls, nuns - and they're all rolling down their car windows, craning their necks to watch the show.

But you're somewhere else. All of your broken bones suddenly feel like a walk in the park and somehow you've gone past the pain ... because you've seen your father as Jesus on his cross just as plain as you see me sitting here ...

I selected you because you understand pain, Dennis ... and if some-thing goes wrong today, you'll understand why I had to do this ...

Am I right, Dennis ...?

... Am I? ...]

" ... because we're always upping that ante, Dennis. Pain exists on a continuum, and maybe there's no real end to the physical endurance of it short of death."

The student mulled the professor's point over, spotting the flaw in his mentor's reasoning and taking the bait as Mangus had hoped.

"Pain alone doesn't cause death. It can't ... can it?"

"Shock and trauma can, but pain without the accompanying life-threatening injury generally won't. Pain is a warning from your brain and central nervous system, your neurons and dendrites playing 'Whispering Down the Lane.' Pain asks us, *'How much can you take, eh? Well, then how about some **more** ...?'* We're all Jesse Owens going for the burn. Our natural perseverance takes us to the next hierarchy; it allows us to endure more. But have you ever wondered where agony to the nth power ultimately leads us, Dennis? To complete desensitization? To nothingness? Maybe it's a door to Nirvana."

The man's esoteric ramblings caused his young disciple to look as if he wished this discussion would rewind to the fall foliage. Julian Mangus' hypothesis could turn most students' brains into hashed browns, but Dennis Possner's was not wired like the others.

"You make the struggle with pain sound like a video game, Professor. Defeat the agony demons in the dungeon, then enter Level Two and confront the evil Wizard of Suffering in the castle ..."

Mangus considered this. The kid's analogy was as good as any he had come up with himself.

And Mangus knew why.

Dennis Possner had seen his father on the cross.

He had met that wizard and had come home limping from the castle ...

~

From the notes of Dr. Julian Mangus : "On Pain and Endurance"

Physicians traditionally have viewed pain as finite, believing that it reaches a nexus at which point the healing process begins and physical suffering levels off. This opinion is rooted in the belief that pain's only function is that it is the forewarning of injury, the body's precautionary signal to 100 billion neurons, the connections and supporting cells of which make up roughly

three pounds of massive nerve tissue. A body's injury can either be cured or it cannot. In either case, once pain has warned the body, its function is fulfilled and its intensity bottoms out or disappears completely.

However, concerning pain the bar can be raised considerably ... if physical injury is not severe enough to become life threatening, we can theoretically impose more pain to this massive nerve tissue without inducing genuine physical harm. We can take pain to its next plateau, and beyond even that.

SAYING NOTHING, Julian Mangus unbuttoned his shirt. The morning had proven gonzo enough, and had the professor gone any further Dennis would not have bothered with ceremony before he was out the door. The man turned full around so that his back faced the young collegian.

"You're looking at the reason I asked you to come today, Dennis."

He removed the shirt. A silver chunk of metal - longer than a nail and as thick as a railway spike - protruded from the center of the professor's back. His was not a muscular physique and the metal could easily have traveled beyond the man's flesh straight to the bone. Mangus looked like an absurd wind-up toy.

"*What the -?*"

It took a moment to sink in, but Dennis grimaced with his realization. The agony of a foreign object inserted directly into one of the most sensitive parts of the body would be considerable. Driven in deeply enough it could be crippling. He knew what the steel bolt had made direct contact with.

"*... the spinal cord? That thing is rammed into your spinal cord?*"

"Correct."

*"Jesus Christ, Professor Mangus ... How can you be walking around with ...? You're telling me that you put that thing into **yourself** ...?"*

Mangus did not have to offer further explanation. Any pre-med student worth his spit knew the spinal cord connected directly to the brain through the brainstem which in turn controlled practically every vital function inside the body. Cranial nerves conveyed sensations along the stem back to the brain. If there were a terminus for pain in the body, that spike protruding from Mangus' back was Grand Central Station.

Dennis reached to touch the metal stud, but withdrew.

"This is crazy! How can ... *How can you - - **Why** would you subject yourself to that kind of--?"*

" ... agony? Rest assured I'm no pain freak, Dennis. It's just a pinprick to me now. The metal isn't in deeply enough to cause serious damage; just enough to provide an interesting buzz whenever I apply pressure to it. Like this ..."

With both palms behind him he pushed the bolt hard into his flesh. The man should have winced and then screamed in agony. But Mangus did not even flinch.

"It was excruciating initially, of course. I felt pretty sure I would pass out the moment I inserted the pin last week, and that's just what happened."

"That thing isn't a pin ... it's a goddamned rivet ..."

"I think of it as a pin. It helps in dealing with the pain. Mind over matter and all that. It's been inside me for over a week now. I've slept with it, taught class with it, felt it tapping at my spine during your entire visit. It's part of me now. That's why you're here, Dennis. As you put it, I think I'm prepared to confront that wizard. I need your help to pull it off."

"I don't under-"

"I think you *do* understand, Dennis. I think you understand better than most. Pain speaks to each of us differently. You told me about the time yours spoke to you. I want to know the secret my pain is telling *me*."

Dennis Possner did not seem interested in unlocking this particular secret from the universe. He looked more likely to woof his danish and bolt through the door as fast as his ruined legs would carry him.

"Don't speak yet, all right? Watch me and listen to what I'm going to tell you. Absorb it and keep an open mind. Then if you want to leave, I'll hold the door myself. Will you do that for me?"

Mangus did not wait for an answer. Instead he lifted the DIEHARD he had set in the corner, carrying it to the roll top. From inside his desk he removed a small black cube with "Lionel" written on it. He held an old transformer box, the kind used to control a set of vintage '50's electric trains. Mangus busied himself with a handful of multi-colored wires some of which he connected from the transformer to the battery; the rest he connected to holes carved into the chunk of metal embedded in his flesh. It was an awkward business reaching behind himself, but he performed this act as methodically as a man about to give his stalled Honda a jump.

"Can't rely on your standard AC electrical outlet for this maneuver, Dennis. Blowing a fuse would be decidedly uncomfortable. The rest of this apparatus I found at an antique store. Model trains used to be big when I was a kid, but you don't see those old Lionels around much any more, do you?"

"I don't see a train set here, Dr. Mangus."

"An open mind, remember? See this red dial? 'Left' is slower; turn it right and the choo-choo goes faster, up to one hundred miles per hour. Got it so far? Because the next part is tricky."

Possner mumbled something unintelligible, but he was listening.

"Think in terms of degrees, Dennis. Keep the dial turned slowly to the left and you've got maybe a bad headache, a throbbing tooth. Turn it clockwise and you're into back ache, migraine, maybe a broken bone or two, and eventually the last twenty minutes of 'Braveheart.' This transformer tells those pounds of nerve tissue what hurts, and the further you turn the switch the more you increase the dosage. The tissue itself remains undamaged, receiving the message from the brain but suffering none of the effects."

The shock wave of Possner's initial reaction had passed. Now he was curious.

"You're telling me you created this gizmo to control pain?"

"Not exactly. It creates pain. A lot of pain."

"Sort of a home-kit for your basic Marquis de Sade wannabe?"

"Only in the wrong hands. I don't exactly plan on marketing this device for the Christmas holidays."

"It doesn't cause injury to your system?"

"No threat to anything inside me at all. Just a whole lot of hurt."

The student took a moment to piece this together.

[How much can you take, eh? How about some more ...?]

"Agony to the nth without having to pay the freight, right?"

"You get an A+, Mr. Possner."

"Just how far have you turned that dial, Professor?"

"Almost half-way. About the equivalent of the pain you experienced during your accident. Today I want to take it full tilt boogie." Mangus went back to his desk and pulled out a small Sony camcorder. "And I want you to get it all on video for me. I need you to push the dial of that transformer, to describe what you see since I won't be in any position to be objective. You're Leonard Nimoy today, Mr. Possner, and together we can go In Search of Human Chutzpah."

Mangus had managed to coax an ephemeral smile from the student but it fell far short of convincing. Dennis picked up the small black transformer and placed a finger on the red dial.

"Okay, so what if I turn this sucker all the way up? What happens if you do pull off full tilt boogie? Will your hair stand on end while you go a round of Final Jeopardy with God? Why would any clear thinking man want to do this to himself? And why would I want to help him?"

"I'd like to think I'm not doing this either to myself or for myself. Do you want my 'It's For the Good of Humanity' speech? Or maybe the one that says I'm doing this because God told me to? I'm a researcher, Mr. Possner. And so are you."

"Is there a textbook answer that goes with the humanitarian one?"

There was no point to shucking and jiving with this kid.

"I believe that anything taken to its extreme becomes its opposite. It's a law of nature, the yin and yang of our being. White agony, I like to call it, like hot ice or the cold blue of a flame. Pain that allows for no relief whatsoever can't become anything but its own antithesis. Today we can find out what that means. Isn't that what medical research is all about?" His eyes bored in on the young apprentice. "See what I just did? I never even mentioned the good of mankind."

Julian Mangus did not come off as the mad scientist type. It would have made Possner's decision easier if he had.

"So? Have I made a sale? Are we off to see the wizard?"

For a moment it appeared Dennis might suddenly hot foot his way to the exit. He placed the transformer gently on the rolltop, careful not to jiggle the attached parti-striped wires, then went eyeball to eyeball with his mentor.

He suddenly smiled one huge shit-eating grin.

"You said something about an A+, Professor Mangus?"

THE STUDENT SET the camcorder on its tripod, taking his seat behind the small black transformer cube. Mangus sat before him in the soft chair, squirming slightly struggling to find comfort, eventually stiffening himself corpse-like with his arms on the rests. For a moment Dennis felt an enormous sense of power, wondering what might follow if suddenly he flicked the red lever all the way to the right. Maybe Julian Mangus would become airborne and go rocketing through the ceiling like Daffy Duck.

Possner imagined the actual result would be a whole lot worse.

"I'm ready, Dennis."

"You're not expecting any other visitors today, are you Professor? If someone drops in now I'm going to have a hard time explaining that we're not into something pretty damned kinky."

He turned the red lever slowly clockwise. Mangus' body twitched but his expression remained the same.

"You okay?"

"Fine ... A little more ... Go slowly ..."

He turned the lever almost imperceptibly, taking several minutes to complete twenty percent of the transformer's measurement crescent. Stopping to study Mangus' face Dennis did not notice any change other than a tightening of his lips. When he moved the lever further Mangus uttered a low moan, but it lasted only a second or two. The man was a stoic, no doubt about that. Dennis pressed the dial another notch, waited, then advanced it again.

"The transformer says this train is doing about 40 MPH. Almost halfway there. You're doing fine, Dr. Mangus. You're sweating a bit, but --"

"*Argghhh ...*"

A louder moan this time. More of a growl than a moan, and it lasted longer than the first one.

"You're sweating quite a bit, Professor. Becoming flushed too. Can you hear me?"

Mangus spoke a single word through clenched teeth. It took an effort to get the word out.

"*... More ...*"

Dennis' hand was trembling, but he slid the lever carefully to the next numeral. He waited a full minute before he continued.

"50 ... 55 ..."

[*About the equivalent of the pain you experienced during your accident, Dennis ...*]

" ... You're up to 60. Are you okay? We're going to 70 ..."

[*Slowly ... Slowly ...*]

Mangus' twitching turned violent. He performed a mad dance in the chair while his fingernails tore into the soft black arm rests, leaving thick wavy streaks in the leather. His face went purple.

"*Ggggnnnnnnngh ...*"

Now Dennis was sweating.

"*M-M-More ...*"

"I'm not sure about this, Professor. Let's wait a minute or two, okay? Let the pain bottom out. You need to adjust-"

"*... M-M-More! ...*"

A road map of plum colored veins filled the man's face, fading for a moment, then reappearing darker and more pronounced. He stiffened in the chair, then began sliding out of it.

"I'm going to stop this, Professor ... I'm not sure you can take any --"

"*Jssst ... apnnnnn ... naaapnnnn ...*"

"What? I can't understand what you're --"

"*... Jussst .... a .... pinnnnnn ...!*"

Mangus slid to the floor, twitching wildly like a man on fire, chewing at each hand in his spasm. Smoke belched from the metal spike in his back.

Dennis moved towards him, but Mangus was pointing with a shaking finger at the camcorder. He had slipped out of its scope and even in agony still found a way to remind the student to keep his mind focused on the research of the moment.

"All right ... *All right!* ... But no more of this, Dr. Mangus. I'm not taking you any higher."

Dennis busied himself resetting the video camera's tripod.

Mangus managed a crawling run, thumping on his knees to the roll top. He grabbed the transformer from the desk and sprawled crab-like across the floor.

Possner spun around. His eyes bugged like an insect's.

"*Don't do it, Dr. Mangus! You don't have to do this ...*"

The student made a move towards the black cube but Mangus was clutching it close to his chest with hands that looked gnarled and arthritic. His words spilled through teeth that had drawn blood from his lower lip.

"*W-W-White ... a-a-g-go-ny ... D-D-Denn-isss ...sss ...*"

In one motion he twisted the dial to 100.

"Oh damn. *Damn!*"

Julian Mangus did not utter a sound.

But Dennis screamed.

"Open wide, Julian. That's it, son ... It's just a little novacaine ... This won't hurt a bit ..."

"*Owww! Owwwwwww!*"

"*Rock-a-bye baby, on the tree top ...*"

"**Cry baby, cry baby! Look at the cry baby!**"

"*And when the bough breaks the cradle will ...*"

"Did you fall, son? Let's have a look at that arm..."

"***That hurts! It hurts so bad, Mommy ...***"

"Julian's crying! Julian's crying! Look at the baby crying ..."

" ... train is doing almost forty miles per hour ..."

"*... and down will come baby, cradle and all ...*"

"Looks like you're going to need a few stitches there, lad ..."

"**Ouch! Ouch!**"

"*Don't cry, dear. Mommy is right here.*"

Floating ... Floating ... up and up and up and up ...

Up-up-up-up ...

"**Ahhhhhhh ...** "

"50 ... 55 ..."

"Damn, look at that lump! Baseball smacked the poor kid right in his head ..."

"*Big boys don't cry, do they Julian? There's a good boy ...*"

"**M-M-More ...**"

"You're sweating quite a bit, Professor ..."

"Christ, Jules ... You took a bad fall there, honey. Can you get up?"

"It's just a pin!"

"Oh my God, Doctor. It looks like the man's broken every bone in his body!"

"Nurse! Nurse! Get this man prepped now ..."

"Aaaaaarghhhhhhhhh!"

"It's all right ... It's going to be all right ... "

" ... but no more of this, Dr. Mangus. I'm not taking you any higher ..."

"M-M-M-M-More!"

"Is he gone, Doctor? How could any man survive something so horrible? ..."

"Better the poor guy dies ... much better if he just lets go ..."

Cry baby, cry baby, crybabycrybabycrybaby ...

"It's all right to cry, baby ..."

"Don't do it, Dr. Mangus ... You don't have to ..."

"We can't do anything for him, Nurse ... No one can ..."

"Poor man, poor poor man ..."

"Aaaaaaaaaarrrrrggggghhh!"

"Much better this way ..."

"White agony, Dennis! White agony!"

"So much better this way ..."

"Oh damn.. Damn! ..."

Up and up and up and up ...

"Off to meet the wizard ..."

"Feeling so much better ..."

And up and up and up ...

"I'm here, Julian ..."

"Dad? Is that you?"

"I'm here, son ..."

"Father? ..."

"Rock - a- bye-baby ..."

up ... up ... up ...

... here for you, son ...

... on the treetop ...

... . my son ... .

∾

" *... I'M HERE FOR YOU.*"

A gentle hand touched his shoulder.

White. Everything white. Too much white ...

"Where am I? Who are you?"

"You know who I am, Julian."

The man's voice seemed familiar, but Julian could not place it. The figure stood before him dappled in blinding white light making it difficult to see his features clearly.

"My pain is gone. It's completely-"

"Yes. I know."

The voice soothed him. Something inside him made Julian feel certain that this man had removed his pain, that the mere touch of his hand had brought him comfort and --

Impossible! Impossible!

"Am I dead?"

"You have endured great suffering, Julian. More suffering than any other man, including myself. You and I share much in common. I have waited a long time for you to come."

The stranger held out his open palms before him. Blood dripped from each of them.

"This is crazy. I'm dreaming, or in a coma. I'm not even a religious man."

"It was never necessary that you believe in me, Julian."

"Why am I here? Am I dead? Is this heaven?"

"Not dead. Not heaven ..."

"Then where is this? Why am I here?"

"In time, Julian ... all in due time ..."

The stranger again held out his palms before him. The blood had gone. The man's wounds had completely healed.

He was smiling.

"You end my suffering as I end yours. I have waited for such a very long time ..."

Not a man at all ... something else ...

The voice faded.

"Here for you ... always here for you ..."

"Wait! Wait!"

And then there was nothing ...

Nothing except the light ...

Nothing except time ...

A very long time ...

"PROFESSOR MANGUS? Are you all right? Say something! Can you hear-?"

He gulped for air from the floor. It took a moment to get his lungs going again, and he coughed powerfully. But he felt no pain, no pain at all.

"Dennis?"

"Thank Christ, Professor. I thought you were dead."

"I'm not dead ..."

Not dead ... Not heaven ...

"You threw one hell of a scare into me, Dr. Mangus. I don't think you ought to be pushing any more dials for a while. You must have been out for over two minutes."

It felt a lot longer than two minutes. More like a lifetime. With the student's assistance he pushed himself from the floor and noticed the metal spike there. It had somehow become dislodged from his back.

"I pulled it out, Professor. I'm sorry, but I just couldn't let you--"

"It's all right, Dennis." Mangus coaxed a wooly memory from deep within his brain. "I had this crazy dream you wouldn't believe ..." He stopped himself. The kid didn't need any more reasons to think of him as a man gone crackers.

"You're going to need some carpet cleaner to get those stains out, Dr. Mangus. But I guess that's a small price to pay considering what you've been through, huh?"

Mangus studied the beige carpet where his palms had left damp crimson prints, then stared at his hands. Blood dripped from each of them. He held his open palms before him to verify that what he saw was really there.

"You bit your palms during that last phase, Professor. You were pretty far gone and you must've drawn blood. It'll be on the video, but there won't be much else to see except for you doing the funky chicken until you passed out. Have you got a first aid kit in the house? Your back is bleeding pretty bad too. "

Mangus placed a bleeding hand on his young mentor's shoulder leaving another palmprint on his sweats. He studied the moist stain as if it contained a secret message.

"In a moment, Dennis. But I need to ask one more favor of you. You've helped me today. Will you allow me to do something for you?"

The kid looked skeptical. Who could blame him? He had spent the last hour performing his professor's torture on request.

"Your legs, Dennis. They've been badly scarred for quite a while now, haven't they? And I know that limp has been a nuisance to you. A young man like yourself should get out and play a little touch football on the quad once in a while, maybe hit the dance floor with a co-ed or two, am I right?"

"I guess so. But I don't see what–"

"*Shhhh ... don't speak. This won't take but a minute.*"

In a day filled with insane occurrences, the student readied himself for one more. Julian Mangus placed each of his bleeding palms upon Dennis Possner's legs. He could feel the flesh beneath the kid's denims begin to tingle.

And then he waited ...

∽

About the Authors

Originally from Asheville, NC, **Dawn Wilson** has more than 20 years of experience as a professional writer. Her short stories and articles have appeared in *Writer's Digest, Evangel, Byline, Levitate, The Rush, and Dr. Hurley's Snake-oil Cure*. She is the author of two traditionally published novels: *Saint Jude* and *Leaving the Comfort Cafe*.

In 2021, her short play "I'm Not a Therapist But Have Seen One for 24 Years" was presented in New York City as part of a mental health fundraising project by Recover Me. Proceeds benefited the Trevor Foundation.

She resides on the North Carolina coast.

Aidan Alberts' first novel, Age of the Titan, is the first installment in a series. Alberts holds a Master's degree in English Literature and is the author of numerous short stories published in print and online literary magazines. He lives in California's Bay Area. He has an active social media presence on all platforms under the username ageof-thetitan where he shares book updates.

Derek Go is an aspiring writer from the Philippines. He enjoys exploring themes of identity and memory in his fiction.

Elaine Crauder's fiction is in *The Saturday Evening Post*; *The Commuter* at Electric Literature; *Cleaver*; *Scoundrel Time*; and elsewhere. One of her short stories earned The Westmoreland Award and another is in *Wigleaf's* Top 50 Very Short Fictions.

Ten of her short stories are finalists or semi-finalists in contests, including finalists for the Tobias Wolff Award (in 2015 and 2021), the Mark Twain House contest (in 2015), and the 50th *New Millennium* Writing Awards (in 2020 and 2022).

Her story in this anthology, "Picking Up Shards", was a Notable Story in *Gemini Magazine's* 2022 Short Story Contest. Under a different title, it was a finalist in *Bellingham Review's* Tobias Wolff Short Fiction Award (2015); a finalist in Salem College Center for Women Writers' Reynolds Price Short Fiction Award (2012); and a semi-finalist in William Faulkner-William Wisdom's Creative Writing Competition (2014). She is working on a novel.

Riza Maria Rojan is a 19-year-old writer and college student from Dublin, Ireland. Her work explores identity, isolation, and quiet rebellion. When she isn't writing, she can be found baking, watching documentaries, or noticing the small stories hidden in everyday life.

Jerry Purdon writes horror and dark fantasy. Graveyards, Bars, and a Graveyard Bar came out in the summer of 2025. Recently, "Bloodlines" in Incurable: Stories from the World of CURE came out in October of 2025. Also "Monster" was published in the summer of 2025 in an annual short story anthology by Running Wild Press. He has several short stories published such as "Vandora" in Magpie Messenger: Halloween Issue 2024 by Curious Corvid Publishing.

Previous works include "Ghosts in the Graveyard", "Beer in a Bar" and "Graveyard Game". The short story "Mr. No-Name" in Gaba-Ghoul from October Night's Press came out in Spring of 2025. Jerry spends a fair amount of time grilling and loves an awesome bowl of chili. His favorite activity is to sit in the Madhouse Pub engrossed in a great book along with his favorite companions, Shelby and Cayenne. He resides in Texas and is married to his ideal reader. You can find Jerry at www.jerrypurdon.com.

∾

Holly D. McCarthy is an American writer of speculative fiction. Her characters transcend preconceived limitations and moral dilemmas, set in the backdrop of horror, urban fantasy, science fiction and supernatural genres.

∾

Daniel Ruefman is a widely published author of poetry and prose. His short works have been featured in more than 100 periodicals, including *The Barely South Review, Blue Mountain Review, Chapter House Journal, DIALOGIST, FLARE: The Flagler Review, Gravel Magazine, Hamilton Stone Review, Minetta Review, Red Earth Review, Sheepshead Review, and Thin Air Magazine,* just to name a few. He is the author of six books, including three collections of poetry, a memoir, and two children's books. When not writing, he teaches the craft as Professor of Rhetoric and Composition at the University of Wisconsin—Stout. For more, please visit https://www.danielruefman.com/.

∾

Evelyn Griffith is a children's author, opera singer, and literary editor writing from Norfolk, VA. Her work explores themes of faith, resilience, and the human spirit. She is currently writing a Middle Grade Fantasy Novel centered around intergenerational musical magic, and is passionate about crafting stories that resonate with readers on a deep emotional level. Evelyn has been published in the Literary Anthology *Constellate*. When she's not writing Evelyn is the Editor-in-Chief of the *Barely South Review*, and enjoys running, baking fresh sourdough bread, and reading YA Fantasy Novels.

Holly Redell Witte lives and writes in La Conner, WA. Born and raised in New York, for many years, she wrote for newspapers and magazines, turning to fiction and creative nonfiction in 2023. Since that turn, her work has appeared in *Blood+Honey*, *Screamin Mamas*, *Sudden Flash*, and the Red Wheelbarrow Press Anthology *A World Unsuspected*. I Have Always Loved Pigeons is from a longer work that she workshopped as a two-time attendee of The Yale Writer's Workshop.

Edward Tyndall is a writer and documentary filmmaker whose award-winning work has been featured internationally, including at the BFI London Film Festival and on PBS. His short fiction and films explore themes of place, identity, and the human experience, illuminating the intersections of culture, environment, and social issues. Tyndall is a member of the Film and Television faculty at the University of Colorado Denver, where he teaches writing for the screen. He's happiest traipsing through the Rocky Mountains with his wife and daughter—telling tall tales that earn big eye-rolls.

Lauren Lang is a former broadcast journalist and current freelance photographer and videographer living in Denver, CO. In her spare time, she writes fiction, cooks, bakes, crochets hats for stuffed animals, gardens with the intent of taking pictures of the flowers should they live and terrorizes residents by pretending to be a wildlife photographer and running through area parks with her camera screaming, "Birds!". Occasionally, she does take a picture of a bird.

More information about Lauren and her work can be found by visiting: https://www.facebook.com/AuthorLaurenLang/

❧

Lauren Robinson is a longtime copywriter based in Chicago. She has a Master of Science in science journalism from Northwestern University and enjoys using fiction to imagine the human side of future—or altogether imaginary—worlds. She lives with two small, furry editors who supervise her while she works.

❧

Christi R. Suzanne was nominated for Best Small Fictions 2023. Her work appears in Invisible City, Harpur Palate, the online journals Variant Literature, and Foliate Oak, and elsewhere. She is a member of The Order of the Good Death founded by Caitlin Doughty and is currently working on a gothic novel set in the Pacific Northwest. More of her work can be found at www.christi-r-suzanne.com.

❧

Elaine Bernstein Partnow is an actor, public speaker, photographer, and author, especially noted for the nationally acclaimed book *The Quotable Woman, The First 5,000 Years,* and for her living history portrayals of notable women, which she's presented to tens of thousands of women, men, and children internationally at more than 500 venues. Among her 17 published books are *The Female Dramatist*, *The Little Book of the Spirit*, *The Complete Idiot's Guide to Your True Age*, and, with her sister, Susan Partnow, *Speaking with Power, Poise & Ease*. Her starring role in the feature film *Slipaway* (2017), shortlisted for the Oscars, earned her six Best Actress Festival Awards. Elaine began photography during the pandemic in 2021. She captures all her images on the bark and roots of trees (ElainePartnowPhotography.com). In 2023, she was honored as one of the top ten emerging artists in Culver City.

Krista Ruffo lives in Orlando, Florida, and works as a Content Coordinator for a local family magazine. She graduated from the University of Central Florida in December of 2024 with a BA in English. She writes poetry, fiction, and nonfiction, and this is the first piece of fiction she's ever had published. A big bookworm, Krista's favorite pastime is reading, although she also loves hiking, photography, living with four cats, and trying to keep plants alive.

Trish MacEnulty is the author of the historical mystery series, Delafield & Malloy Investigations, as well as the award-winning coming-of-age historical novel *Cinnamon Girl* and two memoirs. A child of the 1970s, one of her favorite books is *Fear and Loathing in Las Vegas*.

Amanda Cupp is a writer and behavior technician based in Boise, Idaho. She earned her bachelor's degree in Narrative Arts from Boise State University and is currently pursuing certification as a Registered Behavior Technician. During her studies, Amanda developed a deep fascination with storytelling and the intricate nature of human connection—an interest that led her to child-led ABA therapy, where she helps children with autism find and use their voices to express their wants, needs, and desires. Her story "Knowing When to Say Goodbye" explores the complexities of family dynamics, personal discovery, and identity through the lens of being a mother, daughter, and, above all, a woman.

Scott Taylor hails from Raleigh, North Carolina. He is a writer and a musician, and an avid world traveler. His short stories and poetry have appeared in numerous print and online publications; his novels 'Chasing Your Tail' and 'Screwed' have been released with Silver Bow Publishing, and his novellas 'Freak' and 'Ernie and the Golden Egg' are slated for inclusion in an upcoming anthology with Running Wild Press. He graduated from Cornell University and was a computer programmer in a past life.

R.R. Davidson is the pen name for Raighne Kotrla (she/her), a neurodivergent mother, writer, and artist. She earned a Bachelor of Science with High Honors from the University of Texas at Austin. Raighne has always been a storyteller, originally through movement, spending the first twenty-five years of her life as a classically-trained ballerina then earning a second-degree black belt in Tae Kwon Do after college. When diagnosed with Bipolar Disorder as an adult, writing became her creative outlet of choice. Raighne credits her writing and artistic work as her greatest tools for healing and understanding her mental illness. She lives in Los Angeles, CA with her husband and four children. 'Sushi in Space' is her first published short story.

~

Danny Arthur is a writer from New York, currently living in London. He writes whenever he is not at his day job.

~

Ben White is not so much of a writer than a witness. Raised in graveyards and baseball dugouts, he is always ready to share stories that capture the human experience. He is the author of 10 books including *The Recon Trilogy +1* and *Always Ready: Poems from a Life in the U.S. Coast Guard*. Look for his forthcoming collection of poetry, *Down Along Highway 90*, coming out in April 2026.

~

Kimberly Parish (K.P.) Davis was once upon a time an adrenaline junkie. Director and founder of Madville Publishing, Kim grew up in Texas, but sailed around the world as a chef aboard private yachts for fifteen years before returning home. Her short fiction, nonfiction, and poetry have been published in literary journals, anthologies, and online. She has a short story collection, Trust Issues, (Cornerstone 2025).

~

Lucy Zhang writes, codes, and watches anime. Her work has appeared in Virginia Quarterly Review, Shenandoah, The Massachusetts Review, and elsewhere. Find her at https://lucyzhang.tech or on Instagram @Dango_Ramen.

~

Gretchen Cortez is a college student studying something completely unrelated to writing. When she's not in class, she can usually be found hidden in her room trying to improve her stories.

Ken Goldman, former Philadelphia teacher of English and Film Studies, is an Active member of the Horror Writers Association. He has homes on the Main Line in Pennsylvania and at the Jersey shore. His stories have appeared in ove 990 independent press publications in the U.S., Canada, the UK, and Australia with over twenty due for publication in 2024. Ken's tales have received seven honorable mentions in The Year's Best Fantasy & Horror. He has written six books : three collections of short stories, YOU HAD ME AT ARRGH!! (Sam's Dot Publishers), DONNY DOESN'T LIVE HERE ANYMORE (A/A Productions) and STAR-CROSSED (Vampires 2); and a novella, DESIREE, (Damnation Books). His first novel OF A FEATHER (Horrific Tales Publishing) was released in January 2014. SINKHOLE, his second novel, was published by Bloodshot Books August 2017 and redistributed by Chrystal Lake Publishing June 2025.

ABOUT RUNNING WILD PRESS

Running Wild Press publishes stories that cross genres with great stories and writing. RIZE publishes great genre stories written by people of color and by authors who identify with other marginalized groups. Our team consists of:

Lisa Diane Kastner, Founder and Executive Editor
Joelle Mitchell, Licensing and Strategy Lead
Reuben Tihi Hayslett, Acquisition Editor, RIZE
Benjamin White, Acquisition Editor, Running Wild
Peter A. Wright, Acquisition Editor, Running Wild

Resa Alboher, Editor
Angela Andrews, Editor
Rebecca Dimyan, Editor
Aimee Hardy, Editor
Cecilia Kennedy, Editor
Barbara Lockwood, Editor
Kelly Ottiano, Editor

Evangeline Estropia, Product Manager
Iseabail Lane, Interior Design
Pulp Art Studios, Cover Art

Learn more about us and our stories at
www.runningwildpublishing.com.

Loved this story and want more? Follow us at
www.runningwildpublishing.com,
www.facebook.com/runningwildpress,
on Twitter @lisadkastner @RunWildBooks